A

Bittersweet Betrayal

Book 1: Fighting Destiny

Grace E. Summers

A Bittersweet Betrayal is a work of pure fiction. Names, characters, places, and incidents are the author's imagination to create a fictional story. Any resemblance to actual persons, living or dead, businesses, companies, events is entirely coincidental. The content is intended for a mature audience and might contain forms of events that may be a trigger for some.

Without the help of each individual below, this book would not have come full circle. To each one of you, know that I am grateful for helping me make this dream come true.

Ellen West
Heather O'Brien
Daphne Matthews
Christina Rupe
Jeremy Menefee
Quinne Darkover
Douglas Pershing

Through my own life's journey, God gave me the inspiration for this story. Without Him, this would never be possible.

We all have a destiny. Sometimes we have more control over it than we realize.

Out of nowhere, life detoured me.
I didn't understand why.

...Rachael

Chapter 1: Wednesday Afternoon

Leaving town would be the hardest decision of my life, but not as hard as leaving my little girl behind. I only had a minute to tell her goodbye. It was imperative everything seem normal, even though our lives would never be the same.

"Jilly?" I approached my little girl sitting on the couch in Mandy's living room.

She glanced my way. Those adorable blue eyes followed me. "Mommy, are we going home now?"

"No, sweetie. I need to talk to you." I lowered the volume on the television and motioned for Jilly to scoot over. Then I sat on the couch and pulled my little girl onto my lap. "I, um, have to run an errand. Mandy said you can stay with her."

Jilly's eyes were void of concern or alarm when she asked, "Where are you going?"

I stroked the back of her head and let my fingers trail through her hair, struggling to tell her without her sensing something was wrong. "You'll see. Mandy's going to bring you to where I'll be."

I would have to explain things to her later. At the moment, our safety was my only concern.

"Is Daddy gonna be there?" Her eyes reflected hope that he would. She loved him so much.

"No, baby girl." I shook my head and tried not to cry. Once we were safe, I'd have to tell her she was never going to see him again. "Daddy won't be there. It'll just be you and me."

Jilly's gaze fell to her lap where she held her little stuffed doggie. She bounced him a few times before she nudged him into my hand. "Fumbles said he wants to go with you."

"He did?" I looked at Fumbles and frowned. "You'd rather go with me than watch cartoons with Jilly?" I nodded his head with my finger and then turned to Jilly and gasped. "Did you see that? Fumbles *does* want to go with me."

Jilly drew her shoulders in and giggled. "See, I told you."

Fumbles was Jilly's best friend. She had this immediate

connection with him the second she saw him. Even though I hesitated to take him, I didn't have the heart to refuse her sweet gesture.

Mandy entered the living room and cleared her throat. "Rachael, it's almost four o'clock."

I looked at my best friend standing next to the coffee table. Her wide eyes darted to the door and then back to mine, signaling it was time for me to leave. I held Jilly even tighter. Every instinct in me clawed at my gut and warned me not to go through with Mandy's plan, but if I didn't, I could lose my daughter forever. I kissed the top of Jilly's head and struggled to project a false sense of normalcy. "Who loves you?"

"You do."

My arms drew her closer, and I rested my cheek on her head. "Please don't ever forget that."

I don't know why I said that. Even though it would only be a couple of hours until I held her again, it might as well have been a lifetime.

"I won't forget."

"Rachael?" Mandy gruffly interrupted a second time. "The sooner you leave, the sooner *we* leave." She turned to Jilly. "You want a snack after your mom leaves while I take care of something in my room?"

Jilly sat up, ready to leap from the couch. "Uh-huh. Those cookies with M and M's on them."

Mandy's smile even convinced me everything was as it should be. "Okay, but not until your mom leaves." She glanced my way and mouthed a warning, "Andrew's probably at your house by now."

This was it. Time to leave. As hard as it was, the sooner I did, the sooner I would have Jilly back in my arms. Then we would be safe.

"You be good for Mandy." I kissed her cheek over and over.

Jilly turned her face from me and giggled. "I will."

"I know you will, sweetie." I moaned, squeezing her one last time and then I placed her on the couch. Then I stood and raised the volume so she could watch her cartoons.

Mandy headed for the door and motioned for me to follow. "It shouldn't take me long to pack."

The closer I got to the door, my heart pounded with fury. Like it was warning me not to do this. I had second thoughts about her plan. "Um, Mandy, it's not too late to go back to the house and call the police and explain what happened."

She stopped and turned to face me. "Rachael, you know there's a chance they won't believe your story, but if that's what you want to do, then go home and call them."

Tears slid down my cheeks like condensation on a cold window. My hands trembled, holding my face. "I don't know what to do. I'm so confused."

Mandy wrapped her arms around me. "I know you are. I would be too. I'm here for you no matter what you decide." She leaned me back and placed her hands on my shoulders. "Look, if you want to leave Jilly here and go back to the house, then that's what you should do. Like I said, if something does go wrong, I'll take Jilly to your mom's."

My gut warned me to go home, but if Mandy turned out to be right and the police didn't believe me, I would never see Jilly again. I couldn't risk losing my little girl. I grabbed Mandy's wrist and pleaded, "Please hurry and get to the cabin. I don't want to be there alone."

"As soon as you leave, I'm going to grab some clothes and a few other things and head out. We'll meet you at my parent's cabin in an hour."

I wrung my hands and nodded.

"Listen, whatever you do, *do not* stop anywhere on the way for any reason."

"Don't worry. I won't."

I looked over my shoulder for one last look. Jilly was lying on her stomach, rocking her feet in the air and watching television.

Mandy opened the door, causing the bright sunlight to pierce inside.

I blinked from the glare and turned to her, then swallowed hard. "Um, my car seat?"

"No, I have mine, remember? That's the reason I bought one. So I don't have to keep using yours."

"Oh, that's right. I forgot," I mumbled, still having second thoughts. "Mandy, are you sure we're doing the right thing?"

"I wouldn't let you do this if I didn't think it was your only choice."

"Guess I'll see you at the cabin." I rushed out of the apartment and ran to my Jeep.

"Be careful." Her voice was a mere whisper, then the door

closed. I would never forget that sound.

I buckled up and watched a little girl ride her bike on the sidewalk. Her mother protectively ran alongside her with her arms outstretched ready to catch her should she fall. That's all I was doing, trying to protect my little girl, even though I knew going on the lam was wrong. My husband was dead. There was no way I was letting his rich family take my daughter.

~ *Three Days Later* ~

Mandy's parent's cabin was not what I expected. The roof consisted of rusted aluminum nailed over a wooden frame. The crawl space was exposed with corner piers layered in stones. It was small; one room with no plumbing or electricity.

With my arms crossed over the porch railing, I watched a bee hover over the wildflowers next to the wood steps. Two squirrels chased each other. A hawk's screech echoed between the many trees. Mandy was right when she said the cabin was secluded deep in the woods. I turned and looked at the narrow driveway. For three days I stared at it, waiting to see Mandy's BMW come barreling down and leave a cloud of dust in her wake, but she never showed up.

Fearing something had gone wrong, I got in my Jeep and went looking for Mandy. I didn't know if she'd had an accident or was still in Rockingham or what had happened. About fifteen miles from the cabin, I turned around and drove back. If there was a chance she was simply delayed meeting me, I needed to be there. I never lost faith in Mandy and believed she would eventually show up with some lame excuse why she was late, but that never happened.

Not that I drink, but I compared my lack of good judgment Wednesday on an inebriated brain intoxicated from too much of Mandy's influence. Now I brooded in the hangover stage with regrets I let Mandy talk me into such a stupid plan. In a lucid state, I would have never considered such an unrealistic future. Not to mention her plan had failed within two hours. My only choice was to return to Rockingham, find my daughter, then turn myself in to the authorities. What I had done gave the Greyfells all the ammunition they needed to take Jilly from me. I had no one to

4

blame but myself.

Mandy said we could only stay at the cabin for three days, so my time was up. I had to leave. I tore my eyes away from the driveway. The screen door screeched when I pulled it open. The stifling heat took my breath while surveying the cabin. Mandy's parents would think a hurricane had come through if they saw the aftermath of my destruction. I had a meltdown last night and took it out on everything in the cabin. Even the musty old mattress on the floor. Staring at it, I remembered how I fell asleep in a fetal position crying my heart out, begging God to help me find Jilly.

I set the small wooden table upright, then picked up my purse and a picture of Peter; my dead husband. For three days, I stared at his picture, replaying the phone call I overheard.

"Who were you talking to, Peter?"

And last but not least, I picked up Fumbles. "I'm sorry you were caught in the crossfire last night." I swiped at the dust on him. "Jilly is going to be lost without you." I looked at Fumbles and smiled with sadness. He was all I had left of Jilly.

My wedding rings caught my attention. I retracted my hand and slid them off my finger. I stared at them and thought about my marriage and how it had been nothing but a lie. I slammed them down on the table. The last thing I wanted was a reminder of the man I still loved, even after what he had done.

"Okay, Fumbles. Time to leave."

The sun's rays set my back on fire as I moseyed toward my Jeep Grand Cherokee. The humidity was thick. I lifted my chin and ran my hand across my neck, wiping the sweat before it dribbled down my chest. When I opened my door and glanced at Jilly's empty car seat, my gut twisted with regret and worry. Was she somewhere safe with Mandy, or had something terrible happened?

The gravel crackled beneath my tires, cruising along the narrow tree-lined driveway. A few country roads later, I was on Highway 74 heading home. The air conditioning gave me some relief. It was unseasonably hot for May. I tried to swallow, but my mouth was parched, and my empty stomach growled for food.

"Fumbles, do you want to listen to some music?"

While a song played, instead of distracting me, an unsettling thought hit me—what if a news alert came through about Peter's shooting? It was enough to send my heart racing into next week. I turned the radio off. In the silence, I mocked a news alert in my head. *Authorities in Rockingham are still looking for a missing housewife,*

Rachael Greyfell, and her three-year-old daughter, Jillian. Her husband, Peter Greyfell, a thirty-two-year-old prominent businessman was found shot to death in their home Wednesday.

"News flash. I don't have my daughter. Mandy has her."

The light turned red.

I came to a stop. While waiting, scenarios ran through my head of what could have happened to Mandy. What if her plan hadn't failed, and it was only a matter of finding each other? What if I turned myself in and Mandy was somewhere in hiding with Jilly, looking for me?

The light turned green, and I continued. The beautiful farmland that lined the highway couldn't distract me from my loss. Three days ago, I was a happily married woman, a mother to a beautiful little girl and lived in a gorgeous house. Within thirty minutes, I was a twenty-seven-year-old widow without my daughter and on the run.

When I looked down and saw I was speeding, I eased off the gas. "Don't worry. I'm slowing down," I told Fumbles as if he cared. "I know what'll happen if the cops stop me." I rolled my eyes and laughed, sounding like Chuck from the movie *Cast Away* talking to Wilson.

I nervously made my routine check in the rearview mirror for flashing blue lights. Undoubtedly, one day I would see them. Surely every deputy was on the lookout for my vehicle. I could see it now. Every sheriff's car in town would surround my Jeep with their weapons drawn. A news helicopter would hover and film me being placed in the back of a deputy's car. Then they would trample my neighbor's manicured lawn and ask personal questions for added coverage.

The gas icon dinged, bringing me out of the scenario. I would have to stop at the next town. I wasn't sure I could handle such a simple task. My trembling hands would probably spill gas everywhere.

A sign up ahead read: *Maxton, 10 miles.*

At Exit 191, I left the highway. A convenience store was on my right. I pulled in, but if any cops were there, I would have to abort and go somewhere else. I pulled up to an isolated pump and killed the engine. After getting some gas, maybe I could run inside and grab something to eat and get some water. My mouth was desert dry, and my lips were beginning to chap.

As I rifled through my wallet for a credit card, I couldn't

shake the feeling someone was watching me.

While the gas pumped, I scanned the area. If someone noticed me, I needed to know so I could leave. That's when I saw it. What are the odds I would stop where there was a payphone? My heart raced with hope I could call Mandy and find out where they were.

The pump stopped.

With unsteady hands, it took me three attempts to get the nozzle into the cradle. After doing a full scan of my surroundings, I reached into my console and grabbed some coins.

"Fumbles, keep your paws crossed that old thing still works."

After sprinting across the parking lot, I grabbed the hot receiver and dropped a quarter into the slot. Surely Mandy would answer her phone. She had no reason not to. And, she had to know I would eventually call her—she had my daughter. I dropped the second coin and punched her number, grateful it was easy to remember.

The phone rang, causing my heart to pound, anticipating her voice.

The second ring sounded.

I clenched the metal cord with my other hand. "Mandy, answer."

It rang again.

"The number you have dialed is no longer in service. Please try your call again."

What? Her phone's disconnected?

I ran to my Jeep as fast as I could. After slamming the door, I pounded the steering wheel once. "Mandy, how many times have I told you, you *have* to pay your bills? Of all the times to have your phone disconnected."

Distraught, I left the store without paying attention to where I was going and ended up on a secondary road in the middle of nowhere. When I rounded a curve, the sun blinded me. I quickly raised my hand to shield my eyes. Since I couldn't see from the lingering glare, I feared I might have an accident and slammed on the brakes so hard it threw me forward. After coming to a stop, a cloud of dust surrounded me. I was thankful not to have wrecked and situated myself back in my seat. Soon as the dust cleared, I was able to see I had left the road and went into a ditch but missed the embankment. Before I continued on, I closed my eyes, needing a minute to let my heart settle from the frightening incident.

Chapter 2: A Stranger in Brown

"Ma'am, are you okay in there?" A muffled voice called out, preceded by someone tapping against the glass.

I flinched and opened my eyes to see a strange man peering into my window at me. Terrified and unable to speak, I nodded before I could get out the words, "I'm fine."

"Do you need help?"

I shook my head and looked away, fearing he might recognize me and call the police.

"It's too hot to sit in there. At least roll your window down for some air."

My head was so foggy, I didn't remember killing the engine, but it was hot and getting harder to breathe. Something possessed me to open the door and step out instead of rolling down the window. It was probably the better choice. It was much easier to breathe.

"I noticed your Jeep on the side of the road and wanted to make sure you're alright." His voice carried a warm Southern drawl. "Are you broke down?"

"No." When I closed the door and looked at him, my vision was a bit blurred. Perhaps I stepped out too fast. Once he came into focus, the man appeared to be my age. Maybe a few years older. I thought he was a UPS driver wearing that brown uniform. "The sun blinded me. I couldn't see, so I slammed on the brakes and ended up in the ditch." Perhaps it was the heat or dehydration that made me dizzy or feel like I was going to throw up. I leaned against my Jeep for support. "I'm more startled than anything."

He pointed at me. "Ma'am, you have a knot on your forehead."

Did I hit the steering wheel? I felt for the spot and found it. *Ow*. That's what I get for not buckling up.

"Are you sure you don't need me to call an ambulance?"

"No, I'm fine. In fact, you can leave. I'm sure you need to get back to work or...something."

"Is there anything I can do to help you?"

Since he refused to leave, I would. He might recognize me from the news as the missing woman. I shook my head and reached for the door handle. "No. Thanks for stopping, though."

"Wait."

I swallowed hard before I looked over my shoulder. "Really, I'm okay."

"Let me take a quick look at your Jeep before you leave." He headed to my passenger's side as I watched. "Just to make sure everything's okay and you're not stuck."

Stuck? I followed him with my hand on the Jeep to steady me. By the time I rounded the front end, the good Samaritan was halfway underneath it.

"You're stuck in the ditch, but you also ran over something. Stand away from the side of your vehicle."

He flung a piece of wood against the embankment. It wasn't a big piece. Maybe the measurements of a baseball bat.

"Did it mess up anything?"

He wiggled his way from underneath my vehicle, stood, and dusted the back of his pants. "It's hard to tell without putting it on a lift."

A lift? That wasn't an option. I had to find my daughter.

He reached into his back pocket and pulled out a greasy red rag to wipe his hands. "You need to have your mechanic check it out."

The humidity and blazing sun showed no mercy on me. I was already weak from not eating and dehydrated. Three days at the cabin had taken a toll on me. I didn't feel good and thought I might pass out in front of him.

He tucked the rag back into his pocket. "Are you *sure* you're okay?"

"It's really hot...and I don't know what to do about my car."

"I can tow it home for you."

"Thanks, but I don't live here. I'm just passing through."

I headed back to the driver's side and gasped at what he was driving, and it wasn't a UPS truck. How could I have missed his wrecker? Maybe I did need help.

The stranger followed me. "Ma'am, um, no offense, but you don't look okay."

Of course not. My clothes were dirty. My hair was a mess.

My face was pale, and I had to smell worse than a dead horse. Three days sweating in the same clothes would make even Mother Nature cover her nose.

"No offense taken." I leaned against the driver's door and thought about my options. Not that I had one. I just wanted to go home and find out where Jilly was.

"Is there someone I can call for you?"

"No."

He placed his hand on my passenger's door and his other hand on his hip. "Then tell me what I can do to help you."

There was one thing he could do, and I reluctantly asked him, "If you could pull my Jeep out of the ditch, I would appreciate it."

"That, I can do." He gestured with his hand toward the wrecker and nodded. "I'll need you to sit inside for safety reasons."

If he only knew how hard that was for me, but I respected his concern. I didn't know saying "Okay" could be so difficult. I walked toward his wrecker with him by my side. He was a gentleman and opened the door for me. When he reached out his hand to help me inside, I climbed in without his assistance.

"Be careful," he advised when I stepped over some tools.

Before I knew it, he was in the driver's seat. He pulled around to the front of my vehicle and then backed up while a metal bar lowered. When it bumped my tires, he stopped. With the push of a toggle knob on a small metal box he held, the front end of my Jeep lifted. He pulled forward, and my Jeep was out of the ditch. "Stay here." He reached for yellow work gloves on the console. "I'm gonna check it out while the front end's off the ground." He jumped out of the wrecker before I could say anything. It was a kind offer, and I needed to know, so I waited.

It was only a matter of minutes when my door opened. He cleared his throat. "I hate to tell you this, but there is some damage."

"Can I still drive it?"

He wiped the sweat from his forehead with his upper arm. "No. I'm afraid it's not going anywhere until it's fixed."

I rolled my eyes and sighed loudly. "Of course not."

He nudged the toe of his work boot into the dirt as he thought. "Here's what I can do." His eyes met mine. Droplets of sweat ran down the sides of his temples. "I can tow it to my shop." He nodded toward his right. "It's, oh, ten minutes up the road. I have a room in the back. You're more than welcome to stay there tonight, and I'll look at it tomorrow for you."

"Thanks, but I don't want to impose."

He chuckled. "You wouldn't be."

I detected a familiar odor. Then I noticed a name stitched on his shirt. *Daniel.* Underneath read: *Daniel's Automotive and Towing.* How in the world did I not recognize the guy was a mechanic? My dad used to work on cars. He would come home with the same smell of grease and oil. I remembered how my mom hated when he washed his greasy hands in the kitchen.

The stranger seemed like a nice guy, but there was no way I was staying at his shop. What if he went home and saw me on the news?

"Um, thanks for your generous offer, but I'm not sure that's a good idea."

"Then you need to call a friend to come and get you. I'm not leaving you here by yourself." With his hands on his hips, he looked me over. "Personally, I think you need medical attention. You look like you're gonna pass out any second." With his eyes on me, he reached for his phone that was clipped to his belt. "I'm going to call for help."

"No, you can't." Panicked, I grabbed his arm to stop him. "Please don't."

We stared for a brief moment before he offered me his phone. "Then call someone."

I looked at his phone and exhaled with defeat. There was no one I could call. Going home would have to wait one more day. I cleared my throat and looked at him. "Are you sure it won't be any trouble to stay at your shop?"

With a look of relief, he sighed and returned his phone to his belt. "Not at all."

I wondered what I had gotten myself into while watching him put on his work gloves. "I appreciate you doing this."

"I need to strap it down and then we'll head over there." He ran the back of his hand across his forehead and closed my door.

While I waited, I tried to imagine his backroom. It couldn't be worse than the cabin. At least there would be plumbing and electricity. And, air conditioning.

The driver's door opened. "Okay, we're good to go." He jumped in and settled in his seat and offered me a cold, wet bottle of water. "Here. Drink this."

I wanted that water more than anything. Even the droplets that fell on his console from the condensation. I looked at him but hesitated.

He nudged the bottle closer. "Don't worry. I have plenty in my cooler."

I flashed a shy smile and reached for it. "Thank you. It's a scorcher today."

"Yes, it is." While buckling up, he watched me gulp the water.

I tried not to embarrass myself and stopped, even though I could've taken that bottle all at once. I wiped the wetness from my lips with the back of my hand. It was the best tasting water I had ever had in my life.

"Ready?" He put the wrecker in drive.

"As I'll ever be."

We headed down the country road.

He reached out his hand to me. "I'm Daniel."

I shook his hand. It was still cold from holding the bottle. "I'm Rachael." Dehydration must have dried out my brain. It sure wasn't paying attention. What fugitive uses her real name?

We traveled the country road. The wind blew my hair everywhere. I tried to corral it to the back of my head. "I appreciate you stopping and helping me."

"It must've been meant to be," he sang as if it were a tune. Then he laughed at my puzzled look. "I was on my way to a call," he explained, turning his eyes back to the road. "I never go this way to Mill Creek Road, but something told me to today."

"Was it a little birdie?"

Daniel laughed. "Maybe."

I chugged the cold water. My poor body was pleased with the gift and felt immediate relief.

"Do you need me to turn on the air conditioning?" he asked over the roaring wind as it penetrated through the open windows.

"No. It's fine."

"Let me know if you get too hot." His phone rang. He leaned to his left, freeing it from his belt and answered. "What's up, Seth?"

I scooted closer to the door and leaned my head against the side while Daniel talked.

He chuckled. "Again?"

I noticed a patch of wild daisies. They always reminded me of my dad.

"Call me when you get back in town, and I'll head out there."

After passing an intersection, Daniel turned right. A huge sign written in big brown letters: *Daniel's Automotive and Towing,* told me we had arrived. His uniform was brown. His wrecker was brown. It must've been his favorite color.

The shop was a dingy concrete building with two bays and an attached office. It sat alone, surrounded by a field of newly sprouting corn.

"No problem." Daniel ended the call and parked sideways, claiming three parking spots. He glanced my way and killed the engine. "Let's get you inside. I'll drop your Jeep once you're settled." He opened his door and added, "Maybe get some ice for your forehead. That knot looks bigger."

I stepped out and motioned to my Jeep. "Can I get something out of there?"

"If it's within reach." Daniel opened the door for me.

My Jeep was elevated, so I had to stand on my tiptoes to reach for my purse. It was on the floorboard. So was Fumbles. I grabbed him and stepped back. "Thank you."

"No problem." After shutting my door, Daniel led the way to the office and unlocked the door. I stepped inside and was met with a strong scent of grease. Being in his shop reminded me of my dad and the times he took me to work with him.

The office was bland and in disarray, which was typical for a shop. To my immediate right was a sitting area with two old metal chairs. A wood shelf lined the wall with auto-mechanic books. An L-shaped desk with scattered paperwork claimed the far-right corner. There was a metal door to my left, which I assumed led to the shop.

Daniel guided the way through the office. "Please overlook the chaos. My partner left, and I'm not into paperwork." We walked through the office and turned left. I followed Daniel down a narrow hallway. He entered the second room on the right. "It hasn't been used in a while, but you should be fine for one night."

When I walked in, my eyes widened in awe of the room and was pleasantly surprised. "Wow. You turned this into a real bedroom."

"It was one of my projects last year." He corralled personal items on the dresser and slid them into a drawer. Then he sprinted past me. "Make yourself at home. I'll be right back."

I rested my purse and Fumbles on the headboard. Daniel probably thought I looked silly carrying a stuffed doggie, but he was all I had to my name. I patted his head. "Just for tonight." A chill ran through me, remembering Peter used to do that to make Jilly laugh. For some reason, she thought it was the funniest thing.

I went to the bathroom to investigate, then practically drooled when I saw a bathtub. *If only...* I stared at it like it was a Rembrandt, imagining hot water running down my filthy body. That, or a hot bath, would've done wonders for me.

Nosy, I mosey to what I thought was a closet. When I entered, my jaw dropped. It was a mini kitchen. I opened the refrigerator to see if there was anything to eat.

"I only keep water bottles in there, but feel free to help yourself."

My body sprung upright with my bug eyes finding Daniel's. "I'm good, but, um, thanks."

Daniel had me blocked in, and I was petrified, although I thought I did a good job appearing unfazed. That is, until he approached me. I flashed back to Peter coming toward me with a gun and backed away, panting.

Daniel immediately stopped and held up his hands. "It's okay. I was only going to get some ice." He smiled and wiggled the plastic bag in his hand as though to say, *"See."*

I looked into his eyes, still terrified, but I wasn't threatened by his presence. "Oh, you're fine." My high-pitched voice wasn't convincing. Not even to me. "Let me get out of your way." I bolted past Daniel and sprinted back to the bedroom.

Had I made a mistake accepting his offer? Daniel was a complete stranger. What if his nice-guy persona was a trick to get me there? For all I knew, he could've been a serial killer.

"I don't have an ice pack, but this should work."

"Huh?" I spun around, unaware he was in the bedroom.

Daniel squinted with concern. "Are you sure you're okay?"

"Yeah, it's been..." Wringing my hands, I shrugged and laughed once. "You know, one of those days."

Daniel pointed to the recliner. "Have a seat."

I did as he instructed. It was surprisingly comfortable. My body was quite pleased sinking into it. "I could've done this and let you do your business."

"Gosh. You're making it sound like a big deal." He handed me the bag of ice while suppressing a laugh trying to escape. "Here, then. I'll let you do this part."

"Thanks." I rested the bag on my forehead and smiled.

Daniel smiled back, but his was genuine. And for that short moment, I considered him a kind and harmless Southern guy.

"Do you have a headache?"

"A little one." I lied. My head was killing me.

"I can run to the store and get some Tylenol."

"Um, I think I have some in my purse."

Daniel went to the closet and returned with a bottle of water and handed it to me. "Where is your purse?"

I pointed at the bed. "It's on the headboard."

Daniel fetched it. "You should take some."

He was right. While I took some Tylenol, he pulled a blanket from a dresser drawer and offered it to me.

"The air is sometimes cooler back here."

"Thank you." I accepted the blanket with a gracious smile.

Daniel ran his fingers through his wavy, tousled, dirty-blond hair. "I've gotta drop your Jeep and take care of that call. I should be back in an hour."

I covered my yawn. "Okay."

After Daniel walked out, I let my fatigued body collapse in the comfort of the recliner and fell asleep.

Chapter 3: Biting the Apple

The office door closed, startling me. A bit nervous, I lifted my head from the recliner and listened. Footsteps in the hallway announced someone approaching.

Daniel poked his head in the doorway. "Okay to come in?"

"Sure."

He stepped into the room, holding what resembled carry-out boxes from a restaurant. I sniffed the air and detected a pleasing aroma, triggering my hunger.

Daniel lowered the boxes in front of me. "Thought you might be hungry. The one on top is yours. I sure hope you're not a vegetarian."

It was food? My lips parted, then morphed into a smile, reaching for the box. "No, but I'm so hungry I'd eat anything right now."

"There's nothing here to eat, so I stopped by a diner to get you something."

"Thank you." My feet forced the recliner into a sitting position, and I was ready to devour whatever was in the box.

"I know the owner, so I practically get it for free."

"Whatever it is, smells so good." When I raised the lid, I gasped at the huge cheeseburger with lettuce poking out and the crinkle fries next to it. I was so thankful to see food, I almost cried. "This looks *so* good."

Daniel sat on the bed with his box and a bottle of water. "Dig in and enjoy."

That was my plan. I lifted the cheeseburger with both hands and took the biggest bite I could. I chewed it slowly with my eyes closed. Not only was it mouthwateringly delicious, but my stomach was mighty pleased to have something in it.

For some reason, I reminisced about a time when I was young. Dad and I were walking through the woods like we often did. We heard a strange noise and searched for it. Dad found a baby squirrel hiding underneath a log. Because it was injured, he suggested we let nature take its course.

Dad and I rarely differed on our views, but that was one of them. When he saw my brows narrow and my arms cross, he knew I wasn't going to leave it there to die. Dad rolled his eyes, removed his ball cap, and scooped up the poor thing. We took it home. I was determined to save its life. Mama diced an apple while I searched for a box. My heart broke when he cowered in the corner, terrified. His little eyes stared at me like he thought I meant him harm. My parents watched while I offered him a piece of the apple. I nudged it toward him. His nose twitched, but he refused to take it from me. He eventually ate it after we left him alone. I was like that squirrel: starved, scared, and unable to trust.

Daniel gathered the trash after we finished eating and stuffed it into a cardboard box near the door. He gulped the last of his water and twisted the lid on the bottle. "I need to work on the car I just brought in. The owner's coming by later to pick it up."

"Okay."

He shoved the bottle into the cardboard box. Before he walked out, he told me, "Don't stand up too quick, or you might feel dizzy."

"Don't worry, I won't." I leaned back and forced the recliner into the horizontal position.

"I'll check on you before I leave." Daniel walked out of the room.

Drinking two bottles of water and having food in my stomach did wonders for my body. My life, however, was still a calamity.

I dozed off for a while, then just laid there resting.

Muffled voices came from the shop. Then the clanking of what I assumed was a bay door closing. It was silent until footsteps padded the tile hallway, drawing closer. Then Daniel walked into the room. "How's the headache?"

I shrugged. "Um, not too bad."

"That's good." He looked away and scratched the back of his head. "Guess I'll head home. Do you need anything before I leave?"

"No thanks." I remembered the food and reached for my purse. "Oh, I need to pay you for the cheeseburger."

Daniel waved his hand in protest. "No way."

I still searched for some cash. "Yes. I want to pay you."

"I'm not taking your money."

My eyes darted to his, and my tone was laced with suspicion. "Why are you being so nice to me?"

He shrugged with his lips parted. "That's what I do. I like helping people."

I set my purse back on the side table. "Please know how much I appreciate it and everything else you've done for me."

"You're more than welcome." Daniel pointed over his shoulder. "I have to lock the doors. If you need to step outside, just make sure you lock it when you come back in."

"I don't plan on leaving this room."

"If, for any reason, you need to call me, my number is on the office phone. I only live a few minutes from here."

"Okay."

Daniel headed out of the room. "Oh, I forgot to mention..." He stopped at the doorway and turned to face me with one hand on the doorframe. "Help yourself to the shower. Everything's in there you'll need."

How embarrassing. Did I smell that bad for him to offer? "Thanks, but I wasn't planning this trip and, um, well, I don't have any clothes with me." I wanted to pull the blanket over my head and die of humiliation.

Daniel's eyes darted to the dresser and then back to me. "There's some clothes in there that should fit you."

Was he serious? Wear *his* clothes? That wasn't going to happen.

"Thanks, but I don't—"

"You can wear them long enough to wash yours." He pointed to his right. "There's a washer and dryer in that room." His lips pressed together, fighting a grin—probably at the thought of me wearing his clothes.

"Have a good night." I waved my fingers. His cue to leave. "Thanks again for the food."

That grin escaped along with a chuckle. "I'll see you in the morning." He waved with his back to me and walked out.

After Daniel left, my thoughts turned to Jilly and Mandy. There had to be a good reason why she never showed up at the cabin. Then I scolded myself for listening to Mandy. How could I be so foolish and let her talk me into leaving town? Tired, I closed my eyes and thought about that day, having so many regrets.

"Rachael, I still can't believe it." Mandy shuts her bedroom door and rushes to me. "Why would Peter want to shoot you?"

Crying, I shake my head and babble, "I told you. I don't know why." I cross my arms and pace. "When I tried to get the gun from him, it went off." I stop and look at her, then cry harder. "Mandy, he's dead."

She scowls. "I'd rather it be him than you."

I pace again. "I had to get Jilly out of the house. I couldn't let her see her father like that," I whisper, remembering she's in the living room watching television.

Mandy's eyes widen, then she covers her lips with her fingertips and mutters, "Oh no. Do you think his family's involved? Maybe Andrew was the one Peter was talking to."

"I don't know what to think anymore." I blow my nose and head toward the bedroom door to leave. "Watch Jilly for me. I need to get back to the house so I can call the police and let them know what happened."

Mandy catches up with me and blocks my path to her door. "You're going back to your house?"

"Yeah, why wouldn't I?"

"Are you serious?" She lowers her voice at my glare and continues. "Rachael, if you go back over there, they're going to arrest you."

I scowl at her. "Arrest me? For what…defending myself?"

"Noooo, because there's no way the police are going to believe your story." Mandy shrugs, laughing. "Heck, *I* don't even believe it."

My mouth opens, shocked. "And why not?"

She does her infamous snarky eye roll. "Duh, because Peter was a saint in his community, that's why. And he doesn't have a history of abuse or mental illness. You have nothing on him to convince *anyone* he decided to go psycho and shoot you. To the police, it's going to sound like you overheard Peter on a business call, but you, *you're* going to sound like a crazy wife who lost it and shot her husband without a good reason." Mandy walks to her dresser and reaches for the box of tissues, then offers me some.

"I *had* a good reason." I grab some fresh tissues and wipe my closed eyes and mumble, "That could be me lying on the floor."

After returning the box of tissues on the dresser, Mandy looks at my reflection in the mirror. "What are you going to tell the police? How you guys were happily married and didn't have any problems other than for some strange reason Peter decided to shoot you? Do you hear how *insane* that sounds?" Her eyes are as sharp as her tone. "Don't fool yourself, girlfriend. Peter's the one who's going to look like the victim, not you."

"Look." I glare at her reflection and growl, "I'm going back over there. Are you going to watch Jilly for me or not?"

Mandy turns and leans against the dresser with her palms gripping the edge and squints at me. "Did you guys like, have a fight or something?"

"You know we never fought. We were happy."

Mandy pushes away from the dresser. "Don't let the cops hear you say that." Her eyes meet mine as she paces. "First, you tell them you were happy, then you tell them you don't know why he pulled a gun on you and was going to shoot you? You'd be better off making up something like he hit you."

"Stop talking like that." I sit on her bed before my wobbly knees buckle on me.

"Face the facts, Rachael." Mandy approaches me and counts off on her fingers. "One, you shot your husband—a Greyfell from Lansdale. Two, you didn't call the police and report it. Three, you freaking leave the house and then you return. Four, you can't answer one question the cops will ask you." Mandy shrugs with her palms up. "Do you have any idea how guilty you look?"

"Guilty?" I raise my shoulders and squeal, "Mandy, he pulled a gun on me."

She waves her finger. "Uh, that's your word against Peter's. There's no proof that happened." She points her finger at me. "Rachael, you messed up big time when you left the house and didn't call the police."

I slap my hands on the bed and bark, "I was going to call them until I remembered Jilly was upstairs. Can you blame me for wanting to get her out of that house?"

Mandy eyes me. "Was Peter having an affair?"

"Okay, that's it." I stand from the bed and glare at her. "I'm done here. We're leaving." I sprint toward the bedroom door, slinging my arms. "Thanks for being a friend when *I* needed one."

"Think hard, Rachael. If you go back over there...you *will* be arrested."

Her words bring me to an instant halt, but I can't face her.

Mandy stands next to me. "You need to pull your head out of the sand. What do you think Peter's family is going to do when they find out?"

I side-eye Mandy and growl, "I've always gotten along with the Greyfells. You know that."

She laughs mockingly. "Don't tell me you expect them to hold your hand when they find out you shot their son. Girl, they're going to turn on you and pull strings to have you arrested. Have you forgotten who their clientele is? Try starting with judges and lawyers."

I reach my breaking point and cry out, "*Why* are you doing this to me?"

She yells back, "Because you don't see the whole picture." Mandy gives me her sad face. "Sorry I had to be so hard on you, but you have to see where this is going. Your nightmare has only begun, my friend. This town is going to burn you at the stake."

Knowing she's right, I burst into tears. "But, Mandy, it's the truth. I swear."

She tenderly rubs my forearm. "I know it is. I believe you. It's just…" She sighs. "Rachael, come on, no one is ever going to believe Peter pulled a gun on you, and you know it. And his family won't rest until they get revenge *and* Jilly."

"Surely the police will be impartial and see it was self-defense."

She raises one eyebrow and crosses her arms. "And if they don't?"

Mandy's words frighten me more than I let her know. She's right. My story doesn't make sense or add up. Even though it's true, it doesn't mean the police are going to believe me. Holding back another round of tears, I shrug, not sure what she expects me to do. "It's not like I have a choice. I have to go back over there."

"No you don't." Mandy squints, deep in thought. "That's not your only choice."

"Oh no. I'm not running away, so don't even suggest it."

"What if I go with you? You, me, and Jilly. We can start a new life together. I can work, rent an apartment, go out in public. I can do all the things you can't."

I scowl at the idea. "That's insane."

She hisses back, "Not as insane as you thinking they're going to believe your story." Mandy looks away and takes in a deep breath.

After releasing it, she turns back to me. "Look, I hate this town. You're the only reason I'm still here. Let's go somewhere and start over. Rachael, it's the only way you're going to raise your daughter."

"No. I'm not going to become a fugitive. I came here to see if you'd watch Jilly, not listen to some ridiculous plan."

Her wide eyes tell me she is insulted. "Is it really *that* ridiculous?"

"Yes. It is."

She points at my chest. "I bet when you sit in that cold jail cell tonight, you'll wish you could have this moment back. And, while you're sitting there, guess who'll have Jilly and tell her how Mommy shot Daddy?"

My hands clench. "Stop it!"

"Fine." She strolls away but keeps her eyes on me. "It's your life. But, if you go back over there and the police don't believe you, Jilly will lose both of her parents tonight."

The thought is gut-wrenching when I visualize Jilly crying for me. Overwhelmed, I lower my face into my hands and cry. "You're confusing me. I don't know what to do."

"Rachael, if you don't leave town, you're going to lose Jilly."

"Mandy, I can't run from the law. You know I'll eventually get caught."

"Maybe, maybe not. Is it not worth the risk to raise your daughter instead of the Greyfells? Even if you're not arrested, you know they'll stop at nothing to take Jilly from you." Mandy rests her hands on my shoulders. "Listen, my parents have a small cabin they rent in Laurinburg. It's about forty miles from here. Dad mentioned the other day it's empty until Sunday morning. Charlie and I went there once. Trust me when I say it's secluded. We can stay there for three days and figure out what we're going to do. No one will ever find us."

I wipe my face with my palms. "Mandy, this is *not* a trip to the mall."

Her eyes widen, and she fires back. "I *know* it's not. Geez, I'm only trying to help you. Do you really expect anyone to believe you?"

"No, but I didn't do anything wrong. I'm not a criminal."

"Oh, like innocent people don't go to prison. You don't even have a story anyone is going to believe." She marches to her dresser and adds, "And you won't make one up."

I fold the frayed tissues and wipe my eyes. "Because it's

wrong."

Mandy opens a dresser drawer and rummages through it like a chicken clawing at the dirt. "What's 'wrong' is you going to prison. I know my key is here somewhere."

Exhausted, I sit on the bed and think about Mandy's plan while she rifles through a second drawer.

I can't go on the run. It's wrong. Me, a fugitive? No. But she's right. If the police don't believe me, I'll go to jail. The thought of Jilly losing both of us...

"Ah, here it is." Mandy slams the drawer shut and then approaches me. "Take this." She hands me a pink sticky note with an address and a key, and I take it without thinking. She settles on the bed next to me. "I need you to listen to me."

Absentmindedly, I tuck the key and note with the address to the cabin into my back pocket. "What now?"

"You need to leave. Andrew will be at your house any minute and find his brother. I need to pack and then stop by a grocery store. There's nothing at the cabin for us." She places her hand on mine and grips it tight. "Go on to the cabin, and I'll be there as soon as I can."

Confused, I leave the bed and pace the floor, wondering what to do. I can't go on the run, but Mandy is right about everything she said. I should have never left the house. And I haven't even called the police. They're not going to understand I reacted in the moment and got my daughter out of the house. The only story I have doesn't have any merit. No one is going to believe me. The Greyfells are going to make sure I'm arrested and never see my daughter again. But run from the law?

"Rachael, you guys need to leave. You're not safe."

"Not safe?" I stop pacing and look at her. "What's that supposed to mean?"

Mandy stands from her bed and throws her hands up. "Geez, Rachael. Do I have to spell it out for you? Peter wanted you dead. So did the person he was talking to on the phone. How do you know that person isn't going to come after you to finish the job?"

"That's nonsense."

"Uh, it took you the whole ride over here to convince me Peter tried to shoot you because it sounded like nonsense."

"You watch *way* too many crime shows."

She throws her hands in the air and screams, "That's how I know how these things end and that's with you behind bars. I've watched how detectives handle cases like this. They want answers, and you don't have any, unless there's something you're not telling me."

"No. I told you everything I overheard Peter say."

"Look, right now, we need to make sure you're safe. Andrew is on his way to your house. He's going to find his dead brother. That means whoever Peter was talking to is going to find out and come after you."

I rub away the goosebumps on my arms, listening to her. "Whoever Peter was talking to, he told them I overheard what he said before he hung up."

Mandy covers her open mouth. "Oh my gosh. Rachael, you have to leave. Now. Before the other person finds out he's dead and comes after you."

Any other time I would laugh at Mandy's imagination. Someone coming after me sounds ludicrous, but so does the thought my husband would ever try to shoot me. I can't decipher what is real and what is Mandy's overactive imagination.

Mandy points to her bedroom door. "Rachael, *go.*"

"Mandy, stop it. You're scaring me."

"Good." She grabs my wrist and drags me to the door. "You should be scared." Mandy stops before she opens the door and turns to face me with a concerned look. "Jilly?"

"What about her?"

"She's not safe with you. Why don't you let her ride with me?"

I shake my head and make it clear my answer is, "No."

"So, you brought her here to protect her from what happened at the house, but you're going to take her with you knowing you're not safe?"

"She'll be okay with me."

Mandy shouts, "Rachael, your husband just tried to kill you. And he was planning it with someone else. If that person is looking for you, do you want your daughter with you? God forbid something happens to you, I'll take Jilly to your mom's. At least the Greyfells won't have her."

"No, Mandy."

"Fine." She opens the door but won't look at me. "If something happens to you or Jilly…"

"Mandy, do you honestly think I'd put Jilly in harm's way?"

She looks at me so seriously. "You answer that question, Rachael, knowing what just happened."

I exhale, frustrated. "Mandy, sometimes you *really* drive me crazy. Like right now. But she can ride with you."

"You know I'll do anything to protect her."

I nod. "Yes. I do."

"We need to get to the cabin."

"What about Mama and Grandpa?"

Mandy nudges me out of her bedroom and walks me down the hallway. "You can call them tomorrow on my phone and explain everything. There's no reason for the police to question my calls to them. I'm just calling to see if they've heard from you." She reaches out her hand. "Leave your phone with me. You can't use it anyway."

I reach into my back pocket and hand it to her. "What if the police come here?"

"If you hurry and get out of here, I'll be gone before they have a chance to come by."

"They'll call you."

She shrugs like it's not a big deal. "I'll tell them I haven't seen you. That I'm in Tennessee visiting my parents." She pops my forearm with the back of her hand and smiles. "Maybe we should go there instead of staying at the cabin. They have a guest house in the back, remember? I could hide you there for a while."

We come to the end of the hall.

"I have to talk to Jilly before I leave."

"Make it fast. You need to hit the road."

When I see Jilly engulfed in her favorite cartoon, I have to convince myself I'm doing the right thing.

~ *Daniel's Shop* ~

I awoke from the flashback in a cold sweat and looked around the room, trying to remember where I was but wishing I were back at Mandy's apartment. I wanted a chance to go back and change what I had done. Leaving town was stupid. My gut warned me not to listen to Mandy. I would rather be in prison and know Jilly was safe than to worry where she was.

I let my body sink into the comfortable recliner and stared at the ceiling. "Where are you, Mandy? Where is my daughter? Why didn't you meet me at the cabin?" I looked at the time on the clock.

It was almost two. I made a trip to the bathroom, turned off the lights, then crawled into bed.

Chapter 4: How Bad Is It?

The next morning I was so desperate for a shower and clean clothes, I took Daniel up on his offer and rummaged through his dresser. I held up a blue T-shirt and eyed it. "Fumbles, you watch. Daniel's going to laugh when he sees me wearing this." I grabbed a pair of sweatpants and closed the drawer. "There's no way I'm wearing his underwear." I quivered at the thought, heading to the bathroom.

After worming out of my filthy clothes, I stepped into the shower. The hot water pelted my face and chest while washing my hair. My body felt renewed with the water washing away four days of sweat and dirt.

After drying off, I swallowed my pride and tried to be grateful to have clean clothes. They were baggy, but they smelled good. I could deal with it until I washed my things. After Daniel checked out my Jeep, I would head back to Rockingham. I had to find Jilly.

"Good morning."

Daniel's voice startled me, unaware he was at the shop already.

Towel-drying my hair, I turned and faced him. "Good morning."

"Hungry?" He held a white paper bag in one hand and a tray with two cups of coffee in the other.

"Did you bring food again?"

He handed me the coffee tray. "There's nothing here to eat, remember? So I stopped—"

"By the diner." I couldn't resist finishing his sentence.

"Not today. It's closed on Sundays." He looked me over, wearing a half-grin. "Nice outfit."

"This old thing?" I tried to hide my modesty behind a playful tone, because I was uncomfortable wearing his clothes with him standing there gawking at me.

"They sure look better on you than they ever did on me."

I handed him a cup of coffee. "You didn't have to do this."

He offered me a biscuit in return. "I couldn't let you starve."

I settled in the recliner. My nose hovered over the coffee lid. I had forgotten the smell of the sweet aroma.

"Your forehead looks better."

"Oh, yeah. Thanks for making me put ice on it."

Daniel looked different in jeans and a T-shirt. I could see an Abercrombie guy sitting there.

"As soon as I finish eating, I'm going to put your Jeep on the lift."

"I sure appreciate it, because I need to hit the road." I took a bite of my sausage biscuit.

"It'd probably be fine if you hadn't run over that piece of wood," he teased.

I stopped chewing and wrinkled my nose at him. "You're funny."

He sipped his coffee and set it on the headboard. "I don't think it'll be anything major."

"I hope not."

"You said you're passing through, but I see you live here, in North Carolina."

My eyes widened. I stopped chewing, fearing he knew who I was.

"I noticed your tag when I strapped down your Jeep."

I let out a sigh of relief he didn't know who I was. "Oh, yeah."

"What city are you from?"

I sipped some coffee and tried to think of an answer without telling him exactly where. If Daniel found out I was a fugitive, surely he would turn me in.

"Um, from a small town in the western part of North Carolina."

And that wasn't a lie. Perhaps not as western as I wanted it to sound, but Rockingham is west of Maxton.

Daniel took his last bite, then wadded the wrapper and did a three-point shot into the cardboard box. "Are you heading home?"

"That's the plan."

His phone rang, and he reached for it. "Hey. I tried calling you yesterday."

While Daniel carried on his conversation, I finished eating and thought about my plans. Mandy said if anything went wrong, she would take Jilly to the farm. I would go there before turning myself in. I had to see Jilly one last time and explain what happened to Mama and Grandpa.

"...and see what's going on."

I turned my attention to Daniel when I realized he was talking to me. "I'm sorry. What was that?"

He pointed to the shop. "I'm going to check out your Jeep."

"Okay. Thanks again for the breakfast."

"You're welcome."

While Daniel looked at my Jeep, I washed my clothes along with the sheets and the blanket after gifting them my four-day-old scent.

An hour later, after I made the bed and put on my clothes, I decided to see how things were going in the shop. I pushed through the metal door, hearing Luke Bryan's "Country Girl shake it for me" coming from the radio. As I crept closer to my Jeep on the lift, I noticed Daniel was underneath it.

He saw me approaching and turned the radio off, then he pointed to a hose running across the floor I didn't see. "Watch your step."

"Okay." I crossed my arms and kept my distance. "Hope I'm not disturbing you."

Daniel motioned for me to approach. "Come here. I wanna show you something."

"Please tell me it's good news." I cautiously made my way underneath my Jeep.

"Well, it's good and bad. Which one do you want to hear first?"

"I guess the good news."

Daniel pointed at the passenger's wheel with a long screwdriver. "That piece of wood got caught up on this tie rod arm and broke it." He poked at the broken part with the end of the screwdriver. "See that?"

"And that's good news?"

"Yeah." He looked at me and puffed. "It's an easy repair."

"What's the bad news?"

Daniel motioned for me to follow him from underneath my Jeep. "That's not something I stock. I'll have to order it."

"I know it's Sunday, but is there a parts store where we could get it today?"

He pushed a button on the wall, and my Jeep descended. "Afraid not. They'll have to order it too."

My eyes burned with tears. I had never felt so defeated. "How long will it take?"

Daniel tossed the screwdriver into a toolbox. "If I order it tomorrow, it should be here…Thursday. Friday at the latest."

Four days? There was no way I could wait that long to find out where my daughter was.

My Jeep settled on the concrete.

Daniel sat on his little mechanic's stool on wheels. "You're more than welcome to stay here if that'll help. A hotel would be expensive."

I sighed, still in a daze. "Thanks, but I can't keep imposing on you."

"Maybe we can work out a deal." Daniel leaned over with his elbows on his knees and put his fingertips together. "How good are you with paperwork?"

I raised an eyebrow, not sure what he meant. "Paperwork?"

Daniel grinned comically and tapped his fingertips together. "I sure could use some help getting my office in order."

"Your office?"

"Yep. I don't do paperwork, and since my partner left…" Daniel raised his shoulders and gave me a helpless grin.

"Oh, *I* see." I tilted my head and squinted. "You want me to clean up that mess in your office?"

"Hmm…" With a slack jaw, he scratched his stubble while in thought, then he crossed his arms and grinned. "If you do, I'll fix your Jeep along with letting you stay here. What'd you think?" In my hesitation, he sweetened the deal. "I'll even feed you."

"Interesting offer."

Daniel left his stool and approached me, extending his hand. "Do we have a deal?"

Like I had a choice. Daniel had me again. I shook his hand and exhaled. "Guess we have a deal."

He shook his head and whistled. "You sure drive a hard bargain."

I smacked my fingers over my mouth, remembering something. "Oh shoot."

Daniel laughed at me. "Already having second thoughts?"

I shook my head with my fingers still covering my mouth. "No, it's not that."

His brows narrowed. "What's wrong?"

I tucked the hair behind my ears. "I need to run to the store, and I just realized I can't with my car disabled."

Daniel nodded toward the door. "Come on. I'll take you."

"Let me grab my purse." I sprinted toward the metal door that led to the office.

"I'll lock up and meet you outside."

Since it was his day off, Daniel drove his personal truck; a Dodge Ram 2500 diesel. It was a beast, but it purred like a kitten.

I climbed inside. "What a nice truck."

Daniel flashed a prideful grin. "Thanks." Not that I was trying, but a country man is truly impressed when a girl compliments his truck. He watched me buckle up. "Where do you need to go?"

"Um, anywhere low-key is fine." I wrinkled my nose and confessed, "I'm not a big fan of crowds."

"I know just the place."

Fifteen minutes later, Daniel pulled up to a drugstore. My heart began to race for no reason. Then a horrible feeling of dread came over me like something terrible was about to happen. It was so intense it paralyzed me. I had to force my body to move and walk inside. While grabbing the things on my mental list, I feared customers might recognize me and let my hair dangle to hide my face.

While the cashier rang up my items, a little girl behind me begged her mother for a candy bar.

"But, Mommy, I want dat."

"No. It's almost lunchtime."

"But I wan it."

"No, Tiffany."

"Can I have dis one?"

Listening to the little girl reminded me of Jilly and the times she begged for candy at the checkout. What I wouldn't give to hear her whine for a bag of M and M's. My arms ached to hold her and to know she was alright.

"Here's your change." The cashier handed me the money.

I stuffed it into my purse, grabbed my bag, and walked out. When the automatic doors closed behind me, I froze, remembering the sound of Mandy's door shutting that day. I stood in front of the store, staring vacantly as my eyes pooled with tears.

Daniel called from his window, "Rachael? Is everything okay?"

The mother and little girl whizzed by me in a playful race.

"Let's hurry so we can beat Daddy home."

I watched the mother let the little girl beat her to their car. Tears ran down my cheeks, worried about my little girl. How could a heart endure so much pain without completely stopping?

"Rachael?" Daniel stood next to me, blocking me from everyone. "What's wrong?"

I wiped my face and cried. Even though I was a strong person, I thought I was going to have a breakdown and end up in a mental hospital. As much as I hated needing Daniel, I sucked in a deep breath in between sobs and pleaded with him, "Please g-get me out of he-here."

"Come on." Daniel took my forearm and led me to his truck. I let my hair dangle to hide my face from the world. After he opened the door, he helped me inside.

It was a quiet ride back to the shop until Daniel asked, "Is there anything I can do?"

"No, but thanks." I cowered against the door and looked out the window and tried to focus on the cows grazing, the beautiful old farmhouses, and people relaxing on their porch on a lazy Sunday.

Daniel's phone rang.

"Hey. Sorry I haven't called you back." ... "I don't know." ... "Can I call you later? I'm trying to take care of something." ... "You too. Bye."

We arrived at the shop. I wanted to run inside and hide under the covers, but I had to wait for Daniel to unlock the office. He got out of the truck. My eyes followed him, making his way to my door. When he opened it, I looked away.

"Are you sure there's nothing I can do to help you?"

The tender way in which he asked caused my eyes to water even more. Daniel seemed to genuinely care, and in that vulnerable moment, I wanted to tell him, but I couldn't.

"I'm sure."

"Is your head still hurting?"

I wiped a runaway tear without him noticing and then unbuckled. "No, it's not that." I sniffled and added, "My life is falling apart, and I don't know why."

"I'm really sorry to hear that."

I took in a deep breath. My body trembled, slowly releasing it.

Daniel raised his foot and placed it on the running board and rested his crossed arms over his knee. "Last year kind of sucked for me. We can swap stories if you want to."

"Trust me. You *don't* want to hear mine."

"You're not like…an ax murderer, are you? I mean, it's not like I'm afraid or anything. I don't have any lying around, so I feel pretty safe."

I couldn't help it. Daniel made me laugh. "No, I'm not an ax murderer."

"Hmm, you can't be too sure these days, you know. Just because you're a woman don't mean you can't be one."

Again, I laughed. "Stop making me laugh."

Daniel had the warmest, kindest smile. "Why would I wanna do that?"

"Because I don't deserve to laugh after what I've done."

"I hope you don't believe that." He grabbed my bag on the floorboard. "Come on. Let's get you into the air conditioning."

Daniel refused to leave until he knew I was alright. He found a chess game in the bottom of the filing cabinet, and we played for the longest time. He was pretty good. When he offered to order a pizza, I accepted. While we were eating, guilt set in. It was his day off, and I had intruded long enough. Even though he didn't wear a wedding band, he could still have a family or a girlfriend, so I sent him home after we ate.

For the longest time, I sat at the desk, worried sick about Jilly. What if Mandy had been in an accident? The thought tugged at my heart so hard, I picked up the receiver to call Mama. After punching three digits, something in my gut warned me not to call her. At least not today. Torn, I reluctantly replaced the receiver.

An orange notebook amongst the clutter caught my attention. I opened the drawer and searched for a pencil so I could draw. Within a few strokes, I had Jilly's profile. Her face came to life right before my eyes. She looked at the corner of the page with her little hands reaching up. I captioned it: *Find me, Mommy.*

Around ten o'clock, I crawled into bed. Fumbles was on the headboard. I reached for him and looked at those tiny black eyes. "Did you know you almost didn't become a part of our family?" I shook his head. "You didn't?" The memory made me smile. I ran my thumbs over the fuzzy white dog with brown ears and paws and thought about that day.

It was three months earlier. Me, Mama, and Jilly went to Walgreens to get Grandpa's prescriptions. We stopped in the cosmetic aisle, because I needed more eyeliner. Mama handed me a cheap version of what I was looking for. She doesn't know much about makeup, because she never wears any. She doesn't need to. If she did, it would cover up her natural beauty. When her hair is short and layered, she reminds me of Princess Diana.

Jilly was sitting in the cart, begging to look at the toys. We made a deal. If she let me find what I was looking for, we'd skim the toy aisle. Her birthday was in a week, and I needed ideas for game prizes at her party. While browsing makeup, I noticed this blood-red lipstick and asked Mama what she thought. She said I'd look like a floozy if I wore that. I wasn't sure what that meant, but from her tone, it wasn't something I wanted to be. I told her I was only joking, but she didn't think it was funny.

My eyes misted over, remembering that precious day and missing my family.

Jilly screamed. I looked to see what was wrong. She reached over and grabbed Fumbles off the shelf, screaming she found a doggie. When she held him up and asked if she could have him, I told her no. She had enough stuffed animals in her room collecting dust already, but that didn't faze her. Nope, she threw a hissy-fit. The kind where the whole store hears that one child screaming.

The memory made me laugh.

I tried to explain her birthday was in a week, and she'd get all kinds of toys then. But noooo, she wanted *him*. Jilly had Fumbles secured to her chest, pouting and her brows narrowed. Then she pointed her finger at me and warned me not to take Fumbles from her. When I called her by her full name, 'Jillian Denise Greyfell!' she knew I meant business, but she was defiant. She kicked the shopping cart and guarded him with her life. I tried to take him, but he's so tiny that I didn't stand a chance with him in her grip. Mama realized how much Jilly wanted Fumbles and asked if she could buy him as her birthday present. Jilly gave me that adorable, innocent smile. The one I couldn't say no to.

I lowered Fumbles to my chest and let the tears run down my temples. Jilly wanted him more than anything, and I almost kept her from getting him. And now, he meant the world to me.

Chapter 5: A Week in Maxton

Monday morning

I headed to the office to start on my part of the deal. Yawning, I sat in the plush chair and watched the darkness transition into daylight. As always, my thoughts were on Mandy and Jilly. How could I ignore the possibility she was out there somewhere trying to find me?

Daniel's wrecker whizzed by the front windows. It wasn't long before he waltzed in with a brown bag and a tray with two coffee cups. "Good morning," he sang, wearing a big smile and sat everything on the desk.

I swear he took happy pills. "Morning. You really like that diner, don't you?"

Daniel chuckled and grabbed a chair from the customers' area and sat across the desk from me. "I'll have to take you there for lunch one day."

I reached for a coffee cup and inhaled the steam. "This smells so good."

"I call it my morning fuel." Daniel handed me a biscuit.

"Thanks." I set a cup of coffee in front of him. "Do you have a lot of work to do today?"

He winked while unwrapping his biscuit. "Not as much as *you're* gonna have."

"Go ahead and laugh. When I leave, you'll be the one doing all this work."

"Don't remind me. I *hate* doing paperwork."

I covered my mouth while chewing. "I can tell."

"Is someone being funny?"

I smiled and motioned over the desk. "Just saying."

While chewing, he pointed to the scattered papers that covered the desk. "If you'll separate who's paid and who hasn't,

35

then I'll show you what to do. There are some bills in there I need to take care of, then we'll order your part."

"Sounds simple."

"Guess I'm going to have to break down and hire someone part time."

"You should hire a woman this time."

"My ex-partner *was* a woman."

"Oh, I just assumed. What happened? I mean, if that's not too personal." I sipped my coffee watching Daniel, although he had his eyes on the desk.

He shrugged one shoulder. "Like I said, she left."

"That must've been difficult, I mean, running a business together."

"Life happens, I guess." He sipped his coffee, still avoiding eye contact.

"Was she a family member?"

His eyes met mine. "She was my wife."

I covered a cough while leaning forward to reach for a napkin. "Daniel, I'm so sorry. I didn't mean to pry." I wiped my lips and mumbled, "Me and my big mouth."

"Don't worry. It's fine." He put the last of his biscuit in his mouth and brushed his hands together. "Trust me. I'm over her. It wasn't the best five years of my life."

Daniel had asked if I wanted to swap stories. Something told me that was his.

"Did she leave because she didn't want to be a part of the business anymore?"

He shook his head while wiping the crumbs off the desk and into his palms. "No." He dumped the crumbs into the bag. "I came home early one day from a long run and caught her ex-boyfriend at our house."

"What?" I squealed, almost choking on my coffee.

"Yep. I offered her a settlement so she'd sign divorce papers." Daniel never looked at me, but he raised his eyebrows and sighed. "She took the money and left town with him. I never stayed in the house after that day. I moved in here until I sold it."

"So *that's* why you have a bedroom in the back." After putting the last bite in my mouth, I balled the wrapper and dropped it in the bag. "I figured someone had lived here."

"Yeah. Once I sold the house, I bought the one I have now."

I crossed my arms and rested them on the desk. "Good for

you."

"But, paperwork isn't my thing." Daniel gazed at me with a playful look while wadding his wrapper into a firm ball. "I'm sure you'll do a *much* better job." He threw it at me, hitting my collarbone.

"Really?" I reached for the wrapper still spinning on my desk and was going to toss it in the bag, but I couldn't resist throwing it back at him instead. Unfortunately, I overshot my target.

Daniel threw himself back in the chair and laughed hysterically. "You missed me and I'm this close?"

Squinting at him, I grabbed my wrapper out of the bag. "I won't miss this time."

Daniel leaped out of his chair and ran to the shop door still laughing at me.

I stood and barreled the wrapper at him. It hit the arm he raised to block my throw. I laughed victoriously. "Ha-ha. Told ya I wouldn't miss."

"Guess who has to pick that up?" He bolted through the door.

I plopped down in the chair, smiling. Daniel had a way of making me forget my world had ended. Then I scolded myself for laughing.

After compiling the papers in one neat stack, it was time to sort them. At least Daniel was diligent about noting what was paid or pending payment. One thing I noticed about Daniel, he loved to draw smiley faces.

His name was in the letterhead. "So, his last name is Brown."

I came across a work order that had, *No charge/single mom*, scribbled across it. "Awe." I smiled and continued sorting. Then I came across one for Colt Myers. *Abigail's vendor/payments.*

"Wonder who's Abigail? She has to be someone at the diner. Maybe she's his girlfriend, and that's why he goes there so much. He mentioned knowing the owner and getting his food for almost nothing."

I continued sorting. Daniel's kindness touched me, but I wondered how he made a living being so charitable.

When I flipped to the next invoice, an enormous smiley face caught my attention. *Mom's friend. Never a charge.* "He's so sweet." I glanced at the name–Annie. My smile faded. That was my mama's name. My hands weakened, and the invoice fluttered out of my grasp from the sudden spur of sadness. I never got to use Mandy's phone and call Mama. Not only did I miss her, she and Grandpa had to be worried sick about me.

Daniel walked through the metal door. "I need to run to the parts store." He approached the desk, wiping his hands on a blue towel. "Are you okay?"

"Yeah, um…I was mentally in another place for a second." I didn't want to elaborate and feared he might ask, so I forced a smile. "See you when you get back."

"Are you sure you're okay?"

No, I wasn't. "Excuse me." Before my emotions leaked out in front of him, I headed to the backroom to escape life. My miserable, broken life. Once in my room, tears trickled down my face.

A firm knock on the door startled me. "Rachael, I'm not leaving until I know you're alright."

I had to think of something to tell Daniel that would explain my mood. My face was next to the door when I replied, "I'm okay. It's 'that time of the month.' I'm just hormonal."

He was married for five years. Surely it wasn't a shock to hear a woman had her period. And it was true. I had gotten my period that morning, so I didn't feel it was a total lie. And it was a blessing. Peter and I were trying to have another baby. With everything that happened, it wasn't meant to be.

"Oh. Um, okay, then," he answered uncomfortably.

The thought of Daniel blushing made me grin. "Don't worry. I'll be good to go in a few minutes."

"Call me if you need anything."

"I will."

His footsteps gradually disappeared. Then the office door shut, and it turned a lonely silence. I teared up, missing my family, worried about my daughter, having regrets for running away, my dead husband, and someone possibly looking for me. Overwhelmed, I slid to the floor and curled up, crying.

That night while brushing my teeth, my thoughts were on Mandy, still wondering why she never showed up at the cabin. I replayed that day over and over. Then it hit me what had gone wrong. My eyes bugged, looking at my reflection in the mirror. I leaned over the sink to spit, then poked the toothbrush in the holder. After haphazardly rinsing, I wiped my mouth on the towel, then ran into the bedroom to share the news.

"Fumbles, I know what went wrong." An adrenaline rush had

taken over. I paced. "It was her battery. I bet you *anything* her car didn't start when she went to leave. We were at the mall earlier that day, and she told me it had died on her that morning."

I lifted the covers and crawled into bed. "I *know* that's what happened. I just know it." I turned off the lamp and pulled the covers over me. "Mandy probably had to get the maintenance guy to give her another jump. That's why she was late." I rolled over on my side and released a long sigh. "She probably showed up at the cabin while I was out looking for her. When she didn't see my Jeep, she probably freaked out and left. I didn't even think to leave a note. I can't do anything right, can I, Fumbles?"

~ Tuesday morning ~

I only slept three hours, replaying the scenario in my head. If Mandy was late because her battery had died, she wouldn't go home without trying to find me first. She just wouldn't. That meant she could still be out there trying to find me. How could I go home if there was a chance I was only a phone call away from having Jilly back in my arms?

The orange notebook caught my eye. I picked it up and pulled the pencil from the spiral. Perhaps drawing something positive would brighten my mood. Stroke after stroke, a kitchen table with one plate appeared. Then I drew two pancakes with strawberries on top and syrup running down the sides. The tip of my thumbnail was held captive between my teeth, eyeing Jilly's favorite breakfast. I captioned it: *Strawberry pancakes, Mommy.*

I flipped back to the first page and stared at the drawing of my little girl. "Where are you? Should I look for you instead of turning myself in?"

Jilly had to be asking questions. 'Where's Mommy?' 'Where's Daddy?' 'When are we going home?'

While doodling, I thought about Peter. My husband was dead. I had spent little time grieving for him. Not that he deserved it, but I still loved him. Even though I considered myself more compatible with a country man, that rich city man somehow stole my heart. Peter was a handsome man. He could have been a GQ model. His hair was always styled to perfection. The sides were short, but longer on top with every hair combed in place. Peter

39

could have had any woman he wanted, but he chose me—a poor country girl from Lilesville.

My thoughts drifted to the day we met. It was my last year in college. After a long day of classes, I stopped by the campus café like I often did. It was my only escape from life and a codependent roommate. A few minutes changed my life that day…and a confident man who made a bet with me. One I was glad I lost.

~ *Seven Years Earlier — The Campus Café* ~

"Come on Mandy. I just got here." It has to be her texting me. I continue to dig through my book bag for my novel. Once I locate my guilty pleasure, I reach into my back pocket for my phone and read Mandy's message.

What time you coming home?
You know the answer to that.
Just tell me.

I lay my phone on the table and mumble, "Geez, can I just have thirty minutes before I come home?" I open my novel and leave reality.

"Hello."

I look up from my book to see who spoke. A man sits at the table next to me, which seems odd since the café is practically empty. Assuming he has spoken to me, I smile. "Hi."

The handsome man holds a steaming cup of coffee next to his lips. "Interesting?"

"Excuse me?"

"Your book. Is it interesting?" He sips his coffee and sets it on the table.

"If you like romance."

"It sure had your attention."

My phone vibrates.

"Excuse me." I look at the message. *Are you mad at me?* I ignore Mandy's text and raise my gaze back to the handsome man, glancing at his attire before our eyes meet. "Are you a professor?" I smile innocently to excuse my intrusive curiosity.

He wraps his hands around his coffee cup. "No, I'm not, but my brother is. Andrew works here part time in the business department when he's not working with me and our father. Dad

40

owns Greyfell's Menswear and Accessories. It's in the Lansdale community," he announces with pride and offers his hand. "I'm Peter."

"I'm Rachael." Blushing, I shake his hand and wonder why a rich city guy wants to talk to a girl in jeans, T-shirt, no makeup, no jewelry, and her hair in a ponytail. When I tell him where I'm from, he'll surely take his coffee and suddenly need to rush off for some fancy appointment. With the same pride in my tone, I announce, "I'm from Lilesville. My grandpa has a farm on ten acres." My family doesn't own some classy business like Peter's, but I'm not ashamed of where I come from. Now that he knows I'm a poor country girl, I return to my novel and wait for him to excuse himself. His suit probably cost more than my old Ford truck.

"Do you live with your grandpa?"

My gaze meets his, and I shake my head, surprised he's still here and eager to talk. "No. I live in an apartment with my roommate, but I used to. After Nana died, Mom sold our house and moved in to take care of him."

Peter sips his coffee. "What are you studying?"

"Art. I love to draw and paint."

His eyebrows rise, and he sings, "That means you're talented and gifted."

My smile widens from his praise just as my phone vibrates again. Mandy has lousy timing. I close my book and tuck it into my bag. "Well, Peter, it was nice talking to you, but I guess I should be going."

"Could I talk you into staying if I offered to buy you a cup of coffee?"

I zip my book bag. "Maybe another time. I have a needy roommate at home." I hold up my phone to let him know that's who texted me. "I think she's having one of her meltdowns and should probably check on her."

"Just ten minutes." His alluring eyes are hard to ignore. "I mean, it's cold out there and with traffic, it's a matter of sitting here or in your car."

Peter's charm is somewhat…irresistible. I can't say no. And I don't want to.

"Okay, ten minutes, but I need to check on my friend."

While Peter orders my coffee, I call Mandy with a visual of her sitting on the couch, snacking away her sorrows. She's probably had a bad day at work and wants to complain. She answers immediately, which means she was more than likely composing another text to send.

"Why are you ignoring me?"

I fire back. "Why are you blowing up my phone with messages? You know I stop by the café before I come home."

"Because...I need you."

"What's the emergency?"

"Mom called. We had another fight."

"What about this time?" I hear the crunch of what sounds like a potato chip and roll my eyes.

"What'd you think? 'Mandy, your life is going nowhere.' 'Mandy, you'll never amount to anything.' Blah, blah, blah." Another crunch.

"Why do you listen to her?"

"I don't know." Another crunch.

I lean back in my chair and exhale. "I can tell you fifty times a day how smart you are—*and you are*. You can do anything you put your mind to, but one word from her and you throw a pity party *and* invite me. I know she's your mother, but her words are toxic."

"I know I should ignore her, but..." Another crunch.

Peter is on his way back.

"I've gotta go. I'll be home later—*and stop texting me*."

"Wait. Don't go."

I cup my mouth and whisper-shout into the phone. "Call Eric and tell him to come over for a while."

"I don't want Eric," she grumbles like a pouty toddler. "I want you."

"You'll be okay until I get home. I'm hanging up. Bye." I lay my phone on the table as Peter sets a cup of coffee in front of me. "Thank you."

"You're welcome." Peter pulls a chair from my table and sits across from me. "I hope a large is okay."

"Sure, that's fine."

Peter's gaze lingers. The longer I stare back it makes me smile.

"Is everything okay with your friend?"

"Yes, she's fine. She doesn't like being by herself. She's had a rough life. Her parents never wanted kids, so she's always felt unloved or unwanted." I ramble on without thinking. "I'm sorry. I shouldn't talk about her like this to a stranger."

"I'm just glad she's alright."

I cup my coffee and slide it closer. "So, your dad sells expensive men's clothes. What does your mom do?" I blow the steam from my coffee. Even though it gives me goosebumps, I could stare at Peter all day.

He reaches for his coffee, still sitting on the other table. "She owns a jewelry store in town and one in Charlotte."

"I don't wear jewelry. I'd much rather get dirty and have fun."

Peter spits his coffee at my comment and covers his cough. "Dirty?" He dabs his expensive jacket with a napkin.

I lean closer like I have a secret and whisper, "You'd have to grow up on a farm to understand what that means."

Peter eyes me, grinning as he rests his crossed arms on the table. "Well, I could take you out to dinner, and you could enlighten me." His hazel eyes are full of confidence. I like that in a man. Those perfect dark eyebrows rise at attention. Then he adds a playful half-grin, waiting for my response.

I cross my arms and rest them on the table, mocking him. "Come on, Peter. I'm sure I'd only bore you. It's not like we have anything in common."

"Oh, I'm sure we have a lot in common," says the man with confident eyes.

I counter. "A smart man like you can see we come from different worlds, and we certainly live different lifestyles."

Peter slides his cup to the side with the back of his hand as those warm eyes penetrate mine. "Bet I can name something we have in common. And if I do, you have to go out with me on a date."

Those hazel eyes do something to me. I can't stop smiling, and my stomach feels funny. The longer I stare into those beautiful eyes, they dare me, and I can't refuse. It's not in my nature. Besides, he won't name anything.

"Okay." I lift my wrist and glance at my watch. "You have five seconds to name one thing. Go."

"We both have to eat."

With my wrist still in front of my face, my eyes dart to his. "That's so…not right."

Peter sits back wearing a proud grin and reaches inside his jacket for his phone. "I'll need your number so I can call you regarding the details."

I sit back and cross my arms with a sore-loser pout. "You don't play fair."

He chuckles, looking at his phone, obviously preparing to add my number to his contact list. "You need to remember that when I ask you for a second date."

"Second date?" I laugh, amused. "Oh, Mr. Greyfell. You're a little *too* confident. How do you know I don't have a boyfriend?"

Peter looks up from his phone. "Because you would've put me in my place by now if you did." He gives me this sexy half-grin. "Your number, please?"

"But...I-I don't know you."

"If you're not comfortable with me picking you up, meet me where we're going, or, I'll have Uber pick you up."

The handsome man in an expensive suit has an answer for everything. I think I like that.

"Be careful not to let that confidence convince you I'll go on a second date," I add playfully after giving him my number.

"Why not? It got me the first date." After slipping the phone inside his jacket, he leans closer, into my space. His eyes pierce into mine, making my legs weak, even though I'm sitting. He smiles, and it makes me smile like I never have before. "All I ask is you don't decide until after our first date."

"You're gonna be disappointed."

Peter not only has confident eyes but one heck of a smile. "As long as you're not."

~ *Daniel's Shop* ~

Meeting Peter was more romantic than any encounters I had read in my novels. Heartbroken, I burrowed my face into my hands and cried at the memory. It was my first time feeling butterflies. When I agreed to stay ten minutes, that was my intention, but something held me captive in my seat. When we finally said our goodbyes, two hours later, it felt like Peter was a good friend and we were simply catching up after a long separation.

A few days later, Peter picked me up for our date. Dressing up only happened on Sunday mornings, but I wore my Sunday best. When we arrived at the finest restaurant in Rockingham, I was excited. It was as though he had taken me to another side of life; into his world.

The evening was perfect. Peter knew how to treat a lady and made me feel special, but I never lost sight of the fact we were so opposite. Our lives were very different. That was the reason I had no intention of going on a second date. Something told me it would be better if our lives continued the way they were—on separate paths.

Peter stood at my front door that cold January evening to bid me a goodnight and asked for that second date. I looked into his eyes, ready to decline, but I found it hard to resist Peter. Maybe it was the way he kissed me before he asked.

Chapter 6: Time to Leave

Thursday afternoon

A FedEx truck pulled onto the lot. The brakes squealed as the driver came to an abrupt stop. The part for my Jeep had arrived. After the driver left, I leaned back in my chair and stared at the package. I could be in Rockingham by dark. Although that was my original plan, over the past few days a heavy tug in my heart told me to search for Mandy and Jilly.

I opened my notebook and began to sketch. A large daisy claimed the center of the page. I etched a small one for each pro and con in favor of listening to my heart. The pros went to the right of the large daisy, and the cons on the left. The visual disappointed me. I didn't have the means or the resources to follow my heart. I captioned the drawing: *Home it is.*

Daniel's wrecker whizzed by the glass windows. I closed my notebook and placed it inside a drawer. It had been a long hot day for him, so I went to the back and grabbed a bottle of water from the fridge to offer him. The memory of being dehydrated at the cabin still haunted me. On my way back to the office, a horrible sense of danger swept over me. My brisk walk turned into a shuffle, flashing back to the day I shot Peter. How ironic I was carrying a bottle of water to him. I settled in my chair and looked over my shoulder, sensing Peter was near.

Daniel walked in, wiping the sweat from his forehead. "Boy, it's hot out there."

I pointed to the bottle. "You need to drink some water."

"Thank you." Daniel reached for it and twisted the cap off. "I wasn't expecting that long run, and my cooler's empty."

"You have a package from FedEx."

Daniel gulped the water, then looked over the package, catching his breath. "That's the part for your Jeep." He raised the bottle and finished off the water.

I swiveled in my chair, grinning. "I know. Now I can finally get out of your hair."

Daniel tossed the empty bottle in the trash and glanced at me without a smile. In fact, he looked upset with those brows narrowed. With it being late and Daniel exhausted, I didn't have the heart to ask him to fix my Jeep.

"Why don't you call it a day? My Jeep can wait 'til tomorrow."

"Are you sure?"

"Of course."

Daniel pinched his shirt to fan himself. "You *sure* you don't mind?"

"Go home," I ordered, motioning him to leave.

He locked the shop door and looked over his shoulder at me, suddenly smiling. "Wanna come over to my house? I'll fix supper if you're not afraid to eat my cooking."

Go to his house? Why did that seem like a bad idea?

Daniel approached the desk and ran his fingers through his sweaty, limp hair. "Or, I can run get you something."

The guy was harmless, so I eagerly countered, "I'll come to your house if you let *me* fix supper."

"Hey, I'd be a fool to pass up that offer." With a spring in his step, he headed to the backroom. "If you don't mind, I'd like to take a shower before we leave. I'm sure you don't want to smell me going home."

As he walked out of the office, I mumbled to myself, "You smelled me all sweaty, remember?"

Although Daniel seemed to think he had gotten the better end of his offer, he didn't know how much I wanted to be in the kitchen. I was homesick and missed my life.

On the way to Daniel's house, we stopped at the grocery store and bought some steaks, potatoes, and a salad. When we pulled into his driveway, I liked what I saw. His house sat alone off a country road. On one side was a thick patch of woods and a cornfield on the other. It was a modest ranch home: white wood with black shutters, a large porch with two columns, and wide steps made from stones. A huge oak tree towered over the porch, offering shade. A shelter was next to the shed where he parked his truck I had named—The Beast.

I walked inside and scanned the living room, impressed everything was in place and tidy for a man. Curious, I searched for signs of a woman in his life, but all I saw was a bachelor pad. If he had a girlfriend, he never mentioned her, although someone called him every day. Straight ahead was the dining room and the kitchen, separated by a counter with bar stools.

While we enjoyed our steaks, Daniel shared a little bit about himself. In high school, Daniel's shop teacher mentored him when he saw he had a passion for working on cars. I imagined him more interested in tinkering on motors than having eyes for girls. I saw him as a shy teen who turned to the only thing he was comfortable with—working on cars.

Daniel told me he was born in West Virginia but moved to North Carolina when he was five after his parents split up. Since he chose not to elaborate on the details, I decided not to ask, because he seemed to still harbor some sadness over it. Although he never said it, I got the impression it was because his dad was not a part of his life growing up. That was hard for me to imagine, knowing I had a loving father until I was fourteen. Daniel shied away from the personal topics. He had things he couldn't share as did I.

Around nine o'clock, he drove me back to the shop.

That night, I sat on the bed with my back against the headboard and sketched Jilly in a princess bed. Stroke after stroke, she came to life. Her tiny fingers clutched Fumbles. I made sure to draw her face peaceful and captioned it: *Sweet dreams, my baby girl.*

I set the notebook on the nightstand, turned off the lamp, and snuggled under the covers. "Are you ready for tomorrow, Fumbles? Looks like we're going home." I sunk my head into the pillow and mumbled, "Kind of hard to look for Mandy when I'm indigent, homeless, and phoneless. Oh, and don't forget I'm a fugitive."

~ *Friday* ~

Daniel worked on my Jeep while I cleaned up the backroom. I told Fumbles how I would miss him.

"Am I interrupting anything?"

When I turned, our eyes met. "No. I was just straightening up." I really was going to miss Daniel. His laughter. His kindness. But most of all, his smile. "Is everything okay?"

He leaned against the doorframe and crossed his arms.

"Yeah, I wanted to let you know your Jeep's ready."

"That didn't take long."

He scratched his temple with his index finger. "I also checked the air in your tires, your oil, and the water in your radiator."

"You didn't have to do that."

"You're traveling alone. I wanna make sure you make it home safe."

Daniel's kindness never ended.

I tucked Fumbles inside my purse. "You don't know how much I appreciate it. Thank you so much for everything you've done for me."

"Glad I could help."

The moment seemed to turn awkward. I really was going to miss Daniel, but it was time to leave.

"Well…" I smiled, somewhat nervous. "Guess I should head out and let you get back to work."

Daniel stood from the doorframe and cleared his throat. "Um, I never did take you to the diner. Any chance I could take you there before you head out?"

It wasn't safe for me to go there. Someone might recognize me. However, looking into those blue eyes I could tell it meant a lot to Daniel if I went. After everything he had done for me, the least I could do was accept his kind offer. With Maxton being a small country town, I would have to pray no one watched the news unless it was local.

I smiled and threw the strap to my purse over my shoulder. "Sure. Why not?"

The way Daniel's face lit up, I was glad I agreed to go.

With an outstretched hand, he turned sideways and offered me a clear path. "After you."

I walked past Daniel and teased him. "Make sure you lock up." His famous last words before leaving the shop. I sure was going to miss that smell of grease.

~ ~ ~

The diner was on the corner of a busy intersection. It was small but impressive. Layered stones bordered up to four feet and then nothing but glass. It was easy to see everything happening inside.

The flat roof overlapped the front, doubling as an awning. The sign above read: *The Red Door Diner.*

We walked inside and faced a long counter with red vinyl bar stools. The kitchen was behind the counter, but it was only visible through a ten-foot opening in the wall for passing the prepared food to the waitress. A large burly man wearing a white apron worked hard over the grill. The longer we stood there, the louder the noise became. Forks scraped plates. Coffee cups tapped saucers. The mixture of dialogue intruded into my head. I couldn't shake the feeling everyone was staring at me, although no one looked our way.

Daniel nodded to his right. "Follow me. I always sit at the same table."

"Lead the way." My hair dangled to hide my face, weaving through the tables.

Daniel stood next to one in the corner and gestured with his hand. "Is this okay?"

"Yes. This is fine."

I quickly grabbed a chair and sat before Daniel had a chance to pull one out for me. He would, being the gentleman that he was, but I needed to sit with my back to everyone.

"If you didn't have to eat, I'd probably never see you."

Startled, I looked up to see who had spoken to us in a less than warm and inviting tone. Our waitress stood at our table, holding menus to her chest. She was tall and slender with her sandy-blonde hair in a ponytail. Although she was a pretty woman, the aggressive look she gave Daniel made me wonder why he came there.

Daniel sat back and crossed his arms. "Are you going to give me a hard time?"

She shifted her hands to her hips with the menus in one hand. "Hey, I fixed a big supper last night thinking you were going to come over."

Daniel, unfazed by her intimidating behavior, looked at me and nodded. "Yep, she's going to give me a hard time."

"I even cooked your favorite."

Daniel's eyes darted back to hers. "Did you save me some leftovers?"

She squinted. "Why? Are you going to come by tonight?"

He flashed his pearly whites. "I'll try."

She whacked his forearm with a menu and then placed it before him. "You better."

Daniel chuckled, rubbing his arm. "Ow. What's got you so riled up today?"

"I'm running the floor by myself, that's why. Missy called out sick again," she replied in an irritated tone and handed me a menu. "Hello."

If she knew I was the reason Daniel stood her up last night, she would probably hit me with my menu as well. The feisty Southern lady had to be his girlfriend, and her sharp glare told me she didn't like me.

"Hi." I smiled and reached for the menu.

"Abigail, this is Rachael."

She reached for his menu to whack him again, but Daniel slid it out of her reach before she could. He laughed, but she scowled.

"You *know* you're the only one I let call me that."

"And, Rachael, this is Abigail." Still laughing, Daniel leaned away from her and raised his elbow in defense.

"Will you stop it?" She popped his forearm and then looked at me. "Everyone calls me Abby."

"Table nine."

I flinched at a man's loud voice echoing over the diner. It had to be the big burly guy working at the grill.

"Great. I'll be right back." Her frustrated voice trailed off as she scurried to the kitchen.

With my eyes wide, I sat back and exhaled. "*That* was interesting."

Daniel chuckled, always so happy. "My sister can come off strong sometimes."

"Sister?" I scolded him. "Why haven't you mentioned her?"

"Oh, I'm sorry." He frowned, looking a little sheepish. "I thought I did last night."

I caught a glimpse of her serving customers. Their sandy-blonde hair should have been a clue. "Is she always this…nice?"

"Please don't take it personally. She's overprotective. Especially with everything that happened with my ex."

I grinned and teased him. "Are you the younger brother?"

His cheeks turned a cute shade of pink. "Yeah. She's three years older."

"You realize I was afraid for my life, right?" At least I tried to sound afraid.

His smile immediately faded. "Why?"

"Your sister is *very* intimidating."

He laughed and waved me off. "Oh, she's harmless."

"It's not funny. I thought she was your possessive girlfriend."

Daniel laughed harder. "Girlfriend?"

"Yes." I whispered over the table, "And if you'll remember, I was with you last night."

"I don't have a girlfriend."

"How was I supposed to know?"

He flashed an apologetic smile. "I was about to tell you who she was before she interrupted me."

I reached for the small red vase and sniffed the flower, surprised it was real. "It's not hard to tell how close you are."

He nodded as his smile weakened. "We are. Our mom died a few years ago, so it's just the two of us now."

"Oh, I'm sorry. I-I didn't know."

"It's okay. Since we never really knew our dad, she was the only family we had." Daniel's eyes darted at the kitchen and then back to me. "Well, besides Jory, the cook. He's family. He's Abigail's husband."

I tried to pronounce it correctly. "Jor-re?"

Daniel grinned like he expected my reaction. "Yeah. His parents couldn't decide between Jordan and Cory, so they split the name and came up with Jory."

"So, they run this place together?"

"They *own* this place."

I smiled, surprised. "Oh."

Daniel rested his arms on the table. "Mom had a life insurance policy. Abigail built this diner with her money, and I started my business with mine."

"It looks like you two have done well for yourselves," I commented, impressed.

"I don't want to sound like I'm bragging, but everything I own is paid for. The business is something I love doing to help people."

That explained how he could afford to be so charitable.

"I don't think that's bragging. I think that's a big heart talking."

He smiled like my comment meant the world to him. "Thanks."

"You're a good person. I'm sure your mom would be very proud of you."

Daniel's eyes radiated with sadness as though he still grieved.

"She was a good mom. She worked at the bank for twenty years. Everyone who knew her loved her."

"It's not hard to imagine what she was like when I see how kind you've been to me."

As for Abby, perhaps she took after their father.

Daniel had the warmest smile that traveled to his blue eyes. "Mom would've liked you."

"Your mom would want you to live your life and be happy. She wouldn't want her passing to take away from that."

"Yeah, I know," he mumbled and glanced at his hands, rubbing his palms together. "It's hard sometimes. We were close. I miss her."

My heart ached listening to him, remembering my own loss. "I know what you mean. When my dad died, I was devastated."

Daniel gasped, his eyes meeting mine. "You lost your dad?"

I nodded, trying not to tear up. I hadn't said those words in a long time, but they still pierced my heart with the same raw stab. "When I was fourteen. A man ran a stop light and plowed into the side of his work truck. He died instantly. I didn't get to say goodbye."

"I'm sorry to hear that."

I exhaled with sadness, thinking about him. "My dad was a mechanic too."

He smiled, intrigued. "Really?"

Abby returned and reached for a pad and pencil from her red smock, then she exhaled, exhausted. "Sorry about that you guys, but it's just me today."

Daniel sat up straight, doing a drumroll with his fingers on the table. "You already know what I want."

"You're so predictable." Abby picked up Daniel's menu and then mine. "What would you like, Rachael?"

"Your BLT's are really good, so I'll have one of those." I eased out of my chair and stood. "Um, where's the ladies' room?"

Abby pointed her pencil in the direction. "Next to the counter. You can't miss it."

"Thanks." I lowered my head and excused myself.

On the way back to the shop, Daniel didn't say a word. Unlike his sister, he guarded his feelings. The wind blew my long ginger hair into a frenzy. After corralling it, I poked my hand out the window and let the wind force it backwards. I glanced at Daniel. For someone I didn't trust six days earlier, he had become a good friend.

When we arrived at the shop, Daniel handed me a key to the office and told me he would be in shortly. I walked inside. The phone rang. I had forgotten to forward the calls to Daniel's cell phone. I settled in the chair and jotted down the caller's information. Daniel walked inside as I hung up the phone. "You had a call for a tow." I slid the work order across the desk.

Daniel picked it up and glanced over it, pacing. After folding it, he stuffed it into his pocket and looked out the window. "I'll take care of it in a minute."

There was no use prolonging the inevitable. It was time to go back to Rockingham, even though that tug yanked at me, telling me not to. As much as I wanted to listen to that tug, I didn't have a way to look for Mandy. Without any cash and not able to use my credit cards, I had to go home.

"Um, guess I should leave." When I stood, something was missing. Of all things, it was Fumbles. He was in the bedroom. I headed back there to get him.

"Rachael?"

I turned and looked at him. "Yeah?"

Daniel rubbed the back of his neck. "I, um…" He rested his hands on his hips and exhaled. "I was serious about hiring someone. The job is yours if you want it. You can even stay here."

My eyes widened. "What did you say?"

He shrugged. "The job. It's yours if you want it."

My lips parted, but nothing came out. I didn't know what to say. In my moment of hesitation, Daniel turned and sprinted out the door, leaving me standing there confused. Perhaps he had changed his mind. I headed to the back to get Fumbles. For some reason, I detoured and went out the back door instead. After kicking an empty five-gallon bucket a few times, I sat on it and lowered my face into my hands and massaged my temples. "I can't believe Daniel asked me to work for him. Why didn't I say no and leave?"

Because I was tempted by his offer. If I stayed and worked for him, I could look for Mandy. I bit my bottom lip and wondered if his offer was a sign to stay.

"But if I do, then I won't get to see Jilly or Mama and tell her what happened or let her know I'm okay. She and Grandpa will worry about me."

I picked up a rock and threw it at a rusty transmission. Frustrated and confused, I picked up another rock and threw it at the picnic table.

"If I work for him, he's going to ask questions. How am I supposed to answer them?"

"I won't ask you any."

Scared half out of my wits, I sprung up from the five-gallon bucket and spun around to face Daniel standing in the doorway.

"I didn't mean to listen." He stepped outside, raising his hands in defense. "Honest. I went back inside the office, but you weren't there. I went to check your room and saw the back door was open and heard your voice."

"How much did you hear?"

He lowered his hands to his hips. "Rachael, I'm not trying to pry into your business, but I know you're in some kind of trouble. You were starving and dehydrated when I found you—among other things." His eyes softened, and his voice weakened with concern. "Does your family know where you are? I haven't seen you call or talk to anyone since you've been here."

Mentioning them brought tears to my eyes. I looked away to keep from crying, because I missed them so much.

"I want to help you. You don't have to take the job. The offer still stands. But if you don't have a place to go, stay here."

"I can't work for you. If I'm on your payroll…"

"Then I'll pay you cash."

Struggling with what to do, I paced with my fingers running through my hair, lifting it to the top of my head.

"I came looking for you to tell you I need to do this run. It's an elderly lady I know. Your keys are on the console. You don't owe me anything, so if I come back and you're gone…" He looked at his feet and exhaled. After a moment, he looked at me. "I hope you'll stay, but I have to respect your decision. Just know that you always have a place to stay if you ever need to come back." He turned and went back inside the shop.

Forty-five minutes later, Daniel's wrecker pulled in with his tow. I stood from the chair so I could see where he parked. He stepped out of the wrecker and made his way to the office. For some reason, I freaked out and ran to my room and paced with my hands together under my chin.

The office door closed. His footsteps drew closer in fast strides. When I turned to look, Daniel stood in the doorway.

"Does this mean you're staying?"

I tucked the hair behind my ears, wondering the same thing. "I want to, but what if I'm making a mistake?"

"Rachael, if you're in trouble, maybe staying here isn't a mistake. At least you'll be safe here."

Daniel had a point. I pinched my bottom lip and thought, considering his offer. Maybe I could stay for a week and look for Mandy. If my instincts were wrong, then I would go home.

"Can I ask what's keeping you from staying?"

There was another concern. Daniel was divorced, alone, and maybe looking for someone.

"If I stay and work for you, we keep this strictly a boss and employee arrangement. You focus on your life, and I…well, I'll deal with mine."

Daniel smiled. It was the first time since we were at the diner. "That's not a problem."

"Are you *sure* you're okay with not asking me any questions?"

Still grinning, he nodded once, back to his happy self. "Absolutely."

"Why did you walk out of the office after offering me the job? You didn't even give me a chance to answer."

"Let's just say…" His lips parted, hesitating like he searched for a suitable reply. "Because I was going to try to talk you into staying, and it had to be your decision."

I shrugged and accepted his answer. "Okay."

"I have a question for you."

"Go for it."

"What convinced you to stay?"

"A little birdie told me to."

Daniel chuckled. "Wonder if it's the same one that told me to take Mill Creek Road last week?"

"Maybe." I winked without realizing it.

His eyes were as blue as the Caribbean waters. "I've got to work on this car and then I have to tow it to her house."

When he turned to leave, I called out to him. "Daniel?"

With one hand on the doorframe, he looked over his shoulder at me. "Yeah?"

"Thanks for everything."

Daniel nodded before he walked out. He was like my angel in a brown uniform.

Chapter 7: A New Life

Determined to find Mandy while under the radar, I accepted Daniel's offer to work for him. With the resources at hand and getting paid, I just had to think like her. At the same time, Rachael Greyfell needed to disappear by eliminating any evidence of my identity. Daniel knew my first name, but that would be all I let slip out. After he left to tow the car to the elderly lady's home, I started with my Jeep. I put Jilly's car seat in the cargo area. Then I gathered everything into a trash bag.

Once I had the Jeep taken care of, I headed back inside and went through my wallet. I cut every credit card and form of identification into tiny pieces. While rummaging through a part of my purse I rarely used, I came across an old keychain with a picture of Peter and me in New York City. Peter, along with his father and brother, went there once a year for a convention. When he invited me to go, I eagerly said yes to the adventure of a lifetime.

Peter took me on a carriage ride around Central Park. I thought it was because he knew how much I loved horses. I was wrong. He pulled a red velvet box from his pocket and asked me to marry him. Later, I found out he had paid the guide a big tip to take our proposal picture.

"Stupid memory." I grabbed the scissors and cut the picture into tiny pieces. They fell in the trash can along with my tears.

Over the next few days, I began to feel like a caged animal. My mind could barely function, staring at the dingy concrete walls all day. I needed out of the office, and I didn't care where I went. Desperate, I asked Daniel if we could order something from the diner and offered to run get it.

It was my first time driving since running off the road, which added to my anxiety.

Before walking into the diner, I had to work up the courage by taking in a deep breath and then letting it out, then I entered, grateful no one looked my way. Still, my heart raced. I didn't know who might be an off-duty cop and recognize me. Instead of sitting at a table, I straddled a stool. While waiting for someone to take my order, I glanced through the kitchen opening. Jory was hard at work, flipping burgers. In his younger days, not that mid-thirties are old, I could see him as a biker. Even though his hair was short, I imagined at one time it was long. His arms were thick and covered with tattoos. A greasy white apron covered the beginnings of a growing belly.

He glanced my way, and our eyes met. My heart skipped a few beats, but when he smiled, it made me smile. Perhaps I had misjudged his appearance. Jory probably had a big heart behind that tough exterior.

"Hi. I'll be right with you."

I heard the young lady before I saw her. Then she hurried past me and rushed behind the counter. The timid girl who looked fresh out of her teens set a coffee pot on the burner. She was thin with long black hair clamped to the back of her head. She turned and faced me with her green eyes sparkling under a black curtain of blunt-cut bangs. "Sorry to keep you waiting."

With my hands on the counter, I intertwined my fingers and straightened my back. "You're fine. I just got here."

She reached for a pad and pencil from the front pocket of her red smock. "What would you like to order?" She brushed her bangs to the side and forced a tired smile.

"Two cheeseburgers without onions, and two orders of fries, please. Oh, and it's to go."

As she scribbled the order, I noticed her name tag: *Missy*. She was the one Abby had fussed about calling out sick.

She ripped the ticket from her pad and glanced at me with the same weak smile. "It shouldn't be but a few minutes." She walked to the kitchen opening and shoved the ticket on a carousel.

"Rachael, right?"

Abby's voice came out of nowhere before she ended up behind the counter and punched some buttons on the register. Her tone wasn't friendly, and neither were her penetrating blue eyes.

"Um, yes."

She glared at me and closed the register drawer a little too hard. Then she made her way directly in front of me and crossed her arms. "How long are you staying in town?"

"I'm not sure. Daniel offered to let me work for him."

"So I heard." Abby smacked her palms on the counter and

leaned closer. "Let me tell you something. My brother's been through a lot, and to be honest, I don't trust you. *Especially* since no one's allowed to ask you questions."

"I respect that, but I'd *never* repay Daniel's kindness with anything other than the same."

Abby stood straight, her eyes still glaring, perhaps gauging my sincerity. "Daniel has a tender heart. *Don't* mess with it."

"I have no intention of doing that. I made it clear that I only work for him."

Missy approached, holding her stomach. "Abby, it's slow. Would it be alright if I leave early? I've been sick twice this morning."

"Sure. It's fine. Thanks for hanging in as long as you did."

Missy removed her smock. "If I could hold down some food, I think I'd feel better." She walked away and disappeared through the swinging kitchen door.

"Is she okay?"

Abby sighed, rolling her eyes. "She found out she's pregnant. That's why she's been sick."

"Oh, wow."

"I know. We're happy for her, but I can't keep running this place on my own not knowing which morning she's too sick to come in."

"If you get in a bind, let me know. I'll come in and help." Me and my big mouth. What was I thinking? I couldn't work for her.

Abby's eyebrows shot up. "Are you serious?"

"Um, sure." I smiled but hoped she wouldn't take me up on my unintentional offer. She obviously didn't like me, so why would she want me working in her diner?

Abby squinted, staring hard at me. "Do you have any experience working in a diner or a restaurant?"

"No, and you can't pay me either." Two good reasons not to take me up on my offer.

"Legally, I can't do that." She looked me over, still deep in thought. "But I'm desperate, so I'll take you up on your offer."

"Abby. Order up."

We shifted our gaze to Jory. For someone who looked intimidating, he sure had a sweet smile and a warm voice. The biker look was deceptive. He was probably a big teddy bear in disguise.

Abby fetched my order and set it on the counter, smiling like she had just won a bet with me. "I'll call the shop the next time

Missy's sick."

"Okay. How much for the food?" I stood and reached for the ten-dollar bill from my pocket Daniel had given me.

Abby nudged my order closer, her grin even wider. "This one's on the house."

I handed her the money, not wanting her charity. "Please let me pay."

"Table four," Jory announced as we stared.

Abby laughed, looking over her shoulder, heading for the opening. "Keep the money. I have a feeling you're going to be working it off." She reached for the plates on the divider and carried them to the customers.

I grabbed the to-go boxes and headed for the door. "Rachael," I mumbled to myself. "You have a big mouth."

That night, I couldn't sleep thinking about Eric Jackson. He's the only person who would know where Mandy was. He was her guy friend she met in college. When I moved in with her, Eric and I became friends. Then we became a couple. Eric was a free-spirited guy. He didn't have a lick of sense, but he sure was full of life. He loved anything to do with the outdoors, as did I. We were always doing something: hiking, fishing, camping. Eric talked about getting married, but I didn't feel that kind of connection with him. I hated to break his heart, but I couldn't give him mine.

~ ~ ~

The next day, as soon as Daniel left for a run, I decided to call Eric. The first two attempts were wrong numbers. It was the third time I was successful.

"Hello?"

My heart pounded at his familiar voice. "Hey, Eric."

"Rachael? Rachael Baylen?"

He never did call me by my married name, but I was okay with that.

"Yes, it's me. Listen, I wish I could talk longer, but I only have a few minutes. Have you talked to Mandy lately?" I closed my eyes and mouthed, "Please say yes."

"No. I haven't heard from her in…I guess, almost a year now. Why? What's going on?"

With my elbows on the desk, I lowered my forehead to the palm of my free hand and sighed. The disappointment clawed at my heart. "We kind of lost contact, and I need to talk to her."

"Have you tried her folks?"

"No. I called Mandy a couple of weeks ago, but her phone was disconnected. You know how she is about paying her bills. Is there any way you could call her?"

"Yeah, I'll give her a ring. Rachael, what's wrong?"

I sat back in my chair and debated how much to tell Eric. Although I trusted him, I didn't want to involve him more than I had to for his sake. "I can't go into details right now. I just need to find Mandy. Eric, I wouldn't ask you to do this if it wasn't important. I'm sure she's had her phone turned back on by now, but I can't call her again."

"I will, the first chance I get, okay? Gander Mountain has me working fourteen-hour days, trying to get this store remodeled. Some days I collapse when I get back to the hotel."

Happy tears pooled in my eyes. My feet tapped the floor, doing a little happy dance. "You have no idea how much this means to me. Tell Mandy I'm looking for her. To name a place and time where we can meet."

"Is this your new number?"

My wide smile faded. "Um, no. I lost my phone. I'm using someone else's, so I'll have to call you back."

"Okay. Give me a call Sunday afternoon."

"Eric, I owe you for this—big time."

He chuckled. "I'll keep that in mind."

I tucked the hair behind my ear. "Please don't tell anyone I called you. Not even Mama."

"Rachael, you know I won't."

I nodded, releasing a sigh of relief. "Thanks. I need to go, but I'll call you Sunday."

"It was good to hear from you."

"You too. Bye."

After hanging up, I spun around in the chair, relishing in my victory. However, before the chair came to a stop, my excitement faded and curiosity stole my joy. Why didn't Eric know what had happened? It didn't make sense, even if he had been out of town. And why hadn't Mandy called him? Eric was the perfect go-to guy.

Abby tossed a red smock at me. "You sure you're up for this?"

I laughed, threading my arms through the sleeves. "How hard can it be?"

Abby pointed to a table, and I glanced that way. "Go take their order, and we'll just have to wing it."

I asked how hard it could be, and I found out. Abby worked my butt off. At least the customers were patient. I constantly explained it was my first day. Besides trying to do a job, I was terrified someone might walk in and recognize me. However, from the conversations I overheard in passing, it seemed the only concern was the weather, what crop was in rotation, or who had died. Typical small-town country talk.

I had this one customer who was creepy. Skip was at least six-foot-tall, slender, and appeared to be in his mid-forties. Tattoos of skulls and guns covered one arm and a rebel flag on the other. He rolled his sleeves up to his shoulders and wore his hair in a low ponytail. His face was narrow and sunken in. It wasn't his looks that made me uncomfortable, but how he crossed the line and flirted.

After the last rush, Abby told me I could leave. She thanked me profusely and asked, "You sure I can't pay you something for helping?"

I removed the smock and reached for my purse underneath the counter. "I'm sure. Have a good evening."

"Wanna go with me to Target tomorrow?"

My brows shot up with surprise of her invitation. "Um, I'm not sure I—"

"Good. We close every day at two, so I'll pick you up around three." She brushed past me, leaving me standing there before I could say anything.

~ ~ ~

While sitting at a red light, Abby glanced in the rearview mirror and fluffed her bangs.

"Why did you invite me to go with you? It's no secret you

don't like me."

She swiped on some lipstick lightning fast and pressed her lips together. "Maybe I want to get to know you since you're spending so much time with my brother." Her eyes darted to mine, and she gave me a snarly glance-over. "And, you need new clothes. Time to stop wearing Daniel's T-shirts."

"Thanks for your concern, but I don't have any money to buy clothes."

A mocking half-smile appeared. "But I do."

I smirked. "Thanks again, but I'm not letting you buy me clothes."

"Oh please." She looked at her vanity mirror and pulled the band from her ponytail, freeing her hair. She fluffed it with her fingers. "It's not a big deal."

"To me it is."

"Don't worry about it. You can work it off if it bothers you *that* much."

My irritation grew. "That's *not* the point."

Abby's sparkling blue eyes met mine, and she flashed a taunting grin. "I heard women with red hair have fiery temperaments. Are you by chance Irish?"

Smirking, I countered. "Are the jokes about blondes true?"

She flipped her hair past her shoulder and sang in a sassy tone, "Yes, blondes have *all* the fun."

I thought she was going to tell me she wasn't dumb. She got me. I didn't have a comeback.

The light turned green. Abby proceeded with the traffic. I looked out the window and wondered what her agenda was. Keep her enemy close? And what part of our little adventure had Daniel's name written on it?

~ ~ ~

"No, Abby. Stop. That's *way* too many." I watched her toss shirt after shirt over the side of the red cart. "I said, stop."

Abby sorted through them like she was on a mission. "Oh hush. We're not getting all of them." She held up a yellow and white shirt and eyed it. "Nope. It won't go with your *red* hair." She giggled, placing it back on the rack. The next shirt she held up was sleeveless and low-cut.

My eyes widened, and I pointed at the rack. "No way. Put it back."

Abby looked at my chest and then the shirt. Her brows narrowed. "I guess not. Your girls might accidently escape. Can't have that in front of my brother."

Finally, it was my turn to grin. "Guess you don't have that problem."

"Hey, my girls might be small, but they like the freedom of not having to wear a bra all the time." She grinned with pride. "Like right now."

I admired Abby's witty humor as a comeback, but I wouldn't let her know that.

"Let's hit the dressing room." She pushed the cart and looked over her shoulder at me. "You coming or not?"

As I privately tried on each article of clothing, I stared at my reflection. The old Rachael stared back at me. It was a boost to my self-confidence seeing the old me again. Even though I resisted Abby's offer, she was right. Wearing Daniel's T-shirts had overshadowed my femininity.

Abby drove me back to the shop after our little shopping spree. The first thing I did was put on makeup. I hadn't worn any since leaving Rockingham. Abby was eager to advise me as she watched. By the time she left, I was confident our status had been upgraded to a possible friendship. I liked Abby once she let her guard down. Perhaps she realized I wasn't a threat to her brother.

Daniel stopped by later with burgers and shakes. He said he was in the neighborhood, but something told me he wanted to see how our little adventure went. I caught him staring at the new me and hoped he didn't get any ideas. I only had one thing on my mind and that was finding Jilly.

~ ~ ~

Daniel didn't work on Sundays, so I had the whole day to myself. It gave me privacy when it came time to call Eric. I got excited at the thought of him telling me where Mandy would be. I had my hopes up that I would have Jilly in my arms before the sun set. Around two o'clock, I couldn't wait another minute and called Eric.

"Rachael?"

"Hey. I hope this isn't a bad time." I gnawed at a thumbnail, unable to sit still, desperate to know if he had talked to Mandy.

"Actually, I'm in the middle of something. Hold on a sec." The loud noise in the background became stifled. "Listen, I called Mandy. Her phone is still disconnected. I even tried her parent's home, but no one answered. Don't worry. I didn't leave a message."

Overcome with disappointment, my eyes watered and my body deflated into the chair. I choked up the words, "Thanks, Eric. I appreciate you trying."

"Tell me what's wrong. You know I'm going to worry about you."

With my hand over my mouth, a few tears trickled down my face. "I wish I could, but I can't."

"Are you and Mandy in some kind of trouble?"

"Eric, please don't ask. I'd give anything to tell you, but I can't." I hated to ask, but I was desperate. "Is there any way you can call her parents again?"

"Sure, but since I can't call you back, can you give me a week? I got word yesterday we're moving on to our next store in three days, and things are hectic here."

Another week? He might as well have said a year. At least there was still some hope. Surely over the next week, he would speak to her parents and then call Mandy.

"Of course that's fine. But please don't tell anyone we've talked. Please."

"You know you can trust me. Are you going to be okay?"

"I will once I find Mandy."

"*Coming*," he yelled away from the phone. "Hey, I hate to cut this short, but I need to get back to the crew so we can finish this store by Wednesday. Call me Sunday, okay?"

"I will, and thanks for everything."

~ ~ ~

Abby called. Missy was sick and needed to leave early. She asked if I would come in and finish her shift. Within fifteen minutes, I walked into the diner. Abby was at the counter talking to a man. The young guy was tall, muscular, and had long blond hair like corn silk.

"Rachael, I want you to meet Colt. He's one of our vendors."

I tried not to smile too wide at the energetic surfer-looking dude bobbing his head. "Hi. Nice to meet you."

"You too, but as they say, 'back to work'." He grinned with a somewhat goofy disposition that made me laugh. Colt reached for a clipboard off the counter. "See ya next time, Abby."

"Tell your dad I said hey," Abby shouted just before he pushed through the swinging door.

An hour later, the lunch rush began to dwindle.

I sighed, shoving a ticket on the order carousel. "Boy, lunch was crazy."

Abby reached for two plates on the divider. "I *hate* 'free slice of pie' days."

I snorted. "You should complain to the *owner.*"

"Oh hush." Abby rolled her eyes and scurried away.

I reached for the next order on the divider and headed toward table four. While I served the customers, I noticed Skip walk in. When he headed for my section, I cringed. Once I finished serving the two ladies, I headed to his table.

"Well hello beautiful," Skip sang when our eyes met. "How's my favorite waitress today?"

"Fine," I answered in a short tone and placed the menu before him, although I wanted to hit him with it the way his eyes perused my body. "What would you like to order?"

"Honey, I think I'm gonna have the special. You can omit the free pie, and I'll take you for dessert instead." He cackled and handed me the menu.

"I'm sure you'll enjoy the pie." I yanked the menu from his grip and walked away. At the kitchen opening, I shoved his ticket on the carousel and let out a sigh, not realizing how loud it was.

Jory eyed the next ticket in line. "Everything okay?"

"What's up with that guy Skip?"

"All I know is he started coming in here a few weeks ago." Jory's eyes darted to mine. "Why, did he say something out of line to you?"

I shook my head. "Oh no. He's just weird."

Abby approached. "Ignore him. We get weirdos from time to time." She took her order from the divider and scurried away.

Someone walked in that made me smile. "What are you doing here?"

Daniel waved at Abby and then looked at me with those blue eyes. "I was in the area. Thought I'd stop by and see how you're doing."

"Tired." I exhaled and let my shoulders drop. "It's been busy. It just slowed down a few minutes ago. Have a seat, and I'll get you something to drink and put in your order."

Daniel sat at his usual table. I brought him a glass of tea and was going to sit with him, but Jory announced Skip's order. While serving him, Skip tried to engage me in a conversation. Uninterested, I attempted to walk away, but he grabbed my wrist.

"Wait. Don't leave yet. I ain't done telling ya my story."

I turned and roared, "Let go of my arm."

"Sit here for a minute. I haven't gotten to the good part yet."

"No. Let go." I tried to jerk my arm free.

"Ah, come on. One minute won't hurt. It's slow."

I looked him in the eye and whisper-shouted, "I *don't* socialize with customers, and if you don't let—"

Daniel slapped his palms on the table and glared at Skip. "I suggest you let go of her by the time I count to three. And think fast, because I started counting on my way over here."

Skip released my wrist, glaring back at Daniel and said in that gargled voice of his, "Mind your own business, *boy*."

I raised my hand to Skip. "Stop, or you're out of here." I turned to Daniel, hoping to avoid a scene. "Go back to your table."

Daniel pointed at Skip. "You *ever* touch her again, I'll—"

"Stop." I stepped into his view of Skip and eased him backwards. "Let it go."

Thankfully, I managed to walk Daniel back to his table without anyone noticing what happened.

He took my wrist and looked it over. "Did he hurt you?"

"No. I'm okay." I pulled my wrist from his hands.

Daniel looked at Skip. "I'm going to tell Abigail to ban him from coming back."

"No. Let it go." I popped his stomach with the back of my hand. "And stop staring at him. You're only going to provoke him."

Daniel looked at me with his blue eyes suddenly gray. "He has no right putting his hand on you."

"I know, but listen to me." I leaned closer, lowering my voice. "Please don't make a scene. I can't have the cops coming here."

"That guy is trouble."

I squared my shoulders. "I can take care of myself, you

know."

"Table seven," Jory called out as we stared.

"That's your order." I pointed at his chair. "Sit down, and I'll sneak you a slice of pie."

Daniel raised one eyebrow. "Are you going to eat a slice with me?"

"If you sit down."

~ ~ ~

My shift was over. Before leaving, I fixed a glass of iced tea and sat on a stool to cool off. Summer was in full force.

Abby sat on the stool next to me and pulled the tip money from her smock. She separated the denominations. "I sure appreciate you filling in for Missy again."

"You know I don't mind. Morning sickness can be rough." I lifted the glass and gulped the cold sweet liquid.

"Oh hush and let me thank you since you won't let me pay you," she grumbled, flattening the singles on top of each other. When she came across a ten-dollar bill, she tossed it at my hand and giggled. "Oops. I think that's yours."

"Will you stop?" I laughed and tossed the money back at her. "Look at all the clothes you bought me."

"Whatever. I appreciate it." She gathered her tips into one stack. "You guys want to come over tonight for supper? Jory bought a new grill and wants to try it out before our Fourth of July party."

I lifted the cold glass to my cheek. "Sure. That sounds nice. I'll let Daniel know when I get back to the shop." Abby looked at me suspiciously, and I laughed. "What?"

"My brother seems more like his old self since you've been around." She grabbed a menu and fanned her neck. "Did he tell you about Nikki?"

"Who?"

"His ex."

I ran my finger down the side of the glass and wiped away the condensation. "He mentioned her."

Abby growled. "I wanted to strangle her for what she did to him."

"You should thank her."

Abby popped me with her menu. "Bite your tongue."

"Oh come on. Daniel would still be with her if she hadn't left him, and you know it. He deserves someone a lot better than her."

"You know he likes you."

I waved her off. "Stop it. He's happy someone's sitting behind that desk instead of him."

"Abby, are you taking another break?"

Two customers stood behind us.

She turned and scolded the gentleman while taking his ticket. "Larry, if you and Steve didn't run us so ragged, then we wouldn't need to take a break, now would we?"

Chapter 8: Snowball

Late June

Even though it was hot, I went outside and laid on the picnic table to think and make a decision. The oak tree towering above me offered shade but little relief from the sweltering heat. A puffy cotton-white cloud slowly sailed across the blue sky.

Eric was expecting me to call him, but the more I thought about it, it seemed too risky. Some of the things he said the previous Sunday caused me not to trust him. Eric acted strange, setting off red flags. Why did he pretend he didn't know about the shooting and the fact I was a fugitive? I expected him to question me endlessly about what happened, but he didn't ask one question. And why wait a week for me to call him? Was he setting me up? Something wasn't right, and I couldn't risk contacting him again.

Since calling Eric was a bust, I was at a dead end and depressed. It was time to go home. So much time had passed, if Mandy was out there, she had probably given up on finding me and returned home.

The next day, Daniel left me alone, brewing in my misery, which surprised me. He always tried to make me laugh or smile when I was sad. Maybe he was tired of having a whiny-butt hanging around.

"Get ready. I need you to go with me on a run," Daniel ordered in a bossy tone, entering my room.

"I don't want to go anywhere." I pulled the covers over my head.

"Too bad. It's working hours, which means you're on my time." He pulled back the covers in one swift jerk. "Get out of those pajamas and meet me outside."

"Daniel, *please.*" I gave him a sad face and recoiled from the cool air. "Not today, okay?"

71

He rested his hands on his hips as we stared. "I wouldn't tell you to go if—"

"No." I pulled the covers back over me and rolled over, facing the wall.

"Ten minutes," he warned, his footsteps announcing his departure. "Or I'm coming back and carrying you out to the rollback in your pajamas."

From his tone, Daniel meant what he said. I threw back the covers and growled. After I changed, I locked up and met him in the rollback.

"Where are we going?" I yelled over the roaring wind, putting my hair in a ponytail.

"You'll see," he answered in a dry tone.

I rolled my eyes, still mad at him. "Why did you make me come with you?"

He glanced my way, lacking his usual smile. Did someone forget to take his happy pills today?

"A little birdie told me to."

"I *hate* that stupid bird. If I see it—*I'm gonna shoot it.*" I raised my eyebrows and tightened my lips at him.

Daniel turned his attention back to the road and covered his laugh.

"It's not funny. I didn't want to come."

"You've made that clear."

Daniel turned down a long driveway of a beautiful farm. Four horses grazing in the pasture to my right caught my attention. I crossed my arms and rested them on the door, watching in awe with my face out the window and my cheek kissed by the wind. In unison, they raised their heads and looked our way as we traveled the driveway kicking up dust. A beautiful white horse took off running. The others followed. They ran along the fence beside us like we were in a race.

I looked over my shoulder at Daniel. "Horses."

His own grin seemed to say he took pleasure in seeing the thrilled expression on my face. "I take it you like them?"

My heart raced with excitement I hadn't felt in a long time. Something in me had come back to life. "Mmm, I guess you can say that." I turned my attention back to the horses and watched with admiration. Their manes danced in the wind. Their muscles accentuated power.

When we came to a stop between the house and a barn, the

horses came to a stop at the corner of the pasture, bumping each other.

"What's *up*, Daniel?"

The voice of an energetic man caused me to turn and look. A gentleman in his late thirties made his way to us. The sweat-stained baseball cap covered most of his dark hair. From the size of his swollen cheek, he had dip in his mouth. He leaned over, crossed his arms, and rested them on Daniel's door.

Daniel killed the engine. "Doing okay. How about you?"

"Who, me? I can't complain." He turned to spit. "'Cept for that truck over yonder." He pointed at the barn and laughed frustrated. "Darn thing gave up the ghost on me."

"It sounds like the fuel pump. I'll take it to the shop and check it out." Daniel was cute when he talked business. "Seth, this is Rachael. She works for me." Daniel looked at me and laughed. "Rachael, this is Seth. He keeps me in business." Daniel was so free-spirited and happy.

Seth reached his hand inside the cab. "Nice to meet ya, ma'am."

While shaking his hand, I could only think of one thing. "You sure have some beautiful horses."

He chuckled, adjusting his baseball cap. "Thank you. I appreciate that. You're welcome to walk down there and pet 'em. They're gentle and love attention. Especially Snowball." He turned and spat.

I reached for the door handle, ready to bolt, my heart racing with excitement. "Are you sure it's okay?"

Seth waved me off. "Absolutely."

I looked at Daniel and opened the door. "You know where to find me." Before he could respond, I was out of the rollback. My legs couldn't carry me fast enough. With their heads over the fence, the horses watched me run toward them. Snowball wasn't shy, so I approached him and sang, "Hey there." I stroked his nose. In my shattered world, it seemed therapeutic, running my fingers over his soft hair. "It's been a long time since I've done this."

Daniel rested his arm on the fence and watched. "I think he likes you."

"He sure is a beauty."

Daniel patted the paint horse in front of him. "That little birdie told me you might like to come here."

I laughed, needing that moment. "That birdie was right.

Guess I shouldn't shoot him after all."

Daniel chuckled. "I'm sure he would appreciate that."

I looked at him and smiled with appreciation. "This is really nice, Daniel. Thanks. You have *no* idea how much I needed this." It was sad to think it would be the last time I saw a horse since I was going to prison.

"I figured it would cheer you up."

Snowball snorted like he wanted my attention, so I turned back to him.

Daniel cleared his throat. "Do you know how to ride?"

"Of course," I replied with passion in my voice. "I used to ride when I was young."

"Just wondering."

A loud whistling caught the horse's attention. They bumped each other trying to turn around and then took off running. Their departure roared like thunder. I smiled, watching them head to the barn.

"Would you like to ride Snowball?"

I covered my mouth and squealed like a little girl. "Are you serious?"

Daniel chuckled. "Very serious. Seth is going to saddle him up for you. That's why he called them to the barn." He nodded in that direction. "Go ahead. He's waiting for you. I've got to load his truck."

"Thank you *so* much." I gave Daniel a quick hug and ran to the barn.

~ ~ ~

Seth tightened the last strap on the saddle and steadied Snowball. "He's ready when you are."

The stirrup squeaked when I inserted my foot and threw my leg over the saddle. The smell of Snowball made me inhale deeply, taken back to my childhood.

"Do you know how to ride?"

Nodding, I placed both hands on the horn. "Yes. I grew up on a farm."

Snowball lifted his front ankle at the swarming flies.

"Alright then. Take these." Seth handed me the reins and

threaded his fingers around the bridle, then led Snowball out of the barn. "There's a riding trail you should follow. It goes all the way around the property. Stay on it, and it'll lead you back here."

"Okay."

Seth stopped once we exited the barn and looked at me. "You'll see blue plastic barrels. Make sure they're on your left when you trail by them." Seth reached for the bill of his cap and lifted it. He wiped his forehead with his upper arm and replaced the cap on his head. "Think of the barrels as bread crumbs."

"Sounds easy."

"Lead him down the east side." Seth pointed in the direction. "You'll come back on the south end." He moved his hand in that direction.

"Got it."

"When you come to an open field, he'll probably want to graze a bit." Seth turned and spat and then looked at me. "Any questions?"

I grasped the reins with readiness. "No. I think I'm good."

"Have fun. *Yeeeehaw.*" Seth spanked Snowball on the hind leg, and he took off.

Snowball trotted gracefully down the trail like he knew the routine. When he picked up the pace, I leaned forward in sync with his gallop, bouncing in the saddle. It was such a release from life that I forgot it was in shambles. Even forgetting the pain of not having Jilly. With the wind in my face, the sound of his hoofs, and the power of that beast underneath me, I couldn't think of anything else. And in that moment, admittedly, I didn't want to.

We came to the area Seth mentioned, and Snowball decided to graze, which was fine with me. The small patches of grass were sparse, but Snowball made his way along the barren field nipping at them. The leather saddle spoke when I shifted with each step. His tail swished, swatting at flies.

I patted the side of his neck. "Good boy."

Snowball made his way toward the woods. When we neared the trail, I pulled back on the reins and guided him on the right side of the barrels, away from the grass. I laughed when a rabbit ran out of the woods and sprinted right and then left, then right again. When we came out of the woods, a trail led to the barn, and reality awaited.

"How was the ride?" Seth finger-hooked the bridle and walked us into the barn.

"That was *so* amazing." Once we stopped, I threw my leg over Snowball and dismounted. My feet hit the ground, and I brushed my hands together. "Thank you for letting me ride him."

"Aren't you the pro?" Daniel commented, entering the barn.

The giddiness came out, and I giggled like a little girl. "Oh my gosh. That was so much fun."

Seth threw the saddle over a horizontal post and glanced our way. "You guys should come back one day and ride with me and Tonya."

I gasped with hope, looking at Daniel with my lips pressed together.

"Might take you up on that offer," Daniel replied to Seth, winking at me.

~ ~ ~

On the way back to the shop, guilt riddled my body like standing in front of a firing squad; my punishment for taking a break from life regardless if I needed it.

We arrived back at the shop. Daniel unloaded Seth's truck. As though I had weights around my ankles, I dragged myself inside the office and plopped down in my plush chair and leaned back, tossing my arms over the sides, then stared at the ceiling. I was more depressed than before I left. Since my plan with Eric had failed, I had to tell Daniel I was leaving after we closed up.

Daniel walked through the metal door. He stopped and rested his hands on his hips and squinted. "Is there any apple pie left?"

"Yeah. I think so. Do you want me to cut a slice for you?" I stood, preparing to head to the backroom.

"If you'll eat some with me."

"Okay. I'll be right back."

We sat at my desk and enjoyed two slices of pie each. A food coma threatened my next hour, but I didn't feel as depressed.

A car pulled up.

"We have company," I announced and tried to tidy up the desk.

Daniel stood as a young lady wearing white shorts and a hunter green tank top walked in with a model smile. There's no way she weighed more than ninety pounds.

She lifted her sunglasses over her head with her eyes deeply locked with Daniel's. "Hey, it's been a while," she murmured with a hint of seduction, tucking her beautiful chestnut curls behind her ears.

"Um, I guess it has." Daniel ran his hand through his hair, barely looking at her. "How you been?"

"Oh, you know me. Busy, but good." She reached into the front pocket of her shorts, squaring her shoulders as if to entice Daniel to look at her boobs. She pulled out folded cash between her fingers and offered it to him. "Dad wanted me to stop by and pay you for fixing his truck." When she glanced my way, she did a double take, her brown eyes flashing green.

Daniel tucked the money into his breast pocket. "Um, Heather, this is Rachael. She just started working for me." His eyes met mine, barely. "Rachael, this is Heather."

She smiled like I asked to take her picture for a beauty contest. Perhaps she was relieved I was introduced as an employee and not Daniel's girlfriend. She clearly wanted more than to hand over some cash.

Her eyes flashed back to brown. "Hi. Sorry I didn't notice you when I walked in."

"No need to apologize." I sat back, eyeing her. "I don't mean to stare, but your hair is *so* pretty."

She smiled at my compliment, reaching for a tendril and twirling it. All she needed was some gum to blow a bubble. "Thanks, but it sure is a lot of work. Especially in humid weather."

I leaned forward, cupped my mouth and whispered, "Men have no idea how lucky they are. A two-minute comb in the morning and they're good to go for the rest of the day." I glanced at Daniel and caught his half-smile as he rolled his eyes, knowing he heard me.

She waved me off and batted her eyelashes. "Oh, don't you know it? If they only knew what we go through to look good for them." She glanced Daniel's way, and I wasn't sure if she was talking to him or me.

"Trust me, they know." I laughed. Maybe a little too loud.

Heather's phone whistled. She pulled it from her back pocket and glanced at it. "Really?" She rolled her eyes and shoved it back into her pocket. "I need to go." She looked at me and smiled as though our three minutes had suddenly formed a friendship. "It was nice to meet you, Rachael."

I waved. "Stop by one day to chat."

"I just might do that." Heather flicked the hair over her shoulder and turned her eyes back to Daniel, flashing him a flirty smile. "Call me sometime." After giving him a seductive once-over, she lowered her sunglasses and walked out with her head held high.

The minute the door closed, my eyes darted to Daniel, laughing at what just happened. "Okay, what's the deal with her?"

Daniel reached for a pie crumb on his plate. "I dated her a few times after Nikki left."

"Only a few times? Why?"

"Because…" He picked up an invoice and looked it over. "I wasn't ready to date anyone. That's why."

"She seems nice. She's *really* pretty, and she *obviously* likes you," I teased.

His eyes met mine, letting the invoice free-fall and placing his palms on my desk. His brows narrowed. "If you try to play matchmaker, I'll fire you."

"Come on. It's time you start dating again."

"I will." Daniel stood, straightening his back. "When the right one comes along."

I countered, trying not to laugh at him blushing. "And how are you going to meet her if you don't go out and mingle? You should give Heather another chance. That girl has the hots for you."

Daniel pointed at me and gave me a warning glare. "Don't mention her again."

"You know she's going to come back."

Without saying anything, he bolted for the shop door. While opening it, he looked over his shoulder at me. "Isn't there a rule about you focusing on your life and not mine?"

Before I could answer, the metal door shut.

Ouch. I frowned at his harshness, unlike Daniel. Still, he was right. I had to focus on my life, not his. And he didn't have to worry about me playing matchmaker. After we closed, it was time to go home and find out where my daughter was. Hopefully, with Mama and not the Greyfells. If my in-laws had Jilly, I wouldn't get to see her before I turned myself in. I might not ever get to see her again for that matter. Horrified by the thought, it pierced my heart. Before I had a cryfest in the office, I left my chair and ran out the back door.

The heat enveloped me, running to the picnic table. Once I

sat on top of it, I let go of my tears, missing my little girl and facing an uncertain future. That night, when I told the detectives my story, would anyone believe me? Not that I could explain what happened. All I could do was tell them the truth—what really happened that day.

Chapter 9: A Normal Day

Peter enters the kitchen, tugging his tie in place. "Something smells good."

"It's banana and nut muffins." I motion to his chair. "Have a seat and join us."

Before he takes his seat, he kisses Jilly on her cheek while stealing a marshmallow from her cereal. "Morning, sweetie."

"Hey, Daddy."

After taking his seat, Peter sips his coffee. "I'll be home early. Since Dad is going to be at the store, I'm going to come home and work on the contract for the new store. Andrew said he'd come over around four to help me."

I pinch a bite from my muffin. "I can't believe your father is going to retire, and you'll both have a store once this one is ready."

"I know. Andrew is hoping to open his by the end of June." Peter reaches into Jilly's bowl and steals another marshmallow.

"No, Daddy." Jilly watches him to make sure he doesn't try to steal another one. Then she picks out one of the tasteless oat rings and offers it to him. "Here. You can have these."

"But I like the marshmallows." Peter attempts to steal another one as his hand inches closer.

Jilly guards her bowl, sliding it closer, her eyes warning him not to take another one. Just as Peter goes for a marshmallow, she squeals, "No."

Peter chuckles, reaching for a muffin. "Would it be alright if I invited Andrew and Patsy to have dinner with us?"

"Of course. I'll need to run to the grocery store and pick up a few things." I lower my mug to the table and watch Peter take a bite of his muffin. "Um, you know…it's the anniversary of Mandy's accident this month. Would you mind if I invited her?"

Peter's eyes dart to mine. "Rachael, look, I know she's your friend, but that girl has issues."

"Who doesn't?" I take my mug and head to the sink. "If

something like that happened to me, I don't know if I could handle it either. She's still grieving, Peter." I turn the water on, plug the sink, and add some dish detergent. "She has no one else but me. Her parents don't seem to even care about her." I wash the dishes, frustrated at Peter's lack of compassion.

Peter stands behind me and threads his arms around my waist and kisses my neck. "Rachael, you know there'll be a lot of business talk this evening. Mandy's going to be bored. Why not invite her when we can give her our full attention?"

He's right.

I dry my hands and turn to face him with a pleased smile. "Can I invite her to come over this weekend?"

"Yes."

I finger his belt loops and tug him closer so I can kiss him.

Instead of kissing me, Peter lifts my chin and stares into my eyes. "Do you love me, Rachael? I mean, only me?"

I laugh at his insecurity. "Don't be silly. Of course I do. Now kiss me, Mr. Greyfell." I pucker my lips.

"Yes, Mrs. Greyfell." He brings his lips to mine and kisses me.

After Peter finishes his coffee and muffin, he tells Jilly goodbye. She laughs when he taps Fumbles on his head and tells him to be good. Then he holds me tight and tells me how much he loves me and kisses me goodbye. I watch him walk out the door like I do every morning.

Once I have the kitchen cleaned, we head upstairs to change. If Patsy and Andrew are joining us for supper, I have a lot to do. Since it's Mandy's day off, I invite her to meet us for lunch.

~ ~ ~

We stroll through the mall after eating at Chick-fil-A.

"How's work going?"

"Same crap as always." Mandy sips her soda and adds, "That Mildred, geez, she's *always* on my back. And Keith, oh my gosh. That guy drives me crazy. He's always telling me how to do my job. I can't stand him. Sometimes I hate life. I had to get the maintenance guy to give me a boost this morning, because my battery was dead. It's always something. I can't win."

"Oh please. A dead battery isn't the end of the world." I look at her and notice she's had her hair cut again. "You should let your hair grow out. I've never seen it long."

"No. It's too much trouble." Mandy scowls. "How can you stand that long hair in the summer?"

"It's called…a ponytail."

We approach the center of the mall where there's a play area for kids.

Jilly pats my leg. "Mommy, I wanna go slide."

"Okay, but only go where I can see you."

"I will." Jilly runs to the slide and waits in line.

"Did you talk to Peter about going to Disney World this summer?"

We sit on a bench.

"Yeah, I mentioned it." I sit back and watch Jilly. "It would be nice to go, but you know once Andrew opens his store, Peter will be by himself. He can't just take off and go to Florida for a week."

"Figures. He never takes you anywhere."

I wave at Jilly. "Give him a break. He's a hard worker. You can't fault him for that."

"Rachael, do you ever feel like a trophy wife?"

I turn my eyes to her, lean away and scowl. "Excuse me?"

She shrugs with the straw between her lips. "Just wondering."

"Mandy, watch what you say." I grimace, giving her a warning eye. "I know you two don't get along, but don't say anything else about Peter. I mean it."

"You have to admit…" She rifles through her purse and takes out the enormous sugar cookie she bought earlier. "All you do is stay home and play the perfect housewife and dress up for those fancy business dinners."

"Why do you hate Peter so much? Why can't you two get along?"

She side-eyes me, bending the cookie in half. "Because he does nothing with you. I can't believe you gave up everything you love doing to be a rich man's wife. That's not you, Rachael. I still say you should've married Eric." She bites her cookie, raising a snarky eyebrow at me.

"Are you taking your meds?"

"What's that got to do with it? Either Peter is the most boring man alive, or he's having fun somewhere else."

"That's it. I've had enough." I stand and motion for Jilly to come to me so we can leave before I say something I will regret. "You're in a bad mood for some reason, and I'm not sitting here and being insulted." I look over my shoulder at her. "I don't know what's bothering you, but you're not going to take it out on me. Peter would never cheat on me."

"Mommy. I'm not ready to leave. I only went down the slide one time."

I turn to see Jilly standing in front of me with a pouty face and slouched shoulders. I kneel and tie her loose shoestring. "Sweetie, we need to run to the grocery store. We're out of orange popsicles, remember?"

She rests her hand on my shoulder while I tie her shoestring. "Okay."

Mandy whines. "I'm so sorry." She's always sorry—after the fact. "I didn't mean it." Now the remorseful stage. "You know I say things without thinking." All the time. Mandy doesn't have a filter when it comes to saying what's in her head.

When I look at Mandy, I notice she's wearing the bracelet I gave her in memory of Hannah. That's why she's being so insensitive. The month of May is hard for her. It's been two years this week since the accident.

I stand and gently warn her. "You need to stop saying things like that."

"Don't be mad." She looks up at me with the saddest eyes. A tear runs down her cheek. She wipes it with the tip of her finger and sniffles. "*Please*, Rachael. It's been a hard week." The pain in her voice and the look in her eyes make me want to cry.

I exhale and mumble, "I know it has. Let's talk tomorrow. Okay?"

She takes the shoulder of her shirt and dabs her eye. "Come over to the apartment and hang out."

"I can't." I grab my purse from the bench. "Andrew and Patsy are coming over for supper, so I don't have time." I remember Peter's offer. "Hey, I want you to come over this weekend. You wanna grill out?"

"I guess." Mandy closes her eyes tight.

"Are you having one of those headaches?"

"Yeah."

"Do you have something to take?"

She opens her eyes and shakes her head. "I'm fine."

"Okay." I nod at the exit. "Are you coming or staying?"

"Staying. I might get an ice cream cone before I leave."

"I thought you were going on a diet." I only remind her out of concern.

"I know I'm fat." She snarls and takes another bite of her cookie.

"Stop putting yourself down."

With her mouth full, she fires back. "I'm not. I *am* fat. I know I've gained weight since the accident. I'll go on a diet. I just don't know when."

"Please take your meds. I don't want to see you go back into a deep depression."

Ignoring me, she smiles at Jilly and opens her arms. "Can I have a hug before you leave?"

Jilly throws her arms around her neck. "Bye, Aunt Mandy."

"See ya later, kiddo."

"Let's go," I tell Jilly and reach for her hand.

Mandy waves. "Call me tomorrow."

"I will. See you later."

~ ~ ~

The security alarm beeps, alerting me the garage door opened. A few minutes later, Peter enters the kitchen. Without saying anything, he walks around the counter while I put up the groceries.

"Is everything alright?"

He reaches into the cookie jar. "Everything's fine."

"You sure?" I put the canned food in the cabinet. "You seem distracted."

He leans against the counter and bites into the cookie, still not making eye contact.

"Did something happen at the store?"

Perhaps that is the reason he seems a million miles away.

"No," he answers in a monotone voice.

I approach Peter and cross my arms. "Does it bother you that your father is giving the new store to Andrew and not you?"

"No. I'd rather have this one. Where's Jilly?"

"She's taking a nap." I search his eyes to see if he's with me or lost in his thoughts. "Peter?"

84

He blinks like I startled him. "What?"

"Please tell me what's bothering you."

Peter pulls me close, and I lean against him. "I need to know you love me, and I make you happy."

His words pierce my heart with sadness at the same time alarm.

"Why would you question my love for you? You did that this morning too." The red flags tell me something is wrong. I push back and look at Peter. "Something's been bothering you for two days, and I know it's not the new store."

Peter nods, and I see the weight of the world on his shoulders. "Tonight, after Andrew and Patsy leave, we need to talk. There's something I have to tell you."

As much as I want to know right then, I'm mindful Peter has work to do.

His phone vibrates, but he ignores it.

"Are you not going to answer that?"

Peter takes my face in his hands and rests his forehead on mine. "I know who it is. It's not important." He kisses my forehead. "Andrew will be here soon. I'm going to my office to work on the contract."

"Would you like for me to fix you a sandwich or a snack?"

A forced smile appears, then he shakes his head. "No, but if you want to bring me a bottle of water once I get settled, that would be great." He kisses me with force and passion like it might be our last.

After our kiss, I watch Peter walk down the hallway until he turns and disappears into his study.

~ *Daniel's Shop* ~

"*No, stop,*" I screamed, pulling myself out of the memory. I turned my focus on the car parts scattered in the back of the shop, taking deep breaths and slowly releasing them. It was ninety degrees, but I shivered like it was freezing.

"Rachael?" Daniel's voice grew louder as he approached the picnic table from behind me. "I heard you scream. What happened?"

"Nothing." I quickly wiped each cheek with a long stroke

from my shirt. "I'm fine."

Daniel stood next to me. "Why are you out here in this heat?"

"I needed to be alone."

"Look at me."

I tucked the hair behind my ear and turned my eyes to his.

His brows tightened. "What's wrong?"

"Nothing."

"Talk to me."

Still shaken from the memory, I jumped off the picnic table and paced, hugging myself.

"Rachael, what happened since we got back from Seth's?"

My mind was a mess. I couldn't think and wanted to run until I collapsed and didn't feel anything. To purge my body any way I could from the guilt that tortured me. I couldn't face him when I told him, "I'm going to leave. Today. I have to go home."

Daniel quickly took my arm and stopped me from pacing. Those blue eyes stared into mine. "Rachael, what happened? Talk to me, please."

I couldn't tell him, even though I wanted to.

Daniel wrapped his arms around me. "Whatever it is, it's going to be okay."

I rested my head on his shoulder and threaded my arms around him.

"Rachael, I can't stop you if you want to leave." He leaned his head against mine and held me tighter. "But I *will* keep you from leaving while you're upset." His voice comforted me the way I needed, and I let my body sink into his even more. "Why won't you let me help you?"

"'Cause there's nothing you can do."

"Let's get out of this heat." He took my hand and led me into the shop and then to my room. He disappeared into the closet and returned with a bottle of water. After twisting off the cap, he handed it to me. "Drink, but slowly." He headed to the bathroom.

I gulped the cold liquid with my weak, trembling hand.

Daniel returned with a wet cloth. "Close your eyes." When I did, he wiped my face, washing away the dried tears and warmth from the heat. I allowed my body to receive what he offered. No man had ever washed my face, and it felt good.

"Drink some more water." Daniel headed to the bathroom to discard the wet cloth. When he returned, he stood in front of me with his hands on his hips and waited.

I had all I could drink and gave the bottle back to him.

He twisted the cap on without breaking our gaze. "Lay down on the bed."

I did what he asked. Maybe I needed someone to take over, because I sure didn't feel in control.

Daniel pulled the curtains together, darkening the room. Then he reached for the blanket on the recliner and covered me. "Take a nap. After you wake up, if you still insist on leaving, I can't stop you. But you'll have to convince me you have a safe place to go. If not, I don't wanna hear any more talk about you leaving." Daniel walked out of the room and closed the door.

I laid there too tired to move, staring vacantly. I blinked a few times before surrendering to the exhaustion and fell asleep.

When I woke up, I was still in the same position. I looked at the time. I had been asleep for almost an hour, but it felt like minutes. I left the bed and shuffled to the bathroom. After doing my business, I fixed my hair and touched up my face, then headed to the shop to see if Daniel was there. Soon as I entered the office, I came to a sudden stop. Daniel was sitting in my chair. His elbows rested on the arms with his fingertips together under his chin like he was praying.

"Feel better?"

"A little." I leaned against the doorway and crossed my arms. "How long have you been sitting there?"

"Since you've been sleeping."

"You've been sitting there the whole time? Why?"

"Do you still want to leave?"

"I have to. It's time."

"Can you at least wait until tomorrow?"

"Daniel, I *really* need to go home."

He didn't say anything, although his eyes pleaded for me to stay.

I exhaled and dropped my shoulders. "Fine. I'll wait until tomorrow."

Daniel scratched his jaw as though to hide his smile. "I don't know about you, but I'm suddenly hungry." He stood and stretched, raising his hands behind his head. "Care for some Mexican?"

Sometimes Daniel and I would go to town and grab a bite to eat. He would go in, order the food, and we would sit in his wrecker and people-watch. He was my only window to the world.

87

I flashed a tempting smile. "Chinese?"

He motioned to the door and bowed. "After you."

I led the way, looking over my shoulder. "Don't forget to lock up."

An hour later, we had finished our meal, parked in the corner of the restaurant.

"That was really good." I guzzled the last of my soda and tossed it in the trash bag. "Thanks."

"You're welcome." He offered me a fortune cookie and a tongue-in-cheek grin. "Here. See what your future holds."

Like I didn't already know. Still, I reached for it. "Read yours first."

"Let's see…" Daniel broke the shell and pulled out the strip of paper. "Before the next full moon, someone from your past will come knocking."

"Oooo," I cooed in a spooky voice. "Who do you think it will be?"

"There's no one in my past I want to see."

Daniel stared at the tiny piece of paper with a burning gaze. I thought it might combust. My smile faded, realizing he probably thought about his dad.

I remember Daniel telling me about his high school days. "Wouldn't it be cool if it was your old shop teacher?"

"He died three years ago."

"Oh."

Daniel tossed the paper in the trash bag and looked at me while resting his hand on the back of my seat. "Your turn."

"Here goes." I broke the shell and pulled out the strip of paper and cleared my throat. "Be wise with your next decision. There's no going back." Now *I* stared at the piece of paper. Was the message a sign? A warning?

Daniel grabbed my arm. "Hey, are you alright?"

Shaken, I let the paper free-fall to the floorboard and looked at him. "My next decision was to leave, remember?"

He released my arm and sat back, raising his eyebrows. "Then maybe you shouldn't."

"You don't understand. I *have* to go back."

"Then why are you so upset and letting it bother you? Those things are just for fun."

"I'm not laughing."

"Can I suggest something?"

"What?"

"Stay a few more days and see what happens."

"Daniel, I have to make sure someone is okay."

"Maybe that's why it's not meant for you to go home."

When he said that, my heart skipped a few beats. Was the message a sign not to go home and continue to look for Mandy and Jilly? What if they were still out there but in danger?

Chapter 10: A Smiley Face

I made the decision not to leave Maxton, but only until the end of the week. If nothing changed, I would head back to Rockingham. When I doubted my decision, I read the message from the fortune cookie. Otherwise, I worked feverishly on a new plan to find Mandy.

"Wisconsin." I wrote the word in my orange notebook but second-guessed my memory. "Or did Mandy say she was born in Washington?"

My skimpy page embarrassingly held little details about someone I had known for nine years. Mandy's past was not her favorite subject, and she rarely talked about it. When she did, it put her in a sour mood.

"A private investigator."

I drew a dollar sign and wondered how much it would cost to hire one. With the money I had saved, maybe it was time to find out.

A FedEx truck arrived. The driver rushed in. I closed my notebook. Daniel pulled onto the lot while I signed for the package.

Daniel walked in as the driver walked out. "Is that the part for Jason's truck?" He stood in front of the oscillating fan in search of relief from the sweltering heat.

"Yes."

"Good. He called me this morning to see when it would be ready."

The phone rang. I reached for the receiver like I had done so many times. But when I glanced at the number of the caller, Eric, I retracted my hand as though it were a snake I had almost touched.

Daniel rushed to the desk. "What's wrong?"

"Um…" I looked up at him. What was I supposed to do?

The phone continued to ring.

"Rachael?"

When I didn't answer, Daniel leaned over the desk and

reached for the receiver.

"*No, wait.*" I quickly blocked him. We stared. "It's for me. Please tell him you don't know where I am, and you haven't seen me in a week."

He nodded and brought the receiver to his ear. "Daniel's Automotive and Towing. Daniel speaking."

I cupped my hands and covered my mouth, trying to control my breathing.

"No, she's not. I haven't seen her in a week." Daniel's eyes were on me as he listened. "No. I sure don't. When she left, she didn't say where she was going."

Why was Eric calling me? I told him not to.

"Uh-huh." Daniel mouthed, "He has something urgent he needs to tell you."

I shook my head frantically and mouthed, "No."

"Sorry I couldn't be of any help. If she shows up again, I'll give her your message." Daniel hung up the phone, looking at me, obviously for an explanation.

"What did he say?"

"He said he had some news for you, but it was something he had to tell you personally. If I hear from you, to tell you to call him. He's worried because you never called him back. Who is he?"

"An old friend. I called him because I thought I could trust him, but I turned out to be wrong."

An older gentleman walked into the office. "Daniel Brown," he roared with enthusiasm and offered his hand. "What have you been up to?"

Daniel grinned from ear to ear. "Same old thing, Robert."

"I came by to pick up Kathy's car. She said it was ready."

"It is. I finished it this morning." Daniel nodded at the shop door. "Come on, and I'll show you what was wrong with it." He glanced at me and mouthed, "You okay?"

I nodded. After they disappeared into the shop, I went to my room and laid down. My body still trembled at the thought of Eric calling. He was someone I trusted with my life. Why would he betray me?

After the customer left, Daniel asked me to go on a run with him. He taught me how to hook up to a car. I completely understood why Daniel enjoyed what he did. Getting dirty and greasy was always a plus.

We arrived at the customer's house, but no one was home.

Daniel let me hook up to the car, which made me smile. While I was strapping it down, the tow bar moved. It was only a jolt but enough to scare me. When I looked at Daniel, fearing I had damaged the car, he laughed at me. I finished tightening the strap. "You did that, didn't you?"

Daniel continued to laugh at his little joke. "Sorry. I couldn't resist."

"Ha-ha. That was real funny."

He checked the straps to make sure I had the car secured properly. "You should've seen the look on your face."

The infamous red rag in his back pocket caught my eye, and I jerked it. Daniel turned to see what I had done. That's when I tried to reach for his face and giggled. "I'm gonna wipe that smile off your face."

"I don't think so." Daniel ran away, laughing.

I chased him around the wrecker and the car three times before I had to stop. He was in better shape than I was. I leaned over and tried to catch my breath. A sudden bolt of guilt struck me hard. I went from laughing to crying in a matter of seconds.

"You're giving up?"

When I looked at him, I couldn't speak.

His jaw fell. "Why are you crying?"

Guilt-ridden, I turned my back to him and wiped my face. "Because I don't deserve to laugh when…"

When my child is out there, and I don't know if she's okay. When I don't know if I'm doing the right thing.

Daniel gently turned me around. I clung to him before he had a chance to wrap his arms around me.

"The first time I laughed after my mom died, I felt guilty."

"But this isn't the same. I've done something, and, and…" I cried, missing my little girl.

"Rachael, laughing helps us not to lose our sanity. It's not a bad thing."

"I still feel guilty."

~ ~ ~

It was Friday afternoon. I folded the clothes on my bed I had just washed when Daniel entered my room.

"Do you have a minute?"

I looked at him, folding my shirt. "Sure."

"I have something for you." He handed me a yellow bag.

"What is it?" I peeked inside.

"I added a new line to my cell phone plan and bought you a phone."

I lowered the bag and looked at Daniel. "Why? You know I'm leaving."

Daniel leaned against the dresser and crossed his arms. "I wanted you to have one while I'm gone."

"Gone?"

He nodded. "Seth found a truck on Marketplace in Atlanta he wants to buy and asked if I would drive him down in the rollback and check it out. If it's in good condition, I'll haul it back."

I carried my shirts to the dresser and looked at him as I put them in a drawer. "You didn't have to buy me a phone for a day trip."

"It's overnight."

"Oh." I shut the drawer and headed back to the bed. "When are you leaving?"

Daniel followed me. "In a couple of hours. Seth wants to leave this afternoon and get a hotel. He's going to meet the owner in the morning."

I folded my jeans. "Can I do anything to help?"

"Follow me to the house and stay there tonight."

I giggled at the thought. "I'd feel funny staying at your house by myself."

"Then stay with my sister."

I reached for my socks and sorted them. "Daniel, I'll be fine here."

"I know, but I'd feel better if you stayed at my house. Please reconsider."

We closed the shop early so Daniel could go home and pack. I decided to spend the night at his house and followed him home. While he showered, I made some sandwiches.

After we ate, Daniel cleared the table while I washed dishes, which didn't take long. Once I finished, I took the dishtowel and dried my hands. Daniel stood in front of the sink and gulped the rest of his tea, then set the glass in the sink. He had a sneaky grin and reached for the towel.

I laughed and jerked the towel back. "Hey. Get your own."

"But I want yours," he sang and reached for it again. Daniel was so fast, he had one end in his hand, and we ended up in a tug-of-war.

"Give me." He chuckled, pulling his end.

I laughed all girly but was determined to get the towel. "No fair. You're stronger."

Daniel encouraged me. "Don't give up. You've got quite a pull there."

I backed into the refrigerator and lost my grip. "Ah, dang it."

"Ta-da," Daniel sang, twirling the towel in the air.

I pouted with a sore-loser frown. "Oh hush."

Daniel had that playful grin. "Too bad you weren't watching where you were going."

"Ah, you know you wanted me to."

With my back still against the fridge, my smile weakened, watching him step closer and closer until he was in my space. My heart fluttered with him so close. Our eyes locked. He had me so nervous because I just knew he was going to kiss me. At least that's what his eyes told me. Surely he wouldn't cross that line. Regardless, I wasn't giving him the chance and attempted to step away.

Daniel quickly placed his palms on the fridge to keep me there. "Where you going?"

Nervous, I squealed, "I don't know."

"I sure don't mind standing here until you decide."

Speechless at his deep, flirty voice, all I could do was stare into his gorgeous blue eyes, and he stared into mine. They told me he definitely wanted to kiss me. The thought of his lips touching mine scared me, because I think I wanted them to.

His phone rang.

Daniel's penetrating gaze never left mine as he pulled his phone from the holder on his belt.

With one hand removed from the fridge, I stepped away. That moment, whatever it was, should have never happened. My heart fluttering the way it did should not have happened either.

"That was Seth." Daniel's voice distracted me from my thoughts. The ones of him kissing me. "He's ready whenever I am. Guess I should be going."

I turned, and our eyes met. Why did my heart race simply looking at him? I crossed my arms and tried to ignore whatever was happening between us. "You guys be careful, and have a safe trip."

The way Daniel looked at me, I couldn't help but wonder if

he was thinking about that moment too. Then again, I probably overreacted to something completely innocent.

"You have a phone if you need to call me."

"Don't worry about me. I'll be fine."

When he headed toward the door, I followed. "I'll call you when we get there." Daniel picked up his duffel bag and tossed the strap over his shoulder. He looked handsome in his blue jeans and white button-up shirt with blue pinstripes. "You have a key to the house and the shop, right?"

I nodded. "Yes. I have both."

Daniel opened the door. "I should be home tomorrow around this time."

"Guess I'll see you then."

He walked out, and I followed him. I stood on the porch and watched him get into the rollback. When he waved his hand out the window going down the driveway, I waved back until he disappeared.

Over the next hour, I played with my new phone until boredom set in. Then I decided to sit on the porch. Listening to nature was peaceful. At dusk, the mosquitoes came out, so I headed back inside. Around ten o'clock, my phone whistled a cute tune.

I muted the television and quickly answered. "Hey. Did you make it there okay?"

"Finally. The traffic on I-20 was horrible. We walked into the room about ten minutes ago. Seth went next door to get us something to eat."

I sat up and pulled the blanket over my bended knees. "I know you must be tired."

"I'm more worried about you sleeping on the couch. Sorry I don't have the spare bedroom cleaned out. It's still full of boxes from when I moved in a few months ago."

"The couch is fine. Trust me. I've slept on worse."

"What are you doing?"

I yawned. "Watching a boring movie."

"I have some DVDs in the basement if you like guy flicks."

"That's okay. I brought a book with me, so I'll probably read it."

"Please make yourself at home."

I covered my feet with the blanket while glancing around the empty room. "I am. It's just…quiet here without you."

"Ah," he cooed. "So you miss me?"

Smiling, probably blushing, I rolled my eyes. "You wish."

"I miss *you*."

The way he said it went straight to my heart and caused it to flutter. "I miss you too."

"I wish you were here."

"Why?"

"Because I'd throw you in the pool."

I spit laughed. "You *think* you'd throw me in the pool."

"Oh, I *know* I would."

"You're *way* too confident, Mr. Brown."

"And if you were here, you'd be wet."

"I'd probably be in the hot tub."

"Hang on a second." … "You still there?"

"I'm here."

"Seth just walked in with some burgers."

"You guys go eat."

"Rachael?"

"Yeah?"

"Lock up, okay?"

"I will."

"I really do miss you."

Smiling, I twirled a lock of hair. "I miss you too."

"I'll call you in the morning."

"Just be careful."

"Always."

"Goodnight, Daniel."

"Goodnight, Rachael."

Even our phone call seemed different. I didn't want to hang up. And I did miss him. More than I should have. Tired, I leaned against the arm of the couch and flipped through the channels. My thoughts drifted to Jilly. Her little doggie sat on the coffee table looking at me.

"Fumbles, you're too quiet. Talk to me." I yawned and pressed the button on the remote to turn off the television, leaned back, then covered up with the blanket. "Yeah, I was stupid for thinking that fortune cookie was a sign to stay here. When Daniel gets back, I'm going home."

An hour later, I was still wide awake. I threw back the blanket, stood, and stretched. I decided to go outside, hoping some night air would relax me.

After shuffling across the porch, I crossed my arms on the

railing and leaned forward, taking in the peaceful nighttime harmony. Crickets chirped like they were in a symphony. Frogs intermittently croaked a few choruses of their own. Then an owl hooted, letting everyone below know he reigned over the night as the ultimate hunter.

A cool breeze graced my face. Sometimes I would tell myself that was Dad's gentle touch. Thinking of him, I looked at the sky and admired the twinkling stars. When I was young, Dad and I would sit on the back porch at night and hang out. We would watch for deer, listen to the animals, and stare at the stars. Dad told me to imagine the darkness was a big black curtain. On the other side is heaven, where the bright light is. Then he said to imagine the stars are holes in the curtain, and our loved ones can peek through and watch us. We used to pick one and pretend it was Nana watching. Now I had to pick one and pretend it was him watching me.

Sadness exploded inside of me, and I cried out at God, "Why did my dad have to die?" I caught my breath and screamed harder, "He was the best dad in the world. You *took him* from me for *no* reason." Tears left my eyes with visuals of my father and the memories we shared and for the ones I would never have of him.

The sadness turned to anger. I squinted at the sky and growled at God, "You're taking everyone I love away from me. *Why?* What did I do to deserve this?" I yelled at the sky with everything I had in me. "Why, God? Am I being punished for something?"

In the east, a star caught my attention. It twinkled brighter than any star I had ever seen. I wanted to believe it was my dad telling me he was watching me. I wept, staring at it. "Daddy, I miss you so much."

~ ~ ~

The next day dragged by, waiting for Daniel to come home. Even though it was hot outside, I swept the porch of the debris that had fallen from the tree above. Then I rearranged the patio furniture and gathered all the spare car parts to the side. I was quite proud of myself.

Abby stopped by for a visit. We sat on the porch with a glass of lemonade and talked. She picked on me about how bad I must have it to sit in the heat and wait for Daniel.

I laughed and sipped my lemonade. "You're delusional."

Abby snickered. "I'm not the one delusional. You're both too stubborn to make the first move."

I looked away and mumbled, "I have no idea what you're talking about."

The mood turned heart-wrenching when Abby shared her mom's battle with breast cancer. The first time Leah was diagnosed, Abby was young. It was right before her parents divorced. The second time Leah was diagnosed, she passed within eighteen months.

"I'm so sorry to hear that. I can tell you were extremely close."

Abby stared with sad eyes. "Yeah, we were. I miss her every second of every day."

I placed my hand on hers. "Thank you for telling me about her. I wish I could've met her."

Like Daniel, Abby avoided the subject of their dad. Perhaps some wounds hurt more when you talk about them.

Daniel's rollback came down the driveway.

"Here he comes." Abby punched my arm. "Should I leave so you guys can be alone?"

I dug an ice cube from my glass and threw it at her. "If you don't stop talking nonsense. I told you we're just friends."

Abby laughed. "And I'm a redhead."

Daniel pulled up to the house and parked. We stood, ready to greet him. When he stepped out of the cab, it made me smile to see him. After he grabbed his duffel bag, he made his way to the house.

Abby nudged me. "Here's where you run and greet him with a hug."

With my face tight, I punched her forearm. "Would you stop it."

Daniel marched up the steps, two at a time. "What are you doing sitting out here in the heat?"

Abby pointed at me. "It was *her* idea."

I huffed. "And what's wrong with sitting outside?"

"It's hotter than satan's living room out here. I'm going back inside," she grumbled, heading toward the door.

Daniel chuckled. "She never did like the heat."

"Yeah, that's why she's never in the kitchen at the diner. Are you hungry, or would you like something to drink?"

"Um, some water would be nice."

"Come on, I'll fix you a glass." I held the door for him. "How was the ride home?"

"Good since it wasn't a weekday." He walked through the kitchen. "I'll be right back. I'm going to take this bag to my room."

I poured a glass of iced water and set it on the counter.

"I'm telling you, someone needs to make the first move," Abby whispered as we leaned across the counter next to each other.

"If you don't stop with that nonsense, you're going to see the fiery temperament of this redhead come out," I warned her playfully.

She laughed as if to dare me. "Bring it on."

Daniel walked into the kitchen and rubbed his chest. "Boy, it's so nice to be home."

I pointed to the glass. "There's your water."

Abby jumped in front of him. "Give me a hug first. I've gotta go."

After their hug, Abby gave me one. "See you later."

"Thanks for coming by."

When she released me, she gave me a little push into Daniel. He grabbed my forearms to steady me.

My eyes scolded her as did my voice. "Why did you do that?"

"Someone had to make the first move. You guys have fun." She waved so cutesy and headed for the door.

I screamed, "Abigail Goodman."

Her laughter ended when she walked out of the house.

Embarrassed, I looked at Daniel, still holding my forearms. "Sorry she did that."

"I'm not."

Daniel touching me was probably not a good idea, because I liked it more than I should have. The deeper he looked into my eyes, the harder my heart pounded, fearing he would kiss me for sure that time.

"Come here, you."

Instead of kissing me, Daniel wrapped his arms around me and gave me a tender hug. I timidly threaded my hands to his back and held him. It made me feel safe, and I couldn't resist that feeling.

"I'm glad you're home," I mumbled with my cheek against his shoulder.

"Speaking of, I have a surprise for you."

Daniel released me and reached into his pocket and pulled out a folded napkin. "When I stopped to get some gas, I saw this and thought of you, so I had to buy it." After carefully peeling back the corners of the napkin, he lifted a necklace. A smiley face dangled on the end.

With my lips parted, I cooed, "It's so cute. Thank you."

While he unclasped it, I lifted my hair. Daniel did the honors and put it around my neck. Something told me I was playing with fire by letting Daniel into my heart, but he seemed like the air I breathed. And how do you just stop breathing?

~ ~ ~

That night, I sat at my desk. Instead of going home, I came up with plan B; hiring a private investigator. I searched the cities in Wisconsin and Washington to see if any resembled the one I thought Mandy said was her birthplace. Nothing caught my eye.

I sat back in my chair with one elbow on the arm and my fingers tracing my jaw, pondering what to do next. Curious, I leaned forward and typed Amanda Sue Ross in the Google search bar but didn't hit enter. Mandy told me everything you google could be traced back to you. All she ever watched were those crime shows and talked about how people get caught. I stared at the monitor, still tempted to hit the enter key. One tap and all of my answers might appear right before my eyes. However, I feared I would be the ultimate one searched and couldn't bring trouble to Daniel if the cops found me.

"Damn you, Mandy." I threw myself back in the chair and rubbed my temples, fighting a headache. "What happened that day? Why didn't you show up? Why haven't you turned your phone back on?"

There had to be a reason why. What was I missing?

"Okay, let's say your battery died again, and that's the reason you were late. I was gone when you got to the cabin, so you left." I gnawed at a fingernail and thought. *But what about her phone being disconnected? Coincidence?* I spit out the nail and growled. "Or not?"

A surge of anger coursed through me at a new scenario streaming through my head.

"No. Mandy wouldn't do that to me. She just wouldn't."

100

Or had she?

"No." I pounded the desk with my fist. "*No. No. No.*"

Of all the reasons I had for Mandy not showing up at the cabin, there was one that never entered my mind until then—Mandy ran off with Jilly.

When Mandy had the car accident two years earlier, she was eight months pregnant. She and her boyfriend, Charlie, were in Maryland visiting his parents. Sadly, her baby she had named Hannah, passed a few days later. Since they had to do an emergency hysterectomy, Mandy would never birth children.

Mama and I drove to Maryland to visit her. My heart broke for Mandy, because she wanted that little girl so much. A month later she returned home, but she was a different person. Some days she was angry, and some days she was like a zombie. Mandy was so depressed, there were times I feared she would even try to end her life. Charlie and I finally convinced her to get some help. Unfortunately, a few months later, he left and moved back home with his parents.

Perhaps Mandy saw my situation as her only chance to be a mother and decided to start a new life with my daughter instead of meeting me at the cabin. No one would even look for her. There was no reason to. Everyone assumed I had left town with Jilly.

It was the perfect plan. Mandy could live a free life anywhere she wanted and pass Jilly off as her daughter. Was Mandy so desperate to be a mother she would take my child? Would she use the tragedy of Peter's death to plan such a betrayal? Even though I didn't want to believe she would do such a thing, it made sense. I shut down the computer and headed to bed.

"Fumbles, there's no way I'm going home until I know for sure Mandy didn't run off with Jilly." I crawled under the covers and found a comfortable spot on the pillow. "If she did, I'm going to hunt her down and make her regret the day she betrayed me. If I'm going to prison for shooting Peter, what do I have to lose?"

Chapter 11: The Ex and the Creep

I yawned, sitting at my desk in a sleep-deprived stupor and doodled while thinking of ways to find Mandy. Or at least outsmart her. That's when I realized I had her password to Sprint. I paid her bill a few months earlier because she didn't have the money. If she hadn't changed the password, I could check her statement online. Even though it wouldn't tell me where Mandy was, maybe it would tell me something. But was it safe to do it? Surely the authorities were not monitoring Mandy's phone bill. It didn't matter. I had to find my daughter.

After pulling up Sprint's home page, I typed in Mandy's username and then the password, knowing there was a chance she had changed it. Especially if she had betrayed me, which I wasn't convinced was the case.

After tapping the enter key, her account pulled up. I couldn't believe it.

"No way."

I leaned closer and perused her statement. Something in the upper corner caught my attention. A credit of thirty-two dollars and six cents. A credit to her account meant Mandy's phone hadn't been disconnected due to nonpayment, but she cancelled her service. There was only one reason Mandy would do that. She indeed, had betrayed me. Fuming, I had to look away. The anger had my heart racing so hard my chest hurt. My breathing was so fast it hissed.

"Mandy, I swear I'll hunt you down."

Once the shock settled, I looked at the monitor and clicked on the previous page to see what else I could find out. The last day of service was the day I left town.

"What did you do, disconnect it the second I left your apartment?"

Betrayal had a bitter taste, and I was on fire, ready to spew it on Mandy.

I needed to draw to expel my anger and opened my orange

notebook, almost tearing the pages until I came to a blank one. My hand quivered as the pencil aggressively marked the page, stroke after brutal stroke. The drawing reflected a dark and eerie ambiance. Mandy stood on the edge of a cliff and faced a raging ocean with rising, powerful waves. Gray clouds of evil filled the sky above Mandy as though to haunt her. Then I sketched my hands behind her, ready to push her over the edge. I captioned it: *When I get my hands on you.*

By lunchtime, I was a lit fuse ready to explode. I needed out of the office and told Daniel I was going to the diner to get us something to eat. On the way there, I cussed and screamed, trying to defuse my anger from homicidal thoughts to putting on my hunter's gear. I was so glad I had not turned myself in. Somehow I would find Mandy, and I couldn't do that behind bars. She would regret the day she used a tragedy to steal my child.

I walked into the diner and sat on the last stool at the counter and smiled as though nothing was wrong. "Hello, Missy. How's the morning sickness?"

She poured fresh coffee grounds into the metal funnel and turned on the machine. "It's a lot better now."

Jory poked his face through the kitchen opening. "Hey, Rachael. The usual?"

"Yes, please." My smile was fake. Inside, I was a mixture of hate, hurt, and raging anger.

Zack, Jory's helper, walked by the opening and sang, "Hey, *hey*, hey."

"What's up?" I waved at the twenty-year-old.

Daniel told me how Jory had mentored Zack. At fifteen, he was removed from his mother's custody because her boyfriend hit him. Sadly, she relinquished all rights. Zack ended up in foster care, followed the wrong crowd and found trouble. That's how he and Jory crossed paths. Zack broke into his truck, and Jory gave him a choice between going to juvenile hall or working at the diner to pay for the damage and the property he stole. That was five years ago.

Abby whizzed by and didn't even acknowledge me. Then she recklessly threw menus into the basket on the counter. Something had ruffled her feathers too.

"What's up with you?"

"You're *not* going to believe what I just heard."

"Abby?" Colt interrupted, offering his metal clipboard. "I've put everything in the stockroom. Want to do a count?"

"No, silly. You know I trust you." She reached for the clipboard and signed the invoice.

Colt glanced my way with those big green eyes, flashed his goofy smile and rested his arms on the counter. "How you doing this beautiful day?"

I faked a big smile. A pro by now. "I'm doing just fine. And you?"

"Bummed. My car died a few days ago."

"Aw, sorry to hear that."

He jerked his head to the right, causing his silky blond hair to shift. "It's cool. I found another one I *really* like."

"Here you go."

"Appreciate that, Abby." Colt reached for the clipboard and turned his eyes back to me. "I was going to call Daniel to see if he could look at it for me Friday. You know, to see if it's in good shape and all."

Abby huffed. "Just go over there. You don't have to make an appointment."

Poor Colt looked scolded. Abby did come off a little strong.

I nudged his arm and gave him a smile to counter Abby's harsh tone. "Yeah, just come by whenever you have time."

Colt flashed his goofy grin again and rocked his head. "Okay. I'll stop by sometime Friday." He waved, walking backwards. "Gotta run. See ya next week, Abby."

"I'll be here."

Once Colt disappeared through the swinging kitchen door, I asked Abby, "So, what did you hear?"

Her face tightened and turned red, remembering why she was so upset. "If she comes here, so help me—"

I grabbed her arm and raised my eyebrows. "Who?"

"Nikki. The slut's back in town."

I sat back feeling like I had been kicked in the chest. My heart beat a little off-key. "Are you sure?"

"Yeah. A customer just told me she talked to her in the mall the other day."

"But…she's with that ex-boyfriend, right?"

Abby shook her head slowly. "Nope. Not anymore."

My eyes bulged. "What?"

Abby reached into her smock and pulled out her tips. "Yep. She came back to town by herself." Abby opened the register and put her tips underneath the money drawer, then slammed it shut.

"Word is, the ex-boyfriend dumped her when all the money Daniel gave her ran out, so she came back home to her 'mommy.'"

Daniel's fortune cookie was about someone from his past coming to see him. And, it was a full moon. It was enough to send goosebumps across my arms.

"You think she'll try to contact Daniel?"

"Probably." Abby wet a cloth. After corralling the condiments, she aggressively wiped the counter. "I'm sure she'll try to worm her way back into his life. He's always taken her back, but he better not this time, or I'll strangle *him* instead of her."

"How are you fine ladies doing today?"

Skip's gargled voice caused every muscle in my body to constrict.

"We're doing good." Abby tossed the wet cloth next to the sink behind her.

Jory poked his head through the kitchen opening and sang, "Abby, dear? Your services are needed in the back."

She put her hands on her hips and cocked her head. "I thought the deal was—I run the front and you run the back."

Jory's eyes widened, and his voice deepened. "*Now*, please."

Abby threw her hands in the air and stormed toward the kitchen.

Skip sat on the stool next to me and rested his arms on the counter. "You working?"

"Nope." I kept my eyes on my hands, tapping my fingertips together.

Skip cackled. "Ha, I guess my timing is perfect. Let's get a table."

"No. I have lunch to-go for me and Daniel."

"Then I guess we can talk here."

"I told you I don't socialize with customers." I turned my head and scratched the back of my neck, refusing to make eye contact.

"But you're not working, so, technically, I'm not a customer to you."

"Rachael, your order's ready." Jory placed the take-out boxes on the divider.

I rushed to the opening and poked my head inside. "Thanks. See you guys later."

"Bye," Skip sang when I walked past him.

Before I left the diner, I sat in my Jeep and thought about

Mandy. I couldn't wait another minute to call a private investigator and reached for my phone. I googled the nearest ones and tapped the first choice without hesitating.

"Flynn and Flynn Locators. How can I help you?" The woman's soft, professional voice was welcoming.

"Hi. I have a few questions about your services. I need to locate someone, and to be honest..." I exhaled, preparing for a letdown. "I don't have a lot of information."

Her slight laughter put me at ease. "I understand. That's what we're here for. My husband has a very high success rate. If you want to leave your name and number, I'll have him return your call. He's the one you'll need to speak with."

"Can you give me an idea how much this might cost?"

"We ask for a five-hundred-dollar retainer, and his hourly rate is seventy dollars. Of course, we return any funds that remain once the job is complete. However, if more time is required, then we would ask for a second retainer. Regarding the overall cost, it's hard to say. There may be expenses he'll incur. Some cases take a day. Others take longer. We just never know."

I rubbed my forehead and wondered what to do. "I see. Um, I can't leave a message. I'll have to call back later. Thank you for your time."

"You're more than welcome. If you do decide to use our services, we inform any potential clients we ask for a valid state ID."

"ID?"

"Yes. My husband had a situation last year, and it's to make sure we don't put an innocent person in harm's way."

My eyes burned with tears of frustration and anger. When would I ever get a break? It took all I had to mumble the words, "I understand. Thanks."

After hanging up, I aggressively shoved my phone inside my purse, defeated once again. If they required ID, that was a dealbreaker. Even if another investigator didn't, hiring one was a risk. Surely he would figure out I was a fugitive and turn me in while Mandy remained at large—with my daughter. It was like losing Jilly all over again. Mandy knew exactly what she was doing. She knew my hands were tied. I started my Jeep and headed back to the shop.

I received a frantic call from Abby. Missy was stuck at home with a flat tire. Daniel was on his way to change it, but she needed help with the breakfast rush and asked me to come in. Within fifteen minutes, I was taking orders.

Missy showed up forty-five minutes later. Poor thing was so upset about being late it took me ten minutes to reassure her the world was not going to end. Since the rush was over and Missy was there, I decided to leave as soon as I cleared my last table.

"Hello there, gorgeous." Skip stood at the table and watched me pile the dishes. "You sure are a ray of sunshine on this cloudy morning."

I ignored him and didn't care how rude it was.

"Kind of slow in here. I'm sure the boss won't mind if ya take a break and sit with me. I'll buy ya breakfast."

I corralled the condiments all nice and neat in the center. "No. I'm leaving as soon as I'm finished with this table. Have a seat, and someone will be there shortly."

"At least have coffee with me."

I gathered the dishes in one scoop, stood tall, and looked Skip in the eye. "I think I've made myself clear. I'm *not* interested in socializing." Before he could respond, I walked away and took the dishes to the kitchen. When I walked out on the floor, Abby was at the counter, ringing up a ticket.

"What's wrong with *you?*" she teased, but I wasn't in the mood.

"Nothing." I removed my smock.

"Hey." She grabbed my arm, and our eyes met. "What is it?"

"It's that guy Skip. He's always here."

"Yeah, he comes in every day. Did he say something to you?"

"No, he's just...he really gives me this uneasy vibe."

She closed the register and took me to the side. "If he makes you that uncomfortable, say the word, and I'll tell him not to come back."

That seemed too extreme for paranoia. I shook my head and sighed. "No. Maybe I'm just overreacting." I reached underneath the counter and grabbed my purse.

"Are you sure?"

"Yeah. I'll see you later." I gave her a quick I'm-okay smile and headed to the door.

"Wait." She ran after me. "I wanted to ask you something." She caught up with me at the front door.

"What's up?"

"I need to let Daniel know about Nikki before she tries to contact him." She rolled her eyes. "If she hasn't already. I'm going over to his house tonight and tell him. I want you to be there."

"Oh, Abby," I muttered, shaking my head. "That's not a good idea. It'll feel like I'm butting into Daniel's personal life, and we agreed not to cross that line."

"Then look at it like you're going with me as my friend."

"That might be misleading to Daniel. You can handle this." I gave her a smile and punched her forearm. "I'll see you later."

Chapter 12: Let Me Go

It was almost closing time when a car pulled up. A female stepped out and approached the door, swaying her hips. It looked like she had a hot date all dolled up in that tight, black, low-cut dress. When she reached for the doorknob, I thought one of her boobs was going to fall out.

Miss 'Barbie' pranced into the office with her black stilettos tapping the tile floor. I bet Mama would call her a floozy with her blood-red lipstick. Her bleached-blonde hair was straighter than dry noodles. Miss 'Barbie' surveyed the office as though she was an inspector.

"Can I help you?"

Miss 'Barbie' twirled her head and looked at me. Then she gave me a quick glance-over and wrinkled her nose. "Who are you?"

She sure stole my smile lightning fast with that rude and entitled attitude.

"Rachael. Can I help you with something?"

She threw her hands to her hips and lifted her chin. "Is Daniel in the shop? I want to talk to him."

"He's working."

"So?"

Before I could respond, Daniel nudged the shop door open just enough to see me. "I'm closing up."

"Daniel?" she called out seductively.

He pushed the door open and stepped inside the office to see who had called out to him. When he saw her, he scowled. "What are you doing here?"

"I came by to talk to you."

"We have *nothing* to talk about." Daniel looked her over and snarled. "And you have no business coming here either."

"You wouldn't answer my calls." She flicked her hair over her shoulder and crossed her arms. "So, I decided to stop by."

"You left, remember? We don't have a reason to talk. Now,

or ever."

Nikki? My heart rate tripled, and my eyes almost popped out.

She smiled and batted her eyelashes. "Ah, come on. Just give me a few minutes."

Her boobs trying to pop out begged more than she did. It was obvious where she spent some of the money Daniel gave her.

"No," Daniel snapped, causing me to jump.

Nikki approached him, seductively swaying her hips. When she stood in front of him, she ran her index finger down his chest and poked out her lip. "We had a good thing. I know you still have feelings for me."

He pushed her hand away and smirked. "Oh, I have feelings for you, but not the ones you think."

"I'm sorry. He didn't mean anything to me."

Daniel's eyes widened, then he laughed. "How can you stand there and say that?"

Nikki rolled her eyes.

"How many other guys did you screw who didn't mean anything to you?"

Nikki placed her sprawled hand on Daniel's chest. "Let me make it up to you."

Daniel moved her hand. "Don't touch me."

"Remember the good times we had?"

"What I remember is seeing Josh naked in *our* bedroom." He pointed to the door and yelled, "Get out of my shop."

Nikki looked my way and curled her upper lip. "Is that your *girlfriend?*"

"Get out, Nikki."

She grabbed his shirt and brought her face to his. "Let's go somewhere private and finish this conversation."

Daniel pushed her hand away and stepped back. "I told you not to touch me."

"I remember a time we couldn't keep our hands off each other."

When she said that, something in me snapped. I stood from my chair so fast it hit the wall behind me. Nikki was nothing more than a vulture circling Daniel's kind, forgiving heart, ready to devour it again. How dare she think she deserved another chance with him. I stared her down, about to become her worst nightmare.

Nikki looked me over and laughed insultingly. "You must be the stray he picked up on the side of the road."

Taunting me was a mistake. With the anger I had stuffed inside, she sure didn't want to be the one to pull the plug and release it.

"Best thing you can do is turn around and walk out that door and use that slutty outfit to entice someone else."

She laughed, reaching for a lock of hair and twirled it. "Just because you sit in my chair doesn't mean you can take my place. Especially in bed." She looked at Daniel. "I *know* she doesn't take care of you like I can."

Without saying anything, I ran toward Nikki with every intention of putting a country licking on her. When she saw me coming, her eyes were wide as could be.

Daniel jumped between us just in time to keep me from punching her and forced me backwards. "No, Rachael. This is what she wants."

"Let *go* of me." I struggled to break free from his hold while trying to look around him. "This is between me and her now. Leave." I finally got a glimpse of Nikki and yelled, "I'm gonna shut that smart mouth of yours, you hussy."

Daniel looked over his shoulder. "I suggest you get out of here."

He couldn't hold me back much longer. I was quite a handful when I was on fire.

"Let me go." My hair got in my way, trying to get free.

Daniel somehow managed to get me in a bear hug from behind. "She's not worth it. Listen to me, please. She only said that to hurt me, because she's not getting what she wants." He whispered, "And you don't need the police coming out here."

That's all he needed to say for me to stop struggling. I had to let it go. At least I got a little satisfaction watching Nikki fear for her life.

Daniel, still restraining me, looked at her. "I didn't call you back because I don't want anything to do with you. I'm over you and have been for a long time. This is *my* business now, so don't *ever* come here again or call me. Understand?"

Nikki stood in shock with her lips parted. The air of rejection on her face was a sweet reward.

"Leave, Nikki."

She lifted her head with a look of pride and marched toward the door, stabbing the heels of her stilettos into the tile floor.

Daniel had a firm hold on me as we watched her drive away.

He lowered his lips next to my ear. "If I let you go, promise me you're not going after her."

"I'm not going after her."

"You promise?"

With Daniel's face so close to mine, I forgot all about Nikki. My attention was on his cheek and how it practically brushed against mine and the tingle it sent through my body.

"I promise, but she better not ever come here again."

Daniel released me. "After what you just did, she's probably in South Carolina by now."

My shirt was contorted from his hold. While straightening it, I realized what I had done was wrong. "I'm sorry I lost control like that. We had a deal, and I crossed the line."

"Don't you *dare* apologize."

Although his hand was on my forearm, it was my heart that felt his touch. I found myself breathlessly staring into his blue eyes but didn't understand why. I had looked at Daniel so many times, but my heart had never beat the way it did staring at him in that moment.

"But I shouldn't have interfered. You have every right to talk to her if you want to."

Daniel pulled me closer. My hands instinctively landed on his chest, causing my heart to palpitate. Something warned me to move out of his personal space, but I ignored that inner voice because I wanted to touch him. Maybe even more than I realized.

"I think Nikki got the message. I don't want to talk to her." He tucked the hair behind my ear, causing my breath to catch. "What will it take to convince you?"

The way he muttered those words and looked deep into my eyes, I knew he was going to kiss me. All he had to do was lean in a few more inches. When he slowly did just that, my body froze. I should've turned my cheek to gesture not to, but I wanted him to kiss me. I wanted to feel his lips touch mine. The more distance he closed, the harder my heart pounded with anticipation. My eyes closed, and I raised my lips to meet his. Just before he kissed me, Abby's ringtone broke the passionate moment.

I turned my cheek and covered my lips with my fingertips. "You should probably answer that." Without looking at him, I walked away and settled in my chair.

"Hey, sis." Daniel ran his fingers through his hair and paced. "What about?" He gripped his neck with his free hand and acted like he was choking, making me laugh. "Alright. See you in an hour." Daniel returned the phone to his belt and locked the shop door. He looked over his shoulder at me. "Come with me to the house."

"I'll pass." I explained what Abby wanted to tell him.

Daniel stood in front of me with his hand extended, ready to lift me from my chair. "Please. Please. Please."

I laughed at his silliness and took his hand. "Fine. I'll go with you." When he helped me to my feet, I ignored the tug my heart felt at his touch.

After we arrived at his house, Daniel took a shower while I sat on the porch. When he stepped outside wearing a white form-fitting T-shirt and jeans, I had to force myself to look away. Daniel had worn that outfit many times. Why was it suddenly so hard to ignore how good he looked in it?

Abby and Jory showed up and sat on the porch with us. Daniel had to share all the details, while laughing, of Nikki's surprise visit and my attempt to go after her. Abby did a celebratory dance.

After we had supper, Daniel drove me back to the shop. As we traveled the peaceful country road, I glanced at him and wanted to deny I had feelings for him, but it would have been a lie. If it ever became a distraction, I would have to leave Maxton.

Daniel pulled up to the front of the shop.

I looked at him and unbuckled. "You know I'll be okay going in by myself."

"And you know me better than that."

"We got out of the truck and walked to the office. While standing in front of the door, Daniel hesitated to unlock it and looked around as though he had lost something.

"What's wrong?"

"I think someone's been here." His eyes met mine, then he pointed to the parking lot. "I want you to get back in my truck and lock the doors."

I hugged myself, getting alarmed, remembering what Mandy told me. "Someone broke in while we were gone?"

Daniel took my forearm and walked me to his truck. "I'm not sure, but I want you to wait in the truck until I check inside." He opened the passenger's door, and I jumped in. Daniel opened the glove compartment and pulled out a handgun. Seeing it triggered the day I shot Peter.

"Stay here."

The door shut—another trigger.

The anxiety intensified. I rocked back and forth, wiping my sweaty palms across my thighs. With my eyes closed, I tried to slow down my breathing, but it only escalated, remembering what happened that day. My footsteps—I saw them, heading toward Peter's study with that cursed bottle of water. My heart pounded faster, anticipating the danger.

~ *Peter's Study* ~

"Stop calling me. I told you *I'm* going to handle this."

Peter is so angry. I hesitate to enter his study and consider going back to the kitchen until he is finished with his phone call.

"I'm not going along with your plan, so get over it and leave me alone."

What plan? Is Peter arguing with his brother?

"I'm not..."

Unable to hear him, I lean closer to the partially open door.

"...wrong and because I'm not going to hurt her like this."

Hurt her? Who?

"It doesn't matter. I'm telling Rachael about you after Andrew leaves. I can't do this anymore. It's gone on long enough."

I cover my mouth to silence my gasp. *Is that what he wanted to tell me tonight? That there's someone else?*

"My guys are waiting to hear from me. One call, and they'll go after her. That's what I pay them the big bucks for."

Go after me? Oh my God.

"Then I'll deal with that when I tell her tonight."

This can't be happening. Peter would never... My eyes burn with tears, refusing to believe Peter would cheat on me.

"I'm *not* listening to you anymore."

Peter's tone startles me, causing the bottle of water to slip from my hand.

"Rachael?"

I reach for the bottle on the floor, trying not to cry, not knowing what to do.

"She just heard everything."

A few tears almost escape, but I stop them. They can come later, after I kick him out of the house. For now, the anger wants to come out. I pull myself together and march into Peter's study to confront him and find out who he was talking to.

He stands and stretches his neck to loosen his collar. I slam the bottle on his desk. As much as I want to fire questions at him, the anger mutes me as though to seal my lips together.

Peter aggressively pulls his tie free and tosses it on his desk. "Guess we need to talk now instead of tonight. I can't hold this in anymore because…"

I zone out and imagine what's going to happen after Peter confesses there's someone else. I'll ask him to leave. I'll cry myself to sleep tonight. I'll have to get a lawyer. We'll get a divorce. Shared custody. Shared holidays. Peter will marry the other woman.

"…should have told you that day she…"

My eyes widen in shock. *She? Oh my gosh. There is someone.*

Peter has blindsided me. I thought I had a fairy tale marriage. Mandy was right. He was having fun somewhere else.

"…tell you what she…and I didn't know what to…"

What is he saying?

It's so hot in here, I can't breathe and on the verge of passing out.

"Rachael, say something."

I open my mouth to say, "What," but nothing comes out. Why can't I speak? What is happening?

"Fine. Don't talk to me. I've got my answer."

What answer?

Why am I only hearing bits and pieces of what he's saying? I can't shake this fog and focus. It's like a bad dream. Maybe it is. This has to be a terrible nightmare, because Peter would never cheat on me.

"…take Jilly from me?"

Oh Jilly. This is going to break her heart.

"I didn't want it to come to this, Rachael, but if you…

I blink, trying to focus. *If I what?* Why can't I hear him? Am I in shock?

Peter reaches for something in his drawer, but things are slow motion. He walks around the desk, each step he takes in sync with me blinking slowly. Then he stands in front of me, holding a gun at his side.

Oh my god. He's going to shoot me.

I command my body to run, but nothing happens. Peter raises the gun, and I blink harder, fearing for my life. Just when I think he's going to pull the trigger, his eyelids flutter like he, himself is in a bad dream or in a state of confusion. Something comes over me, maybe instinct, and I lunge for the gun, struggling with all I have in me to get it from Peter. With him gaining control, I knee him in the groin. Peter grunts and doubles over from the pain. When I try to take the gun from him, it fires. I watch in horror as Peter falls to the floor and rests on his side.

My hand weakens, and the gun hits the floor. I fall to my knees next to Peter and sob. My hands hover over his chest, hesitating to touch his stilled body. Blood pools through his almond dress shirt.

"*Nooo.*"

I quickly get to my feet and reach over the desk for the receiver to the landline. The ringing in my ears distracts me, pulling the phone closer. While punching the numbers, I remember Jilly is upstairs. She had to hear the gun. The motherly instincts take over. I drop the receiver and run to her room. The adrenaline carries me two steps at a time to the second floor, and I rush into her room.

Jilly, coming out of her nap, lifts her head, her hair all messy. "Mommy."

Although she appears unscathed from the horrible sound, I have to take her away from the tragedy. I can't let what happens next be a part of her memory. After scooping Jilly up and leaving the house, I call Mandy on the way to her apartment.

~ *Daniel's Shop* ~

"Rachael, what's wrong? What happened?"

"Mandy." I cried hysterically with my eyes closed, although I saw my dead husband. "It's Peter. I sh-shot him. He's, he's *dead*," I babbled and covered my face.

"Rachael, it's me, Daniel." He took my wrist and helped me out of his truck, then held my forearms. "You need to calm down. Look at me and take some slow breaths. You're okay."

When I looked at Daniel and realized where I was, I threw my arms around his neck. "Please hold me."

He held me tight and whispered, "It's okay. I'm not going to let anything happen to you."

I inhaled deeply and released it slowly through my parted lips, trying to calm and shake the memory. After a few minutes, my breathing became normal and the shakes had stopped, but I was so tired.

"Are you okay?"

I licked my dry lips and swallowed. "I think so. Please tell me you don't think I'm some crazed killer." My words slurred like I was drunk.

"Not a chance." Daniel stroked the hair away from my face and guided it to my back. "Do you want to talk?"

"I've said too much already."

"Then let's head back to my house."

"Your house?" I pushed back and looked at him. "No. I'll be alright here."

"No. You're going home with me." He took my hand and led me to the shop.

"I'm okay. Really."

"Rachael…" Daniel opened the office door and led me inside. "Someone tried to break in while we were at my house earlier. It's not safe for you to be here."

"What?" I had forgotten about that. "Did they get inside?"

He led me to the backroom, still holding my hand. "No, but they tried to."

I cringed at the thought Mandy was right, again, and Peter had someone coming after me. Had they found me? "Daniel, has anyone tried to break in before?"

"No. It's always been safe out here. If it wasn't, I wouldn't let you stay here by yourself." He released my hand. "Sit down for a minute." He headed toward the bathroom.

I sat on the edge of the bed and rubbed my forearms. So, nobody had tried to break in until I happen to stay there. Surely it was a coincidence and not what I feared.

Daniel handed me a wet cloth. "Wipe your face. It'll relax you."

I wiped the dried tears and handed the cloth back to him. "Thank you."

He extended his hand and helped me to stand. "Grab what you'll need, and let's head back to my house."

In the truck, we sat for a moment.

"I'll have a security system installed. Until I do, it's best you stay at the house."

Still a bit shaken, I nodded.

Daniel started the truck, eyeing me with concern. "Rachael, are you sure you're okay?"

"Yeah. Just tired." With a jittery hand, I tucked the hair behind my ears. "Guess you know why I'm hiding from the police. I'd understand if you wanted me to leave."

"The only place you're going is to my house." Daniel put the truck in gear, and we left the shop. He looked my way. "If you ever need to talk, I've got two shoulders."

"I know. Thanks."

The glow of a full moon as we traveled the five-minute ride to Daniel's house was hypnotic.

"I'm not so sure it wasn't Nikki trying to break in."

"Do you think it was her?"

"It could be if she's desperate for money. She knows I keep some at the shop for emergencies."

Daniel pulled up to his house and killed the engine, then he looked at me. "I have to go back and call the police to make a report."

I nodded with understanding. "You should."

After Daniel made sure I was settled inside, he drove back to the shop. I still had a nagging feeling it was someone Peter had looking for me, not Nikki.

Chapter 13: Summer Fun

Colt walked into the office, looking like a California surfer dude in his cargo shorts, tank top, and flip-flops. He approached my desk, smiling with his lips parted and his blond hair dancing. He's one of those guys you just have to smile at because he always smiled.

"What's up, Rachael?"

"Nothing much. Just the usual." I leaned to my right and stretched my neck to look out the window. "Is that your new car?"

He bobbled his head. "Yep. That's it."

"It looks nice from what I can see."

"Come out and take a look at it."

"Okay." I headed for the door with Colt on my heels.

"It has a lot of miles, but I think the owner took good care of it."

Once outside, I strolled around the Ford Fusion. "I like this color of blue."

Daniel came out of the bay and teased Colt. "Hey, man, I heard about your car."

Colt stood with his feet apart and crossed his arms. "Yeah, old Jed finally died on me." When he glanced at the Ford, Colt flashed a wide smile, and his eyes sparkled with pride. "But I sure am enjoying this car. It's fully loaded. Oh, and it's quiet. I won't wake my neighbors anymore with that loud muffler."

Daniel laughed, giving the car a glance over. "You want me to check it out for you?"

"If you're sure you have time."

"Guys, I'm going back inside," I announced and left them to do their business.

While trying to figure out an order, the office door opened. Colt walked in. "Hope you don't mind if I wait in here while Daniel takes the car for a test drive."

"Don't be silly." I abandoned my work and swiveled my chair to face him. "Pull up a seat and chill."

"Okay." Colt dragged a chair to my desk and sat opposite me.

Every time I had seen him in the diner, it was always rushed, so I enjoyed getting to know him. Colt was a sweet guy. He told me his mother's birthday was in two days, and he didn't know what to get her.

"Well, flowers never disappointed me."

"What kind of flowers do you like?"

Daniel stood in the doorway. I glanced at him, not sure how long he had been listening.

"Um…"

Colt noticed my attention had been diverted and looked over his shoulder. He quickly stood with a look of surprise. "Oh, you're back."

Daniel headed for the shop door and motioned Colt to follow him. "Yeah, come on, and we'll go over the car."

He invited Colt into his shop? He never allowed anyone in the bay when he worked on a car. Daniel was religious about safety.

"Oh, cool." Colt slid the chair against the wall. Poor guy had no idea he had caused Daniel's blue eyes to turn green. Colt smiled at me and followed Daniel. "I enjoyed talking with you."

"Remember what I suggested."

An hour later, Colt and Daniel came through the shop door. I closed my novel. "You guys finished already?"

Colt smiled as though he had won the lottery. "Yeah, Daniel said it was in great shape, so I guess I'll be buying a car tomorrow."

I sat back and swiveled. "Congratulations. I'm excited for you."

"Me too. Now I don't have to worry about getting stranded anymore." He turned to Daniel and reached for his wallet. "How much do I owe you?"

He waved him off. "This one is on me."

Colt's eyebrows shot up. "Are you sure?"

"I'm sure."

Colt extended his hand. "Man, I sure appreciate it." He turned my way. "See ya, Rachael."

I waved my fingers. "Bye." After he walked out, I caught Daniel staring at me and laughed. "What?"

"That guy has a crush on you."

"He's nineteen years old."

"So?"

I squinted. "Did you know your eyes look green instead of

blue?"

"So, what's your answer?"

"To what?"

"What's your favorite flower?"

I frowned, almost laughing. "Oh come on. He was asking because he wanted ideas for his mother's birthday. Not for me."

Daniel exhaled and scratched the back of his neck. "You didn't answer my question."

"Daisies, if you must know."

A FedEx truck pulled up and interrupted the moment. The driver rushed in, and Daniel signed for the package. The driver left, and Daniel disappeared into the shop.

That night, I couldn't stop thinking about daisies. When I was a little girl, sometimes I could talk my dad into going to the field next to the woods. It was a small, barren spot of land. Nothing ever grew there except wild daisies. The first time I saw them, I was in awe. Like a first snow. There must have been thousands of them. They were so beautiful in such a lifeless spot. The little white flowers became my favorite. I always picked a handful and carried them home for Mama. She would smile when I handed them to her. Then she would put them in a vase and set them on the kitchen table. Every time I saw a daisy, I thought about my dad and all the times we walked through that field.

With thoughts of my dad, I went outside and laid on top of the picnic table. It was a muggy night, but the sky was clear, and the stars twinkled. I smiled, thinking they were loved ones on the other side of the black curtain peeking through the holes. Then I cried because I missed my dad so much.

~ ~ ~

Plan A; calling Eric—failed. Plan B; hiring a private investigator—also failed. I stared out the window in a daze, trying to come up with a plan C. I was limited on what I could do to find Mandy. Not to mention staring at the office walls all day made it difficult to think. When lunchtime came, I headed to the diner. It was my escape. Sometimes Abby had a way of unknowingly lifting my spirits, and they needed lifting.

I sat on a stool and looked for Abby.

"Hey, Rachael?" Jory called with a curious tone.

I looked at the kitchen opening. Zack stood next to Jory. They grinned like something was funny.

"What's up?"

Zack mocked a fistfight. "How's things going, Rocky?"

I wrinkled my nose. "Ah, ha-ha."

Zack squinted. "Were you really going to fight Nikki?"

"No. I was simply going to rearrange her makeup and hair. I figured she needed a real woman's touch." I held up my fist to represent the word 'touch'.

Jory and Zack faced each other and cackled at the same time.

Jory held his stomach as he laughed. "I'll have your order ready in a minute."

He and Zack headed back to the grill, still laughing.

"Hey, Rachael. How are you doing?" Missy set an empty tea pitcher on the counter.

"Great. How about you? Still having morning sickness?"

She rinsed the tea pitcher while looking over her shoulder at me. "No. I think I'm finally past that part."

"Oh, that's good. I know you were having such a hard time."

Missy laughed. "Yeah, it was no fun." She measured the sugar. "I lost a few pounds, but I'm finally gaining some."

"That's good to hear." I needed my best friend and scanned the diner looking for her. "Is Abby around?"

"No. She ran an errand while it was slow, but she should be back soon." Missy grabbed a full pitcher of tea and walked away.

A few minutes later, a hand rested on my shoulder. Thinking Abby had returned, I looked up, but then scowled and pushed Skip's hand off my shoulder. "What do you want?"

He gave me a sad face with his lips puckered and his forehead wrinkled. "You look like you could use a friend. Come sit with me at my table."

"No."

"Then I'll sit here with you." Skip straddled the stool next to me and turned to face me, resting his arm on the counter. "How about I take you out tonight and cheer you up? You can sure bet we'll do something fun."

If I could only turn him into dust. "I don't need cheering up."

"Then let's just go out and have some fun."

"No." I slammed my palms on the counter as my glaring eyes met his. "I told you, I'm *not* going out with you."

"Why? Is it my age?" He nudged my arm and scrunched his nose. "Trust me. I'm young at heart."

Since I couldn't turn him into dust, I ignored him.

"Ahhh, she's thinking about it."

I rolled my eyes. "No I'm not."

"Are you and Daniel a couple?"

"No. I just work for him."

"Promise I'll dress up and look all spiffy for you."

Do I get points somewhere for remaining calm and not knocking him off the stool?

"The answer is still no."

"I wish you'd go out with me just one time."

"Look, I don't want to go out with anyone, and I'd appreciate it if you didn't ask me again."

"Just one time?" he begged in a playful tone.

The anger in me rose like a pressure cooker ready to send its lid across the kitchen. "For the last time..." I wanted to swat him like a fly. Step on him as though he were a spider. "Don't talk to me anymore. I want you to leave...me...alone."

Surprised he didn't respond, I made the mistake of looking at him. A different Skip stared back with dark and piercing eyes. It was unsettling. Flirting was one thing, but that guy was scary. And it takes a lot to scare me. Daniel was right about him.

"Here's your order, Rachael."

Skip had me so creeped out I couldn't even look at Missy when I took the boxes from her. "Thank you."

"You're welcome. See you later."

When I slid off the stool, I don't know why I looked at Skip. Those cold eyes went right through me. I was going to take Abby up on her offer and have him banned from coming back.

By the time I arrived at the shop, I was mentally drained and sluggish. When I stepped out of my Jeep, I noticed Daniel leaning against one of the bay entrances with his arms crossed, watching me like a hawk.

Why is he standing there like that?

He continued to gawk at me with a mischievous grin while I made my way to the office.

He's up to something.

I figured Daniel would walk through the shop door and meet me in the office, but when I stepped inside, he was nowhere to be found. However, he left me a surprise. My desk was covered with water bottles, each one filled with wild daisies. They were the most beautiful sight in the world. I had a mini field of daisies in front of me. I took in each one. My heart melted with a mixture of sadness and awe.

"You said they're your favorite, right?"

I didn't even notice Daniel was next to me. "Yeah, I, um…"

He took the boxes from my trembling hands and set them on the corner of my desk. "I see them all the time on Mill Creek Road. When you said they're your favorite, I had to go pick some for you."

With my palms on my cheeks, still in shock, I side-eyed Daniel. "I, I can't believe you did this."

He grinned so proudly and sang, "So, you like them?"

"You have *no* idea." I looked at each precious one and struggled to hold back my tears. They escaped, meeting my hands still on my cheeks. "They remind me of my dad. We used to have a field of daisies behind our house." I cried harder at the memory and babbled, "I miss him so much."

Daniel wrapped his arms around me and laughed. "Ah, I didn't get them so you'd cry."

"It's okay. They're good tears." I threaded my arms around his waist and held him.

"I just want to make you smile."

"You do. You always know what to say or do."

"Do I? Really?"

"Daniel, you're so good to me. I don't know what I would do without you."

His hand lowered to the small of my back. A little too low for a casual hug. My eyes widened with surprise. Had I said something to mislead him? That inner voice told me to move his hand, but his touch awakened my body, and I found it hard to move it. In fact, I closed my eyes and relished in his touch, guilty of wanting more. That inner voice scolded me and reminded me my only focus was Jilly.

I cleared my throat. "Our food."

Daniel broke our embrace and walked away without looking at me. "I apologize if I was out of line."

"No need to apologize." I settled in my chair and placed his to-go box on his side of the desk.

Daniel dragged a chair across the floor to my desk and sat. "I've got a run I need to take care of after we eat. I want you to come with me."

"Where?" I lifted my BLT sandwich, took a bite, then smiled at my flowers.

"Have I disappointed you yet?"

I covered my mouth while chewing. "No." Then I grinned and added, "Not yet."

"Let's just say, I don't think you'll be this time either." He lifted his cheeseburger and took a big bite, then winked at me.

I winked back. "Oh really?"

"Yes, really."

After we finished our lunch, I forwarded the calls to Daniel's phone and locked up while he waited for me in the wrecker.

Our ten-minute ride ended when Daniel turned into the driveway of a beautiful two-story house. The landscape was immaculate with perfectly placed flowers, shrubs, and outdoor décor. We passed the detached garage, left the property, then traveled a dusty path. Our bodies shifted in unison with the wrecker, enduring the potholes. When the path ended, my eyes widened with surprise.

"A pond?" I looked at Daniel, grinning with excitement and unbuckled, ready to have some summer fun. "Are we going fishing?"

We came to a stop in front of the dock. Daniel parked and looked at me, shaking his head. "Nope. We're going swimming."

I frowned, scolding him and settled back in my seat. "You know I don't have a bathing suit."

Daniel reached behind his seat and pulled a duffel bag up front and unzipped it. "I have a shirt and some shorts you can wear." He tossed them at me and added, "I'll change outside while you change in here."

I scanned the area. "But won't someone see us? Where are we?"

"Mr. Sumpter is a customer. That's why we're here. I need to pick up the car he tows behind his RV." He pulled some shorts from the duffel bag. "I went to school with his son, Alan. We were good friends growing up." Daniel zipped the duffel bag. "His twin sister, Ana, had a crush on me in high school." He lowered the duffel bag to the floorboard. "And, we're out in the middle of nowhere."

I held up the shirt and eyed it to see if it would fit. "Is anyone at the house?"

"No. Alan lives in Georgia, and Ana lives in DC. Their

parents are traveling in their RV and won't be back until tomorrow. Trust me. It's okay. I used to spend my summers here. They let me come any time I want. So…are you game or chicken?"

The grin on my face probably answered before I did. "Step out so I can change."

Daniel's thrilled smile widened, and he opened his door. "Oh, she's game."

"No peeking," I yelled just before he shut the door.

After I changed, I stepped out of the wrecker and couldn't help but sneak a peek at Daniel's chest. Maybe it was more than a quick glance. Daniel had a hot body underneath that brown uniform. He grabbed two towels from the cab, then we headed to the dock. It was so hot I was ready to jump in immediately, but Daniel wanted us to dive in at the same time.

We stood at the end of the dock, poised for a dive. I smiled, listening to Daniel.

"On the count of three. One… Two… *Three.*"

When I dived into the velvet water, my body instantly cooled from the summer heat. Once I surfaced, I looked for Daniel. He was still standing on the dock. "*You jerk.*"

He pointed at me while laughing hysterically. "Ha-ha. You fell for that old trick."

I swam back with a bruised ego. Really bruised. When I got to the dock, I treaded water and looked up at him. "Just so you know, I have a good memory, and I *will* remember that. Mark my word."

"Oh," Daniel cooed. "If that's a threat, bring it on." He had the nerve to dive in right over me.

"Don't think I won't." I swam out, and the minute Daniel surfaced, I splashed him continuously with all the force I could muster while laughing. When he swam toward me, I let out a girly scream and swam back to the dock to avoid his more powerful splash. Still laughing, I climbed the hot aluminum ladder and made my way on the dock and watched him approach.

Daniel climbed the ladder. "Why did you get out?"

"I'm coming back in, silly."

His glimpse at my wet T-shirt didn't go unnoticed. Embarrassed, I crossed my arms to cover my chest. Once he stood on the dock, he tugged his wet, droopy shorts away from his legs. Water beaded on his body. His fluffy hair surrendered to the water. Droplets fell from the ends.

He reached out his hand to me. "Come on. Let's jump together."

"Oh, yeah, right. You think I'm going to fall for that again?"

Daniel wiggled his fingers. "We'll hold hands."

If we held hands, he would have to jump, so I took his hand, then we faced the water.

"On the count of three. One..."

Grinning at him, I took a runner's position with my knees bent and counted. "Two..."

With our hands gripped, he hollered, "*Three.*"

We took off running, hand in hand. Just as we neared the end of the dock, we leaped at the same time and plummeted into the cool, refreshing water. When we surfaced, Daniel was in front of me.

"Let's do a cannonball."

And show off my wet shirt again? Wasn't going to happen.

"Maybe later. The water feels so good I don't want to get out."

"Chicken." Daniel splashed me, but it was a teaser.

I splashed him with the same force. "No I'm not."

"Yes you are." He splashed a little harder, and I did the same.

It turned into an all-out splashing war until I became tired. We swam back to the ladder. Daniel held onto one side, and I held the other. He shook his head and tried to sling water on me.

"Hey, stop it." I laughed, trying to shield my face with my hand. "You're acting like a dog taking a bath."

"Have you ever been skinny dipping?"

"Of course I have."

"With who?" He filled his mouth with water and spat it out like a fountain.

"Eric. I used to date him when I was in college. His parents had a pool." I pushed away from the dock to tread water. It hurt thinking about him. Eric was the last person I thought would turn on me.

"Would you mind if I did?"

I smiled with my lips parted and thought he was teasing me. "I dare you."

Daniel took off his shorts and tossed them on the dock. When he swam by me, he winked. "I could dare you too."

I swam back to the ladder and leaned my head against the railing, watching Daniel enjoy the water. I was jealous and envied his free spirit. Then something possessed me to take off my clothes. I lowered my chin and looked at my body. The water wasn't clear enough to see anything. I pushed away from the dock. My legs kicked, and my arms thrashed. The cool water against my skin was priceless under the blazing sun, and I was able to escape life.

"Rachael, you need to head back."

Unaware how far out I was, I twirled like a dolphin and swam back to the dock. By the time I got there, Daniel already had his shorts on, and his eyes scolded me just before he looked away. "Why did you take your clothes off?"

I laughed. "Because I wanted to go skinny dipping."

Daniel handed the shirt to me while still looking away. "Put it back on."

His scolding wasn't so funny anymore.

"Are you mad at me?" I took the wet shirt and struggled to tread water while putting it over my head.

Once I did, Daniel handed me the shorts. "No, but put your clothes back on, please."

I took the shorts. "Yes, you are mad." I struggled to thread my legs through the opening. "Why? What's wrong?"

"I'm not upset with you." Daniel turned and splashed me. "Forgive me for being a man. We have dirty minds, you know."

"Then why did you tease me?" I mocked his earlier words. "'I could dare you too.'"

"I didn't think you'd do it. I've never met a woman like you who isn't afraid of a challenge."

I smiled, proud that was how Daniel saw me. "You should keep that in mind." I pushed away from the dock and used both hands to splash him.

"Duly noted." He encircled a wave of water with his hand and splashed me.

We sat on the dock, resting and drying off. Daniel volunteered to towel-dry my hair. I lowered my chin on my bended knees and wrapped my arms around my legs. Thoughts of Jilly consumed me. Then the guilt set in.

"You're quiet. What are you thinking?"

"How I shouldn't have come here. I shouldn't be having a good time."

Daniel stopped drying my hair and scooted in front of me, but I didn't look at him. "Rachael, I care about you, and if I can take you away from whatever is haunting you, then I will. I'm sure when we get back to the shop, you'll continue to punish yourself. But give me a chance to convince you that you *do* deserve this."

With my chin still on my knees, I looked at Daniel. The way he raised his eyebrows and smiled struck an emotion in me. I threw my arms around his neck and held onto him, sniffling and trying not to cry.

Daniel held me tight and rested his head against mine. "Rachael, talk to me. I don't know that I can change anything for you, but holding it in is obviously hurting you."

He was right. All the vile emotions stored in me were like poison. And I didn't have to tell him everything, only something to feel a release. There was no way I could talk about Jilly. It would put me in a bad place, but he knew I shot Peter.

After releasing a long sigh, I began. "When it happened, I wasn't trying to shoot him."

"Peter?"

I nodded and closed my eyes tight, fighting the visual of Peter lying on the floor and his shirt soaked with blood. "Yeah."

"Was it an accident, or was he trying to hurt you?"

"He was—"

Daniel's phone rang.

I broke our embrace and turned away from him.

"Ignore it." He scooted closer and gently moved the hair away from my face, trying to make eye contact. "Please finish telling me."

With the urge to run, I stood as his phone continued to ring. "It's business hours. You should answer it." I grabbed our towels and headed to the wrecker, fighting every tear and memory of that horrible day.

Daniel cupped my wrist and brought me to a stop and then took me in his arms. "I'm sorry. I should've left my phone in the wrecker. Tell me what I can do to help you."

As I shed the tears with my face against his chest, I gasped for air and pleaded, "Can we please leave? I don't feel good."

"Of course we can."

In the silence, we traveled the dusty path back to the house. While Daniel hooked up to the car we came to tow, I curled up against the door and stared at nothing. The guilt of what I had done consumed me. Why did I leave town? Why did I listen to Mandy? I would rather be in jail than not know where my little girl was.

Chapter 14: Just for Today

*July, 5*th

It was three in the afternoon, and I was still in bed. Sundays were always boring, but that Sunday was boring *and* depressing, because it was my birthday. I had never felt so alone in my life. I stared at the ceiling and wondered what my mom was doing. She had to be thinking about me.

In the silence, the office door opened and then closed. It couldn't be Daniel. He didn't come to the shop on Sundays. Terror washed over me, fearing it was the person who had tried to break in the day we were at Daniel's. That time, they were inside the office, and I was alone. Each step that squeaked over the tile floor caused my heart to pound faster and harder. I cowered against the headboard and pulled my knees to my chest and hugged my legs.

Someone was in the hallway, careful to silence his footsteps. I visualized a masked man in black appearing in the doorway. He spots me like a hunter, slowly raising his rifle with both hands. Then he looks down the barrel with his head cocked, eyeing his target— me. The shooter would smirk before pulling the trigger. Peter's death; avenged.

By the time the footsteps stopped at the doorway, I was hyperventilating and had the covers pressed against my mouth. The silence haunted me, knowing someone was standing there. Any minute the intruder would look inside, and our eyes would meet.

"Rachael, are you dressed?"

My breath caught, then I gasped. "Daniel?"

"Is it okay to come in?"

I cried uncontrollably with relief it was him and not an intruder.

Daniel stormed into the room. The mattress shifted as he quickly crawled across the bed, then he sat in front of me and moved the curtain of hair away from my face. "What happened? Are you hurt?"

"No, I'm not hurt." I swallowed and patted my chest. "I...I thought you were the person who tried to break in that day we were at your house."

Daniel exhaled, the sound of guilt flowing from his nostrils. "Oh, Rachael. I'm so sorry I scared you."

"I didn't think it was you, because you never come by on Sundays."

He guided the hair past my shoulder. "I wasn't thinking. I'm so used to just coming in."

"Will you hold me?"

Daniel pulled back the comforter, exposing my quivering body, and crawled into bed. "Come lay next to me." He held up the covers, inviting me.

I stretched out my legs, scooted next to him, and tenderly rested my head on his shoulder. "You just scared me half to death."

He covered us. "You know there's a security system."

"I was so scared, I forgot." Still quivering, I curled up next to him. "Peter has someone after me. I thought it was him breaking in."

"Who was Peter?"

"My husband."

"Was he abusive?"

"No." I shook my head aggressively, reassuring him that was not the case. "Peter loved me, but he..." My voice lowered from sadness. "I don't know why he pulled a gun on me."

"He didn't love you if he pulled a gun on you."

Those words hurt, even though Daniel was right. "I overheard him talking on the phone in his study. He said he has people who can come after me. I think the person he was talking to pressured him to shoot me, but I don't know why. I'm pretty sure he was seeing someone else, because it was a woman he was talking to."

Daniel took a lock of my hair and twirled it. "I'm sorry. You didn't deserve that."

"I walked into his study to confront him. The next thing I know, he's standing in front of me holding a gun."

"What happened?"

"He hesitated, so I lunged for it. We struggled, and it went off."

Daniel stopped twirling my hair in midstream. "You realize that's self-defense? I mean, technically you didn't even shoot him."

"That's what I told Mandy, but she said I couldn't prove it, and no one would believe me."

"Who's Mandy?"

"She was my friend. After I shot Peter, I panicked and drove to her apartment." I couldn't tell Daniel why. If I talked about Jilly, it would upset me more. "When I told Mandy what happened, she convinced me I'd go to prison, because Peter would look like the victim. I was an idiot for listening to her, but she had me so scared I didn't know what to do." I lifted my head and looked at Daniel, ignoring how close our faces were. "I know I shouldn't have run away. Please don't think I'm a horrible person."

"There's nothing you could ever do that would make me think that."

You would if I tell you about Jilly. You'll say I should've known better. You're struggling with your own issues and what your father did. How can you possibly understand?

"Daniel, you're harboring a fugitive."

"Let me worry about that."

"If someone's looking for me, I could be putting you in danger by staying here."

He huffed, not concerned. "Oh please."

"But I can't do that to you."

"Rachael, promise me you won't leave. If someone's after you, then you could be in more danger out there by yourself."

I lowered my head on his shoulder and snuggled as close to him as I could. Not only had I come to trust Daniel, I felt safe with him. "I won't leave."

"Rachael?"

"Yeah?"

"Why are you still in bed this late in the day?"

"Because it's..." I sat up with my back to him. The more I thought about it, it wasn't worth mentioning, so I mumbled, "It's nothing."

Daniel placed his hand on my back. The warmth of his touch penetrated my shirt. Then my eyes closed, adoring the comforting sensation.

"I know something's bothering you."

"Really, it's nothing."

He traced large circles on my back with his fingertips. "Please tell me."

My eyes watered, the feeling of being alone returning. "It's my birthday," I blurted out. Overwhelmed with sadness, I threw my face into my hands and cried. "I miss my family and wanna go home."

"Aw, come here." Daniel pulled me back into his embrace. "I wish you would've told me so I could've done something for you."

"It's not a big deal."

"Yes it is. Happy Birthday."

I wiped my tears with the sheet. "Thanks."

"How old are you?"

"Twenty-eight."

He chuckled. "No you're not."

"Yes I am."

"I thought you were like, oh, maybe…thirty-four."

The way Daniel said it, he was serious. I raised up and looked at him, insulted he thought I was that old. "Did you really?"

Daniel belly-laughed. "Of course not. I was only picking with you."

"You're supposed to say I look younger than I am, not older."

"Okay, then, you look…" His eyes perused my face. "Mmm, twenty."

I popped his forearm. "No brownie points for you, mister." Since we were being personal, I asked him, "How old are *you*?"

"I'm not telling."

"Why not? I told you how old *I* am."

Daniel rolled his eyes and exhaled. "If you must know, I'm twenty-nine."

"When's your birthday?"

"Don't ask."

I poked his side. "Geez, you can be stubborn sometimes."

"Hey." His eyes scolded me, quickly guarding his side. "Don't do that."

"Why? Are you ticklish?"

"Maybe." He grabbed my pillow and covered his torso, then grinned like he was safe.

"Tell me when is your birthday, or I'm going to tickle you."

"No, don't."

I raised my hands in the air and wiggled my fingers. "Tell me or else."

Daniel grabbed my wrists and pinned me down and then straddled me. It happened so fast. Needless to say, I was breathless with him sitting on top of me.

"The answer is February the fifth." He raised one eyebrow. "Any more questions?"

Daniel wasn't playing. He was serious. Perhaps I had offended him in some way. My brows tightened as I shook my head. "I'm sorry if I—"

"Rachael, you didn't do anything wrong, but I am a man. If you touch me in certain places..." Daniel released my hands. He didn't finish his sentence and practically jumped off the bed. Then he walked over to the window, resting his hands on his hips and staring outside.

I raised up on my elbows and looked at him, wondering what he was thinking. "Why are you even here? I thought you had something at home you had to do today."

"I did." He looked at me and laughed. "I got the stump out of the ground, but I sure got the truck dirty. You should see it." He walked toward me, scratching the back of his head. "I came over to wash it because my spigot is broken."

Squinting at him, I growled, "You mean you got The Beast dirty?"

"Yep, I sure did. Since you like the truck so much, why don't you help me wash it?" His eyebrows danced, challenging me.

How could I resist?

"Okay." I scooted off the bed and pointed at his chest. "But you wash and I rinse."

Daniel looked me over, smiling with his lips parted and nodded toward the door. "Let's go."

~ ~ ~

Even though it was hot and muggy, we washed The Beast. I stood in the bed and washed the top, stealing glances of Daniel flexing his muscles while scrubbing a tire. His hot, sweaty body was quite the distraction in flimsy shorts and a loose tank top.

"Can you hand me the water hose?"

He reached for the nozzle and offered it to me. "This is my

last tire, then I'll be done."

"Okay. I'm finished. I just need to rinse it."

Daniel continued to scrub the tire. Shame on me for staring at certain parts of his body. After I rinsed the top, I stepped out of the bed and hosed off the rest of the truck while Daniel rounded up the cleaning items. With his back to me, I bit my bottom lip and smiled, waiting for the perfect opportunity to pay him back for tricking me at the pond. When he bent over to pick up a brush, I aimed the nozzle at his butt and squeezed the handle.

"*Rachael.*" Daniel dropped everything, spun around, and marched toward me.

"Did you fall for that old trick?" My smile disappeared when he didn't laugh. *Oh, he's not happy.* I backed up and pleaded my case. "Come on, Daniel. Don't be mad." I laughed, hoping he would too. "I warned you that I have a good memory, and I'd get you back. Ha-ha?"

I continued to walk backwards, pointing the nozzle at Daniel like it offered me some kind of protection. In no time, he caught up with me. When he reached for the nozzle, I squeezed it as hard as I could. We ended up soaking wet before he managed to take it from me. Once he had, I backed up, ready to plead for mercy that time. If I wasn't in trouble before, I sure was now.

"Don't be mad at me." I raised my hands in defense, laughing hysterically, barely able to get my words out. "You have to admit the water felt good."

Daniel never said a word, but I should've known by the look on his face something was about to happen. And it did. I backed into a junked box truck. I winced in pain and rubbed the back of my head.

Daniel covered his mouth and chuckled. "Oh, did you hit your noggin?"

Embarrassed, I poked out my bottom lip. "Yes, I did."

Although I was upset with him for letting me hit my head, I wanted to smile at his adorable wet face. Drops of water gathered at the ends of his bangs, ready to drip on his face, and it was all my fault.

"Are you okay?"

"Yeah."

"Just making sure." Daniel's eyes went to my chest, then quickly back to mine.

"Hey, I saw that." I crossed my arms in case he was tempted

to steal another glance. "You looked at my wet shirt, didn't you?"

"It was an accident." A sideways grin followed his confession.

I gasped at his ungentlemanly-like behavior and scolded him. "Oh, that's not nice of you."

"It's *your* fault it's wet," he sang.

"I don't care. I'm embarrassed."

"You shouldn't be. Mine's wet, and I'm not embarrassed." Daniel took his shirt and tried to wring out the water. "I want to do something for your birthday."

I looked down and shook my head. "I don't want to do anything."

Daniel lifted my chin, and I looked at him. "I know what you're thinking. Just for today."

"It doesn't feel right to celebrate my birthday."

"Hogwash." Daniel took my wrist and led me around the building. "Let's go take a shower, and then we're going to do something for your birthday." He opened the door for me. "Run in and take yours first."

After we had our showers, we headed to Daniel's house. He caught me staring at him while he drove.

"Were you mad at me when I hosed you down?"

"No. I'm just not used to someone like you." He turned his attention back to the road. "You're fun to be with."

"Fun?" That answer was a shock. "You sure looked mad when I did it." I still thought it was funny and covered my smile.

When we arrived at his house, Daniel instructed me to sit on a stool. The man on a mission grabbed items from the kitchen cabinets, the drawers, and the fridge. He stealthily put everything in a picnic basket, denying me of his intentions. Once the basket was full of his little secrets, Daniel set it on the counter in front of me and exhaled, tired. "Are you ready?"

With a wide grin, I slid off the stool. "Whenever you are."

He nodded to the back door. "Follow me."

We casually walked across the yard until we came to a homemade fire pit. Daniel rested the basket on a picnic table. His smile reflected pride. "Since this is last minute and I can't take you somewhere nice, I guess you'll just have to settle for roasted hot dogs over a fire."

I clapped and bounced on my feet, grinning with excitement. "I *love* roasting hot dogs over an open fire."

Daniel sighed with relief. "Good. I'm glad to hear that." He pointed to a patio chair. "Have a seat and get comfortable while I get things started."

Once the fire was going, Daniel set up the picnic table. There's nothing sexier than a man in jeans and a T-shirt being domestic. He cut two small branches from the oak tree towering over the picnic table. Then he sat next to me and shaved off the ends with his pocketknife like he had done it a million times before. I watched his every move.

After piercing two hot dogs, he handed one to me. "Here you go, birthday girl."

"Thank you."

We roasted our hot dogs while enjoying the fire, even though it was still daylight and hot. Once they were well-done, we sat at the picnic table and ate. It was an intimate moment, just the two of us sitting in the backyard. And then there were four of us.

"*Happy Birthdayyy.*" Voices carried over the backyard.

Startled, I almost choked, my eyes darting in that direction. Abby and Jory stood on the back porch and waved like they were stranded on an island and saw a passing ship.

After forcing the food down, I yelled back, "*Come join us.*" Then I immediately turned to Daniel and threw a potato chip at him. Then another one. "You told them, didn't you?"

"Who? Me?" Daniel grinned innocently, then bit into his hot dog.

Abby scolded me. "Girl, the nerve of you not telling us it's your birthday."

"Don't be upset."

"Well, I am. You know we look for any excuse to party." She straddled the bench and punched my forearm. "*That's* for not telling me."

"Ow." I rubbed my arm, laughing.

Jory patted my shoulder in passing. "Happy Birthday." He settled on the bench next to Daniel. "Abby, I think everyone knows you like to party."

Someone played footsies with me. Not that I had to guess who. When I turned my bug eyes to Daniel, he smiled, chewing his food. I scowled playfully. He winked and took another bite of his hot dog.

"Hush, Jory. You might be sitting across the table, but I can still reach you."

Daniel looked at Abby and then Jory. "Do you guys want a hot dog?"

Jory swatted at a fly. "No thanks. We just ate with my parents."

"Then, how about..." Daniel reached into the picnic basket and pulled out a bag, then he dangled it in the air. "Roasted marshmallows?"

My hand went flying in the air. "Oh, I do. I do."

Abby raised her hand. "Me too."

We gathered around the fire. Abby and Jory sat on one side. Daniel and I sat on the other. By the time we finished the bag of marshmallows, it was dusk. The night was peaceful. I listened to the crickets and stared at the stars. Abby and Daniel reminisced about their younger days and then Abby and Jory talked about buying a bigger house. It hurt listening to them talk about their lives when I had to be silent. I thought about Jilly, Mama, and Grandpa.

Daniel must have noticed I zoned out. He placed his hand over mine.

I looked at him with weary eyes but didn't say anything.

He winked and mouthed, "Just for today."

Abby stood and clapped once. "Okay, everyone. It's time to head inside."

We put the fire out, cleared the picnic table, then went inside. Abby summoned everyone around the kitchen counter and stood in front of a familiar-looking white cardboard box from a deli. She lifted the lid and exposed a birthday cake with red and yellow roses. Instead of my name, there was a smiley face.

Abby poked candles into the cake and lit them, then they sang, "Happy Birthday." With each word it became emotional and hard to hold back tears. How could my husband and best friend betray me, yet three strangers made me feel like family without knowing anything about me? I dropped my face into my hands and cried. Daniel wrapped his arms around me. My face went to his chest like a magnet.

Abby rushed to my side and placed her hand on my shoulder. "What's wrong?"

Jory snickered. "It was probably your singing."

Abby whispered to Daniel, "What can I do to help?"

"Give her a minute. She'll be okay."

"Was it something we said or did?"

"I told you. It was your singing. It's enough to make anyone cry."

"You better hush up." She marched over to Jory and popped his arm. "Stop being so mean."

"Mean?" He laughed with his shoulders raised and his palms facing up. "I'm just being honest. You sounded like a chicken with laryngitis."

The couple were always quite comical and made me laugh.

Abby's face contorted. "You just wait—"

Daniel, laughing himself, cleared his throat. "Guys, can we have some cake?"

"Oh." Abby laughed, embarrassed. She looked at Jory and pointed. "Hand me a knife from that drawer."

He opened it, shaking his head and mumbled, "Okay, dear, but keep in mind it's for the cake." He handed it to her while fighting a grin. "I have witnesses here."

If only Jilly had been there, it would have been the best birthday ever.

Chapter 15: The Visitor

Are you kidding me? It's only one-thirty? I dropped my face back into the pillow and growled. Another night of intense thoughts kept me awake. I had so many pecking at my brain. With Daniel at the shop during the day, I was distracted, but at night, they all came together and fought for my attention. One thought in particular had me wondering—how was Mandy surviving? There was no way she was still working in Rockingham. Her parents probably deposited money into her bank account.

"Fumbles, oh my gosh. Her bank account." I sprung up in bed with my eyes wide and my heart racing. "Why didn't I think of that sooner?" With a burst of adrenaline, I threw back the covers and ran to the office as fast as I could. Then I flipped the light switch, jerked the chair from under my desk and plopped down. Once I fired up the computer, I had to wait for it to load, which seemed to take forever. It was a long shot, but priceless if I could get into Mandy's bank account like I did her cell phone account. It would tell me where she was or had been. I was ready to fist the air at the thought of hitting pay dirt and finding my daughter.

Once the computer loaded, I pulled up the home page for Wells Fargo. I exhaled slowly and typed in the same username and password for Sprint, praying she was consistent. If I could see the location of her transactions, I would know where she was or had been. That time, I didn't hesitate to hit the enter key. Low and behold, my heart almost stopped when her account opened right before my eyes.

"No way," I squealed, doing a happy dance in my chair.

Finally, my luck had changed, and I was on her trail. Perhaps Mandy wasn't as smart as I thought she was. I perused her statement, massaging my jaw, but something wasn't right. The last date of any transactions was the same day I left town. One was at Chick-fil-A when we had lunch, and the other one was at a bar. I scrolled, looking at her past transactions. Everything seemed normal except for one. A week before I left, there was a two-hundred-dollar payment to a Brad Hinson. Mandy had never mentioned him.

I sat back and stared at the monitor. Accessing her account left me with more questions than answers. Who was Brad Hinson, and why did she give him money? Why did her activity stop that day? And if Mandy went to a bar, where the hell was Jilly?

With the new information, I needed time to process it and make sense of it. Even though it seemed like a setback, I was more determined than ever to find Mandy. I even had a plan C.

After shutting down the computer, I shuffled back to my room and crawled into bed. "Fumbles, where do you think she is?" I pulled the covers to my chest. "Where would she go with Jilly?" I released a long sigh, closed my eyes and tried to think where Mandy might have taken my daughter.

~ ~ ~

Why didn't I figure it out sooner? Disney World. Mandy was obsessed with going there. Of course that's where she took Jilly. After walking the park all day, I finally spotted Mandy and Jilly talking to Snow White. That silly disguise didn't fool me. Not the blonde hair or the sunglasses that nearly covered her face. For twenty minutes, I stalked Mandy like a hunter undetected by its prey, waiting for the right second to strike. It was all I could do not to grab Jilly, but I didn't want to frighten my little girl. If only I could have seen her face. She had her own disguise; a theme park hat that robbed me of a simple glance. Mandy might have hidden her face, but she couldn't rob me of my little girl's voice, following them in my own disguise. I lowered my sunglasses with the tip of my finger and peered just below the bill of my baseball cap. Today was the day, my dear friend.

Jilly pointed at the Mad Tea Cups spinning around and squealed. "Let's ride that." She grabbed Mandy's hand and tugged her in that direction.

She stood firm in place. "Not right now, Hannah. Look how long that line is."

Just as I thought. Mandy called Jilly by her deceased daughter's name. The mother bear in me wanted to come out, but

I contained it, waiting for the right moment.

They continued to walk, hand in hand.

Jilly pointed at the flying Dumbos in the air and jumped up and down with excitement. "Then can we ride that? Please. Please."

Mandy stopped and knelt to meet Jilly's eyes. I quickly ducked behind a directional sign.

"Sweetie, I'm kind of hungry. How about we get a funnel cake instead?"

Jilly crossed her arms and pouted. "No. I wanna ride that. You said it's our last day."

Their last day? It was time to make my move. Right then. Before Mandy got to her feet, I ran to her, mindful Jilly was watching. "Amanda Ross?"

Mandy whipped her head around at the same time she raised her sunglasses over her head. "Rachael." Poor thing looked like a deer staring into headlights.

"Long time no see." I stood only feet away from my so-called best friend.

Mandy stood and shielded Jilly. Her lips parted, and she struggled to breathe. I'm sure the sight of me stole what air she held. "How did you find me?"

"You charged a hotel room on your bank card, stupid. You didn't think I'd come looking for you after you didn't show up at the cabin?"

Mandy glanced to her right and then left like she contemplated running. That wasn't going to happen. She wasn't going anywhere with my daughter.

"What's wrong? Cat got your tongue?" My eyes glared into hers, saying the things I couldn't with Jilly standing behind her.

Mandy's eyelids fluttered, telling me she was fighting one of her headaches. And to think I used to feel sorry for her.

"I just wanted to take her to Disney World. We were going to come back. I swear."

"Liar," I mumbled under my breath. "Give me my daughter back."

In her hesitation, it took everything in me not to strangle her, even though people seemed to be paying attention. Some of the stares lingered in passing, but it wouldn't stop me from taking my daughter.

Jilly peered around Mandy's leg. Finally, a glimpse of her face appeared inside the fuzzy hat.

"Mommy, who's that?"

My heart skipped several beats at once. Jilly called Mandy— Mommy. My child didn't recognize me.

"Hannah, please stay behind Mommy."

When she said that, I lost it. The mother bear came out. I pushed Mandy to the side at the same time I grabbed Jilly's arm to catch her. Mandy stumbled before hitting the hot asphalt. I removed the hat and then screamed in horror, "What the hell did you do to my child?" Jilly's long blonde hair had been cut short and dyed black.

Mandy shoved me. Caught off guard, I fell. She scooped Jilly up and raced away before I could get to my feet. I ran after them, fighting my way through the crowd that had poured around me. I called out her name in desperation. "Jilly? Jilly?" I couldn't run. The crowd was too thick. "Jilly? *I'm* your mommy."

I stood in a sea of people giving me weird glances. After looking right and then left, I closed my eyes, took in a deep breath and screamed as loud as I could. "Jilly." My voice echoed for the longest time. Like I was in a tunnel.

"Rachael?" A man called out my name. Although he seemed far away, he pulled on my arm. "Rachael, wake up. You're having a bad dream."

A bad dream? I tried to pull myself out of the nightmare. It felt like I was speeding backwards through a dark tunnel. When I opened my eyes, my chest heaved, and I was drenched in sweat.

"That must've been some nightmare."

My eyes went to Daniel, sitting on the edge of my bed with his hand on my shoulder. "You have no idea." I licked my dry lips and moved my legs. "What time is it?"

"It's almost seven."

I yawned. "Why are you here so early?"

His hand left my shoulder, and he sat up straight. "I got a call from a stranded motorist on his way to work. I had to take him…"

My mind drifted, hearing Jilly call Mandy her mother. It was my worst nightmare. And who's to say that wasn't happening? If I didn't find Jilly soon, that nightmare could be reality. The thought was enough to break me. I wanted my little girl, but I didn't know how to find her. I rolled over and curled up in a fetal position and cried.

Daniel crawled under the covers with me. When his arm wrapped around me, trying to hold me, the floodgate of my emotions released, and I sobbed from the depths of my soul.

"It's okay. Cry it out."

"I don't know if I can do this anymore." My body quivered, and I cried and coughed at the same time.

Daniel snuggled closer and rested his face next to mine. "I want to help you, but I don't know what to do."

I wanted to tell him. The words were there, ready to come out, but I couldn't say them. Daniel was sensitive about his abandonment issues, and if he thought for one second I had walked away from my child, he would never look at me the same. Still sobbing, I wiped my face with the sheet. "I just need you to hold me."

"I will…as long as you want."

~ ~ ~

The morning passed quickly. When it rained, it was always busy. By lunchtime, I needed out of the office and headed to the diner. Maybe a few minutes with my best friend would do me some good.

Abby and Colt were talking at the counter, so I quietly sat on a stool.

"Make sure you tell your boss let's stick with these numbers for now." Abby handed the clipboard to Colt after signing the invoice.

"I'm sure it won't be a problem."

"Hey, girl." Abby flashed a quick smile and reached for a pitcher of tea. Her eyes followed me, walking around the counter. "Let me take care of these customers, and I'll be right back."

"No rush. Take your time." I forced a smile and looked at Colt. "Are you enjoying your new car?"

His proud smile answered for him. "I sure am. I'm driving it to Florida Saturday to visit with some friends for a week."

"Sounds like fun." *Florida? Plan C?* I smiled for real and leaned closer. "Colt, I was wondering if you could do me a *big* favor?"

Colt's pale cheeks turned a pretty shade of pink. "Um, sure. What is it?"

"Is there any way you could mail a letter for me while you're there? You see, I have something I need to mail, and my friend would *love* to see it came from Florida." I bit my bottom lip, anxiously waiting for him to reply. Perhaps that nightmare was about to be overshadowed with some hope.

Colt nodded along with his upper torso. "Sure. I can mail it. Do you have the letter?"

My wide smile disappeared, and I exhaled with disappointment. "No. It's at the shop."

"I'm going to be in that area in an hour. I can drop by and pick it up if you'd like."

My smile returned, even bigger. "Are you sure you wouldn't mind?"

Colt looked at his watch. "No, but I've gotta run if I'm going to stop by." He waved, walking away. "See you in an hour."

While I waited for my order, I thought about the letter to Mama I had started. I needed to get back to the shop and finish it. An hour wouldn't leave me a lot of time to write everything I wanted. After Abby handed me the order, I didn't waste time and hurried back to the shop.

Daniel rushed through lunch so he could finish working on the car he had towed so early that morning. The owner paid him extra to have it towed to his job site before five o'clock so he would have a way home. As soon as Daniel finished his burger, he headed to the shop, and I was on a mission to finish my letter.

Mama,

Sorry I have to make this short. I only have a few minutes to write this letter. Please don't worry about me. I promise I'm safe and okay. God sent an angel my way. Know that I miss you and Grandpa so much. Mama, I need you to call the police and tell them Mandy kidnapped Jilly. She's not with me, and I don't know where they are. Mandy ran off with her. Mama, she's crazy. I'm worried about Jilly. That's why I haven't come home. I can't. Not until I find my little girl or know she's safe.

I didn't mean to shoot Peter. I don't know why, but he was going to shoot me. I grabbed the gun. It went off in the struggle. That's how Peter was shot. I didn't think anyone would believe my story. I let Mandy talk me into leaving town. She convinced me I'd go to prison and never see Jilly again if I didn't. I was stupid for listening to her. I'm so sorry for the heartache it's caused you and Grandpa. I'll find a way to make it right, but I have to find Jilly and I can't. Please don't

let anyone know I've contacted you, because I'm going to write again. I'll come up with a way we can talk. I don't know how, but I will figure out something. Please find Jilly and bring her home. I love you. Tell Grandpa I love him.
Rachael

I stared at my letter and smiled. Mama would hold that piece of paper within a few weeks, or sooner, depending on when Colt mailed it. She would know I was okay and look for Jilly in a way I couldn't. I took a stamp and envelope from the desk drawer. My hand trembled, addressing the envelope. My letter was ready. I sat back and said a little prayer my plan wouldn't fail.

When Colt pulled up to the office, I grabbed the letter and ran out to meet him. The quicker the transition happened, the less chance Daniel would find out.

"This is so sweet of you to do this. You have no idea how happy she's going to be when she gets this and sees it's from Florida."

Colt took the letter. "I can stop and buy a souvenir if—"

"Oh, no, no." I interrupted, waving my hands. "This is way better than *any* souvenir you could buy." I glanced over my shoulder at the shop, afraid Daniel was going to notice he was there. Then I turned back to Colt. A nervous laugh escaped. "I should get back to work, and I know you're on a schedule." With my shoulders raised and my fingers nudged inside my back pockets, I gave him the biggest indebted smile I could. "Have a safe trip and a good time."

Colt opened his door and jumped inside the truck. "I'll see you in a few weeks."

I waved and headed back to the office. My eyes watered for the first time with good reason. Once Mama knew Mandy had Jilly, nothing would stop her from finding them.

Beep. Beep. Beep…

Colt's reverse sensor sounded like a fire truck backing up. There was no way Daniel wouldn't hear it echo over and over. Sure enough, when I walked inside, there he was.

Daniel had just entered the office from the shop door and watched him leave. "Is that Colt?"

"Yeah." *Stupid sensor.*

Daniel glanced at me with his hands on his hips and a curious look. "What'd he want?"

"He's helping me with something." I headed to my desk, hoping he wouldn't push the subject.

"Why didn't you ask me?"

I settled in my chair. "Because. It's complicated." I began to sort through the invoices.

"So, letting Colt help you makes it *less* complicated?"

This is why I didn't want him to know what I was doing. The last thing I wanted to do was hurt Daniel's feelings. He asked so many times to help me, and I turned to someone else.

I lowered the invoices and looked at him. "When I was at the diner, I found out he's driving to Florida this weekend. I need to get a message back home, so I asked him to mail a letter for me so it can't be traced here." I shrugged and raised my eyebrows. "That's it."

The worried look on his face softened. "Is everything alright?"

A small smile escaped at the thought of Mama getting my letter. "I think it will be."

"You know I'll do anything to help you."

"I know, and I really appreciate it. I didn't have any other way to get that letter mailed."

"I need to finish this car if I'm going to get it back to the owner before he gets off work." Daniel headed toward the shop door and looked at me while opening it. "Want to order a pizza after we close up?"

I raised one eyebrow. "With olives?"

He shivered and scowled. "Ew, that's so gross. They look like bugs." He disappeared into the bay.

My body melted into the chair. Even though I smiled at the thought of Mama getting my letter, the nightmare still haunted me. Nothing a drawing couldn't change.

The pencil rested between my fingers while pondering what to sketch. I thought about Jilly. She looked like Peter, so I used his facial features to come up with an image I thought might resemble her as a woman. Jilly posed like a model with her hands on her hips, her chin in the air, and long blonde hair draped over her chest. A giggle escaped, etching her in jeans, a plaid shirt, and boots. Something was missing. After erasing one of her arms, I penciled a cowgirl hat on her head and her new hand holding the bill. I captioned it: *My little cowgirl.*

Around four o'clock, Daniel left to tow the car to its owner.

I was in my own world with my notebook and pencil. Stroke after stroke, Daniel's fire pit came to life with the four of us roasting marshmallows. Smoke rose into the air. With a few strokes of a red highlighter, I had flames. I captioned the drawing: *Just for today.*

I flipped back to a picture of Daniel I had sketched with him standing next to his wrecker. I drew a halo over his head and marked through the old caption and renamed it: *My angel in a brown uniform.*

It was time to call it a day, so I closed my notebook and returned it to the drawer. The office door opened. When I looked up to see who had walked in, I slammed the desk drawer shut. "What are you doing here?"

Skip tucked his hands into his front pockets and shrugged. "I was in the neighborhood. Thought I'd stop in and see ya."

I gathered my paperwork into one stack. Anything to take my eyes off of him. "It might be best if you turn around and leave."

"Something wrong with stopping by to see how you're doing?"

I looked at him with my eyes wide. "You have to ask that after what happened in the diner?"

Skip stroked his unshaven jaw and looked around the office. "Daniel's not here, so I don't see the problem."

I placed my paperwork in the three-shelf organizer. "I'm closing, so you need to leave."

He pointed at the wall. "According to that clock, you're open for fifteen more minutes."

As we stared, the phone rang.

Still maintaining eye contact, I picked up the receiver and answered. "Daniel's Automotive and Towing. How can I help you?"

Skip walked over to the shop door and peered through the window into the bay. He was way too nosy for my comfort.

"Sorry. I must have dialed the wrong number." The woman hung up.

I took advantage of the call and pretended I was talking to a customer. "No, but I'll send him a text and let him know. Hold on." I picked up my cell phone and sent a message to Daniel. *ETA? I have a little situation. Don't speed.* I picked up the receiver and spoke into thin air. "Hey, Ronny? I just sent him a text. Give him a few minutes. I'm sure he'll give you a call." I kept my eyes on Skip as he surveyed the office. "Oh, you're welcome." After replacing the receiver, I reminded him, "I need to lock up."

Skip shoved his rolled-up sleeves higher. "That clock says I have thirteen minutes. After that, I wanna take you out for coffee."

"I'm *not* going out with you. Get that through what part of your brain functions and stop asking me." My phone beeped. I told Skip, "You can see yourself out," then read Daniel's message.

Almost there. You okay?

I thumped a reply. *Yes. Be careful.* While closing out my phone, I looked up to see Skip standing inches from my desk, smiling.

"Now, Rachael, you don't have to get so riled up over a cup of coffee."

I stood and pointed at the door. "Get out, or I'm gonna call the police."

Not that I could, or we'd both end up in jail.

Skip looked me over, amused at my demand. "You sure are cute when you get fired up."

"And you're an ass. Now get out of here, and don't ever come back."

His grin slowly melted as his eyes turned cold and dark. The same eyes I saw that day in the diner. I went from being angry to being afraid.

"You shouldn't be rude when a man asks you out, woman. When a guy asks nicely, which I have, it's polite to accept his invitation."

Even though I was afraid of Skip, I wasn't backing down or letting him sense it. "Maybe in your sick world, but not mine. I suggest you get out of here before Daniel gets back."

Skip's cackle bounced off the concrete walls. "You think I'm scared of a boy?"

Daniel's wrecker flew by the window and caught my attention, but I kept my eyes on Skip as to not alert him.

"It's a matter of respect. I've asked you several times to leave." Without looking at the door, I could see Daniel walk inside.

"And I've told you I—"

The door slammed so hard I thought the glass would shatter. Daniel marched toward Skip and clenched his hands and growled, "What are you doing in my shop?"

Skip looked at Daniel and gave him a casual shrug. "I stopped by to see Rachael. Do you have a problem with that since you're not her boyfriend?"

Daniel stepped back without taking his eyes off of Skip and

opened the door. "Out. Now!"

Skip turned to me and winked. "We *will* finish this conversation later, honey."

I crossed my arms and looked him dead in the eye. "You heard Daniel."

Skip headed toward the door, casually swinging his arms.

Daniel eyed him with his lips tight. Just as Skip approached the doorway, Daniel struck like a snake, cupping Skip's neck with one hand and throwing him against the doorframe. "So help me, if you *ever* come near her again, you'll become a missing person to your family. Do you hear me?"

Skip struggled for air while trying to pry Daniel's hand from his neck. His jaw clenched and his eyes bugged.

I ran to Daniel. "Let him go."

"He needs to know I mean business." Daniel squeezed harder, and Skip's face turned red.

"Please let him go. You're scaring me."

Without looking at me, Daniel asked, "Did he touch you?"

"No. I promise he didn't."

Daniel released his grip on Skip and stepped back, panting from anger. "Get out of my shop, and don't let me catch you near Rachael ever again."

Skip held his neck with both hands and wheezed, staggering out of the office. Daniel slammed the door. We watched until Skip drove away and then Daniel looked at me, breathing hard through his nostrils. How many times was he going to have to save me? Without hesitating, I threw my arms around his neck.

Daniel held me, still breathing hard. "How long was he here?"

"Not long."

He rubbed my back, trying to relax me. "You're trembling."

"Because he scared me."

"Why was he here?"

"He said he was in the area and just stopped by."

"That's bull." Daniel leaned me back. The anger lingered in those gray eyes. "You're coming home with me. I don't care if there's an alarm system. After the nightmare you had and what just happened, I'm not leaving you here alone, so don't argue."

With tears of gratitude and relief, I shook my head. "I'm not going to argue. I wouldn't be able to sleep if I stayed here."

Chapter 16: Alan and Ana

Daniel and I were in the office talking when a black Mercedes pulled up. A young man and woman, around our age, exited the car. The slender woman wore a tan pencil skirt and a white silk blouse. The gentleman wore a teal dress shirt and black slacks. They walked into the office, flashing big smiles.

"*Daniel*," they hollered in unison, running to him.

It was a heartwarming group hug. Laughter filled the office with positive energy. I couldn't help but smile watching them.

"What are you guys doing in town?" Daniel asked excitedly after their hug, although her hands lingered on his arm.

"We're here to celebrate our parent's anniversary," the woman full of bubbly energy sang with her eyes fixed solely on Daniel.

The gentleman glanced at me, then smiled. Without taking his eyes away, he nudged Daniel and scolded him. "Are you not going to introduce us?"

"Sorry, guys. This is Rachael. And Rachael…" He looked at me still smiling, so happy to see them. "This is Alan and Ana. We picked up their parent's car the other day."

Oh, where we went swimming in the pond. The twins.

Alan walked up to my desk and extended his hand. "What a pleasure to meet you." His handshake started with one but ended up with both hands hugging mine.

"You too."

"Hi, Rachael," said the girl who had a high school crush on Daniel. From the looks of her hanging onto his arm, it was still alive and breathing.

I waved so cutesy. "Hello, Ana. Nice to meet you." I cringed, waiting for God to send a bolt of lightning for lying.

Alan turned to Daniel and popped his arm. "Why didn't you tell us you have a girlfriend?"

Daniel and I looked at each other. Such a simple question,

but it seemed to create tension between our gazes. He cleared his throat and turned back to Alan. "Rachael's not my girlfriend. She just works for me."

Alan grinned as though he took delight in Daniel's response. "Oh. Sorry. My bad. Are you seeing anyone since that sorry excuse of a wife?"

Daniel tried to keep his smile from falling. "No. I've been too busy with the shop." He glanced at me, and I looked away.

Ana practically drooled, staring into Daniel's eyes like a lovestruck teenager. "We came to pick up the car for Dad. He wants to hook it up to the RV this evening."

Alan placed his hand on Daniel's shoulder. "Why don't you come to the house for supper? It would be like old times."

"Yes." Ana tugged on Daniel's arm. "Please say you'll come."

"I'll let you know." Daniel nodded to the shop. "I'll get the keys for you."

When he headed toward the shop door, Ana followed him, still holding onto his arm. Once the door closed, I caught Alan staring at me. He had beautiful brown eyes and dark eyebrows. His jet-black hair was short and styled like a professional. He was quite the handsome businessman. Like Peter. And his lingering smile said a lot more than a friendly greeting.

"How long have you been working for Daniel?"

"A little over two months."

"So, Rachael…" He purred my name, casually approaching my desk with his eyes zeroed in on me. "Why don't you join us for supper? We'll have plenty. I promise."

If he were a hunter, his charm would certainly hold his prey's attention. I sure didn't want to run. But I also wasn't going to be devoured.

"That's nice of you to invite me, but…" I scrunched my nose. "It's probably not a good idea." The thought of watching Ana molest Daniel all evening would make me barf.

Alan's smile faded as he lifted his chin and squinted. "I knew it. You have a boyfriend?"

"No. I'm just not comfortable going out in a social setting with my boss."

Alan didn't waste a second reaching into his back pocket for his wallet. "In that case, how about I ditch supper at my parents and take you out somewhere nice?" He thumbed out a business card and offered it to me.

I laughed and took his card. "Wow. You're not shy, are you?"

"When it comes to a pretty woman, not at all." The playfulness in his tone switched to a serious one. "Tell me you're free tonight and what time I can pick you up."

As we stared, Ana and Daniel walked through the shop door. "We need to leave."

Alan ignored his sister. I don't know which one of us grinned the biggest as we continued to stare.

"Anywhere you want to go," he whispered. "You name the place."

Ana huffed. "Come on. We have to go. Dad's waiting on the car."

"I want to take you out," he whispered fervently.

Ana sprinted to my desk and shoved Alan. "Let's *go*."

He turned to her. "You have the keys. Go ahead. I'll be there soon."

She gave him a stern eye. "Okay, but don't be too long." She looked at me and flashed her pearly whites. "It was nice to meet you."

I gave her an Oscar-winning smile. "You too."

Ana made sure to give Daniel a big hug before she left. "It was so good to see you. Please come to the house for supper."

"I can't promise, but I'll let you know if I will."

With Ana gone, Alan turned his attention back to me, grinning a teasing smile. "So, what about tonight?"

"Alan, let's step outside and talk so we don't disturb Rachael while she works."

My eyes darted to Daniel, giving him a scolding glare. *Work? What work?* My work was always finished by noon.

Alan extended his hand, flashing that confident smile. "Again, it was a pleasure to meet you." His voice lowered, and he added, "You have my card. I hope you'll call me."

I flashed a weak smile as to not upset Daniel since he apparently didn't like us talking. "And it was nice to meet you too."

Daniel opened the door. Alan walked out, and Daniel followed. Even though everyone had left, the tension in the air remained—unlike when Alan and Ana walked in.

My orange notebook called out to me. Drawing was my way of releasing stress. With a visual in mind, I opened it and searched for a blank page. A long-flowing waterfall was almost completed when Daniel walked in. He stood in front of my desk and rested his hands on his hips. "What's going on between you two?"

I continued drawing without looking at him. "Nothing. We were just talking."

"Talking?"

"Yes." My eyes cut to his. "Why are you acting like this?"

"From what I saw, there was a lot more going on than talking."

I held my breath and counted to three so I didn't mirror his dry tone. "Daniel, let it go."

"He asked you out, didn't he?"

It was time for us to take a break from each other. After tossing my notebook on the desk, I headed to the back without saying anything.

In my room, I stared out the window and watched a bird hop across the picnic table. In the silence, footsteps licked across the tile floor and then they stopped.

"Were you trying to make me jealous because of Ana?"

The question ran through me, hitting the wrong button. I spun around and scowled. "What makes you think I was jealous?"

He stood at the doorway, staring holes through me with his slate-gray eyes. "Are you going out with him?"

"What difference does it make to you? I'm not your girlfriend. I just work for you."

He rolled his eyes and huffed. "Will you just answer the question?"

My emotions were ready to explode like fireworks. I needed away from Daniel. With my eyes on him, I marched toward the doorway. "I'm going outside. Let me know when you cool down."

Daniel blocked the doorway, causing me to stop. We stared, and he slowly asked, "I want to know if you're going out with him."

My hands clenched, and my eyelids fluttered. "No. I'm not going out with him. *Satisfied?*"

"Rachael, I'm only asking out of concern. Alan has a reputation. You shouldn't let him think you're interested in him."

I crossed my arms and laughed to counter the anger. "Are you saying I led him on?"

"No, I'm not, but…" Daniel paused as though to filter his next words. "From what I saw, you looked like you were interested in him."

"This conversation is over. I don't want to talk about it anymore. Besides, I don't owe you any explanation for what I've said or done. I'm not your girlfriend, remember?"

"Um…" He scratched the back of his head and narrowed his brows. "That's twice you've said that. Did you *want* me to tell him you're my girlfriend?"

My answer came fast. "No. I'm reminding you to stay out of my business."

"Okay." He raised his shoulders and then his hands in defense. "I was just trying to let you know Alan is a ladies' man. That's all."

The way he said it hurt so much my breath caught, then my eyes watered. I placed my fingertips over my lip and swallowed. "Can you, um, please go? I want to be alone."

His eyes reflected remorse. "Rachael, I didn't mean to upset you. I'm sorry." Daniel stepped closer.

I held up my hand for him not to. "Don't. Just go."

"Please don't push me away."

"Don't you have work to do?"

"I don't want to leave you upset. Especially if it's because of something I said or did."

He wouldn't leave, stressing me out more, causing me to snap. "Look, if you don't leave right now, then I will." And the way I felt, I meant for good.

"*Fine.* I'm going home. You can lock up." Daniel turned on his heels and marched out of the room.

I stood there in shock at what happened. Then the office door slammed so hard I flinched. I ran and secured the shop and office. After forwarding the calls to Daniel's cell, I went to my room and laid down. I don't remember falling asleep.

When I woke up, not that I was hungry, I searched the fridge for a snack and grabbed the leftover sub sandwich. In the office, I sat at my desk and nibbled on it, but I couldn't eat, recalling the things Daniel had said. I checked my phone, expecting to see a message: *I'm sorry. Please call me*, thinking Daniel texted me while I was asleep. When I saw the message box was empty, it hurt. The same way it did when Daniel told Alan, 'She just works for me.' It was time to admit there was something between us. Something more than friends. I had broken my own agreement to keep things strictly business.

Ignoring the little releases of pain trailing down my cheeks, I had to face reality. It was time to leave Maxton. If not, my feelings for Daniel would get in the way of finding Jilly if they hadn't already.

Besides, I couldn't offer him anything. I was a fugitive.

Slouched in my chair, I swiveled, staring at the ceiling while in thought. With the money I had saved, I could survive until I figured out a way to call Mama. Since she would have my letter soon and would search for Jilly, I didn't need the resources at hand any longer. In fact, roaming, I could probably call Mama. I thought about going to my room, gathering my things and leaving. When I glanced at the clock, I realized without a plan it would be wiser to set my alarm and leave in the morning before Daniel arrived.

I tried to read my novel, but it was pointless, so I took a hot bath. No telling when I would get another chance. Around nine o'clock, I packed my belongings into a large trash bag and set it at the doorway. I checked my phone; still no messages. I envisioned Daniel at Ana's having a smashing time with her hands all over him. The visual made me want to throw up.

Around ten o'clock, I went outside and laid on top of the picnic table, hoping for some peace and guidance. I gazed at the stars and talked to my dad. Off in the distance, a noise caught my attention. Like a car door shutting. No one should be that close to the shop. I jumped off the table and ran back inside.

After setting my alarm, I turned off the lamp and crawled into bed. "Goodnight, Fumbles." I closed my eyes, ready for the day to end.

Thump.

My eyes opened. Then I sat up in bed, hoping my heart raced for nothing. Maybe it was the raccoon on the roof again.

Thump. Thump.

My heart rate went into turbo speed. It wasn't a raccoon on the roof but someone at the back door. Without turning on the lamp, I reached for my phone on the headboard to call Daniel. I couldn't swipe his number fast enough with my fumbling hands.

"Rachael?" He sounded alert, as though he had not yet gone to bed.

I cupped the side of my mouth and whispered, "Are you here, at the shop?"

"No. Why?"

"Because I heard something outside and—"

Pound. Pound.

"Oh no," I squealed, cowering against the headboard. "Som-someone's trying to br-break in. Daniel, I'm scared. I-I can't call the police."

"I'm on my way. I'll be there in two minutes."

Tap. Tap.

"I can hear them jiggling the office door. *Daniel*—"

"Lock your bedroom door. Right now! Then go to the bathroom and lock that door."

"I can't." My eyes closed, and I babbled, "I-I'm too scared to move."

"Rachael, you're stronger than this. Do it. Now."

"Okay." After throwing back the covers, I ran to the door and turned the knob to lock it. Then I ran to the bathroom and locked it. With my back against the wall, I sank to the floor and whimpered, "I'm scared." I closed my eyes and cried harder. "I don't wanna die."

"Calm down. You know I'm not gonna let anything happen to you."

I lowered my forehead on my bended knees. "What if you don't get here in time?" I pinched my shirt, raised it to my cheek, and wiped my tears.

"You'll be okay until I get there. Are you in the bathroom with both doors locked?"

"Yes."

"Stay in there. You hear me?"

I held my breath, trying not to cry.

"Rachael, answer me so I'll know you're alright."

I nodded. "Yes. I-I hear you."

"Which door are they at?"

"The office door. Not the one that's between the bay doors."

"Listen to me. I just pulled into the back of the shop. Do *not* come out of that bathroom."

"Please be—"

Bloop, came the sound of the call ending.

Crying, I rested my phone on the floor, hugged my legs, and rocked in the silence. "God, please watch over me. Don't let me die. I have to find Jilly."

POW.

"Oh my God." I jerked my head up and listened for another gunshot. Then I feared the worst. What if Daniel had been shot? With trembling hands, I couldn't get the bathroom door opened fast enough. I grabbed my jeans from the floor and shoved my legs into them as fast as I could. Then I left the room and tiptoed down the hall, terrified what I would see. The office door slammed, causing me to stop.

"Don't shoot," a panicked voice pleaded.

After taking a few more steps, I slowly peeked around the corner and into the office. Daniel pointed his gun at a masked intruder kneeling to the floor.

"I'm getting down, *man*. Just don't shoot me."

"Shut up. I should've shot you instead of giving you a warning." Daniel glanced my way and did a double take. "I told you not to come out of the bathroom." He quickly turned his attention back to the intruder, as did I.

"I know, but—"

"Rachael, grab your keys and leave."

"Daniel, it's *him*," I shouted from the doorway.

"Who?"

"It's Skip. I'd know that voice anywhere."

Daniel motioned with his gun. "Take off that mask."

The intruder shook his head.

"One…" Daniel looked down his outstretched arm with both hands on the gun. "Two…"

"Okay! Okay!" The intruder reached for the top of his ski mask and slowly lifted it until his face was exposed. It was him.

"Rachael, leave. Now."

"You *can't* just shoot him."

"Why do you think he's here?"

Skip waved his hands in surrender. "Let me walk out of here. I swear I'll leave town."

Daniel smirked and sang, "Not a chance."

Skip reached out his hands and begged harder. "Come on, man. *I swear.*"

Daniel's phone beeped. While keeping his attention on Skip, he pulled it from his belt and glanced at it. "He tripped the alarm. The security system has alerted the police. They're on their way." Daniel glanced at me with panic in his eyes. "Go to my house. Hurry."

"Okay."

I ran to the room, grabbed my things, then rushed back to the office. I walked along the wall and made my way to the door. When I opened it, I waited for Daniel to look at me. When he did, I pleaded with weary eyes. "Please don't…"

"I won't unless he moves." Daniel turned his eyes back to Skip. "Hurry and go to the house."

I ran to my Jeep and left. Less than a mile from the shop, flashing blue lights headed my way. In a matter of seconds, a sheriff's car whizzed by me in full pursuit. I looked in my rearview mirror and watched as long as I could. Of all the times I imagined seeing flashing blue lights in my rearview mirror, I never thought the day I saw them it would be a relief.

When I arrived at Daniel's, the first thing I did was run to the bathroom and throw up. The thought of Skip breaking into the shop had me purging everything in me.

"Oh my God."

Was he the unsettling noise I heard when I was lying on the picnic table? Then I thought about the day he came to the shop. That's why Skip was so nosy when I was on the phone. He was casing the place.

After rinsing my mouth and washing my face, I headed to the kitchen to fix a cup of hot tea to settle my queasy stomach. While the microwave heated the water, Skip's cackle echoed in my head. His face was a ghostly image in front of me, laughing and taunting me.

I sat on a stool and stared at my mug. The tea turned cold before I had my fourth sip. I pushed the mug to the side and rested my head on my crossed arms.

The front door opened.

I lifted my head.

Daniel walked in and dropped a trash bag at the door, then he headed to the kitchen, yet to have made eye contact with me. After pacing, he approached the counter that separated us and finally looked at me. "Are you okay?"

"No."

"We need to talk."

"Just tell me he's in jail."

"Yes. He's going to be in jail for a long time." Daniel walked around the counter and sat on the stool next to me. "Skip's a wanted man. He has outstanding warrants in Ohio."

I covered my gasp. "What? Warrants for what?"

Daniel rested his elbows on the bar and covered his face with his hands.

I pushed his forearm. "Tell me what for."

His burdened eyes met mine. "For kidnapping and sexual assault. It happened four years ago. After he posted bail, he left town."

Sexual assault? I felt violated hearing that.

"Talk to me."

"I don't know what to say."

"I didn't press charges against him."

I slapped the counter with both palms and yelled, "Why not?"

"Because I can't protect you if news crews and reporters come to the shop asking questions." Daniel left the stool and paced in the kitchen. "I went to your room to grab some clothes for you so you can stay here tonight. I found them in a trash bag at the door and brought it." He turned and looked at me with those dull eyes. "You were going to leave, weren't you?"

With everything that happened, I had forgotten about my plans to leave in the morning. With remorse in my heart, I mumbled, "I'm sorry. I didn't mean for you to find out that way."

His brows tightened. "How was I *supposed* to find out, Rachael? When I went to work in the morning and noticed you were gone?"

I looked at my hands resting on the counter. "I was going to leave you a note and explain why."

He laughed, insulted. "*Really?* A lousy note?"

After everything Daniel had done for me, leaving a note did seem heartless. I lowered my forehead to my fingertips and massaged it. I didn't know what to say.

"You told me on your birthday you wouldn't leave."

I moved my hands and looked at him. "Daniel, after what happened with Alan, I just—"

"Just what, Rachael? Decided to walk out of my life the same way my dad did when I was five?" As we stared, his eyes glazed over with tears. He tried to blink them away. "We were a family. Or so I thought. My parents had this big fight. Dad left. I kept thinking he would come back, but he never did. He left me like I was nothing to him."

That was the most Daniel had ever said about his father. And that's when I realized how painful his past was. My heart broke for what he went through. I didn't know what to say other than, "I'm sorry he never came back."

His lips parted like he was going to say something, but only his teary eyes spoke, screaming abandonment and insecurity. I thought I was looking at a little boy.

I left the stool, ran to Daniel and threw my arms around his waist.

Daniel wrapped his arms around me and let go of his tears. He wept.

"It's okay." I ran my hands across his back to comfort him the way he had done so many times for me. My strong angel broke down in front of me.

"Please don't leave. I want us to talk tomorrow. I can't do it right now."

"I'll stay."

"You promise?"

I leaned back and watched Daniel wipe his cheeks. "Yes. I give you my word I'll stay, and we can talk tomorrow. Okay?"

Daniel nodded without looking at me.

"It's late. Let's try to get some sleep."

"No, please. I need to hold you." Daniel pulled me back to him and secured me to his chest.

"You can hold me as long as you need to." I held him and let him melt in my arms. It was my turn to be there for him.

Chapter 17: I'm Messed Up

During breakfast, Daniel didn't say much other than he thought it was best if I didn't go to the shop, which I quickly agreed. There were moments when I didn't think I could ever go back. Even though Skip was in jail, his presence would still be there, along with the thoughts of what could have happened.

After he left for work, the day couldn't drag by any slower if I held the minute hand on the clock and stopped time. I called Abby and told her what happened. I needed a woman to talk to. She tried to comfort me and encouraged me to be strong, but all I did was cry. However, by the time our conversation ended, my best friend had me smiling and holding my head up high.

After lunch, I sat on the porch and tried to find solace in nature so I could think. How could I have feelings for Daniel when only months earlier I was happily married? Perhaps my feelings were only gratitude for everything he had done for me.

Around two o'clock, Daniel called and told me he was closing the shop and to be ready. I could only imagine where we were going. I stood at the door and watched for him. Things were never going to be the same after our talk, and I didn't know what that meant.

The wrecker crept down the driveway. I locked up and walked outside.

After getting out of the wrecker, Daniel approached me.

I smiled, admiring his shorts and loose-fitting T-shirt with a monster truck on it. "You've already showered and changed."

Even though Daniel smiled, his eyes told me he was still burdened. "I didn't want you to have to smell me."

"I like that shirt."

He looked at it and frowned. "This old thing? Abigail bought it for me years ago." He walked me toward The Beast. "How are you holding up?"

I shrugged. "Okay, I guess. Did anyone show up asking questions?"

He opened my door for me. "No. I know one of the deputies who showed up last night. He said he would do his best to make sure no one found out since I didn't file charges."

After jumping inside the hot cab, I buckled up. "That's good."

Daniel closed the door and headed to his side of the truck as I stared out the window.

The diesel cackled.

"Hey, are you okay over there?"

I looked at him, coming out of a daze. "Where are we going?"

After Daniel turned the air on, he buckled up. "You should know the answer to that question by now."

"Yeah, I know."

At least Daniel smiled. I worried about him after his meltdown last night. His dad abandoning him left such a raw wound, even twenty-four years later.

We traveled the country roads in silence until I realized where we were going.

"Why are we coming here?" Surely he heard the disapproval in my voice.

Daniel turned right and headed down the driveway. "I talked to Alan this morning to make sure no one would be here. Everyone is in Lumberton for his parent's anniversary party."

We passed the detached garage and traveled the dirt path.

"I don't want to be here. Not after what happened yesterday."

"We won't stay long." Daniel turned to me as our bodies shifted in unison, enduring the potholes once again. "I promise."

"Why would you bring me to Alan's house?"

With confidence, he asked, "Have I disappointed you yet?"

I rolled my eyes and looked away. "No, but I don't like how this feels. Can we please go somewhere else?"

He pulled up to the dock and parked. I stared at the pond, remembering the first time we came there. Daniel startled me when he opened my door. I looked away and refused to get out.

"Come with me. Please." He tenderly placed his hand on my arm. "Just for a few minutes. If you still want to leave, we will."

I turned to face him, his blue eyes staring at me.

Daniel offered his hand. "Five minutes."

After unbuckling, I stepped out of the truck and took his hand. Daniel had a tight grip on it as we made our way to the dock.

It was hot, so he suggested we put our feet in the water to cool off. After we took off our socks and shoes, we sat side by side with our feet in the water.

"Why didn't you tell me Skip was still bothering you at the diner?"

Clearly, he and Abby talked after I called her.

I sighed, paddling my feet in the cool water. "Because I thought I could handle him."

"When I think what he—"

My hand went up to stop him. "Please don't say it. That's not something I can think about right now."

"I'm sorry for the things I said yesterday."

I made circles in the water with my feet. "Why were you so angry?"

"Because Alan was hitting on you."

"Daniel, he's not the first man to ever flirt with me. It didn't mean I was going out with him. You know I couldn't. Not that I wanted to."

He looked over the water and exhaled from deep within through his parted lips. "I brought you here to tell you something, but I don't know how. You know I'm not good with talking about my feelings."

A breeze blew hair across my face. I tucked it behind my ears. "Just say it."

Daniel looked at his feet and placed his palms on the edge of the dock. "After Nikki left, I realized our marriage was a mistake. I thought I loved her. Maybe I did. Maybe I didn't want to be alone. I want someone to steal my heart, not just be there to fill the loneliness. I want to find that special woman, you know? But I don't think she even exists."

A giggle tried to escape. "Heather was—"

"Stop." His eyes darted to mine, squinting. "Don't mention her again, or I'll throw you in."

With the serious look he gave me, I believed he would.

"I won't mention her again."

Daniel cleared his throat. "As I was saying, over time, I convinced myself this woman didn't exist. She was only a vision in my head. Then one day I stopped to see if someone stranded on the side of the road needed help. And there she was." Our eyes met at the same time. "She did exist."

"Surely you're not talking about me."

He huffed offended. "How can you *not* know it's you?"

I looked away and pretended I wasn't affected by his comment, although my heart somewhat relished in what he said. "You've never kissed me, even though I made a big deal about me only working for you. Most men would've tried anyway."

"There's a reason why."

"Because you think of me like a sister?" I turned to see his reaction.

Daniel didn't laugh. "No. Because I'm messed up. That's why."

"Messed up?" I frowned. "Why would you say that? You're not—"

"Don't. I *know* what I am."

"And what's that?"

"After what I did yesterday, you have to ask?"

"Um, yes, I do."

"I'm jealous. Insecure. I have no self-esteem. I have abandonment issues. I have a hard time telling people how I feel." He raised his eyebrows. "Want me to continue?"

I shook my head, speechless at his comment. "You're so much more than that. I wish you could see yourself through my eyes."

"That's because you have innocent eyes and always see the good in everyone." Daniel looked over the water. "When I saw your things were packed, a part of me wasn't surprised because you had seen that side of me. But what hurt more was you were going to leave without telling me. Without even saying goodbye. I guess it triggered my dad leaving."

I tried to scoop up water with my toes curled upward. "I didn't mean to hurt you. Please don't think I was going to leave because *you* think you're messed up."

"Then why were you going to leave?"

I straightened my back and looked at the blue sky. If that was going to be our last day together, I didn't want to leave on a lie. "After our…what happened yesterday, I realized I have feelings for you. With everything that's going on in my life, I can't be distracted by that. I'm not even sure if my feelings are real or something else. Even if they are real, it doesn't matter, because I can't offer you anything."

"Are you saying you want to?"

Not sure how to answer, I paddled my feet in the water and

mumbled, "Right now, I'm confused."

"Well, I'm not confused." And his tone confirmed it. "I know I agreed to keep this 'boss-employee' thing between us, but after yesterday, I can't deny my feelings for you anymore."

When I looked at Daniel, it was imperative I chose my words carefully, for both of us. "There's something about me you don't know. Once that's resolved, I have to go home and turn myself in. When I do, I'll be arrested. You know how the rest of the story goes."

Daniel gently tucked the hair blowing in my face behind my ear. "Then I'll be there for you, but not as your boss. I'll find you a good lawyer. I have money. And if I have to, I'll sell my business."

When Daniel said that, my eyes watered from sadness, because there was no doubt it was time to let him go. And I didn't want to. Without saying anything, I lifted my feet out of the water, but before I could stand, Daniel grabbed my arm and kept me from getting to my feet. When I looked at him, it broke my heart to know what I had to do.

"Don't go." His eyes stared into mine with desperation. "Please, Rachael."

I shook my head, raising my eyebrows. "I'm not letting you put your life on hold for me. And I'm certainly not letting you sell your business because of me. That's your passion, Daniel."

"That business means *nothing* to me without you."

My voice broke, trying to say the words I didn't want to say. "I can't offer you a future."

His grip on my wrist tightened. "Please don't leave me. Please, Rachael."

The fear in his words cut through me as did the tormented look in his eyes. I saw a little boy who watched his dad walk away, and I was about to do the same thing.

"But I have to. My life is... Well, I don't have one. It wouldn't be fair to make you wait for—"

He put his finger over my lips. "Not giving us a chance is what's not fair." Daniel placed his hand on my cheek, and his thumb stroked my skin. "Don't walk away like everyone else in my life."

"It's not like I want to."

"Then don't." Daniel leaned in to kiss me.

I quickly turned my face and raised my hand between us. My chest heaved, struggling for air. My head spun, lost in a world of wants, desires, fear, and even hope. "We can't. I'm not the one for you."

"You *are* the one." Daniel took my hand and placed my palm against his chest. "Feel my heart pounding? It's because of *you*. I didn't find you just to lose you."

My own heart pounded, because I wanted him too, but it wasn't meant to be. I ached to touch Daniel and reached up in sessions, then put my hand on his cheek. My eyes teared up. "Daniel, I have to let you go."

"And I have to fight for you." He took my wrist. Still looking into my eyes, he kissed my hand. "I'm not letting you go, Rachael."

Every word he said only made me want him more, but I couldn't give him false hope. I couldn't let him wait for me to be a free woman.

Eyeing me, Daniel eased closer, then stopped. As we stared, I thought my heart was going to come out of my chest, because I knew he was going to kiss me, and I was going to let him. I think my gaze even invited him to, because he eased even closer. I wanted it more than anything and closed my eyes, but Daniel didn't kiss me. Instead, he brushed his cheek against mine. His stubble graced my skin. It left me so weak, I almost cupped his face and put my lips on his.

Daniel whispered next to my ear, "Can I kiss you?"

He should have just taken me. I couldn't give him permission, but I wouldn't stop him either.

"Daniel, I'm scared." Scared because if he kissed me, I wouldn't be able to walk away from him.

"I am too. More than you know. But if you don't tell me no, I'm going to kiss you."

I didn't have any strength to say that one word.

"Rachael?"

"Daniel, please, I…"

He brushed his cheek against mine again. "That's not a 'no.'"

I finally confessed, "I can't say it."

Daniel kissed my cheek. My breath caught when he kissed it again and moved his lips closer to mine. "It's not too late to say it."

It was for me. I would have to deal with my loss of control later, but in that moment, I wanted Daniel. I placed my hands on the back of his head and brought his lips to mine. As I kissed him, it was like a part of him poured into my heart, my body, and my soul, putting me in seventh heaven. Still locked in a passionate kiss, I leaned back until I rested on the dock.

When Daniel pulled his lips from mine, he wore this incredible smile and lowered his body next to me. "Are you comfortable?"

I smiled and nodded, looking into those blue eyes.

Daniel kissed me again and wrapped his leg around mine. My hands went underneath his shirt and up his chest until my palms brushed over his nipples. I wanted to feel all of him, and I wanted him to feel me. Our hands traveled to places they shouldn't have.

Abby's ringtone played.

Daniel swiped and silenced the call.

"Are you sure you should do that? What if it's important?"

"I'll call her back in a minute." He rested his phone on the dock. "I want a minute to hold you and kiss you." Daniel tugged the collar of my shirt to the side, exposed my shoulder, then kissed it. "If you only knew how long I've wanted to do this." His lips traveled to my neck, teasing me in ways he didn't know. "Do you feel the same, or do I need to stop?"

"I want you, but I'm scared."

He leaned back and looked at me with those calm blue eyes and a sweet smile. "Don't be."

"But I am. I've never felt this way with anyone before."

"Not even with Peter?"

My thoughts drifted, remembering the things Mandy had said. She was right. I gave up the things in life I enjoyed doing to be Peter's wife. "I loved him, but something was missing. I didn't even know it until I met you." I couldn't resist trailing my fingers through his hair. Then I looked into those blue eyes. "Now I can't imagine my life without you."

Daniel kissed me, and I enjoyed it like a cool rain in the summer. I could have laid there until the stars came out, but I remembered Abby's call.

I eased him back. "You need to call your sister."

He grumbled and picked up his phone. I sat up with my knees to my chest and hugged my legs, relishing in everything that happened.

"Hey, what's up?" Daniel wrapped his free arm around my neck and kissed my forehead. "I was busy." He kissed me again, and I smiled. "Yeah, Rachael's with me. We'll be there in twenty minutes." He kissed my temple. "You too. Bye."

"What's wrong?"

Daniel swiped his phone and ended the call. "Jory's truck

won't start. They're stranded at the diner." He clipped his phone to his belt and looked at me. "You mind if we run over there and see what's wrong with it? It shouldn't take long."

"Of course not." I reached for my socks and shoes.

"We can come back if you want to. I'll stop and grab some burgers and shakes, and we can eat on the dock." He slipped on a shoe and added, "The sunsets are really nice."

I looked over the water and tried to visualize one. "I bet they are."

Daniel stood and offered his hand.

Once I was on my feet, I covered my giggle. "Oh no. What are we going to tell Heather if she stops by to chat?"

"I warned you." Daniel came after me.

I squealed and ran.

Daniel caught me, then wrapped his arms around me. With his face against mine, he held me tight. "Where do you think you're going?"

I laughed and leaned my head against his. "Nowhere."

"That's right."

Daniel released me, took my hand, and walked me off the dock. Then he kissed me again. It lingered, then I pulled my lips from his and placed my hand on his cheek. "We need to go."

"Did I disappoint you?"

"No. Not yet," I sang.

"Do you trust me? I mean, really trust me?"

"Of course I do."

"Then let me help you."

Why did he have to rain on our moment? Daniel meant well, but my past came flooding back, filling me with guilt and regrets.

I lowered my chin. "I want to, but…give me a little more time. Okay?"

"I understand." Daniel took my hand, and we continued walking.

"Rachael?"

We arrived at the passenger's door.

I turned to face him. "Yeah?"

"Move in with me."

My jaw fell. "What?"

He quickly amended his offer. "I mean, into one of the spare bedrooms."

I inhaled but couldn't release it. "I-I don't know."

He guided the hair past my shoulder, watching his hand. "I worry about you at the shop. And I want to spend the evenings with you."

"I don't know. I grew up in church, and it would feel wrong. Let me think about it, but if I do, you have to be a gentleman."

Daniel took my face in his hands and kissed me. Then he asked, "Does this mean you're my girlfriend?"

I reached up and held his wrists. "Well, since you've kissed me, I guess that means I am."

We left the pond and headed to the diner. The song "Miracles" by JEFFERSON STARSHIP played. Daniel turned it up and sang along with it like he was the happiest man in the world. I swayed in my seat and sang with him. In that moment, we were in our own world, and I wanted to believe in miracles.

Chapter 18: I Thought I'd Lost Him

We traveled the country road with our hands linked together over the console like a couple. My mind was deep in thought while staring out the window.

Daniel squeezed my hand. "What are you thinking?"

"You don't want to know."

"Yes, I do. Please tell me."

"When I turn myself in, I don't know when I'll see you again. It's not fair to you if—"

"What's not fair is you walking away from me because of that."

I looked at Daniel and reminded him, "You know I'm facing some heavy time."

"We'll deal with that when it happens." He glanced my way. "It was self-defense. And with a good lawyer…" He turned his attention back to the road. A moment passed, then he mumbled, "Rachael, *please*," he squeezed my hand, "don't walk away from me."

I turned and looked at the truck in front of us pulling a dump trailer full of debris but thought about my letter to Mom. Once she got my letter, everything would change. "I'm going to have to go home soon." I watched the debris bounce around. "Those boards are going to fall off if he hits a pothole."

"I was thinking the same thing. The idiot didn't tie it down." Daniel released my hand and gripped the steering wheel. "I'm going to back off. Just in case."

"That board on the left is…" It flew out of the trailer and went airborne. "*Look out.*" I crossed my arms over my face.

"Hold on." Daniel swerved into the other lane to miss the flying debris. We left the road, creating a cloud of dust surrounding the truck. Metal crunching and glass breaking sounded like a bomb had exploded when we hit something and came to a hard, instant stop.

"Are you okay?" I spat the taste of dirt from my mouth and waved away the dust.

Daniel didn't answer.

Still blinking from the dust and coughing, I turned to check on him. His limp body rested against his door. "*Daniel?*" He was hurt. Panic set in. I tried to unbuckle, but it wouldn't release. "Don't you dare do this to me."

My door opened, distracting me. I looked to see who opened it.

An older gentleman in worn overalls waved away the dust between us. "Is everyone alright?"

"No. Please call…" I coughed from inhaling the dust. "For help. My friend is hurt."

The stranger leaned over and tried to get a look at Daniel. "Maw's calling nine-one-one. I'll run back to the house and make sure she tells them someone's injured." He scurried away.

Once my seatbelt released, I leaned over the console and took Daniel's limp hand and held it against my cheek. Blood trickled down his forehead. I tried to stay calm and not panic.

"Daniel, open your eyes."

He didn't respond.

"Please look at me," I commanded, still trying to convince myself he would be okay.

Daniel blinked slowly and tried to open his eyes, then he moaned in agony, "*Ah*, it hurts…bad."

"Don't move." I quickly held his face to keep him still.

He looked around until his eyes met mine. "Are you hurt?"

"No, I'm okay."

His eyes closed, and his body slouched. Then his face relaxed in my hands like he had fallen asleep.

"Daniel, *no*. You have to wake up," I demanded, still trying to remain calm, but time seemed suspended in a moment when every second counted. "Daniel. Wake up. Do you hear me? Don't you *dare* leave me."

He blinked a few times.

"That's it. Look at me." I held his head in place. Blood trailed down his forehead. "Come on, Daniel. Wake up. I need you."

With his eyes barely open and his breathing shallow, Daniel struggled for that one word. "Leave."

"No. I'm *not* leaving you."

"Is he alright?"

I turned, hoping it was help, but it was the older gentleman. "No. Is the ambulance here?"

"Not yet, but some volunteer firemen just arrived."

"Please tell them to hurry. My boyfriend needs help." I turned to Daniel. "Stay with me. Help is here."

His face tightened, enduring the pain. "Call Abi…gail"

"I will. As soon as someone's here to help you."

Daniel closed his eyes. A moan seeped out. Then his body went limp. His face became heavy in my hands.

"*No.*" I wept, fearing he had died in front of me. "I can't lose you too." My thumbs rubbed across his cheeks as tears slid down my face. "Please, Daniel. Please open your eyes for me."

"Ma'am, my name's Mike. I'm a volunteer fireman. Are you hurt?"

Sobbing, fearing my world had once again crumbled on me, I babbled, "No, but he is. Please help him. Please don't let him die."

Two men tried to get to Daniel's side of the truck, but it was wedged against a tree.

"We'll take care of him, but I need you to step out of the truck to see if you're alright." The fireman extended his hand and wiggled his fingers. "Come on. I'll help you."

"No. I can't let go of his head."

"It's okay. I've got him." One of the firemen at Daniel's door had managed to reach inside the truck and placed his hand under Daniel's jaw to support his head.

Before I let go, I said a quick prayer. *God, please don't take him from me.* I kissed Daniel's cheek and whispered, "I love you."

The fireman helped me out of the truck. Before he whisked me away, I watched a medic enter the cab. When I turned, I faced a yard full of spectators. The red lights on the ambulance we approached pulled me into a trance. Surely there was noise, people talking, sirens off in the distance, but I didn't hear anything. I just stared, somewhat numb.

Mike helped me sit on the back of the ambulance. A medic tried to put a neck brace on me, but I pushed it away. He was persistent until I informed him I refused medical treatment. He wrapped a blanket around me while I watched the firemen and medics surround Daniel's truck.

The stranger who had opened my door approached with a thin, fragile-looking grandma by his side. "Maw found this on the ground. I think it's yours." He set my purse next to me.

"Thank you," I mumbled with sincerity but somewhat in a fog.

The elderly lady, unable to stand up straight, placed her hand on my knee. "Sweetie, is there anyone we can call for you?"

"Um, Abby." I looked at her with my jaw quivering. "Can you, um, call her, please?"

"Maw, write down the number, and I'll run to the house and call her." The gentleman reached into the breast pocket of his overalls and pulled out a tiny spiral notebook and a short pencil.

"What's the number, dear?" She smiled, waiting for me to answer.

After calling out the number, I added, "It's his sister."

"Maw, stay here with her." The gentleman reached for the notebook and hurried away.

The medic presented a clipboard in front of me. "Since you refused medical services, I'll need you to sign this waiver."

I scribbled a name no one could read.

He took the clipboard. "You should go to the hospital and be examined."

"Thanks, but I'm alright," I muttered with my attention on Daniel.

Firemen and medics worked frantically to free him from the mangled truck. The deputies asking questions would soon make their way to me. My freedom was the last thing I was worried about. I wasn't leaving Daniel.

It only seemed like seconds since the gentleman had left to call Abby before he returned, winded. "His sister said to tell you she's on her way."

My eyes turned to him, slowly. "Thank you."

The elderly lady, smiling with sensitivity, patted my hand. "Everything's going to be alright."

My eyes watered because I needed to hear someone say those words. That I wouldn't lose Daniel. I sniffled and swallowed the lump in my throat. "He's all I have left." My body shook as though I were cold, even though it was a hot summer's afternoon. "I'm scared he's going to die."

The sweet lady lifted the blanket over my shoulder that had fallen. "They're doing everything they can for him."

"*We need the stretcher.*"

I sat up alert. My heart pounded, and I watched intently. The urgency of the fireman calling out to another one gave me hope

174

Daniel was still alive. Tears of relief filled my eyes, and I breathed a little easier.

Another ambulance backed up to his truck. Medics jumped out as others quickly opened the back doors. The adrenaline kicked in, and I bit my lower lip, watching and waiting with anticipation.

"*Rachael?*"

I searched for Abby through the spectators and spotted her running toward me with Jory and Zack not far behind her.

The elderly lady placed her hand on my shoulder. "Since your family is here, we're going to head back to the house."

Before she walked away, I reached for her arm, and she turned her gentle eyes back to me. "Thank you both so much."

"We'll pray for him."

They headed toward the old farmhouse.

Abby approached the ambulance, winded. "Are you hurt?"

We hugged each other.

"No." I held on to her for dear life, sobbing, finally breaking down. "But Daniel is. I can't lose him, Abby. I just can't."

"We're not going to lose him." She rubbed my back. "Which hospital is he at?"

"He's still in his truck. They're trying to get him out."

Abby leaned me back and scanned the yard. Then her eyes darted to Jory. In her take-charge voice, she told him, "Get her away from here, *now*. I'll ride with him to the hospital."

"No." I panicked at the thought of not being with Daniel.

"Jory…home." Abby took off running to the ambulance and yelled over her shoulder, "I'll call you."

"Rachael…" Jory gently took my forearm as though to keep me from running after her. Our eyes met. "This is what Daniel would want." He looked at Zack. "Ready?"

"Sure."

Zack made his way to my side, and they led me through the spectators. When we arrived at Zack's Kia Spectra, Jory helped me into the backseat. I watched the firemen load Daniel into the ambulance. Tears fell from my eyes, longing to be with him. Abby jumped inside and then two medics. They closed the back doors as we left the scene.

Jory told Zack to head back to the diner.

I stared out the window, worried about Daniel. Perhaps it was the shock, but I couldn't cry. I was numb and lifeless.

We arrived at the diner and went inside. I sat on a stool, still staring.

Jory sat on the one next to me and rested his arms on the counter. "Would you like some coffee?"

"No," I mumbled, still numb.

Zack walked behind the counter and prepared a fountain drink. He looked over his shoulder while the cup filled. "What happened?"

I straightened my back and released a long sigh. "We were behind this dump truck full of debris. A board fell off and came at us. Daniel swerved to miss it but lost control and slammed into a tree."

Zack approached, sipping his Pepsi. "Are you sure you're not hurt?"

"No, I'm okay."

Jory's phone beeped. I think we all jumped. He read the message to us. "At Lumberton Hospital. Will call soon."

My body slouched, my head tilted, then I pleaded from the bottom of my heart. "Please take me there."

Jory put his phone back in his pocket. "You know I can't."

"*Please.*"

He rubbed his forearm. "Abby'll call when she knows something."

The tears came. I jerked a few napkins from the holder and covered my face.

"Look, I know you wanna go there. I'd feel the same way if that was Abby."

My hand clenched, squeezing the napkins as I turned to him. "You *don't* understand. I have to know he's okay."

"Zack, while we're here, would you mind checking the temperature in the freezer to make sure it's still holding?"

"Sure thing, boss."

Once Zack was gone, Jory leaned in. "I don't know what your story is and don't care to know. That's your business. But Daniel made Abby promise to watch over you if something happened to him. And you know her. She'll do anything for her brother. If I go against her, I'm going to be in the doghouse."

"But, Jory..." I stretched out my arms over the counter and lowered my head on top of them. "I have to know he's okay."

He patted my shoulder. "I totally understand."

Zack returned. "Everything's good."

Abby called to tell us she was in the waiting room, but there was no news to report. She refused to let me come to the hospital, so I threatened to walk home and get my Jeep and drive myself. She reluctantly gave in. Zack was kind enough to drive us since Jory's truck was still disabled. With traffic and parking, it took an hour until we walked into the waiting room.

When I spotted Abby, I rushed to her side. "Hey." I lowered myself into the chair next to her and placed my hand on her shoulder. "Any news?"

She lifted her head and looked at me with swollen red eyes. "No. Not yet. They're running tests on him."

Jory kissed her cheek, then settled into the seat next to her. "Did the paramedics say anything?"

"Other than asking questions about his health, no. They were too busy working on him." She turned to me and scowled. "He's going to be *furious* with me because you're here."

And I quickly told her, "I had to come."

She leaned closer. "Rachael, a deputy was asking about you when I got to the ambulance. A fireman told them there was a female passenger. The deputy said he would question Daniel at the hospital."

"I'll be careful."

Abby rolled her eyes and sat back in the chair. "You need to go home."

"Not until I know Daniel is okay."

We settled into the quietness and waited. I held onto my smiley necklace and lost count how many times I prayed.

Jory cleared his throat and stood. "Would anyone like some coffee?"

Zack leaned forward in his seat and raised his finger. "I could go for a Coke."

Abby nodded. "I'd like some. It's going to be a long night." She patted my hand. "Rachael, how about you?"

"No thanks."

"We'll be back in a minute."

Jory and Zack headed to the cafeteria.

I leaned forward and placed my face in my hands, massaging my forehead. The waiting was hard, and all I did was relive the accident.

Abby rubbed my back. "You really care about him, don't you?"

"I didn't know how much until I thought I'd lost him."

"He cares about you too."

I sat back and smiled, thinking about what happened at the pond. "I know."

Abby punched my forearm. "What's up with that smile? What are you not telling me, girlfriend?"

I rubbed my arm, trying not to grin. "Daniel, he, um…kissed me earlier."

Her jaw dropped, and her eyes bugged. "Oh my gosh. You mean he hadn't kissed you *yet?*"

"Shh." I leaned closer, smiling with my lips pressed together. "Trust me. It was worth the wait."

"Does this mean you guys are like, boyfriend and girlfriend now?"

"You can say that."

She punched my arm again. "It's about time."

"Ow. Stop doing that." Abby was my rock, and I trusted her, which made me feel guilty for not telling her what was going on with me. "Sorry I can't tell you my story."

"Hey, as long as you treat my brother right, I don't care what it is." She looked around, then leaned closer and whispered, "You're running from the law, aren't you?"

I nodded.

A lady wearing a doctor's coat scanned the waiting room. "Anyone here for Daniel Brown?"

"Yes," we replied in unison, leaping from our chairs like they were on fire.

We rushed to the Asian woman. I studied her facial expression. Surely someone with really bad news would not greet us with a pleasant smile such as hers.

"Hello, I'm Dr. Lee. I wanted to update you on Daniel's condition. Are you family?"

Abby was quick to answer. "Siblings. How is he?"

Dr. Lee's thick, dark eyebrows tightened. "Well, I was concerned about his head injury, but I just got the results from his CT scan, and everything looks normal, but he does have a mild concussion."

My body slouched with relief, cupping my hands together at my chest. "He's going to be okay?"

Dr. Lee nodded, and her smile was reassuring. "Yes. He's going to be fine, but he does have other injuries."

Abby's celebratory smile faded. "What kind of injuries?"

Dr. Lee tucked her hands into the pockets of her white coat. "Besides the concussion, he has a hairline fracture of his fibula. It's the smaller bone in his leg. He also has a couple of bruised ribs and a laceration on his forehead, which we stitched up."

I wiped away the tears of relief from under my eyes. "When can he come home?"

"With the concussion, I'd like for him to stay overnight so we can keep an eye on him."

Abby exhaled anxiously. "Can we see him?"

With her lips tight, Dr. Lee appeared in thought. "Okay, but only for a few minutes. They're getting ready to take him upstairs to his room." She motioned. "Follow me."

When we arrived at Daniel's room, a nurse approached with urgency. "Dr. Lee, the call you've been waiting for—"

Dr. Lee turned to us and quickly walked away. "I have to take this call. Just a few minutes."

Abby pushed through the door and rushed to one side of Daniel's bed, and I scurried to the other. A large bandage covered his forehead, spiking his hair. His left leg was in a full cast.

I took his hand and brought it to my cheek. "Daniel?"

After blinking a few times, he opened his eyes and licked his dry lips. "You shouldn't be here."

Abby leaned over the bed and popped my arm. "See, I told you." She looked at Daniel. "Don't be mad at me. She's a stubborn redhead."

"Are you sure you're not hurt?"

"Yeah, I'm okay."

Daniel winced in pain, shifting his body. "Please go home. The cops were here asking questions about the passenger."

Abby asked, "What did you tell them?"

"That some girl asked me for a ride home." He licked his lips again. "All I know is her name was Sandy."

"Would you like some water?" I looked for a pitcher.

He pointed to the table next to his bed. "There's a cup of ice."

I reached for it and spooned some for him. "There's not a lot left." I put the spoon in his mouth.

Daniel chomped on the ice. "Please go home."

I offered him more, but he shook his head, so I set the cup on the table. Then I reached for his hand. "I want to be here with you."

Abby grunted. "No. You're going home. I'm going to stay with him."

I scowled. "No, I'm *not* leaving him."

She fired back in her feisty tone. "My brother needs you at home, not in jail. Which is what's going to happen if you don't leave."

"Abigail, can you give us a few minutes to say goodbye?"

Tears pooled in my eyes. I shook my head and pleaded with him, "No, please don't make me leave."

"The doctor said I can come home tomorrow."

I pressed my lips together and looked away, fighting tears.

"I'll see you upstairs." Abby leaned over and kissed Daniel's cheek, then she looked at me. "It's for the best, and deep down you know it. I'll see you in the waiting room." She turned on her heels and headed for the door.

"Rachael, I know you want to be here, but I can't let you risk it."

I watched his thumb rub across my fingers and thought about how close I came to losing him. My chin fell to my chest, and I cried at the visual of him unconscious. "I thought you were dead when they pulled me out of the truck."

"Don't cry. I'm right here." He squeezed my hand. "Can I have a kiss since you're my girlfriend?" He puckered his lips and made a kissy sound.

It was enough to make me laugh. I eagerly leaned over and gave him a quick kiss.

Daniel smiled, gazing at me. "Kiss me again."

And I did.

"Another one." Daniel puckered his lips, waiting.

I giggled. "Okay. If you insist."

When I kissed him that time, Daniel reached up with his free hand and held the back of my head. Our kiss turned passionate and took me away from what happened.

When my lips left his, he looked into my eyes. "Now go home."

My smile melted. I traced my fingers along the side of his face, no longer confused about my feelings for him. Without question, I had fallen in love with Daniel.

A man in blue scrubs walked in and announced he was taking Daniel upstairs to his room. I gave him a quick kiss and headed back to the waiting room.

"Do you want to stay at our house tonight?" Abby sipped her coffee, waiting for me to answer.

I settled in my chair, leaned back and exhaled. "No, I'll stay at Daniel's. My things are there."

Abby placed her hand on my arm. "Don't be mad at me."

My eyes cut to her. "You know I wanted to stay with him."

"Yes, I know. But he's probably going to sleep all night. Go home and rest so you can be there for him tomorrow. I'll have him call you as soon as he wakes up." She turned to Jory and gave him a kiss, then placed her hand on his cheek. "It's getting late. You guys head on home."

"Call me later."

"I will."

Everyone stood, but I couldn't bring myself to leave my chair. Abby held out her arms to give me a hug. After rolling my eyes, I left the chair and hugged her.

On our way home, the accident replayed in my head. The terrifying fear when we left the road, the horrible sound of the impact, and the haunting visual of Daniel unconscious. I hadn't even noticed we had pulled into the driveway.

Zack and Jory walked me inside. Since Daniel would need some clothes, I gathered a few things for him in a duffle bag and gave it to Jory. He and Zach made sure I was alright and left. The house was so lonesome without Daniel. I missed him so much.

After taking a hot shower, I put on one of his T-shirts and laid on the couch, curled up with a blanket, and tried to watch something on TV to distract me. I thought about Mom. She should have my letter any day and would let the authorities know Mandy had Jilly. Even the Greyfells would stop at nothing to find their granddaughter. It was heartbreaking, knowing I wouldn't get to watch her grow up. A fair trial would be too much to ask for, and a light sentence for defending myself would only come from a miracle.

Chapter 19: Recovery

While waiting for Daniel to come home from the hospital, I sat on the porch with a cup of coffee. The warmth of the rising sun devoured the crisp morning air. So much had happened since that day Alan and Ana came to the shop. From having our first fight, to Skip breaking in, to confessing our feelings, and having the accident.

The gravel crackled.

I turned and watched Abby's car come down the driveway. Daniel was home. I stood, anxious to see him just like the day he came home from Atlanta. Once the car came to a stop, I rushed down the steps to meet them. Jory helped Daniel out of the car. He steadied himself on crutches but had his eyes on me. When Jory attempted to walk him to the house, Daniel held out his hand. "Wait. I need a minute." Daniel lifted his chin, motioning for me to approach with a smile that said he needed to hold me as much as I needed to hold him.

My fingers were locked together under my chin, and I raised my eyebrows. "Are you sure?"

Daniel winked. "Come here."

Without hesitating, I carefully threaded my arms around his waist. He kissed the top of my head, and I smiled. I wanted to hold Daniel forever but released him. "Let's get you inside."

Jory took over and helped Daniel up the steps. Abby and I were behind them.

She voiced her concern. "Be careful with him. He has a broken leg, remember?"

Jory looked over his shoulder and laughed. "Which leg?"

Her face tightened, glaring at him. "You want one too?"

Jory sighed. "Honey, I've got him. He's not going anywhere. Besides, with you two behind us, if we fall, you'll cushion us."

Abby popped Jory's backside. "Just get him inside. In one piece."

Daniel hobbled to the couch. Abby was on one side, and I was on the other. We helped him get settled. I placed a pillow under his leg. Abby tossed the blanket over him.

Jory stood next to the coffee table. "Do you need me to do anything while I'm here?"

"I'm fine for now, but thanks."

Jory looked at Abby and nodded at the door. "We need to head over to the diner so I can check on the freezer. I don't want it going out on us over the weekend."

"I know. Give me a minute to say goodbye." Abby stood at Daniel's side and pointed her finger. "Promise me you'll lay there and rest."

Daniel pointed back. "If you knew how much it hurts to move, you wouldn't ask me that."

"Rachael's going to be here, so let her take care of you."

"Oh good. Where's my nurse?" Daniel searched for me and found me standing at his feet. A shameless grin appeared. "You're going to take care of me?"

"Of course I am, silly."

Daniel rested his palms on his chest and moaned in agony while looking around the room. "Oh, I'm in such pain. Nurse Rachael? Where are you? Help me."

We watched his little performance until Abby poked his side. "Stop that."

"*Ow.*" He wailed in pain and turned his wrinkled eyebrows at her. "Watch the ribs."

She laughed. "It's the other side that's hurt." Abby looked at me. "In case you didn't know, he can be a big baby. Are you sure you're up for this?"

I smiled at Daniel and sang, "Absolutely."

With his eyes on me, Daniel motioned them away. "You guys need to leave. This patient needs medical attention—in private."

"Daniel." I scolded him, embarrassed.

Jory laughed. "I think his meds have kicked in. Time to leave, honey."

After kissing his cheek, Abby headed for the door, and I followed.

"We'll stop by this evening and bring you guys some supper. I know you won't feel like cooking anything."

"That's not necessary."

Daniel quickly informed me, "Um, Rachael, I don't have a lot of food here."

I looked at Daniel and then Abby. "Then I guess we'll take you up on your offer."

Abby gave me a bear hug and rocked me. "Thanks for taking care of him."

"You don't have to thank me."

Jory gave me a hug. "We're only a phone call away if you need us."

~ ~ ~

Daniel slept most of the day while I cleaned out the spare bedroom since I would be staying there until he recovered. I carried box after box to the basement. It was like a small apartment, even with a kitchen and private entrance. The previous owner, clearly a Carolina Panthers fan, had turned it into a man cave.

By the time I had the bedroom in order, it was late in the evening, and I was exhausted. And sore from the accident. The recliner looked inviting, so I took a break. After positioning it horizontally, I closed my eyes and relaxed. For some reason, I thought about my house and wondered who was living in it. Someone's wife was in my kitchen. A little girl was probably in Jilly's room.

My phone chirped. Abby texted to let me know they would be over within the hour. That gave me enough time to take a catnap.

Abby and Jory arrived with pizza. We gathered at the table and filled our bellies. Daniel ate three slices. The pain meds must have been working. He was more like himself and even mentioned going to work Monday. Abby and I let him know that was not going to happen.

Before going to bed, Daniel needed his bandage changed and ointment applied to his laceration. I counted five stitches. After he took his meds, I helped him to the restroom one last time. Once he was settled in bed, I sat on the edge, facing him.

"Are you sure you don't need anything before I go to bed?" I reached for his hand and aligned my fingers with his.

"I'm sure."

Our fingers curled and our hands locked.

"You know I'm across the hall if you do."

"I know." His grip tightened.

"Are you alright? You seem like you have something on your mind."

He exhaled loudly. "No, I'm fine."

"It's been a long day. Try to get some sleep." I leaned forward to turn the lamp off.

"Leave it on," he pleaded in a petrified tone that caused the hair on my arms to rise.

I quickly retracted my hand and looked at Daniel, not sure what had happened, but his eyes were wide as could be. "What's wrong?" I placed my hand on his shoulder. "Are you hurting?"

"No."

I attempted to place my palm on his forehead to see if he had a fever, but he grabbed my wrist in mid-air and lowered my hand to his chest. "I just…" He swallowed hard, still trying to catch his breath.

"Just what?"

"I've been having nightmares about the accident. I still see that tree, and I can't avoid hitting it. It gets closer and closer, and there's nothing I can do. I should've been able to regain control, but I couldn't."

"But there was nothing you could've done. And I'm sure the nightmares will go away soon."

Daniel looked at the ceiling and exhaled like my words gave him little or no comfort.

"I'll stay with you tonight in case you have another one." I turned off the lamp.

"Rachael, you don't have to. I'll be fine."

"Don't argue. It's settled." I lifted the covers and carefully crawled into bed. "Don't let me hit your ribs. It's dark, and I can't see anything."

"You're fine."

In sessions, I shifted my body closer to Daniel. "Where's your cast? I don't want to hit that either."

He snorted. "If you hit the cast, it's going to hurt *you* more than it is me."

"Oh, are we being funny now?" I continued to feel my surroundings and touched Daniel in an intimate spot. My eyes bulged. "Oops, sorry about that." How embarrassing.

Daniel chuckled and then winced in pain. "Ow. Don't make me laugh. It hurts."

"Ha. You deserve it for letting me almost touch you like that."

We were on our backs, shoulder to shoulder. Lying next to Daniel made my shattered world seem a little less broken.

"Daniel?"

"Yeah?"

I yawned, pulling the covers higher. "Maybe you couldn't avoid hitting the tree, but give yourself some credit for keeping the truck from rolling. You know, that probably saved our lives."

Daniel was silent except for the peaceful sigh he released while taking my hand in his. That was the last thing I remember before falling asleep. For the first time in two months, I slept like a baby.

~ ~ ~

We made it through the first week. Daniel didn't have any more nightmares, so I slept in my room. We went to the shop for a few hours each day. Daniel only did minor jobs, and that was with my help. I did the things he couldn't. I learned a lot about cars that week and even wore a uniform shirt. We went on calls together, but I had to do everything, which was okay with me. Daniel and I were an unstoppable team.

While taking care of Daniel, I tried not to lose focus on finding Jilly, but sometimes the guilt was heavy on my heart. Like I had put Daniel before her. The only thing that gave me strength was knowing Mama had to have my letter and reported Jilly had been kidnapped. Mama wouldn't waste one minute in her search. I counted on her doing what I couldn't.

I turned on the water and poured some Dawn over the supper dishes. The sink filled with water and created a mountain of bubbles.

"Hey, hey." Daniel rushed to turn the water off before the sink overflowed. "Where were you just now?"

I shook my head with my eyes wide. "Um, I don't know. Guess I got lost in thought." I scooped the bubbles into the other sink and tried to laugh it off, but when I looked at Daniel, he wasn't laughing.

"What's bothering you? You barely said two words at the

table."

I continued to scoop the bubbles. "Remember me telling you I had something to take care of before I turn myself in?"

Daniel shifted on his crutches. "Is this where you tell me you're going home?"

"No, but I need to make a trip to Florida and mail another letter."

My second letter to Mama was ready. I instructed her to visit Ruth's house on the twentieth, and I would call at one o'clock. Ruth was an elderly widow from church, and she didn't hear well. For Mama to answer her phone would only be natural. Ruth would unlikely be able to hear Mama if she spoke softly. She would explain that Grandpa had called needing milk or something.

"Then we'll go to Florida."

I reached for a dishtowel to dry my hands. "You can't go. You're still recovering from the accident. I'll have to go by myself." I shrugged. "Jacksonville is what, seven hours one way? I can do it in a day."

"Are you sure that's a good idea?" Daniel hobbled toward me. "I can't tell you not to go, but a simple flat tire or traffic stop... Your Jeep and a North Carolina tag will catch a state trooper's eye like a hawk."

"I've already thought about that, but I have to do this."

Daniel hobbled closer. "What if we drove to Charlotte or Wilmington?"

I wrapped my arms around him and rested my cheek on his shoulder. "Something tells me to go to Florida."

"I know it's a lot to ask, but if you can wait a few weeks, I'll have this cast off, and we can go together."

"I can't believe you'd go with me all the way to Florida just to mail a letter."

"Baby, I'd go to the moon and mail it for you."

A few weeks sounded the same as eternity, but I remembered Pastor Helms always preached how God works in His time. However, if I had to wait three weeks, when I got to Florida, I would call Mama instead of mailing the letter. The thought of hearing her voice eased the sting of waiting.

The second week rolled around. Daniel had his stitches removed. The scar would be hard to see with his wavy hair dangling over his forehead. Still, Daniel was self-conscious about it. He blushed when I told him it was sexy. The insurance settled, and

Daniel replaced The Beast with a new truck. And, until his cast came off, I got the pleasure of doing all the driving.

~ ~ ~

It was time for Daniel to see the orthopedic doctor. After a tech cut off the cast and they took an x-ray, we sat in the exam room and waited.

An older gentleman with short gray hair and wearing blue scrubs entered the room. "Mr. Brown." He had energy in his voice and a friendly smile. After resting Daniel's folder on the counter, he extended his hand. "I'm Dr. Capshaw. How are you doing?"

"Fine, thank you."

"How does your leg feel?"

"Funny without the cast. And it itches."

"If you don't mind lying down, please."

Once Daniel was on his back, Dr. Capshaw placed his hand under Daniel's calf and lifted his leg, then he cautiously raised his foot. "Does this hurt or feel uncomfortable?"

"No."

He flexed Daniel's leg. "And now?"

"No."

"Awesome. You can sit up." He lowered Daniel's leg back to the table and reached for the folder. "The x-ray shows your leg has healed nicely. What kind of work do you do?"

"I'm a mechanic."

Dr. Capshaw flipped through the chart. "I don't see the need to put another cast on..." He looked at Daniel. "Unless you want one."

He laughed and waved his hands. "Oooh no."

Dr. Capshaw chuckled and scribbled. "Just take it easy until your leg strengthens." He closed the folder, handed it to Daniel and smiled. "Give this to the receptionist on your way out. Nice to meet you. Have a good day." He nodded at me in passing before walking out.

Daniel made his way off the table and took my hand. Without wasting a minute, we checked out and headed to his truck.

"Let's go somewhere and eat to celebrate," Daniel suggested as we strolled hand in hand.

"That sounds like a good idea."

When we arrived at his truck, Daniel cleared his throat and held out his hand. "First things first."

I shook his hand and grinned. "Nice to meet you."

Daniel wiggled his fingers. "Hand them over."

I pouted with my lip poked out, digging through my purse for his keys. Then I smiled. If he wanted them, he would have to come after them. I tucked the keys in my back pocket and leaned against the door, flashing a daring grin. "If you want your keys, come and get them," I whispered seductively and winked.

Daniel parted his lips, looking me over. "If you think I won't go after them, then you don't know me, Darlin'." He placed one hand on the truck and pried the other hand between me and the door. "And I'll do it slowly. And we'll both enjoy every second it takes me."

Daniel seemed too shy to have a tiger in him. Perhaps I had pleasantly misjudged him.

"I'm waiting."

"Oh, Rachael," he purred seductively as his hand inched closer to my pocket, his passionate eyes holding me captive. "I think the anticipation is going to make you remember playing with me." He moved his hand to my butt and massaged it.

I gasped and tried to ease him back. "Stop. People might be watching."

But he didn't stop. Daniel pinned me against the truck and kissed me while his hand teased my body mercilessly.

I pulled my lips away from his, gasping for air. "Okay, I give."

Daniel removed the keys from my pocket and smiled victoriously. "Just so you know, Miss Playful. I have no problem touching you. Anywhere."

"Oh?" I cooed with a naughty grin.

"Yeah, *oh*," he cooed back. "You're lucky we aren't home. I would've done a lot more than take those keys." He leaned in for a quick kiss. "Let's go somewhere and eat."

Chapter 20: Finish Your Sentence

Daniel came to a stop at a red light and kissed my hand. "Oh, I know the perfect place we can eat," he told me with zest in his tone.

"Where?" Just looking at Daniel made me smile. If only I could tell him about Jilly.

"It's a surprise, but I think you'll like it."

"Well, you haven't disappointed me yet." I tucked the hair behind my ear, watching his gaze linger. "Why are you looking at me like that?"

"Because I hope I never do."

The light turned green. Daniel proceeded with the traffic. I looked out the window.

Maybe Daniel would understand if I told him about Jilly. But what if he tells me I should've known better and think I'm a neglectful mother? I couldn't bear to have him look at me with disgust.

Daniel pulled into a construction site for a new bank.

"Is this it?" I looked at him and laughed. "A hot dog stand? Really? We're going to celebrate eating hot dogs?"

"Oh come on. You'll like it." He killed the engine. "Sometimes I stop here when I'm in the area. There's a canopy with picnic tables behind the trailer where we can eat."

I looked at the portable food trailer. No one was there, yet. "What about the construction workers?"

"We have time before they'll take their lunch break."

I unbuckled and smiled at Daniel. "Okay, I'm game."

We got out of the truck and walked up to the trailer. A young lady stood behind the counter, drying her hands. "Hi. Can I help you?"

Daniel placed his arm around me and rested his hand on my shoulder. "I'm not sure yet."

"Take your time. Let me know when you're ready."

Daniel tugged me closer and rested his temple against mine as we decided. "Think I'm going to get the special. What would you like?"

"Guess I'll have the same."

Daniel ordered our hot dogs. After she handed him the change, he wrapped his arms around me and kissed my cheek. I held him, knowing our time together would soon come to an end.

When our order was ready, we walked around the trailer. Thankfully, we were the only ones under the canopy, because I wanted privacy to talk. We sat at a picnic table and unwrapped our food.

"Now that you've been released from the doctor, I need to go to Florida." I bit into my hot dog.

"When do you want to go?"

I covered my mouth while chewing. "Tomorrow."

Daniel held his hot dog with both hands and brought the end to his mouth. "What time?"

I smiled at the thought of talking to Mama within twenty-four hours and hoping Jilly had been found. "Actually, I was thinking tonight." I pulled a potato chip from the single-serving bag and added, "We could be there in the morning."

Daniel peeled back the tab on his Pepsi. "Just let me know what time."

If Mama told me they hadn't found Jilly yet, I would set up a time and call her at Ruth's for an update. However, if Mama told me they had found Jilly and she was home safe, I would go back to Rockingham and turn myself in.

I watched Daniel guzzle his soda. "When we come back, there's a chance I'll have to go home and turn myself in. You know my life's going to be on hold for a long time."

Daniel stopped drinking his soda and set the can down a little too hard. "Don't walk away from me."

"But it's not fair to you."

"Rachael, if you cut me out of your life because of this, it'll hurt me ten times more than having to wait for you."

"But I know you want kids someday, and I won't be able to give you any."

"What's the name of our song?"

"Miracles by Jefferson Starship. Why?"

He reached for a potato chip from his bag, staring at me with those calm blue eyes. "I've always loved that song, because it's about convincing the person you love to believe in what you do. And I believe with a good lawyer, you can—"

"Daniel, I don't have the money for a good lawyer."

"Don't worry about that. I've already talked to someone." Daniel opened wide and inserted a few more chips.

"Wait, don't tell me you—"

Daniel reached for my wrist. "Do you trust me?"

"Yes, I trust you."

He released my wrist and reached for his soda. "How's your hot dog?"

"It's really good. Thank you." I smiled before taking another bite.

After we finished our lunch, Daniel was determined to do some work, so we headed to the shop. I stared out the window with so many thoughts running through my head. Some were pleasant. Like going to Florida and talking to Mama, and the accident finally behind us. The day was off to a good start. And just like that, something stole my joy.

"Hey. What's on that pretty mind of yours? I know you're thinking about something."

"Yeah, sort of."

Daniel merged onto the highway. "So, what is it?"

"I'm glad the doctor released you."

"Me too."

"I just wasn't prepared, I guess."

Daniel glanced at me long enough to ask, "Why does that seem to upset you?"

My words wouldn't come out.

He turned his eyes back to the road. "I think I know what it is."

"Now that you're okay, I have to go back to the shop."

"No you don't."

"You don't understand. I wasn't brought up that way."

"Rachael, there's nothing wrong with you staying in the spare bedroom. Heck, I'll clean out the basement if that's what it takes to keep you there. It's not like you're still married."

Those six words were so painful, I couldn't respond. No, I wasn't married anymore. I wasn't a mother anymore either. Or a daughter. Or a granddaughter. Or even myself. I leaned my forehead against the window and let the tears trail down my cheeks. I was nothing.

"Rachael." He squeezed my hand. "I'm sorry. I shouldn't have said that. It just came out."

But it was true.

Daniel kissed my hand. "Talk to me, baby. Yell at me if you need to."

What I needed was my daughter.

Daniel swerved and left the highway.

"What's wrong?" I held on as the truck came to an abrupt stop on the side of the road.

"I don't want to do this while driving." He forced the truck in park with his left hand. Then he leaned so far over the console, he took my right arm and turned me to face him. His eyes held me captive the way they stared into mine. "I'm sorry. I didn't mean to hurt you."

"It's not you. It's just, when you said that, it reminded me of everything I've lost." I wiped the tears across my shoulder, missing my little girl. As much as I wanted to tell Daniel about Jilly, I was afraid he wouldn't understand.

"If I could give it all back to you, I would."

"I know you would." It was time to tell him about Jilly or break emotionally. I had held it in as long as I could. As I worked up the courage, fear struck me, and it hit hard. I struggled for air, suddenly claustrophobic. The harder I tried to breathe, the less air I seemed to take in.

"Rachael, calm down. It's okay."

"I need some air." After jerking my hand from his hold, I tried to open the door, pressing every button.

Daniel grabbed my arm to stop me. "Rachael, no. Stay in the truck. It's not safe."

"But...but, I can't breathe. I need out of here."

The door wouldn't unlock. In my confusion, I thought I was in The Beast and pushed the wrong buttons. By the time I got it open, Daniel was there with his arms outstretched to block me from getting out of the truck.

"Take short breaths to slow down your breathing. You're going to hyperventilate if you don't."

The way my emotions attacked me, I didn't have any control. Overwhelmed with life, at rock bottom, I wept in agony, missing my daughter.

"Baby, please talk to me. Tell me what's wrong."

Sobbing and my face wet with tears, I babbled, "I can't tell you." I swallowed, caught my breath and added, "I, I want to, but I can't."

"Come here. I want to hold you." He took my forearm and coaxed me out of the truck.

Once my feet hit the ground, broken, I let go and cried. "I'm so tired. I can't do this anymore."

"I know." Daniel held me. "Please tell me what's wrong."

With my face against his chest, I lifted his T-shirt and wiped my eyes. "You won't understand."

He laughed and sang, "Of course I will. You said you trust me."

And I did. It was time to tell him, even if he held it against me. After I calmed, I leaned back and looked into his eyes. With the words on the tip of my tongue, my lips parted, ready to free them. "I, I have a…" My heart raced, igniting the fear again. "Um…" I couldn't do it and looked away.

"No, look at me." Daniel turned my face, and our eyes met. "Finish your sentence."

The words would not come out no matter how hard I tried to force them. Broken, I laid my head on his shoulder and whimpered, "I can't say it."

"Rachael, it's okay," he whispered, holding me as I trembled. "I know you have a daughter."

I immediately leaned back and looked at him, convinced I had heard wrong. "What did you say?"

He shrugged as though it were nothing. "I know you have a little girl and miss her."

"How could you possibly know that?"

Daniel guided the hair away from my wet face and exhaled like he was the one relieved. "When I worked on your Jeep, I saw a hair bow in the floorboard when I powered your seat back.

Jilly's hair bow?

"And you always bring that little dog when you stay with me."

Fumbles?

Daniel laughed playfully. "It's not hard to figure out it belongs to a small child." He kissed my forehead. "Oh, and I also saw a car seat." He grinned like he just answered a prize-winning question.

"You've known this whole time?"

He nodded. "I almost asked you about her several times, because I knew that's why you were crying."

"I can't believe this," I mumbled, still in shock. "You, you've never said anything."

194

"Remember our deal—I wouldn't ask any questions?"

"I remember."

With Daniel knowing about Jilly, surely he would help me find her. Suddenly, there was light at the end of that never-ending tunnel. For the first time, I didn't hesitate to have hope.

"Daniel, that's what the letter is about. My trip to Florida. Except, I was going to call my mom instead of mailing the letter. I have to find Jilly before I turn myself in."

He frowned. "Oh, I assumed she was with your family."

"No. Mandy has her. The one I told you talked me into leaving town. She took Jilly and ran off with her."

Daniel inhaled deeply and looked away.

Fearing what he was thinking, I gripped his forearms and pleaded, "Please don't think I'm a terrible mother. Let me explain what hap—"

His eyes darted to mine, and he placed his finger over my parted lips. "Stop. I would *never* think that."

I looked down and mumbled, "I-I just thought that..."

Daniel lifted my chin. "Baby, we're together now. You need to tell me everything so I can help you. Somehow, we *will* find your daughter."

I threw my arms around his neck. "Oh, Daniel, I miss her so much."

He held me, letting me cry endless tears of happiness. "Don't worry. We'll find her. No mother should be without her child."

After composing myself, I puckered my face and confessed, "I should've told you sooner."

He took my hands and held them to his chest. "Do you want to go to Florida right now so we can call your mom?"

"No. Let's go tonight as planned. There will be less traffic, and I'll feel safer in the dark. And I know you have so much work waiting on you. We can finish out the day, but I wanna leave as soon as it's dusk."

"Are you sure?"

"Yes, I'm sure."

"Okay, but after we close up, we're going home and talk."

I nodded, agreeing it was time to tell Daniel everything. "Sounds like a plan."

"Did you say her name is Jilly?"

"Yes. It's short for Jillian." I giggled all excited, bouncing on my toes. Saying her name, hearing the words come out of my mouth, made it so real.

"When we're at the shop, please don't think I'm ignoring your situation if I get quiet, okay?"

"Oh no. I won't. I know how you are about safety."

"Yes, I need to stay focused."

"Daniel." I frowned. "I know I keep asking this, but why are you so good to me?"

"Are you sure you want me to answer that? Because I will if you're ready to hear it."

Was Daniel going to tell me he loved me? The thought made my heart go all hyper on me. A part of me wanted to hear him say the words, but it wasn't right for us to proclaim our love with my future so uncertain. I answered him by bringing his lips to mine and kissing him.

A passing vehicle blew the horn.

Daniel's lips left mine, and he patted my hips. "Let's go. We need to get out of here before someone calls the law, thinking we need help."

We traveled the open highway. I couldn't contain my happiness—real happiness. My smile stretched wider than it had in months. Why didn't I tell Daniel sooner? His reaction was not what I had expected, but so much more. I smiled at my angel. Mandy didn't factor in Daniel when she betrayed me.

He caught me staring at him. "Are you staying at the house with me?"

My smile left. "You know I can't."

Daniel sighed, shaking his head and turned his attention back to the road.

I threw my head against the headrest. "It's not like I *want* to go back to the shop."

"Then don't." He glanced my way, flashing that happy smile. "I promise I'll be a gentleman."

"You're not making this easy."

He grinned like a Cheshire cat. "Good. Then it's settled."

"You're going to cook supper tonight."

Daniel chuckled. "Remember you said that when you see what we're having."

More hot dogs? I covered my giggle. "On second thought, I'll cook."

He sighed with defeat. "If you insist."

Daniel pushed himself and tried to do too much. Around four o'clock, he called it a day, and we closed the shop. On the way home, I told Daniel I wanted Abby and Jory there when I explained what happened. I would be lying if I said I wasn't afraid to tell them everything.

Abby and Jory showed up at six o'clock. Daniel informed them I had something I wanted to share. He sat next to me on the couch. Abby squeezed into the recliner with Jory and demanded to know what was wrong.

Knowing how hard and intense it would be, I asked they not interrupt but told them they could ask me questions once I had finished. After taking in a deep breath, I started by telling them, "I'm married and have a daughter."

Abby yelled in shock, rhetorically repeating what I had said. Jory told her to be quiet and listen.

I briefly described the past seven years and the happy life I had until that day in May. They listened intently as I explained. "I overheard Peter talking on the phone in his study." I flashed back to that day and wasn't sure I could finish. I wrung my hands, and my knees bounced. My words seemed lost in the turbulent spinning in my head.

Wide-eyed, I stared at the floor and continued. "After Peter hung up, I walked into his study to confront him for cheating on me." My eyes watered when I got to the part, "He pulled a gun on me."

Abby gasped and covered her mouth. Jory lowered his face and shook his head.

It got to a point where I had to pretend I was telling someone else's story, not mine. It made the words come out easier when I told them, "Peter hesitated, and I lunged for the gun." The lump in my throat finally surrendered and moved along just before I told them, "We struggled for it. Somehow it discharged, and he was shot. He died in front of me."

The horrid look on their faces made me wonder if that was the same look I had when I shot Peter. Or perhaps it was because they realized they were looking at a murderer and wanted nothing to do with me anymore. The thought made me want to run out the door.

The hard part came when I explained why I left the house after I shot Peter. "I had to get my daughter out of there, so I took her to Mandy's." I assured them I had every intention of going back and calling the police. However, while there, I let Mandy convince me I would go to jail, because no one would believe it was self-defense. Fearing Jilly would lose both of her parents, I went along with her plan, which included leaving Jilly with her. "Everything Mandy said might happen was true, but she used it against me to run off with my child."

Abby and Jory looked like guests in a theater watching a horror movie. Their jaws dangled, and their eyes looked like a hamster's when you hold them a little too tight. But that was no theater. It was my life they listened to.

One day I would have to forgive myself for leaving Jilly with Mandy, but not one too soon. My punishment was deserving for being so easily misguided when I knew I was doing the wrong thing. I couldn't help but wonder what other fool had succumbed to Mandy's antics. Perhaps I was the only one who had 'Fool' written across her forehead.

After telling them, "Mandy never showed up at the cabin with my daughter, and I don't know where she is," I broke down and wept, remembering that heart-wrenching moment. The regret of my actions strangled my heart, taking my breath. The emotions I held in for so long escaped through my tears and my sobs. I surrendered and didn't fight them.

Abby shot out of the recliner and rushed to the couch. She sat next to me and tried to comfort me. Between her and Daniel, they eventually calmed me when they vowed to find Jilly. Abby was furious at what Mandy had done and told Jory, "We need to do something."

Jory sat on the coffee table and told me, "I have a cousin who would know how to find Mandy."

Unfortunately, he was out of town until Tuesday, but Jory was going to contact him. I made all three of them swear they would not do any searches on the internet or look for Mandy on their own, because I feared being traced. It could wait until Tuesday. Their support was beyond overwhelming.

Daniel and I stood on the porch and watched the taillights of Abby's car travel down the driveway. Daniel stood behind me with his arms threaded around my waist and his chin on my shoulder. My head rested against his.

"What time do you want to leave for Florida?"

I turned and faced him, releasing a long sigh and thought hard about my decision. "Would it be okay if we wait until after we talk to Jory's cousin? Something tells me not to go tonight."

"Are you sure?"

"Not really, but I have to go with my gut on this. The last time I didn't, I made the biggest mistake of my life."

Chapter 21: Let's Go

Saturday

While washing breakfast dishes, my thoughts were on Jilly. Jory called his cousin to brief him before our meeting on Tuesday. Mandy was crazy, but she was smart. What if this guy couldn't find her? The thought held me imprisoned with hopelessness. But then there were moments when I smiled, because I believed my day was coming.

Daniel threaded his arms around my waist from behind and kissed my cheek. "Let's take a drive to nowhere and get you out of this house."

"We haven't done that since the accident." I rinsed the plate and set it in the drain. "That actually sounds nice."

Daniel spun me around, wet hands and all. "We can even have a picnic somewhere."

I reached for a towel to dry my hands, smiling from his tempting offer. "I would *love* that."

"I thought you would."

I placed my hands on the back of his head and lifted my lips to his. Daniel deepened our kiss, pinning me against the counter with his lower torso and his hands roaming a little too far north. I grabbed them before they reached my breasts and pulled my lips away from his. Caught off guard by the tiger in him, I headed to the fridge. "Would you like chicken salad sandwiches or cold cuts?"

"Chicken salad sounds good."

After gathering my items, I headed to the counter. "How many would you like?"

"One is fine." Daniel got the picnic basket and set it on the counter. His phone chimed, and he answered it. "Hey, sis, what's up?" He leaned against the counter next to me while I prepared the sandwiches. "Can it wait? Rachael and I are—" Daniel glanced at me and listened intently with his brows tight. "I'm on my way." He gave me a quick kiss on my cheek and clipped his phone to his belt. "I need to run to Abigail's for a minute."

I held up the mayonnaise-covered knife, watching him practically run to the door. "If you wait a minute, I'll go with you."

"Why don't you finish the picnic basket? When I get back, we'll head out."

"What's the emergency? What did Abby want?"

Without looking at me, Daniel opened the door and muttered, "I'll be right back."

"Daniel?" I huffed, resting the balls of my hands on the counter. He shut the door. Frustrated, I tossed the knife in the sink. Even though I finished packing a lunch, something told me we were not going on a picnic.

~ *An hour later* ~

My smiley necklace reflected in the bathroom mirror while brushing my hair, trying to decide on a ponytail or not.

The front door shut. "*Rachael?*"

The way Daniel called my name sent a harrowing chill through me. I threw my brush on the counter and ran to see what happened. When I entered the living room, I came to a sudden halt. Daniel's eyes were heavy with burden like he didn't know how to tell me what happened, which caused my heart to pound harder than it already did. Slowly, I took a step backwards and prepared to run to my room.

"Wait," he called out to me with dread. "I need to tell you something."

It had to be bad news, and I couldn't bear to hear it, so I headed to my room. Daniel managed to head me off and blocked my path.

"Whatever it is, I don't want to hear it," I told him in a strong voice, making it clear I meant what I said. When I attempted to walk around Daniel, he held out his arms and blocked me. My eyes met his, and I growled, "I *said*, I don't want to hear it."

"It's…" He took in a deep breath and lowered his arms. "It's about Peter."

"Peter? What about him?"

Daniel shrugged with his lips parted, struggling to answer. "I-I don't know how to tell you this."

"Tell me what?"

"Rachael, I don't know what happened that day you shot Peter, but he's not dead."

As the words rang out in my head, it went silent and dark. The next thing I know, I'm lying on my back and trying to open my eyes while something cold and wet caressed my face.

"Rachael, wake up. Open your eyes."

"Stop." I pushed whatever it was away from my face and looked to see where I was. Somehow I ended up on the couch. "What happened?"

"You passed out." Daniel sat on the coffee table in front of me and tossed a washcloth to his side.

I leaned up on my elbows, still coming to.

Daniel placed his hand on my shoulder. "Don't get up. Lay there for a minute, please."

It didn't take long for me to remember what Daniel told me. "What did you mean Peter's not dead?"

Daniel reached into his back pocket. "He's not, and he's looking for you. Abigail called me because Jory's cousin had some time and did a little research." He unfolded a piece of paper and handed it to me.

I sat up and reached for it. "What's this?"

"A missing person's flyer Jory's cousin emailed Abigail this morning."

After I looked over the flyer, I handed it back to Daniel. "What does this prove?"

He raised his eyebrows. "Don't you find it odd you're missing and not a fugitive?"

"No. Peter's family probably thought it would attract more attention if I were some rich man's wife who went missing. Look at the reward. Who wouldn't look for me?"

"There's more." Daniel stood from the coffee table and sat next to me, not breaking our gaze. He took my hand. "Don't get upset, but while I was there, we googled Peter and saw he—"

My eyes widened in anger. "You did *what?*" I jerked my hand from his. "You *swore* you wouldn't."

"I know, but Rachael, it's true. He *is* alive."

Furious, I looked away, shaking my head and mumbled, "I can't believe you guys did this after I *begged* you not to. Maybe it's from my family. Mama would never label me a fugitive."

"Rachael, it was from him. Peter was also on the news. He was begging for the public's help to find you. And there's more."

I leaned back and exhaled loudly. "I don't want to hear anymore."

"Please look at me."

"*No.* I'm upset with you and Abby."

"In the interview, Peter's holding Jilly."

Without moving my head, my eyes cut to his. "I told you I left her with Mandy. There's no way Peter has her because…" My eyes widened. "…he's dead."

Daniel unclipped his phone from his belt. "I didn't want to show you this because I don't know how much you can handle at once." After swiping the screen, he handed it to me. "This is the video of the interview."

I reluctantly took his phone and tapped the arrow. "I'm telling you it's…"

The second the video played, I froze, staring with my eyes wide and my heart palpitating. Peter, holding Jilly, stood next to a young news reporter.

"Good evening. I'm Leslie Newell. We're in the Lansdale community at the home of Peter Greyfell. His wife, Rachael, is missing, and he's asking for the public's help to find her." She turned to Peter and aimed the mic at him as the camera zoomed in. "Mr. Greyfell, when was the last time you saw your wife?"

Peter shifted Jilly. "Wednesday afternoon around three o'clock."

"And what was she wearing?"

Peter shook his head as though he tried to remember. "Um, jeans and a T-shirt."

"And where was she last seen?"

"Here. She left and hasn't been seen since."

Jilly wrapped her arms around Peter's neck and rested her head on his shoulders.

The reporter faced the camera, smiling like a model. "We have a picture of Rachael and her Jeep. If anyone has seen her, there's a number at the bottom of your screen you can call."

The same picture of me in the flyer popped up in the corner. Jilly must have seen it on a monitor. She lifted her head and pointed. "That's Mommy. I want my mommy."

With my trembling fingers over my mouth, tears slid down

my face, watching my little girl.

The reporter asked Peter, "What would you like to tell your wife if she happens to see this video?"

Peter looked into the camera as though he looked right at me. "Rachael, if there's any chance you're watching this, please come home. Your family misses you." His eyes watered, struggling to continue. "I won't give up until I find you. Our daughter needs you to come home."

The camera shifted to the reporter. "Again, if anyone has seen Rachael, please call the number you see on the bottom of your screen. I'm Leslie Newell for Channel Seven News."

The video ended. I couldn't move. I couldn't even blink.

Daniel reached for his phone, startling me. "Are you okay?"

"I, I don't understand. How is he alive?" I looked at Daniel, shaking my head in disbelief. "And how does he have Jilly?"

"I don't know. Maybe they found Mandy."

I stared, taking everything in. A sigh escaped between my fingertips still pressed against my lips. "You mean, she's been with Peter this whole time?"

He shrugged, just as confused. "It looks that way."

"Then where's Mandy?" Before Daniel had a chance to answer, I grabbed his arm and gasped like I had seen a ghost. "Oh my gosh. You know what this means?"

"No. What?"

I squealed with excitement and shook his arm. "I know where Jilly's at." I left the couch and paced, wringing my hands.

"Rachael, what are you thinking?"

"That I'm going to Rockingham to get my daughter."

With so many thoughts firing at once, my head went into overload. I stopped and pressed my fingertips against my temples and tried to focus.

Daniel placed his hands on my forearms. "Calm down. I don't want you to pass out again."

I took deep breaths, then smiled. "She was safe this whole time."

Daniel didn't smile or seem elated with the news.

"What's wrong?"

With a look of dread in his eyes, Daniel released my forearms and shrugged. "You wanted your life back. Now that we know you're not a fugitive, nothing's stopping you from going home."

My jaw dropped. "Do you think I'm going back to Peter?"

He shrugged. "You said you loved him."

"I'm *not* going back to Peter. My home is here with *you*...unless you don't want me here anymore."

"You know better than that." Daniel took me in his arms and held me so tight it hurt. "Am I wrong for needing to hear that?"

Aware of his insecurities, I rested my chin on Daniel's shoulder and gave him a reassuring hug. "Not at all. I'm going home, but only to get Jilly. Peter better not try to stop me either. If he does, I'll kill him for real this time."

Daniel leaned back and eyed me with concern. "Rachael?"

I grinned and poked his stomach. "You know I'm kidding."

He squinted, maintaining a straight face. "Just making sure."

My shoulders slouched, and I brought my hands together under my chin. "Can we please go? I need to see my little girl."

"What'd you say we take a trip to Rockingham?"

I jumped with excitement and clapped. "I say, let's get in my Jeep and stir some dust from here to Rockingham."

Daniel laughed at my giddiness. "Okay, but let's take my truck. It'll be to our advantage if they don't see your Jeep."

"Can you get the car seat for me? It's in the cargo area." I ran toward my room, looking over my shoulder. "Let me get my purse."

"I'll meet you outside."

"Guess what, Fumbles?" I grabbed him off the headboard. "We're going to see Jilly." After snatching my purse from the recliner, I ran out of the room. On the way out, I grabbed the picnic basket off the kitchen counter. Within five minutes, we left a trail of dust in the driveway and headed to Rockingham. Daniel let me watch the video on his phone. I must have replayed it a dozen times. Nothing made sense. How could Peter be alive? How did he have Jilly? And where was Mandy?

Daniel called Abby and gave her an update and then he handed me the phone. We talked, and we cried. It was still hard to believe the police were never looking for me as a fugitive. Then doubt set in. What if it was a trick? What if Peter was indeed dead?

We traveled the highway. Thoughts ran rampant through my head. Could I get back everything I had lost? Should I dare believe I would see my daughter before the sun set? And, since I was a free woman, I could go to the farm and see Mama and Grandpa. My world was changing faster than I could grasp, but only if Peter was alive.

Daniel took my hand. "How do you suggest we handle this

when we get to Rockingham?"

"Peter works half-days on Saturdays, so I'll have to go to the store and confront him there."

He lifted our hands and kissed mine. "Whatever you think is best."

"Daniel?" I watched his thumb rub my hand.

"Yes, baby?"

"I'm scared."

"Don't be. You know I'm here."

"Tell me the police aren't looking for me again."

"The police aren't looking for you again." He glanced at me and laughed.

"Ha, ha. You're funny." I looked out the window at the farmland and the cornfields, wishing it would still my shaky legs and jittery hands. "I don't understand. I know I shot him. There was blood and..." I gasped, turning back to Daniel. "Wait, I didn't check for a pulse. I just assumed he was dead. Maybe he was alive when I left the house."

Daniel came to a stop at a red light. "I've already thought about that, but Peter wasn't a wounded man in that video. And we still don't know why he pulled a gun on you, so please don't ask me to leave you alone with him."

"I was going to ask you not to when we got there." Perhaps food would be a distraction. "Would you like a sandwich?"

"Sure."

After unbuckling, I crawled halfway into the back and dug around in the picnic basket. "Stop that. Keep your hand on the steering wheel. Not my backside."

Daniel chuckled. "I'm sitting at a red light."

"Yeah. Yeah." I grabbed two sandwiches and two bottles of water and made my way back into my seat. "Here."

Daniel took the bottle I offered him.

"What if we're walking into a trap?" I unwrapped a sandwich and handed it to him. "I'm having doubts he's alive."

Daniel took a bite of his sandwich and tried to talk with his mouth full. "Think about holding that little girl in your arms."

What I thought about was calling Mama, but I needed to see Peter first. I had to look him in the eye. Only then would I believe he was alive. Only then would I have my life back.

An hour seemed like a lifetime. Then we passed the sign, *Rockingham*. I went from jumping in my seat with excitement to slouching in my seat to hide from danger. The familiar landmarks caused my heart to race like it was warning me I was about to walk into a lion's den.

"Take a deep breath."

I swallowed hard and announced, "We're ten minutes away."

Daniel tugged my hand. "Are you okay?"

"No," I muttered, looking right and then left. My eyes watered, fearing danger as though it was ready to leap out of nowhere any second. "Pl-please turn around. I-I can't do this." I fanned my face.

"Do you need me to pull over?"

"Turn around. It's a trick." I fanned my face harder, desperate for air. "The police are going to, to..." I gasped deeper. "...to take me away before I, I find Jilly."

He laughed at me and rubbed my shoulder. "Baby, the police don't want you."

I whimpered, "I just want my little girl."

"I know you do. Soon."

I wiped the tears with my shirt and babbled, "But if this is a trick, then I'll lose you too."

"You're not going to lose me. I'd never let you come here if I thought the police were looking for you. Google yourself."

"Oh, I hadn't thought about that." I quickly reached for my phone. After typing my name in the search engine bar, I tapped the button. "The only thing that shows up is that video and how I'm reported missing."

Daniel flashed a proud grin. "Are you a fugitive?"

"No," I mumbled, nudging my phone inside my purse. "It's hard to believe. I can't fathom the thought Peter's alive."

Ten minutes dwindled down, and we pulled into the Lansdale Commons. I directed Daniel through the parking lot. When Peter's store came into view, I broke out into a cold sweat. "Stop here so I can see what's going on."

Daniel parked next to a box truck. We watched through the front glass.

"Is that Peter?"

Gnawing at a nail, I shook my head. "No, it's a customer. Let's wait here until he leaves." I looked at Peter's private parking spot. "There's his Audi."

"What time does he close?"

"In twenty minutes." I tucked the hair behind my ears,

watching the store. "I want you to walk in first and then I'm going to walk in behind you. That way he doesn't see me right away."

Eighteen agonizing minutes later, the customer walked out, causing my heart to drop to my stomach.

Daniel put the truck in drive. "Tell me when."

As soon as the customer's reverse lights flashed, I unbuckled and tucked Fumbles into my back pocket. "Let's do this before he locks up."

Daniel crept closer and parked in front of the store. Someone walked into the backroom, but it was hard to tell if it was Peter.

Daniel took my arm, and our eyes met. "When you get out, walk around the back and get behind me."

Panting with my lips parted, I nodded. "Okay."

After stepping out of the truck, I did as Daniel suggested and followed him. He pushed the glass door open and entered. The sensor chimed, announcing our entrance. I grabbed the back of Daniel's shirt and followed him with my toes to his heels, praying it was not a trick.

Chapter 22: Peter

With my forehead against Daniel's back, we waited for Peter to come out of the backroom and greet us. My heart pounded so hard I was afraid it might explode.

"Good evening. Can I help you with something?"

My breath caught at the sound of Peter's warm salutation. He was alive. Terrified and shaking uncontrollably, I forced myself to step to the side and revealed myself. Peter stood behind the counter, still handsome as ever in his suit, flashing his familiar charming smile. When Peter saw me, he did a double take. His smile faded. His eyes widened with shock as though he were looking at a ghost. I probably flashed the same shocked look at him.

Peter pressed his hand to his chest like he was having a heart attack while hurrying from behind the counter, never taking his eyes off of me. "Rachael, you came home." Peter ran to me with his arms open, calling my name as though it were a heartwarming reunion. The last time Peter came at me, he had a gun. As the memory flashed through my head, I panicked and held up my hand for him to stop.

"No!"

Before he could get close to me, Daniel stepped into Peter's path and shoved him to the side and then pointed at him. "Stay away from her."

Peter shoved Daniel. "This is *not* your business."

Daniel grabbed Peter's lapels, walked him backwards, and pinned him against the counter. "I'm afraid you have that wrong, because she most certainly *is* my business."

"Stop it," I yelled, rushing to Daniel. I pulled on his arm and pleaded, "Let him go. Please don't fight."

They gazed at each other like two angry bulls with their nostrils flaring. Daniel reluctantly released Peter.

Relieved they kept their hands to themselves, I looked at one and then the other. "This isn't going to solve anything."

Peter, giving Daniel the look of death, straightened his jacket and grumbled, "Then maybe he should leave."

"He's not going anywhere."

Peter's eyes darted to mine.

Before he could say anything, I looked him over and shook my head. "Wow. Have to say. You look pretty good for a dead man."

He stepped closer and whispered, "Let me explain."

"Back off." Daniel's fingertips met Peter's chest, and he gave him a warning glare. "I won't tell you again."

Peter knocked Daniel's hand from his chest and pointed his finger. "And I won't tell you again to butt out or get out. This is between me and my wife."

Daniel, calm and composed, shook his head. "Not anymore."

Before it turned into a fight, I raised my hand and roared, "Stop it. I mean it. Both of you."

Peter pointed at the door and barked, "Get out of my store."

Daniel stood his ground and smiled. "Not gonna happen."

"I said, *enough*." My screaming finally got their attention. I came to get my daughter, not watch them fight. I stepped closer to Daniel so Peter couldn't hear me and whispered, "It's okay. I don't think he's going to hurt me, but we have to be nice to him since I don't know where Jilly is. Let me handle this, please." With Daniel defused, I turned and faced Peter like a soldier at attention. "Where's Jilly? I want to see my daughter."

"She's with Mable, her nanny." Peter reached into his pants pocket and removed his phone. As he swiped the screen, his eyes met mine. "She took her to get ice cream. I'll have her bring Jilly here."

One phone call and I would see my little girl? Was I naïve to believe it would go so easily? I looked at Daniel, biting my lower lip from excitement.

"Hi, Mabel. Can you please bring Jilly to the store? Someone's here to see her." Peter gazed at me while he listened. "Yes, that's fine." After ending the call, he slipped the phone into his pocket. "She's eating her ice cream. Mable will bring her here after she's finished."

The wait to see her would be agonizing, but Peter and I had things to discuss.

"Where's Mandy?" The anticipation of finally facing her sent a burning sensation through my veins.

Peter hesitated, releasing a long sigh and then the words flowed from his lips with ease. "Mandy's dead. She died the day you left."

I laughed. "Is she going to come back to life too?"

"It's true. She went to a bar that night, got drunk, then ran her car into the Pee Dee River on her way home. Someone fishing saw it the next day."

That explained why there was no activity on her bank account and her bar tab, but I was reluctant to believe him. "Did they find her body?"

He nodded. "Yes. She was in the car when they pulled it out of the water. Her mother identified her by the bracelet you gave her."

I looked Peter over and fired away my questions. "How can you be alive after I shot you? How did you get Jilly from Mandy? And who were you talking to that day?"

"Can we do this…" He side-eyed Daniel and scowled. "In private?"

Daniel answered before I could. "No."

Peter looked at me and smirked. "So, this must be Eric."

I shook my head, confused. "Eric?"

"Yes, Eric. You're ex-boyfriend, remember?"

"Why would you think he's Eric?"

"I know what was going on."

I threw my hands up. "Peter, I don't have a clue what you're talking about."

He rolled his eyes. "Come on, Rachael. Just admit it."

"There's *nothing* for me to admit. Stop stalling and tell me what happened before Jilly gets here. I don't want her to see us like this, and I know you don't either."

His lips parted, ready to argue, but he didn't. Peter shook his head and muttered, "No, I don't." But he still hesitated to tell me what happened.

My eyes widened. "Well?"

"I'm so sorry. If you only knew how much…" Peter pressed his lips together and looked away, his face tight and struggling with his next words. "It, it was all a…"

Impatient, I snapped. "A what?"

"A plan. It was all a plan," he answered quickly as if to purge it from his mouth.

"A plan? For what? I don't understand."

"You have to believe me. I wasn't going to do it."

"Do what?" My lips tightened, then I squinted. "Peter, what did you do?"

The man I had always known to have such confidence cowered like a frightened puppy in a cage.

"I-I know you'll never forgive me, and you'll probably hate me for the rest of my life, but please hear me out."

"Peter," I yelled, frustrated at his continuous delay. "Tell me what you did."

He raised his hand and inhaled hard. "I *swear* on our daughter's life I wasn't going to go along with her plan until you overheard that phone call."

The word 'plan' hit me like a ton of bricks weighing heavy on my chest, each breath painful. As if my world couldn't crumble any harder, I asked the question, praying the answer wasn't the one I expected. "For the love of everything we shared, tell me that wasn't Mandy you were talking to."

Peter didn't answer, at least not verbally, although his troubled eyes confessed for him.

In a flippant tone, I answered for him. "Yes, Rachael, it was your best friend I was talking to. I was going to tell you that night how we—"

"No." He quickly raised his hand between us. "It's *not* what you think. I swear."

I gritted my teeth. "So it *was* her."

"I-I was going to tell you everything that night, remember?"

"Say it, Peter. Tell me it was her. I want to hear you say the words."

He nodded slowly. "Yes, it was her, but can I explain?"

I crossed my arms, perhaps so I wouldn't take my fist and hit him. "Go ahead. Tell me what you can *possibly* say that'll make this knife in my heart you just stabbed into it hurt any less."

Peter whisper-shouted, "Can we *please* talk alone?"

I shook my head. "No."

We stared.

Peter finally confessed. "After you left Mandy's apartment that day, she brought Jilly back to our house."

In a fit of rage, I pushed Peter's chest, causing him to step backwards. "You're *lying*. I don't believe you."

Daniel quickly grabbed my arm and restrained me from shoving him again.

"Rachael, when I heard the doorbell, I thought it was Andrew, not Mandy with our daughter."

~ *Three Months Earlier* ~

Peter opens the front door and buttons the cuff of his shirt. "What are you doing here?"

Mandy shifts Jilly on her hip and huffs. "Duh. I'm supposed to be here. Are you going to let us in or what?"

After they enter, Peter takes Jilly from Mandy's arms. "Where's Rachael?"

"Mommy said she had to go somewhere." Jilly wraps her arms around his neck and adds, "But I let her take Fumbles with her so she's not by herself."

"I'm sure he's keeping her company." Peter kisses Jilly's temple. "Daddy needs to talk to Mandy for a moment. You can play outside while I do." He glares at Mandy before walking toward the French doors.

Once outside, Peter stops at the edge of the deck and sets Jilly down. He kneels on one knee to meet her eyes and places his hands on her forearms. "I won't be long, sweetheart. Play in your dollhouse or on the swing, and I'll call you in a few minutes."

"What about Mommy?"

Peter stands and smiles, cupping Jilly's chin, her blonde hair floating from a breeze. "Don't worry about Mommy. I'm going to find her." He glances over his shoulder to see Mandy watching from a window. "Go play. I'll come get you in a few minutes."

"Okay." Jilly runs across the yard to her dollhouse.

Peter heads back inside and marches toward Mandy in quick strides with his chin at his chest. "Where is Rachael? I need to explain things to her."

With a proud grin, Mandy claps. "Bravo, Peter. That must've been *some* performance. I didn't think you could pull it off." Mandy backs up as Peter continues to approach her and raises her finger. "Don't start with me. You know why we did this."

Peter reaches for his phone. "Fine, don't tell me. I'll call her."

"Um, I have a feeling she's not going to answer."

Rachael's phone rings.

Peter's eyes dart to Mandy's pocket and then back to her.

"You have her phone? You left her without a way to call for help if something happened? Are you crazy?"

"Oh come on. It's not like she was going to use it."

"You think this is *funny*?" He turns and marches toward the French doors to watch Jilly. "This was wrong. I want my wife home."

"Well, she doesn't want to be here, and I don't blame her. Eric knows how to make her happy. Something money can't buy."

He stares out the window, watching Jilly chase a butterfly. "I should've been a better husband and done things with her."

"Look, I know this was hard." Mandy approaches but with caution. "She was my friend. I'll miss her too."

Peter turns to Mandy and snarls. "Don't act like you care about Rachael. All you did was use her. You were never a friend to her."

Mandy gives Peter a quick glance-over and sneers. "And you were nothing more than a rich husband wanting a pretty wife. If you loved Rachael, you would've done things with her. But no, everything was about *you*. Rachael deserved better. I hope she runs off into the sunset with Eric and lives happily ever after."

"If I've lost her, it's because you butted into our lives. I told you *I* was going to handle this."

"Handle it?" Mandy flails her hands in the air and rocks her head. "Oh yeah, right. Sic your hot-shot lawyers on her and sue for custody."

"At least they would've kept her from leaving town with my daughter."

"You know as well as I do no piece of paper was going to keep Rachael from leaving town if you sued for custody."

Peter turns his attention to Jilly and watches her sit in the swing and push the ground with her feet. "I should've called Rachael the minute you left my store Monday and told her about your surprise visit and the things you told me. I was going to tell her this evening, but you just had to call me, didn't you?"

"How was I supposed to know you had left the store and was home?"

"When I find Rachael, if she tells me you've lied to me about anything, so help me, I'll—"

"Seriously? You're going to stand there and threaten me after everything I've done to help you?"

Peter shakes his head slowly. "No, something's not right.

Rachael was happy."

Mandy throws her head back and growls. "She was happy because of Eric. Not you." She curls her upper lip. "You…you're boring. All you do is work. Work. Work. Work."

"Rachael *never* said anything about my work being a problem. She knew this when she married me."

Mandy steps into Peter's space and glares hard into his eyes. "I know what Rachael told me. You don't think she confides in me? One day Jilly is going to see how absent you are when you make excuses with her too. Like the one you gave Rachael about going to Disney World. Make all the money you want, Peter, but one day you'll come home to an empty house."

"I'll tell you like I told Rachael. I can't leave the store for a whole week, even if I wanted to. Andrew's opening his store next month. It's bad timing."

"You always have excuses, don't you?"

Peter raises his eyebrows and shouts, "It's not an excuse. It's reality."

Mandy steps back and raises her hand between them. "Don't yell at me."

He scoffs. "What did Rachael ever see in you?"

"I've asked myself the same question about you, Mr. Fancy Pants."

Peter watches Jilly swing, her feet lightly scraping the bare spot on the ground. "Why are you still here?"

"Damage control."

"There wouldn't be any if I hadn't answered your call. Rachael wouldn't have overheard me. I wouldn't have pulled a gun on her." He sighs. "I could've talked her into staying and working things out."

"Work things out?" She laughs facetiously. "Peter, have you been listening to me the past two days? Eric got that job in Montana. He's begging her to go with him and start a new life. I see the temptation in her eyes when she talks about going. We had to do something."

Peter watches Jilly go down the yellow plastic slide. "I still have a hard time believing Rachael would take Jilly from me."

"You're such a hypocrite. That's exactly what you were going to do. Your lawyers were on standby, waiting to sue her for full custody, so what's the difference?"

"I wasn't leaving town. *That's* the difference." Peter reaches for the knob on the French door and bolts outside. When he reaches the edge of the deck, he cups his mouth. "Jilly, come inside."

"Just a few more minutes." Jilly's faint voice echoes over the yard.

"When you see me waving, come in."

"Okay, Daddy."

Mandy rushes to Peter when he walks inside. "This wasn't easy for me either, you know. I betrayed my best friend to help you."

Peter brushes past her and mumbles, "Hope I never have a best friend like you."

She follows him with her hands outstretched. "Why are you being so hateful? All I did was try to help you keep your daughter."

"Why were you so eager to betray a good friend who has been nothing but loyal to you?"

"I told you why. I was scared she was going to drag Jilly across the country. She was going to take her away from both of us."

"Us?" He chuckles. "Excuse me, but Jilly's not yours to lose." Peter points to the door and growls, "Get out of my house."

Jilly runs inside. "Daddy, I need to potty."

"Go ahead. Wash your hands afterward, and I'll make you a snack. Uncle Andrew will be here any minute."

"Okay." Jilly scampers down the hall.

Peter turns to Mandy. "How could I be so stupid and listen to you?"

"I'm sorry we had to do it this way, but it worked."

"How can you sleep tonight knowing she's out there thinking she shot me, *and* you didn't show up with Jilly?"

"I understand you're worried about Rachael, but had you not done this, that bedroom upstairs was going to become a vacant bedroom. You won. Why are you complaining?"

Peter gingerly strokes his five o'clock shadow and eyes her, flashing a half-grin. "Boy, did I underestimate you."

Mandy closes her eyes and presses her fingertips against her temple. "Stop being so ungrateful."

"That friend of yours trusted you with her life...and her daughter's. How can you look in the mirror after what you've done to her?"

Mandy opens her eyes, clenching her fists next to her head.

"Look who's talking, Mr. Innocent. You're the one who set this plan in motion, not me. If you'll recall our conversation, I merely suggested you do this if you wanted to keep Jilly." She smirks with a sideways grin. "Okay, so I'm guilty of buying the gun for you. But *you* are the one who pointed it at Rachael, not me."

Peter nods once. "You're absolutely right. But you're the one who convinced me I was going to lose Jilly."

"It's done. Let's move on from here."

"No, it's *not* done. Where did Rachael go?"

"To the cabin. The one I told you I rented from that guy in case you decided to go through with the plan." A smile forms at the corner of Mandy's mouth. "You'll never find it if that's what you're thinking."

Peter smiles with confidence. "Oh, I'll find it. With or without your help."

"Better find it before she leaves."

"Having money has its advantages," he retorts, raising one eyebrow.

Mandy's confident smile vanishes. "No, no. You can't afford to let anyone find out what you did. Not with the name Greyfell."

"Guess what, Mandy?" He leans closer and sings in a mocking tone, "I don't *care* what people say or what they think."

"Well…" She frowns and retorts in the same mocking tone, "What about your family? You gonna take them down with you?"

Jilly runs to Peter. "Daddy, my hands are clean. See."

"That's my girl." Peter places his palm on her shoulder. "I want you to go into the kitchen and get a juice box. Sit at the table and drink it. I'll be there in one minute."

"Can I have a cookie?"

Peter holds up his index finger. "Just one."

Once Jilly is out of the room, Peter turns to Mandy. "Tell me where the cabin is. I'm not playing games with you."

"No. I'm not going to tell you."

Peter points to the door and yells, "Then get out of my house."

Mandy doesn't flinch at his anger and calmly replies, "I'm not leaving."

"Oh yes you are."

"No. We have to stick to the plan."

"Not going to happen. I'll stop at *nothing* to find Rachael."

"And then what?" Mandy shrugs and grins tauntingly.

"Explain how you set her up? You think she'll forgive you after what you've done to her? Rachael won't let you near Jilly after what you did. Even with your money and influence with judges, if you do get visitations, Jilly will hate you for what you did to her mother, so you better think hard. You have a lot more to lose than what you already have. Leave things the way they are if you want to raise Jilly."

Peter straightens his back and exhales, staring hard into her big brown eyes. "You know, you're probably right about everything you predicted. But, Mandy, you see, the difference between us is…*I* have a conscience and want to do the right thing." He points at her. "And if you get in my way of finding Rachel, mark my word, she won't be the only one missing."

Mandy mocks a terrified look and quivers. "Oh, I'm sooooo scared. Should I make sure my life insurance policy is still active?"

Peter rolls his eyes. "Whatever."

Mandy rests her hands on her hips and rocks her head. "Just so you know, your threats don't scare me one bit."

"They're not meant to scare you, but for you to understand I mean what I say. Now, for the last time, get out of my house, and don't ever come back."

"No, the plan was for me to take care of Jilly if she left."

"I *never* agreed to that." Peter storms toward the front door to see her out.

Mandy remains in place. "You'll never cut me out of Jilly's life. *Ever.*"

"I'm calling the police." Peter reaches for his phone and taps the screen. "You have no idea what I'll do to make sure you're never around my daughter or Rachael ever again." When he puts the phone to his ear, he watches in horror as Mandy runs to the kitchen.

Chapter 23: Forgive Me

"You bastard." I slapped Peter with all the force I had in me.

With one arm around my abdomen, Daniel scooped me backwards before I could hit him again.

"You thought I was cheating on you with Eric?"

Peter placed his hand on his cheek as if to soothe the sting.

While struggling to pry Daniel's arm from my torso, I continued my rage. "*That's* why you did this to me?"

"I'm so..." He lowered his face into his hands and wailed louder than my angered words. "I'm so sorry."

"You destroyed *everything* we had because of lies? *Lies*, Peter, because that's what they are."

Sobbing, he parted his hands and looked at me. "She convinced me you were going to run off with Eric."

"Oh please." I looked him over with disgust. "What'd she do, put a spell on you or something? Or, was it enough to walk in here and tell you that?"

"No, she didn't just tell me and I believed her," he retorted in the same cynical tone. Peter ran his hands down his cheeks to wipe away the tears. "I even laughed when she told me you were seeing Eric and let her know I was going to call you."

"So, why didn't you?"

Peter loosened his tie and pulled it from his collar. "It's something I'll regret the rest of my life." He looked over his shoulder and tossed the tie on the counter. Turning his eyes back to me, he exhaled loudly. "Mandy said she had proof. I'll admit, that got my attention. I asked to see it, but she didn't have it with her. She offered to bring it the next day and challenged me not to say anything to you until I saw it."

"What kind of proof did she bring?"

"She didn't come back the next day. She said she had to work late and would come by the following day. I told her not to bother, because I was going to confront you. That's when she offered to email me something." Peter reached for his phone and swiped the screen. "It's a picture of you and Eric hugging." He held up his phone for me to see.

I looked at the picture. It was taken at Mandy's apartment, but I struggled to remember when. Then it hit me. "Peter," I shouted, my eyes meeting his. "He happened to stop by Mandy's while I was there. You know we were still friends. I hadn't seen him in years. That hug was completely innocent."

He shrugged and squealed, "How was I supposed to know?"

"By asking me," I growled through my clenched teeth.

Peter aggressively swiped his phone again. "Then explain this card he gave you." He held up his phone for me to see and recited the message from memory as I read along with him. "'I enjoyed our afternoon. I wish I could see you every day, but I know one day we will be together forever. Until I hold you in my arms again, know that I long for the day I can hold you as my wife.'" He lowered the phone. "Are you going to deny he gave you that card?"

I swallowed hard, breathing breaths of anger through my nostrils. "Eric gave me that card when we were dating. *Before* I ever met you. When we got married and I moved out, I left all of that stuff in my closet, because Mandy said she'd throw it away for me."

Peter returned the phone to his pocket, his eyes flashing shame and humiliation. The longer we stared, the more it hurt. Before I let him see my tears, I turned from him.

Daniel placed his hand on my shoulder but didn't say anything.

"Please tell me this isn't real." Before he could answer, I looked at Peter and screamed, "You put me through hell because of lies."

He immediately fired back. "Rachael, she told me you weren't happy anymore. As crazy as Mandy was, I could see where everything she said was possible. I do work all the time. You did give up a part of who you were when you married me. And no, I didn't do things with you like Eric did."

"Did I ever complain?" My eyebrows raised, waiting for him to answer. In his silence, I taunted him. "Did I? Tell me if I did, because I sure don't remember."

Peter looked down, shook his head and mumbled, "No."

"For two days, you talked to Mandy about this." I started out calm, but then the anger rose, burning my chest as I breathed. "You listened to her lies, and not *once*," I held up my finger, "did you talk to me…your wife." In a fit of rage, I lost it and shoved a mannequin dressed in an Armani suit. Then I clenched my hands and yelled, "I never once gave you a reason to think I would ever cheat on you."

Peter placed his sprawled hands on his head and screamed, "Rachael, I was so confused. I didn't know what to think anymore. Between her lies, the card, and the picture…I, I was an idiot, okay? I fell for it, hook, line, and sinker. She had me scared to death you were going to run off with, with…" He flung his hand. "With what's-his-name and take my daughter from me." He caught a second wind and added in a lower tone, "I was going to talk to you. Honest. Maybe I was scared you would tell me it was true."

I didn't know what to say, so I paced. My fingertips trailed along a display of expensive belts, thinking back to those two days. "So that's why you questioned my love for you." I looked at Peter and let him see the hurt in my eyes. "It was because you believed *her*. For two nights, you laid in bed with me thinking I had betrayed you, and you never said a word."

"But I wanted to tell you," he roared, also hurting. "Honest, Rachael."

"And here I thought *you* were the one having an affair."

Peter gasped. "*Me*? No, Rachael. I love you. I'd never—"

"You love me?" I marched toward him, but Daniel grabbed my arm and held me back, but I still let go of my fury. "You set me up to think I killed you, and you call that love? I cried myself to sleep every night worried about Jilly and was afraid I would never see her again. How *dare* you stand there and claim you love me."

Peter stood tall. "No matter what I did, I love you. I always will."

My hands clenched, wishing I could hit him. "That's not love, Peter. That's hell. All you had to do was ask me if I was seeing Eric."

He shrugged with his palms up. "I did ask you."

I looked at him cautiously. "When?"

Peter looked more confused than I did with his head cocked and his brows tight. "When you were in my study. I told you Mandy came by the store and what she said. I *asked* you several times if you were seeing that guy, and you just stood there like a deer caught in headlights," he sang, insultingly. "I kept waiting for you to tell me it wasn't true, but you didn't." He narrowed his brows at me and barked, "What was I supposed to think, Rachael?"

I couldn't answer, speechless, finally learning what he said when I zoned out.

Peter continued, his words coming fast and with conviction. "When you didn't deny it, I thought it must be true. I was hurt you betrayed me, then I panicked because I was *so* scared you were going to run upstairs and take our daughter." He placed his hands over his face and wept. "I've never been so confused in my life. For two days, I thought I was going to lose you. And then in my study, I thought I was going to lose my daughter."

In that moment, I felt sorry for Peter. Mandy obviously confused him the way she did me that day in her apartment. And he did ask me about Eric. It just happened to be when I had spaced out.

"I didn't hear you ask me that."

Still crying, he lowered his hands, his bloodshot eyes looking at me and asked condescendingly, "How could you *not* hear me? You were standing right in front of me when I asked."

I shrugged, searching for an answer. "I, I don't know why I didn't hear you. Maybe I was in shock and blacked out in those few seconds. Can you blame me after hearing you tell another woman how things had to end? Maybe I didn't want to hear my world was about to fall apart. And you scared me, because you were so angry."

Peter ran his fingers through his hair all the way to the back of his head and roared, "I was angry because you didn't deny it. Because I thought it was true."

"If I had heard you, I would've told you it was all a lie," I replied in a brusque tone. "But you, you should've trusted me. How could you *ever* think I'd cheat on you?"

Peter placed his hands on his hips and eyed me as he countered. "Didn't you just say you thought *I* was the one cheating? I mean, from that short conversation you overheard that's what *you* thought, and it wasn't true."

"Don't turn this back on me," I hissed, pointing my finger at him. "None of this would've happened if you had trusted me. But instead, you trusted my friend who you called a psycho the whole time we were married."

His eyes bulged. "You don't think that haunts me?"

"Speaking of haunting..." I looked him over. "Why are you not dead? I saw the blood."

The confident man who always had an answer remained silent.

I wasn't having it and yelled, "Answer me."

He did, but without looking at me. "The gun wasn't real, and it was fake blood. Mandy bought it and told me to use it."

My jaw fell. "Are you trying to blame Mandy now?"

"*No*, of course not. I take full responsibility for my actions. For thinking about her stupid plan in that split second and reaching into my drawer for that gun."

"What exactly was this plan?"

"Rachael..." He eyed me with hesitation. "Are you sure you want to hear this?"

"Just tell me."

Peter reluctantly continued. "She told me if I could make you believe you shot me, she would scare you into leaving town. Once you were on the run, she knew you wouldn't come home. At least no time soon, because you would look for her and Jilly. When you did finally come home, my lawyers would sue you for abandonment."

I ran my hand over a display of perfectly folded ties, sending them across the store like a gust of wind had blown through. "Do you hear how sick that is?"

"Yes, I do." Peter's voice was equally as loud and defensive. "I live with it *every* minute of *every* day. I'm not making excuses for what I did, but when you didn't deny seeing Eric, my worst nightmare came true." He paused and covered his mouth, then massaged is jaw as though to calm down. "Maybe I was in shock. I don't know. I just saw you taking Jilly from me. Rachael, I panicked and made a horrible choice."

A part of me still didn't want to believe Mandy would ever betray me in such a way. But the ache in my heart told me it was true. "Why?" Tears of betrayal slid down my face. "What did I ever do to Mandy to make her do something like this to me? I was the only friend she ever had."

"Because she wanted Jilly. That's what this was all about. She thought if she got rid of you, I would need her and let her take care of Jilly."

"Did she tell you that?"

"Honey, while I was talking to the dispatcher, Mandy ran into the kitchen and grabbed Jilly. She held me at bay with a knife and tried to leave with her. If Andrew hadn't showed up when he did, I'd hate to think what would've happened."

The visual went through my head. If Mandy wasn't dead, I would have hunted her down if it took me the rest of my life.

"Did she hurt Jilly?"

Peter shook his head. "No. She was scared and crying, but she wasn't hurt."

I still had questions and little time left to ask them. "Who were the people you had coming after me?"

He narrowed his brows with confusion and shrugged. "I, I didn't have anyone coming after you."

"But I heard you say you pay them good money."

"I was talking about my lawyers. How they would go after you for full custody to keep you from leaving town with Jilly."

All of those times I've feared someone was after me, and it was his lawyers.

"What if I had finished that phone call to the police?"

"I would've stopped you and explained it wasn't real. It would have ended right then."

It sounded so simple. All I had to do was press one more digit.

"After you ran out of the study, I realized what I had done was wrong. I got up and saw the phone was hanging over my desk. I put the receiver back in the cradle." He shrugged with his lips parted. "I don't know why I thought you were coming back to the study. I waited for you so you would see I was alright. When I heard the garage door open, I realized you were leaving. I ran out of the study to stop you, but you were pulling out of the driveway. I ran after you, waving my arms to get your attention, but you turned the corner and disappeared."

If only I had looked in my rearview mirror. Another missed chance.

"Why didn't you call me?"

"I did, but it went to voicemail."

He called while I was talking to Mandy? I guess I was so upset that I didn't hear the beep.

"I called you several times, but it always went to voicemail. I left messages, telling you I was alright and to come home."

That's why Mandy wanted my phone. She knew Peter was alive and would call me.

"What if I had taken Jilly with me to the cabin?"

Peter shook his head. "I honestly don't know. I didn't think Mandy could talk you into leaving town, much less leave Jilly with her."

I smirked. "Guess I look pretty dumb right now."

"No, not at all. Mandy knew what to say to both of us to get what she wanted."

I corrected him. "You mean she knew what to say to *you*. There's no way I'd let someone tell me something like that and not come to you immediately."

"That's easy to say until someone gets into your head and confuses you to the point you don't know right from wrong. Mandy did the same thing to you when she convinced you to leave town."

I wanted to tell him he was wrong, but how could I? Peter was right.

"You only had her in your head for what, five minutes? I had her in my head for two days."

"That doesn't give you the right to pull a gun on me." I pointed at his chest, throwing responsibility back at him. "You chose to do that, knowing what it would do to me. Knowing it was wrong."

His confident hazel eyes penetrated mine. "Just like you chose to leave town, knowing it was wrong." Before I could defend myself, he asked, "Tell me, Rachael, in that desperate moment in Mandy's apartment, did you listen to your own gut or what she told you was your only choice?"

I wouldn't let you do this if I didn't think it was your only choice.

The hair on my neck stood up, hearing Mandy's words. How could I argue with Peter? He was right again.

"I tried so hard to find you at the cabin."

"I was there for three days."

"But I didn't know where it was. I had to hire a private investigator." He unbuttoned his collar. "When he finally found it, you had already left." Peter reached inside his shirt and pulled out a necklace. After sliding it over his head, he held it up. "He saw these lying on a table."

"My wedding rings?" With my eyes wide, I stared at them dangling on the end of the necklace.

Peter offered them to me. "I wear them every day, waiting to give them back to you."

I shook my head and raised my hand. "You keep them."

Disappointed, Peter slipped the necklace into his pocket. "You charged some gas that Saturday. After that, it was like you disappeared into thin air."

I didn't hold back my sarcasm. "Wasn't that the plan?"

Peter glanced at Daniel, then back to me. "Where have you been?"

"Maxton." I kept the focus from shifting. "So, everyone thinks I left Jilly and ran off with Eric?"

"That was Mandy's plan, but I told Andrew everything after the cops left."

"Mr. Greyfell?" An older woman's voice called out from the back.

With his eyes on me, Peter informed her, "We're out on the floor."

Chapter 24: Jilly

I stared behind the counter, preparing to lay my eyes on Jilly. She was so close, the mother in me wanted to run to her, ending our time apart. I rested my chin on my intertwined hands and said a prayer she would remember me, still fearing my nightmare that she wouldn't.

An elderly lady appeared in the doorway of the backroom. My breath caught, and I covered my gasp as the moment drew closer.

Peter waved his fingers, coaxing the nanny. "Bring Jilly out front, please."

Mable moved timidly along the counter. The height obstructed my view of Jilly, which only increased my anticipation. By the time they reached the opening to the sales floor, my legs had weakened, causing me to become unsteady. Mable revealed herself first. Biting my lip, I stretched my neck and tried to see past her. When Mable stepped to the side, there she was, my little girl, as adorable as ever in her shorts and pink shirt with sparkles. Her beautiful blonde hair was in a high ponytail.

When our eyes met, it was like my heart had been struck by lightning. Weak and overwhelmed, my knees buckled. Daniel quickly grabbed my forearm. Peter simultaneously grabbed the other one. Unable to stand, they guided my limp body to the floor. Jilly watched with curious eyes, holding her nanny's hand. I desperately wanted to call out her name so she could hear my voice, but I couldn't speak.

Daniel knelt next to me and rubbed my back. "Rachael, take small breaths."

"Mable, get us a glass of water, please," Peter instructed with urgency, still holding my forearm.

The nanny hastened away, abandoning Jilly's side. My little girl gazed at me spellbound, then she looked at Daniel. Her blue eyes studied him.

227

After catching my breath, I called out her name. "Jilly."

Her wide eyes darted back to mine. "Mommy?"

When I heard her sweet voice, my emotions gave way, and I wept uncontrollably. "Yes, baby. It's Mommy." With the deepest longing and ache to hold her, I pulled free from Daniel and Peter's grasp. With my arms outstretched, I invited her to come to me.

Without hesitation, my baby girl scampered to me with her arms equally open. As soon as I had her in my embrace, I closed my eyes and wept, my heart finally whole again.

"Why are you crying?"

I composed myself and leaned Jilly back, looking at her and gently touching her cheek. "Because I missed you so much."

"Thank you. Wait for me in the backroom," Peter told Mable and handed me the glass. "Here, drink some water."

With a shaky hand, I accepted the drink and eagerly gulped the contents. The cool liquid replenished my dry mouth. With a thank you nod, I handed the glass to Peter and quickly turned my eyes back to Jilly. I pulled Fumbles from my pocket and held him in front of her. "Do you remember this little guy?"

She reached for him and giggled. "That's Fumbles."

"Yes it is."

Jilly gave him a quick kiss and bounced him on my arm. "Mommy, are you going home with me?"

I looked at Peter and caught him wiping his tears. "Daddy and I have to talk, sweetie." I held my hand out to Daniel to help me stand while holding Jilly. She was heavier than I remembered.

Jilly whispered, "Who's that?"

"This is my friend, Daniel. Can you say hello?"

She held her old friend in the air. "Hello. This is Fumbles."

"I know. I think he's glad to see you."

"Rachael, do you mind if I take her to the back with Mable so we can finish talking?"

The thought of letting her out of my sight caused me to hold her tighter. Jilly had only been in my arms for a few minutes. However, Peter and I had loose ends to tie up, and the sooner we did, the better. My glorious day was not over yet. Not until I went to the farm.

I leaned closer to Daniel. "Would you mind going to the back with Jilly? I don't want the nanny to leave with her."

"Are you sure it's okay to be alone with him?"

"I'm sure. I promise it won't take long."

Daniel didn't appear thrilled about the idea of going to the back, but he agreed. "If that's what you need me to do."

I turned to Peter with my head held high and announced, "Daniel's going to take her to the backroom so we can talk privately."

My comment put a smile on his face. "That's fine."

When I turned my eyes back to Jilly, I reminded myself it was only for a few minutes. "Sweetie, I need to speak to Daddy. Will you go with Daniel to the back for a minute?"

Jilly's brows narrowed as she looked Fumbles over. "No. I wanna stay with you."

"It's just for—"

She threw her arms around my neck and locked them. "No. I *don't* want to."

I rubbed her back and tried to soothe her panic. "Baby girl, I promise it's only for a minute." Once she seemed okay, I leaned into Daniel, and he reached for Jilly.

"*Noooo.*" She squealed at the top of her lungs and held onto me with all her might. "I want my mommy."

"Shhh, I'm right here." I walked away from Peter and Daniel and paced at the front of the store to give her a moment and to calm my own anxiety of letting her out of my sight. "Guess what?"

"What?"

"After I talk to Daddy, I'm going to the farm. Would you like to go with me?"

"You're going to see Grandma?"

"I sure am."

Her head sprung up, then she nodded. "Yeah, I wanna go with you. Fumbles said he wants to go too."

I laughed. "Okay, but I need to talk to Daddy first." I lowered my chin and looked into her blue eyes. "Will you go with Daniel for me? I promise I'll make it as fast as I can."

She noticed my smiley necklace and lifted it from my chest. "Okay."

I walked back to Daniel. "Wait 'til you see his truck. It's really big."

"How big?"

I grinned. "You'll see."

Daniel reached for Jilly. She went to him, but her eyes never left mine. I smiled and waved as they walked away. Once Daniel was in the backroom, it was only me and Peter. Awkward had a new

229

meaning, staring at the man I thought I had shot. I released a long sigh of relief. "I wasn't sure she would remember me."

Peter flashed a modest smile. "We talk about you every day, and I let her go through the pictures of you on my phone."

I smirked. "Should I thank you?"

Peter's smile melted, and he shook his head. "I'm sorry. I didn't mean to—"

Determined to make it a short conversation, I interrupted and got to the point. "We need to figure out an arrangement."

"Wait, you're not coming home?" He asked like I was going to kiss and make up after destroying what we had.

I laughed, not that it was funny. "Do you honestly expect me to come home like nothing happened?"

Peter's eyes told me that was exactly what he wanted me to do. "Yes. That's your home. You're my wife. I know it'll take time, but we can work through this."

"No. I'll *never* step foot in that house ever again." My body shivered at the thought.

The confident man always had an answer. "Then I'll sell it. We can buy another house anywhere you want. I'll find us a place to stay until we do. Rachael, I want a chance to treat you the way I should have." Hope radiated from Peter's smile, and confidence filled his hazel eyes. "We'll do all the things you like to do. I'll even hire some help to run the store so I can be home more."

Of all the things I tried to be prepared for, Peter begging me to come home was not one of them.

"I'm not coming home. What you did changed everything." I walked past him and considered the subject a closed matter. We had other things to discuss.

"Please, Rachael." Peter stepped into my path and held up his hands. "Look, I know you're hurt and angry, but we have a good marriage."

"We *had* a good marriage until you no longer trusted me." Before he could plead his case for the millionth time, I quickly added in an unequivocal tone, "I told you things are different now. What we had is gone."

The hope in his smile faded, and so did the confidence in his eyes. "You're not going to try to work this out, not even for Jilly?"

"Peter, when you pulled that gun on me, you took everything we had and wiped it away. I can forgive you for not trusting me, even not telling me sooner, but not that. As for Jilly, we would still

Grace E Summers

be a family if you had only come to me and told me what Mandy had said. That's on *you*, not me."

He rolled his eyes and crossed his arms. "You're staying with him, aren't you?"

I refused to feel guilty. "Yes, I am." I walked away and rested my arms on top of the counter.

Peter stood next to me. "Are you—"

"No, I'm not sleeping with him."

He looked at his hands and rubbed his palms together. "I was going to ask if you're in love with him. It's obvious he's in love with you."

I picked up a tie clip and fiddled with it. "We have other things we need to talk about."

"Do you hate me?"

"No," I mumbled with honesty. "But you hurt me more than you'll *ever* know." A montage of the past three months flashed before me. "You have no idea what you put me through. The nightmares. Crying. The guilt of shooting you. Feeling betrayed. Going to prison. Never seeing Jilly again. Fearing for my life. Not knowing why you wanted to shoot me." As much as I wanted to name off everything I went through so he would understand what he had done, I was out of breath.

Peter reached for my hand, but my glare warned him not to touch me. "I can't tell you how sorry I am. How much I regret what I've done. But I know it's only words." The sadness in his eyes deepened from his own pain. "Rachael, please. I'll do *anything* to make this right if you just give me a chance. Anything."

A reconciliation was not up for discussion, so it was time to end our little talk and go see my family. I reached for a pen and piece of paper and jotted down my phone number, then slid it next to his arm. "Here. I guess you'll need this." Our eyes met when he reached for it. "How's your family doing?"

Peter chuckled with a half-smile. "Well, they almost disowned me." He tucked the paper into his breast pocket. "But we're okay. Andrew's running his store. Dad's fully retired now."

"Speaking of family, I want to go see mine. We can talk later since you have my number."

"Mable takes Jilly to the farm on Tuesdays and Thursdays for the day, and then I take her out there for a weekend each month."

My jaw dropped, and I placed my hand on my chest. "Mama's been seeing Jilly this whole time?"

He nodded. "I called her after the police left and told her what happened in case you called her. She's still furious with me, but we worked out an arrangement for her to see Jilly."

For three months I wanted to see my family, and the only thing stopping me was talking to Peter. I wasn't about to waste one more minute. "We'll have to talk later. I'm going to the farm to see my family."

I left Peter standing there, but he quickly caught up with me. "Where do we go from here?"

"Let's take it one day at a time." After we rounded the counter, I stopped and faced Peter. We had a small detail to settle. "I'm taking Jilly with me."

Peter's eyes watered, but he forced a smile. "She needs her mom." He cleared his throat, keeping his composure. "When can I see her?"

"Um…" Maybe there were two details to work out. "I'll come back this weekend. She can spend it with you, and I'll stay at the farm. And, you can call her any time during the week. I'll get a laptop tomorrow so you can video chat with her."

"What about her things? Her car seat?"

"Keep them." I continued to the backroom and added, "I have my car seat with me, and we'll stop on the way home and get whatever else she'll need."

"Is it okay if I call her tonight?"

"You should. She's going to need to hear from you." I stopped before we entered the backroom and whispered, "Peter, let's try to work together and put this behind us. If nothing else, for our daughter."

He hesitated, then nodded.

I walked into the backroom and covered my smile. Jilly sat next to Daniel. Her legs swung, and she gestured with her hands, telling him all about her favorite cartoon. In mid-sentence, she glanced my way and did a double take. She left her chair and ran to me like there had been no time lost between us. I scooped her up and held her tight, kissing her cheek over and over. After introducing Mable, a widow and long-time friend of the Greyfells, Peter explained to her what was happening. I introduced Daniel, but there were no handshakes between him and Peter, only glaring eyes. Somehow, those two were going to have to get along.

Chapter 25: The Farm

We left Peter's store and headed to the farm. When we drove over the Pee Dee River, I visualized Mandy's BMW upside down in the water. It was wrong to wish someone such a fate, but perhaps God had taken care of business. Five minutes from the farm, I called Mama, fearing she might have a heart attack if I showed up out of the blue.

"Hello?"

When she answered, I got all choked up. "Ma-mama?"

She screamed my name before bawling. We cried so hard we could barely understand each other. We were only minutes away, so I told her I would see her soon. Unable to sit still, I called Abby and gave her a quick update. We giggled like teenage girls. She couldn't wait to meet Jilly and insisted on being at the house when we arrived. I couldn't wait to introduce my little girl to everyone.

Seeing the old familiar landscape was priceless. Mr. Thompson, rocking on his porch, waved like he always did no matter who drove by. The Efird's cows huddled under the only shade tree.

"There's a driveway just past that big tree on your right," I informed Daniel. "Turn there."

For three months, I envisioned the day I would come home. Never did I imagine it would be with Peter alive, Jilly safe, and me a free woman.

"We're at Grandma's."

I laughed at Jilly's excitement. "That's right."

When Daniel turned down the gravel driveway, the memories stirred. Grandpa's old tractor was next to the barn. It hadn't been used since he shut down the farm after Nana died. The empty pasture held memories of cattle that once grazed the land. It seemed like a lifetime ago.

"The house is just past those trees." I pointed, although Daniel had to notice it without me announcing it.

The house came into full view. Mama and Grandpa stood on the porch, anxiously awaiting us. I fanned my face, fighting tears. It didn't seem real.

"I see Grandma and Grandpa."

"Me too."

Mama covered her mouth like she was crying. Grandpa stood next to her with the help of his cane.

"Would you mind getting Jilly out of the truck for me?"

"Not at all."

When Daniel came to a stop, I jerked the door open and ran as fast as my feet would carry me. Jilly screamed for me, but in that moment, I needed my mama. She rushed down the steps to meet me.

"*Mama.*" I cried, running to her.

"*Rachael.*" She ran as fast as she could.

When we embraced, I didn't have to be strong anymore. I had crossed the finish line and could collapse. I was finally home. The nightmare was over.

I squeezed her to make sure I wasn't dreaming. "Oh, Mama." The past three months collided with the present, and it overwhelmed me. I cried harder. "Mama, I, that day…" All of my emotions trying to escape made it hard to talk.

"It's okay, sweetie," she whispered in her comforting voice, being the strong woman that she was. "It's okay. You're home now."

My face burrowed in her neck, still holding onto her. "I missed you so much."

Mama held me tighter. "I missed you too."

The more I cried, the more my body purged all that I had stored inside. "I-I was so scared."

"I know you were. I was scared for you and prayed every night. When I got your letter, I knew you'd be home soon." She leaned me back and held my face in her hands. "It's going to be okay."

"Mama…" I gasped for air and swallowed hard. "They-they betrayed me."

Her smile faded into a frown, taking the dishtowel from her shoulder to wipe my tears the way she did when I was young. "What they did was *horrible*," she growled in her feisty Southern voice. "Don't think I didn't give Peter a piece of my mind."

I laughed at the visual.

"I had to ask God to forgive me for the thoughts I had about him."

"Mama, I thought I killed Peter. I didn't think I'd ever see you or Jilly again."

She lifted my chin and looked into my eyes. "I know it was horrible, but you're home now. Don't let what happened steal another second of your life. Your father taught you to be strong, and I'll help you get through this." She glanced behind me and then looked at me and whispered, "Here comes Jilly. Don't let her see you upset."

I wiped my face and composed myself.

Jilly tugged at my shorts. "Mommy."

"Come here, baby girl." I scooped her up and held her tight.

"Grandma, Mommy came home just like you said she would."

Mama tossed the dishtowel over her shoulder and sang, "I told you God answers prayers."

Grandpa and Daniel chatted at the foot of the steps.

I couldn't run to him fast enough. "Hey, Grandpa." The look in his eyes caused more tears of happiness. With my free arm, I gave him a hug. Then I stepped back and looked him over. It broke my heart to see how much his health had deteriorated since I had been gone. He looked fragile, his unsteady hand shaking the cane and his back hunched. The overalls swallowed him whole from the weight loss.

"Your maw and I looked for you, but we couldn't find you."

I rubbed his forearm and smiled to let him know I was alright. "I know you did, but I'm home now."

He rested his hand on my shoulder and leaned closer. "Who is this stranger you're with? He doesn't look like Peter."

It was time for introductions. "Mama? Grandpa? I want you to meet someone special." I glanced at my angel standing next to me and winked. "This is Daniel."

"Hi." Mama extended her hand and smiled. "It's nice to meet you. I'm Annie."

"Ma'am, the pleasure's mine," he replied in that deep Southern drawl, shaking her hand.

"And this is my grandpa, Reece."

Daniel offered his hand and nodded once. "It's a pleasure to meet you, sir."

"Grandma? Grandma?" Jilly waved her hand, trying to get

her attention.

Mama turned to her. "Yes, sweetie. What is it?"

"He, um..." Jilly pressed her finger against her lip and gave me a puzzled look. "What's his name? I forgot."

I whispered, "Daniel."

"Oh yeah," she whispered back and continued. "Grandma, you should see Daniel's truck." She spread her hands wide. "It's dis big."

"I see that." Mama turned to us, fanning her face. "It's awful hot out here. Let's go inside where it's cooler. We can have a seat and talk. Maybe have some iced tea."

One by one, we marched up the wooden steps. The porch squeaked when we walked across it. A familiar sound of home I would never take for granted ever again. No matter how many times we replaced that one board, it always squeaked.

Grandpa settled in his recliner. Mama slid a wooden chair next to him, and Daniel sat next to me on the couch. Jilly nestled in my arms. She refused to let me out of her sight, but I was more than okay with that. However, she watched Daniel's every move.

Mama and Grandpa listened intently while I reminisced about the past three months. After telling them how I met Daniel, I shared how he had taken me in and let me work for him. I rambled on about Abby and her diner, and Jory—and Zack and Missy. As I talked about them, it was clear I had a new home and a new life.

However, some things were not so pleasant. I teared up when I talked about the accident. Without going into details, I told them about Skip and how he broke into the office. It still bothered me more than I would admit. Mama was so grateful to Daniel, she left her chair and gave him a hug. When she said he must be the angel she prayed God had watching over me, I smiled. If she only knew.

The minutes turned into hours. It was late in the evening. Mama and I fixed supper. I caught myself staring at her, afraid I was dreaming.

When it came time to leave, Grandpa had already retired for the day. Mama took me to the side for a private goodbye, and we shed more tears. Even though she wanted me to stay, she told me how much I smiled when I looked at Daniel and knew I was where I belonged.

On the way home, I sat in the back with Jilly until she fell asleep, which was only a matter of minutes. Then I crawled up front with Daniel and called Abby to let her know we were on our way home. I had to pull the phone away from my ear when she squealed with excitement. She and Jory wanted kids, but after several miscarriages, they accepted it wasn't meant to be. She insisted on running to the store for me. I was grateful and gave her a short list of items. I wasn't sure who was more excited, her or me.

Every two minutes, I looked over my shoulder. Jilly slept peacefully with Fumbles in her hand.

"I need to make a quick phone call." I reached inside my purse for my phone.

"Hello?"

"Hey, Eric. It's me. I know it's late, but I—"

"Girl, are you trying to put me in my grave prematurely? What the heck's going on with you?"

I laughed, tucking the hair behind my ear. "A lot, but I can't go into all the details right now. I wanted to let you know I was okay. Sorry I never called you back."

I take it everything worked out?"

"Yes, finally."

"Did you hear about Mandy? I tried to call you and tell you the news, but you disappeared on me."

That was the urgent news Eric wanted to tell me that day he called the shop. If I had only answered his call. The one person I didn't trust turned out to be the only one I should have.

"Yes. I was shocked when I heard she died. Wasn't expecting that."

"I don't think she ever got over the accident, you know, the loss of Hannah. That was such a horrible thing. Then Charlie left her."

I looked out the window and exhaled. "Maybe she's at peace now."

"Did you ever meet her friend, Samantha Penegar? Everyone called her Sam. She rented your room before you moved in."

My brows narrowed as I thought. "No. I never met her, and Mandy never talked about her."

"Well, she went missing a couple of months ago."

"Hmm, that's weird."

"Yeah, I hope she's alright. She's a nice girl, but a little on the wild side if you know what I mean. Always partying and drinking. I think that's why she and Mandy got along so good."

"Maybe she'll show up soon. Sometimes we just need to get away from life."

"Are you sure you're okay?"

I looked at Daniel and smiled. "Yeah. Things are where they should be."

"With that boring husband of yours?"

"Oops, sorry. I forgot to tell you we aren't together anymore."

Eric gasped deeply. "Hey, if you're a free woman, I'm flying home."

I laughed at his playfulness. "No. I'm not a free woman."

Daniel's eyes darted to mine.

"I should've known. Anyway, I'll be home in October. Any chance we can meet and catch up?"

"Sure. Call me when you get to town."

"You can count on it."

"We'll talk then. Bye."

Daniel glanced my way. "Eric?"

"He's the guy who called that day, and I panicked. Remember?"

"He's also your ex-boyfriend." Daniel half-jokingly asked, "Do I need to worry about Eric too?"

"You don't need to worry about anyone." I shoved my phone inside my purse and then held his hand. "I'm all yours."

"I want that in writing one day."

~ ~ ~

It was late when we walked through the front door. Abby greeted us, reaching out her hands to hold Jilly, but she recoiled and hung onto me. She had just woken up and was confused. Her little world had changed, and it had to be overwhelming. When Abby pointed to the toys and clothes on the couch, Jilly couldn't resist the temptation and let Abby walk her to them. Jory feared his burly appearance might scare Jilly, so he stayed in the kitchen with me and Daniel while we snacked on some finger food they had bought.

An hour later, Abby and Jory said their goodbyes. Jilly had warmed up to Abby and let her have a goodbye hug. She even had

Jilly giggling. It was the most beautiful sound in the world. Jory tried to tell her goodbye, but Jilly's eyes grew wide, so he told her from a distance. We tried not to laugh, but it was kind of funny.

I thanked them for going to the store and tried to pay Abby, but she reminded me of all the times I had helped her at the diner. When she added the comment, "Besides, I need to get used to buying baby things," her statement caught me off guard, and I gave her a puzzled look. Abby teared up and fanned her face and announced, "I'm pregnant." Daniel took his sister in his arms and congratulated her. I had to fight my tears, watching them. They were the only ones left in their family, and now there would be three.

Peter called while I was helping Jilly put on her new pajamas. She described them, along with all the things Abby had bought. While they talked, I thought back to my first night without Jilly. I didn't wish that feeling on Peter's first night without her. No matter what he had done, Peter was an amazing father, and Jilly was a daddy's girl. After their conversation, we played with her toys. Abby bought the cutest doll that came with fashion accessories. Jilly named her Lucy.

While I cleaned up the kitchen, Daniel took a shower. I must have looked at Jilly a million times.

Daniel startled me when he entered the kitchen. "I see that grin."

My attention was diverted to the handsome man standing in front of me wearing shorts and a tattered T-shirt. I leaned against the counter and dried my hands. "Can you believe this day?"

"And it's only gonna get better." Daniel placed his hands on my hips and pulled me closer.

"How could it get any better than this?"

He brushed his cheek against mine and whispered, "Your life's not on hold anymore."

I rested my chin on his shoulder and slowly trailed my fingertips over his back and mumbled, "I know. It's still hard to believe."

He guided the hair from my temple and tenderly kissed it. "Maybe we can talk about our future."

A tingle rushed through me, causing me to smile. "Did you have something in mind?"

"We'll continue this conversation when you're free from Peter." Before I could question him, Daniel pressed his lips against mine.

After our kiss, I checked on Jilly. "Hey, she fell asleep. I need to put her to bed." I headed to the couch, relishing in the thought of her sleeping in my bed tonight.

Daniel followed me. "Do you want me to carry her to your room?"

As much as I looked forward to doing it, I was guilty of wanting to watch Daniel hold her. I whispered over my shoulder, "Sure."

He gently scooped up my sleeping angel and carried her to my room. After he rested Jilly on the bed, I pulled the covers over her and kissed her cheek, tucking her in for the first time in three months. Something I would never take for granted ever again. It would be the best night of my life, having her back with me. Still in my happy moment, I gave Daniel a quick peck on his cheek and whispered, "I'm going to take a shower and call it a day."

Daniel pulled me closer and gave me a passionate goodnight kiss. Then he whispered, "You know where to find me if you need anything." As he walked out of my room, certain parts of his body had my attention.

While taking a shower, I still couldn't believe everything that happened. For the first time in three months, I could smile at the thought of my future—one that included Jilly and Daniel. Was he talking about marriage earlier? When the time was right, I would talk to Peter about a divorce so I could be free to be with Daniel.

After drying off, I slipped on a nightshirt and panties. I opted not to put on shorts since I wasn't leaving my room. Exhausted, I slipped into bed and pulled the covers over my tired body and yawned.

Fumbles?

I dragged myself out of bed and tiptoed to the living room to fetch him. On the way back, Daniel opened his door, exposing only his face and part of his bare chest. My cheeks warmed, and I pressed my lips together, smiling at the notion he was naked and hiding behind the door.

"Everything okay?"

"Yeah." I held up Fumbles. "I had to get him."

"Come in for a minute."

"Give me a second," I mouthed, then entered my room. After placing Fumbles next to Jilly, I headed across the hall. I knocked softly before stepping inside and closed the door, minus a few inches in case I heard Jilly. Daniel, with his back to me and only wearing boxer briefs, pulled back the covers on his bed. Shame on me for not taking my eyes away and gawking at him. "Um, what's up?"

When he turned, I forgot how to breathe with his half-naked body drawing closer. Forcing myself not to look at his lower extremity was quite difficult.

Daniel looked me over and smiled. "Don't you look cute."

I had forgotten to put my shorts on. Guess Daniel got an eyeful as well. He stood in front of me, gazing into my eyes and closed the door. The sound was incredibly seductive, however, the room suddenly appeared twenty degrees warmer. My body wanted to melt to the floor like a dry spaghetti noodle sinking into a pot of hot water.

I swallowed the lump in my throat and backed against the wall. "What did you want?"

Daniel placed his palms on the wall but respectfully maintained a distance between us. "If there's anything else Jilly needs, we can run to the store tomorrow."

"Oh, um, okay."

He grinned like he could read my intimate thoughts. The ones of us taking off our clothes and doing more than kissing. "Nervous about something?"

"Why would I be nervous?"

"Well, you never know what might happen," said the man who had been the perfect gentleman.

"So far, nothing."

Daniel leaned back, and his eyebrows shot up. "Oh really?"

"Yes, *really*. How long do you intend on being that gentleman?"

As though I had poked the tiger in him, Daniel attacked, pressing me against the wall and kissing me with force. Now that I had a future, I placed my hands on his face and returned the heated passion, letting him know I was ready for whatever happened next, and that was him throwing me on his bed and making love to me. His fingers slipped underneath my shirt and teasingly trailed up my side until he placed his hand on my breast. His touch left me wanting all of him right then and there. And from the feel of his lower extremity pressed against mine, he wanted me too. When Daniel kissed my neck, I lost all control. If he didn't take me soon, I just might have to take him.

He moved his lips to my ear and whispered, "How long do you intend on staying in that room?"

"Not long. I need to…" It was hard to speak when his hand traveled down my stomach and headed for another sensitive spot. "Um, as soon as Jilly's had time to adjust to that room."

Not only did his hands leave my body, he attempted to walk away.

I grabbed his wrist and pulled him back to me. "Did I say or do something wrong?"

"No. Don't ever think that." Daniel took my face in his hands and kissed my forehead.

I reached up and held his wrists. "Then why won't you make love to me?"

"You have no idea how close I am to ripping those clothes off of you. But when I make love to you, I want you to sleep with me in my bed. Not watch you leave me."

Daniel never disappointed me. His words reminded me why I loved him. He wanted all of me.

His fingertips trailed across my cheek as his eyes followed them. "I said I'd be a gentleman, and I will." His eyes met mine. "When you're ready to take that step and move in here with me, then I'll make love to you…all night long."

Thinking how to move that process along, I had an idea. "Maybe we can decorate the room and make it feel like hers. Once she's adjusted, I'll move in here with you and take you up on that offer."

"Babe, we're getting up early and running to the store." He kissed my forehead. "Be thinking about how you want to decorate her room." He kissed my cheek. "And you can decorate this one if you want to." Daniel wrinkled his nose and shook his head. "Just not pink."

I laughed and reached for the doorknob. "I should probably go."

"Not until I get a goodnight kiss."

I brought my lips to his and kissed him good night.

Chapter 26: What Happened?

Her little fingers twitched. Jilly slept so peacefully, I didn't want to wake her up. It still seemed like a dream. My baby girl was with me. The hair was in her face, so I gently guided it to the side. I couldn't wait to make her favorite breakfast. Three months later, and a nanny, I had no idea what her routine was like. It didn't matter. We would make a new one.

Jilly opened her eyes, yawned and scanned the room.

"Good morning."

"Where are we?"

"At Daniel's house, remember?"

Her sleepy eyes met mine, blinking slowly. "Mommy, you were gone a long time."

My heart felt the sting of her innocent words. "I know, baby girl, but I'll never let you out of my sight ever again."

She didn't smile. "Did you not wanna come home?"

"Oh, sweetie. Of course I did."

"Then why didn't you come home?"

"I didn't know where you were."

"Daddy said you got lost. He tried to find you." She picked up Fumbles and looked him over. "He was sad because you were gone."

"Jilly, please believe me when I say I wanted to come home more than *anything* in this world."

"I'm glad you're not lost anymore." She touched my cheek.

I took her hand and pressed it against my face. "*Me* too."

"If you ever get lost again, you can call Daddy. He'll come find you."

"I'll make sure I call him." I tickled her. "Are you hungry?"

She giggled, fighting my attack. "Yes. I want some pancakes."

"Anything my baby girl wants."

After breakfast, we headed to town. I couldn't wait to spend my first full day as a free woman looking for ideas for Jilly's room. Life was so good. I couldn't stop smiling and talking to strangers. For lunch, we didn't have to sit in the wrecker and hide. I didn't have to fear the police when I saw them. By late afternoon, we called it a day. Our last stop was at the paint store. I decided on a neutral color so I could design a mural on Jilly's wall. Daniel was going to paint the room while we were at the farm.

Jilly warmed up to Daniel in no time. She loved how he tossed her in the air. He showed her around the shop while I placed two orders. Jilly ran into the office and told me how Daniel let her drive the rollback. When my eyes darted to his, Daniel shook his head and let me know that's what she thought, but she was only sitting on his lap, pretending.

Jilly was a big hit at the diner. I didn't care about the questions they asked. I simply explained we were reunited after an unfortunate situation and left it at that. Abby tried to spoil her more than I did. Jory, well, Jilly needed more time to warm up to him, but she would. Jory had a heart of gold behind that tough exterior.

The rest of the week, I only worked a few hours a day at the shop. Jilly helped me do small chores. Never in a million years could I have imagined her taking afternoon naps in the room I once called mine.

Friday came, and we headed to Rockingham. I met Peter at his store. Their reunion was emotional. Jilly was so happy to see him, running as fast as she could with her arms open, calling his name.

I headed to the farm and spent the next two days with Mama and Grandpa. As happy as I was to be there and grateful they were back in my life, I sure missed Daniel. We constantly texted each other. At night when he called, I missed him even more.

Sunday afternoon, Jilly and I headed back to Maxton. When I turned into the driveway and saw Daniel's truck, I was the happiest woman in the world. I had my daughter back and the man of my dreams waiting for me at home. Just as I got Jilly out of her car seat, Daniel came down the front steps. I couldn't wait and ran to him. Daniel caught me when I jumped into his arms. I wrapped my legs around his waist, my arms around his neck and rested my head against his. He twirled me around with my hair horizontal. It was as though life repaid me tenfold for what I had gone through. We were interrupted when Jilly begged Daniel to twirl her.

For two weeks, things were amazing. We went to kid-friendly places, out to eat, and walks in the park. Jilly loved her new bedroom and the mural on her wall; a field of daisies. One day I would tell her the story behind it. She finally adjusted to her room, although it took a little longer than anticipated. I was sure it was her fear of letting me out of her sight. I was ready to move into Daniel's room with him, but for whatever reason, he seemed resistant.

It was my third weekend visit to the farm when things started to change. I came home, and Daniel wasn't there to greet me. Not that it was a surprise. He had become distant and withdrawn. I didn't ask questions and tried to be patient. Having my life back was an adjustment for everyone, so I let him work through whatever bothered him.

By the fourth week, I wasn't so patient. The tension between us was uncomfortable, not to mention I couldn't remember the last time Daniel touched me. We never talked. We either texted, or Daniel would leave a note on the fridge. He always left before breakfast, and he was never home for supper. He was always so late coming home, he went straight to his room and shut the door. I assumed that meant—leave me alone, so I did.

It was sometime during the fifth week it happened. Daniel had slipped into a dark place. I stopped going to the shop. The cold shoulder hurt too much. At night, I cried, not knowing what bothered him. The worst part was feeling like he didn't want me there anymore. One night it got to me, and I decided it was time to confront Daniel.

"Why are you still at the shop? It's almost nine o'clock. Come home. We need to talk about this."

"Go on to bed. You don't have to wait up for me."

"Why are you shutting me out? I can't keep doing this. Talk to me so I can help you."

"I've gotta go." His reply was that cold, distant tone I had come to expect.

"Tell me, is it something I've done?" I sat on the edge of the couch. "Daniel, I need you."

"I have to go."

I wiped my tears and pleaded, "Please don't hang up on me."

"Goodnight."

The conversation was over. I laid on the couch and cried into the pillow. I was losing Daniel, and there was nothing I could do.

After I pulled myself together, I went to bed, determined something had to change. Living in a house where I felt unwanted had worn me down. I set my alarm with the intention of confronting Daniel in the morning.

~ ~ ~

My phone alarm vibrated next to my pillow. I turned it off, already awake, fearing the talk Daniel and I would have. It was time he understood I couldn't keep living the way we were. And I didn't even know what was wrong. After sliding out of bed, trying not to wake Jilly, I tiptoed across the hall. I knocked on Daniel's door and waited for him to answer, but he didn't respond.

I opened his door and gasped at the mess. Daniel was tidy, not to perfection, but clean. His bed hadn't been made, and his clothes were scattered on the floor. So not like Daniel. The blinds were closed, and that concerned me. He hated them closed, because he liked the sun to shine through in the mornings. Now he preferred the darkness. I rushed to the kitchen to see if he was there. He wasn't. When I glanced at the fridge, neither was his typical note saying he had left early for work. Daniel hadn't come home. He slept at the shop. The ache in my heart told me we were in trouble.

By lunchtime, I was antsy, agitated, and wanted answers. I decided to go to the shop and confront Daniel. If he didn't want to talk, that was fine, he could listen to me. Jilly played a game on my phone in the backroom. I stood in the office. My heart pounded, preparing to face Daniel. I pushed through the metal door, not knowing what to expect. Daniel knelt, working on the brakes of an old work van. His eyes met mine for a second, only to see who had entered and then he continued working.

"Hey. We were in the area. Thought I'd stop by."

He ignored me. Not one word.

I crossed my arms and counted to ten, reminding myself to remain calm. By the time I got to seven, I was anything but calm. "How long are you going to ignore me?"

"Not now."

"You didn't come home last night, did you?"

He stopped what he was doing, lowered his head and sprawled his hands. "Rachael, this isn't the time or place."

I flung my hand and screamed, "Then when is the time and place? Tell me so I'll know. You're never home, and you won't talk to me."

Daniel continued to work.

"Is this because Peter's back in my life? Are you upset it's not just the two of us anymore? What is it?"

"You know I don't like to be distracted when I'm working on something."

"Okay, fine. We'll talk when you get home tonight. Can I at least have a hug? Please?"

"I've got grease on me."

I rolled my eyes at his lame excuse and mumbled, "That's never stopped you before."

Daniel stood and walked away, never making eye contact.

I inhaled a deep breath and tried counting to ten again. I couldn't decide between throwing something or falling to the floor and crying. "*Tomorrow is Friday,*" I yelled, pacing, waiting for him to return. "*I have to take Jilly to Rockingham.*"

Daniel banged on a part at his work station.

I made my way there. With his back to me, I continued my tirade. "Look, if you don't want me here, just tell me." When he continued to ignore me, my fiery temperament came out, and I barked, "You don't wanna talk, *fine,* but I've had enough of this. While I'm gone this weekend, you better think hard about what you want, because if I come back home to this, I won't stay. You're not talking to me, but your actions tell me you don't want me here anymore. And if that's the case, I have no problem packing my things and leaving you." I turned on my heels and walked out of the shop.

~ ~ ~

The weekend in Rockingham was a much-needed break from Maxton. At least at the farm I was wanted and not ignored. Mama asked if something was wrong. I told her I wasn't ready to talk about it. I needed Daniel out of my head while I was there.

Sunday afternoon, I met Peter to pick up Jilly and then we

headed back to Maxton. The closer I got, the tighter the knots in my stomach twisted, sending a vile taste to my mouth. The thought of walking into that cold house and feeling Daniel's rejection made me want to turn around and go back to the farm. Perhaps I was going back only to gather my things.

I turned into the driveway and parked in my usual spot. Daniel's truck wasn't there, not that I expected it to be. Apparently, our time apart hadn't changed anything. With the Jeep still running and my hand on the gearstick, I put it in reverse instead of park, but my foot remained on the brake. In my head, it was over, and there was no reason to stay. It wasn't even worth going inside to grab my things. But at the bottom of my broken heart, a shattered piece of it pleaded for me to stay. After killing the engine, we headed inside.

Daniel left a note on the fridge—*At the shop*. I balled it up and threw it in the trash. Even though it was what I expected, it still hurt. The day lingered. Daniel didn't call or come home. At supper, his chair sat empty, and his smile was missing. Although his voice was there, it was only a memory. Perhaps listening to my heart and staying had been a mistake.

That night, lying in bed, I waited for him to come home. For what, I wasn't sure.

The front door shut. At least he wasn't sleeping at the shop. The next sound would be his bedroom door closing.

The minutes passed, but Daniel hadn't gone to his room. Curious what he was doing, I left the bed and cracked my door open to listen. The fridge door shut. Then a drawer. With nothing to lose, I headed down the hall and stood at the entrance to the kitchen. Daniel's back was to me with the loaf of bread and the pack of bologna on the counter. In those few seconds, I pretended nothing was wrong, and the man who loved me and would do anything for me was simply making a sandwich. After coming back to reality, I worked up the courage and spoke. "You're home."

Daniel looked over his shoulder at me. It was the first time in a week I had seen his eyes, and they were dull. He finished making his sandwich.

I approached the counter, not getting my hopes up that all was well between us. "I can do that for you."

"I've got it." Daniel licked the mayonnaise from the knife and tossed it in the sink.

Cautiously, I placed my quivering hand on his forearm. "I missed you." When he pulled away, I muttered, "I see nothing's changed."

"Night." Daniel picked up the sandwich and walked away from me.

Angered, I ran and headed him off, then I held out my arms to block his path. Daniel came to a stop. We stared. My heart pounded and my hands trembled, but my voice was strong and determined. "Talk to me, or I'm going to leave."

Daniel pressed his lips together and looked away.

"Either tell me you want me or tell me to leave."

Still looking away, Daniel sighed like he wanted me to move out of his way.

"I mean it. I will *not* keep doing this." I moved into his line of vision, causing him to look at me. Desperate to break through that wall, I pleaded, "Fight for us. Like the night Skip broke into the office. You begged me not to leave, remember?"

Daniel looked down, holding his sandwich between us.

"Please, whatever it is…" I hesitated, not sure what to say. My eyes pooled with tears at his rejection, but my heart told me somewhere inside was my Daniel and not to give up, to save him from the dark place he was in. "I know you have a hard time talking and sharing your feelings, but at least let me know you want me here."

"I'm tired and want to go to bed." He attempted to walk around me.

"No." I grabbed his wrist, and surprisingly, he looked at me. "Daniel, either tell me you want me right now, or I'm leaving." I desperately needed to hear him say he wanted me, but I feared his answer. Panting, I warned him, "I swear I'll leave."

"If you want to leave, I'm not going to stop you."

I got my answer, and it felt like someone had stomped on my heart. Daniel didn't want me. Crushed and in shock, I swallowed the lump in my throat and struggled to ask the question, "So, you…you don't want me anymore, do you?"

He looked away and sighed with his lips parted.

"The least you can do is look at me."

When he did, his dull eyes were empty as though no one was behind them. My Daniel was gone. Nothing I said would change anything. It was over. Tears seeped from my eyes, letting go of his hand. Daniel walked away from me. Each step he took, I sobbed harder, choking on the air in my throat.

Still not ready to let go of the man I loved with all my heart,

I pleaded one last time. "Why won't you fight for us?" With my hands together at my chest, I watched as he continued walking. It hurt so much I thought I would die.

"I gave you my heart, *and you broke it.*" Devastated he kept walking, I held my stomach and wept.

Daniel disappeared into his dark place. When he shut the door, I melted to the floor on my knees and sat back on my heels, weeping in agony with my eyes closed. I had lost him and didn't know why. The vile tasted in my stomach churned and then it rushed up to my mouth. I forced myself to stand and ran to the bathroom, covering my mouth. As soon as I raised the lid, I threw up.

After it was over, I flushed the commode and lowered the lid. My body was too weak to stand, so I sat for a moment and rested my cheek on the cold lid and stared at the wall. Once I had enough strength to stand, I washed my face, brushed my teeth, and went to bed.

Chapter 27: Disappointed

Yawning, I headed to the kitchen for some coffee. There wasn't a note on the fridge from Daniel. I wouldn't have read it anyway. The last thing I wanted was anything to do with him. I couldn't wait to pack my things and leave. Last night broke me, and I wanted as far away from Daniel as I could get.

Before I started breakfast, I called the only person I could talk to who would give me the strength I needed. The minute I spoke, Mama knew something was wrong. I told her what happened without shedding a tear. Perhaps the exhaustion numbed me, because I wasn't mad, angry, or even sad. Maybe there was a sense of relief it was over. Mama reminded me I always had a place to stay. Before we hung up, I told her I wanted to come home and would be there that afternoon.

Around ten o'clock, Abby called and asked me to come to the diner as though life was normal. She wanted to add new items to the menu and needed my opinion. My tone alerted her something was wrong, and she invited herself over.

"*Rachael?*"

"*I'm in my bedroom.*"

Abby giggled when she entered. "Jilly, you sure like that doll, don't you?"

"Uh-huh. She has to get ready to go to work."

"Okay, have fun. I'm going to talk to your mom for a minute." Abby leaned against the bathroom doorway and crossed her arms. "What's going on?"

While brushing my hair, I looked at her reflection in the mirror. "I wish I knew."

"Did you guys have a fight?"

I turned and faced her, pinning back my hair. "Do you have time for some tea so we can talk?"

Hopefully, Abby would tell me what was going on with Daniel. If anyone knew, it would be her.

Abby glanced at her watch. "Um, I have about twenty minutes before I need to get back to the diner for the lunch rush."

"Come on. I have a new flavor I want you to try." I eased by her. Before I walked out of the room, I told Jilly, "We'll be in the kitchen."

She never took her eyes off Lucy. "Okay."

"So…" Abby pulled a chair from the table and plopped down. "Talk to me. I'm all ears."

I reached for two coffee mugs in the cabinet. "Remember a few weeks ago I told you Daniel was shutting down on me?" While running water in the mugs, I added, "Well, now he's a brick wall."

"With everything that's happened, can you blame him?"

I carried the mugs to the microwave and shot her a what-the-heck glare. "What are you talking about?"

She twirled her ponytail and shrugged. "You have to admit things are not the same since Peter's back in your life."

The mugs landed a little too hard on the glass turntable. "So, this *is* about Peter." After setting the timer, I leaned against the kitchen counter and crossed my arms. "Why can't he tell me that? He's obviously willing to talk to *you*."

Still playing with her ponytail, she rolled her eyes. "Because he knows you wouldn't understand what he's going through if he did tell you."

I approached the counter that separated us and growled under my breath, "What *he's* going through? Are you *kidding* me? He's being a jerk because Peter happens to be alive, which *happens* to be a good thing. Would your brother rather Peter be dead and me facing jail time?"

Abby left the table and made her way to the island bar that separated us, giving me her protective-sister glare while straddling a stool. "You don't know what Daniel's been through, so you don't know how he thinks."

My eyes widened from concern. "Is there something I don't know?"

"Does he talk about our dad?"

I opened the box of tea bags and placed one in front of her on a napkin. "No, but he did tell me he walked out of his life when he was young." The microwave beeped. I returned to remove the mugs and carried them to the counter and set one in front of Abby.

She dunked her tea bag, staring at it. "Our dad left our mom for another woman he was cheating on her with."

I blew the steam from my tea. "I-I didn't know. That's horrible."

"We were a happy family until one day he left and never came back." Staring, sadness filled her eyes. "I'll never forget watching Daniel hang onto his leg, begging him not to leave. Mom had to pull him away. He was only five years old. He never got over that."

"What about you? You seem to have worked through it."

She laughed and set her mug down. "I hate the bastard and hope he rots in hell."

"Abby, don't say that. He's still your father."

Her grin faded, and she flashed an irritated glare. "Daniel still has a hard time dealing with that. Then Nikki goes back to her ex." She raised one eyebrow and challenged me. "Why shouldn't he be afraid history will repeat itself, and you'll go back to your ex?"

I slowly replied, "Because I'm *not* Nikki, that's why. You, of all people know how I feel about Daniel, or have you forgotten the day we had the accident?"

Abby tilted her head and removed the tea bag from her mug. "It doesn't matter what I think. Daniel's convinced you're going to go back to Peter just like Nikki went back to Josh."

I rolled my eyes and mumbled, "Wow, unbelievable."

"Maybe to you, but not to Daniel. You're not widowed, but married to a man you were happy with for seven years. And, you guys have a child together." She lifted the mug to her lips and mumbled, "If I were in his shoes, I'd feel the same way."

"For your information, I shared more with Daniel in the short time I've known him than I did in the seven years I was with Peter. And, I'm here. Doesn't that count for anything?"

"You're here during the week, but on the weekends, you go see Peter."

"We're parents, Abby." I reminded her in a harsh tone, frustrated she continued to question my love for her brother. "You *know* we have to talk. It's not like I go see him, and you know it. How many times do I have to keep saying...I'm *not* going back to Peter?"

"Maybe that's how you feel today. But who's to say a spark doesn't reignite during one of those visits? It could happen."

Defeated, I threw my hands up. "How could he think I'd go back to Peter after what he did to me?"

"Daniel thinks you'll forgive him, then the hurt will go away, then you'll want your family back. You can't argue couples forgive and reconcile all the time, especially when there are children involved."

I laughed, dumbfounded. "What is it with men not trusting me?"

"It's not you." She sipped her tea and added, "Daniel's insecure. Watching you go back to your old life, your husband—"

I pointed at her and raised my eyebrows. "Keep in mind you just said, 'my *old* life'."

"But that 'old life' has a husband, and he wants you back. Daniel's afraid you'll come home from one of your weekend visits and tell him you're leaving him."

So that's why he's not here when I come home.

"Do you hear how crazy that sounds?"

"Rachael, come on. Is it really that crazy to think it might happen?" She tightened her ponytail. "Did you know he's having nightmares that you tell him you want to save your marriage?"

"No. He won't talk to me because of that insecurity of his. Daniel needs to grow up and get over his past and trust me. I'm tired of having to pay for the actions of others."

She leaned over the bar, looked me dead in the eye and lashed out at me. "*That's* why he's not talking to you. If you said that to him, it would break him. You obviously had two loving parents growing up. We didn't. Sometimes in life things happen, and we don't just 'get over it' and move on. Some wounds don't heal, and for you to insinuate it's easy for my brother to forget a horrible event in his childhood is like telling you to get over the death of your father. Maybe we didn't lose our dad to death, but we still lost our dad that day."

Abby's words were harsh, but rightfully so. I saw things from her side and felt bad I minimized what they had been through.

"I, I'm really sorry I said that. It's just—"

"Stop." She raised her hand and settled back on the stool. "I know you didn't mean to say that to be hurtful, but that's a sensitive subject for Daniel." Her hand lowered as she calmed. "Me, I have thick skin, so it doesn't bother me. Look, I know Daniel's acting...difficult, but he shuts down when he can't handle things. The more he's hurting, the more he shuts down. He just can't talk about it."

"But why?"

"That's the way he is. Daniel's scared you're going to leave him like everyone else has."

"It sounds like you're convinced too."

She scrunched her face and shook her head. "No. I know you love Daniel, not Peter. I wanted you to see how my brother thinks. It's hard to understand when you haven't been through what he has. Nikki really scarred him, and it's like a Deja vu thing for him with you and Peter. Trust me. I've tried my best to convince him you're not going back to Peter, but I was talking to the same brick wall you are."

Finally validated, I looked away and fanned my face, fighting the tears coming out of nowhere. "Abby, he's throwing away something special. Daniel means the world to me, but I...I can't handle him shutting down on me."

"Hey, don't *ever* think he's not happy you have Jilly back, but finding out Peter is alive *and* he wants you back is playing with Daniel's head. He's not trying to hurt you by shutting you out. Right or wrong, he's protecting his heart the only way he knows how."

I walked around the counter and sat on a stool next to her and reached for a napkin to wipe my face.

"Don't cry." She rubbed my forearm.

"Why does he want me to leave?"

"He's convinced himself he's lost you, and it's only a matter of time before you tell him you're leaving. It's less painful to let you go now than to sit and wait for that day to come."

I folded the napkin. "I'm *not* going back to Peter."

"Have you asked him for a divorce?"

"I was going to, then Daniel pulled this stunt. Doesn't seem top priority now."

"Daniel believes you're not asking for a divorce because you don't want one."

I rubbed my temples and released a long sigh. "It doesn't matter at this point."

She rested her hand on my shoulder and rocked me. "Hang in there. He'll come around."

It was time to talk about something else, and I knew the perfect subject to lighten the mood. I nudged her arm and grinned. "How's the pregnancy going?"

That sure put a big blushing smile on her face. "So far, so good. I've officially made it past the first trimester. That's why we waited to share the good news. You know, just in case."

"Are you hoping for a girl or a boy?"

"A girl." As though her smile couldn't get any wider, she

added, "I want to name her Leah after my mom."

"Oh," I cooed all giddy, sitting up straight. "That's so sweet."

"But I'm so excited I'll be just as happy if it's a boy."

"You guys are going to be awesome parents."

"Thanks." She left the stool and stretched. "I should probably head back to the diner. Come by after the lunch rush. I need your advice on those new items."

My smile faded, remembering I was leaving Maxton. "I have something I need to do."

"Whatever," she grumbled. "Call me if you change your mind."

I managed a brave smile and stood. It was probably the last time I would see her. "You're like the sister I always wanted."

Abby wrapped her arms around my neck and rocked me. "You *are* the sister I always wanted, even though you have red hair."

Not only did I feel like I had lost Daniel, but Abby as well. It would be too painful for us to be friends, being his sister. After she told Jilly goodbye, I walked her out on the porch. The tears were there, but she didn't see them. When her car traveled down the driveway, I released them. I was going to miss her like crazy. I went inside and wrote her a letter and explained why I had to leave. I let her know I would never forget her, and she would forever be a part of my heart.

By three o'clock, I had everything loaded in the Jeep, ready to leave. The sadness lingered in my heart, but I didn't cry. Before I left, I wrote one more letter.

Dear Daniel,

So many times you feared disappointing me, and now you have, because you didn't trust me just like Peter didn't. You put up a wall I couldn't penetrate. Please work through your insecurity so the next woman in your life won't have to feel the way I do right now. I thought we had something special, but apparently, I was wrong. The Daniel I know would've never walked away from me and left me crying the way you did last night. I'll never forget that image or how much it hurt. When you closed the door, you threw away everything we had. I'm truly sorry for all the loss you've suffered in your life, but I wasn't one of them until you pushed me away. You didn't lose me to Peter, but from what you've done. Like I said last night, I gave you my heart, and you broke it. But I'll survive.

I'm leaving the cell phone since it's in your name and your keys. This will leave nothing left between us but our memories, which I will always cherish, except for the last month. I'm grateful for everything you did for me from the moment you stopped on the side of the road to see if I needed help. I guess I wasn't the one you were looking for after all, but I hope you do find her someday. I don't hate you for how you treated me, but I won't stay and continue to be treated this way. Especially since you couldn't tell me you wanted me to stay. You need to find a way to heal that wound inside. You're not messed up, just still hurting, and you don't have to. I truly wish you all the happiness you deserve. Take care of yourself, Daniel.

Disappointed.

I called Mama to let her know I was on my way, and if I wasn't there in an hour to let Peter know since I wouldn't have a phone to call if there was an emergency. After placing the phone on the counter next to the letters, I placed the key to his house and the office next to it. I reached for my smiley necklace and remembered the day Daniel put it around my neck. It was that very spot. Overcome with sadness, I jerked the necklace, freeing it from my neck, and rested it on Daniel's letter.

"Let's go." I took Jilly's hand, and we walked out the door. As we made our way to the Jeep, I reflected over my summer in Maxton. So many memories in such a short time, but they would last me a lifetime.

When I started the Jeep, my heart skipped a few beats. I expected it. Surely I would feel something. Going down the driveway, I refused to look in my rearview mirror. I was only going to look ahead.

"Mommy, are we ever coming back to Daniel's?"

"No, sweetie."

The drive to the farm was harder than I expected. I would be lying if I said I wasn't heartbroken, but the stubbornness in me refused to let Daniel break me. I never imagined his insecurity could be so extreme he would throw away what we had.

Jilly and I sang songs, cruising along Highway 74. She was so smart. Three months in the life of a growing three-year-old was amazing. Peter had done such a good job taking care of her. I wish he had done a better job at being a husband. But then I would have never met Daniel.

When Jilly dozed off, I turned on some soft music. The

257

memories came flooding back no matter how much I fought them.

"Just put your clothes back on."

I laughed, remembering the day at the pond. But not all the memories made me smile.

"Rachael, why do you think he's here?"

My body tensed, remembering the night Skip broke into the office.

Then I thought about the day Daniel took me to Seth's. I was really at rock bottom.

"Ten minutes, or I'm carrying you out to the rollback in your pajamas."

I laughed, because he would have. All he wanted to do was make me smile, and he did. I flashed back to the day he picked those daisies.

"So, do you like them?"

Daniel's voice made me cry. Why couldn't he trust me when I said I wanted him?

The light turned red. When I came to a stop, I let the tears fall. My heart hurt so much. It wanted me to turn around and go back, but I had to remind it we wouldn't be going back to Daniel. He was lost somewhere in that dark place.

"Rachael."

The visual of me hosing Daniel after washing The Beast was still funny. The look on his face was priceless. Even the happy times made me cry. I snatched a tissue and wiped my face. It was painful going down memory lane, so I shifted gears and thought about 'what now?' Staying with Mama would only be temporary. Once I was settled, I would find a job and get my own place. My only focus was raising my daughter and starting my life over—without a man.

I left the highway and turned onto a secondary road. In no time, I headed down the driveway toward the farm. After everything I had been through, I could put Maxton behind me. My daddy raised a tough country girl, and I wasn't about to lay on the ground and give up. So what if I had to start over? It would be a new beginning, and I would embrace it.

...to be continued

Sometimes the ending of a story can be disappointing. However, this is not the end. It was impossible to finish Rachael's story in one book, so don't hesitate to pick up book two in the series: *A Bittersweet Beginning.*

Things in Maxton heat up with suspense, danger, and even healing. Meet a whole new cast and some old characters that blend in for a truly heartwarming story. You don't want to miss what happens next. A stranger comes to town and changes everything.

The greatest compliment you can give an author is a review. It would mean a lot if you could take a few minutes and write one on Amazon's website. You may also contact the author at janecool777@gmail.com.